For Michelle

With special thanks to Lynne and Dennis for all their help.

Hobson & Co
(Paranormal Investigators)

Part One of The Greyminster Chronicles.

Chapter One

The Dark and Distant Past.

October 31st, 1896. This is not a good night to be out. The rain is beating down upon the stubbled head of Thomas Hobson so hard that it rattles through his skull as hunched against the wind that snatches at his cowl, he makes a steady progress through the narrow Lancashire streets. Every so often his gaunt and ancient frame stops and leans forward on the twisted stick he carries with him, whilst his skeletal fingers wrestle the damp leaves from his sodden clothing. Here he comes now, look, his eyes as hard as steel; alert as a raven's.

The figure stops beneath a wheezing gas lamp on the corner, trying to catch his breath. The cramped and sooted mill-town terrace that bears the blackened nameplate 'Applegate' is momentarily lit with startling detail against the palette-knifed ridge of the Greyminster Fells. Illuminated by lightning as it tears through the storm clouds that crowd against the dark night sky overhead. The same bright light reflects like a serrated blade in Hobson's malicious eyes.

Number 114 glistens, soaked in the autumn rain. The Presbyterian home of long-time colleague Samuel Foster, it stands out like a twisted screaming skull. A fitting sort of house for what will happen tonight.

Taking the brass knocker in his bony grip, Thomas Hobson knocks. A resounding knock that echoes down the entrance hall, rousing Foster from his forty winks into opening the front door.

Time moves forward. A time filled with muttered greetings and trivial observations on the appalling nature of the weather. No-one wants to get bogged down in the small talk of two old gentlemen and, in the interests of economy, neither do I.

One hour forward then. A wheezing catarrh-lined cough rattled up the tall oak bookcase startling a bleary eyed newt. A newt that had until that moment found the rafters of the old house to be a most opportune location for facing the onslaught of winter. It blinked and looked down through the smoke at the two decrepit figures huddled about the oval table below.

The time was slowly approaching nine-thirty and the dimly lit drawing room hung heavy with the smell of burnt kippers. Crowded over their meal at opposite ends of the dark table, Thomas and Samuel ate in a bloated, thoughtful silence, the shadows cast by the solitary candle dancing across the cracked plaster walls, caricaturing grotesque monsters tormenting the souls of the dead.

Thomas always found awkward situations difficult to manage. Tonight's apologetic meal was one of the most awkward for some time. At length he realised that the introspective gnashing of Samuel's gums was simply the old man's stubborn way of making him broach the subject. A subject that he had been putting off from the moment the meal began. So, laying down his cutlery in as collected a manner as possible, he steepled his long fingers into the general shape of a mint humbug and drew in a deep catarrh-filled breath.

'You know, I must admit Samuel. You've taken this rather well.'

'Samuel.' That sounded odd. Over the years Thomas had never bothered with the old man's Christian name.

Perhaps now was a good time to start.

Without moving his heavy eyes from the plate, but with a mouth full of mashed fish—more of which was cluster bombing the surrounding table cloth than actually reaching the gullet—Samuel responded with a voice as contorted as his features.

'Well, *Thomas*. I said *"Let the best man win"* and that apparently happened to be you.'

Thomas snorted down his ancient tar-coated nostrils. At least the old idiot was attempting to be civilised. Now to add a note of genuine sounding sympathy and lose the subject to history once and for all.

'You know, most people in your situation wouldn't have taken things so sportingly. I know how much you desperately wanted that promotion.'

There was a sudden flash of movement from the old man's equally hard and beady eye that almost knocked Thomas off guard. But it was gone in the same instant and the crippled octogenarian crammed another forkful of pulp into his dark mouth with misleading levity.

'What's done is done,' he said, the words indistinct and muffled. 'No point in wasting a good meal.'

'No, no...'

Now that was over Thomas attempted to steer the conversation in an altogether different direction.

'How's Elizabeth?' he said, dredging up some dark memory. 'Couldn't she come tonight?'

'No!' Samuel's voice dropped thoughtfully. 'She's gone to her mother's.'

'Oh, right. I see...'

'Financial troubles. That sort of thing. Couldn't quite make ends meet you know?' Samuel's eyes moved slowly up under the weight of the rhetoric and bore down into Thomas' soul.

'Oh, right. Erm...' An ominous cloud of embarrassed guilt positioned itself above Thomas' crown where it hung much like the storm outside that was currently rattling the loose windows. 'I'm er...sorry Sam.'

'No...No problem.' The rheumatic fingers fumbled with the dusty wine decanter. 'All water under the bridge, eh?'

'Yes, I suppose so...'

A deathly profound silence dropped over the couple. At least, as much of a silence as two aged gourmets with barely a whole tooth between them could muster. It worked its invisible fingers into the cracks and the crevices of Thomas' brain. His better judgement suggested caution; just ride the evening out as he had done with the storm and every thing would look different in the morning.

Unfortunately his mouth had other plans. The awkwardness of the situation seemed to give it a life of its own. He pushed the mocking thoughts of his promotion into a dusty corner of his guilt ridden mind and his mouth moved into gear by itself.

'And er, the children?'

'Ah, now, I must show you this.'

Suddenly animated Samuel's corpse-like hands dug fervently into the darkest recesses of his great-coat pockets, rummaging and rustling for what seemed like an eternity.

'I got some daguerreotypes back from the developers this morning.'

With an uncharacteristic flourish the pallid fingers,

speckled with liver spots, tugged a small black ring-binder from God knows where and proudly waved it in front of Thomas' nose.

'Luckily Elizabeth didn't know, otherwise she'd have taken them along with the children. Bloody women, eh?'

Thomas swallowed once, a bolus that seemed defiantly to crawl back up his scraggy throat. 'Yes...'

'Look. This is Jonathan in the paddling pool. Look at those bony knees. Just like his old father eh? And here's Sarah Matilda at the nursery dressed up as a bumble bee. Can you see all right there, Thomas?'

'Oh yes. Fine.' *In fact if you get any closer, I'll be going home with one of the damn things speared to the end of my nose*, he added to himself.

'Go on. Have a closer look.'

Thomas condescended an etched on grimace and felt the photographs closing in.

'Yes, yes. Lovely children Sam.'

Suddenly his nostrils were filled with the pungent fumes of chemicals that bore down upon him with so much strength he could almost taste them. Blurred beyond his focus Samuel's gums flashed and winked in the candlelight.

'Look! LOOK!'

Thomas felt the gristle in his nose give with a violent snap as the album shut with the weight of a bank vault's doors. It was followed by a delayed bolt of pain, splitting through his adenoids. Although his sight had become blurred by the sudden rush of water flooding his tear-ducts, he could make out the shape of Samuel. It was a hunched and menacing shape, forcing the album back down inside its long pocket. He considered that he really ought to protest at this point but the muscles in his mouth had already gone back into uncontrollable spasms.

'You know, Sam...I really am terribly sorry. I never thought...'

'Oh. No problems, Tom. No problems. These things happen.' Samuel waved him away with a flippant, non-committal gesture.

Then he turned aggressively.

'Er, is that a fleck of dirt on your fork there, Tom?'

Panic took a firm and substantial root in Thomas' mind, becoming a confused focal point for all his thoughts.

'Oh no, I don't think so.'

'Yes...Yes, it is. Look.'

He could see the prongs becoming more unfocused as the gap between his eye and the fork narrowed dramatically.

'No. I'm sure it'll be fine.'

'LOOK!'

This time the pain came swiftly and seemed to rip back and forth from the base of his skull. He struggled defiantly with the object projecting from his left eyeball, twisting and writhing to wrench it free. On the dim edge of his conscious hearing he noted an oddly familiar noise. A clunking that sounded heavy and dangerous coming from roughly the position where Samuel stood.

'I bought this today at Ardwick's Hardware's in town.'

'Oh yes. It's very nice.'

Samuel weighed up the copper-bottomed frying pan in his hands, juggling it meanly from one bony claw to the other.

*The rain is beating down upon the stubbled
head of Thomas Hobson so hard that it rattles
through his skull as hunched against the wind that snatches
at his cowl, he makes a steady progress through the narrow
Lancashire streets.*

'Yes. Nice and heavy.'

Through the already blistering pain and torment that was now turning him mentally numb, Thomas felt a new sensation hit him hard round the back of the head. His neck snapped forward adding whiplash to his ever increasing chain of injuries.

'It's certainly got some weight behind it, Sam.'

'Not bad is it?'

Thomas sagged. The time for reasoning with the embittered old fart was over. It was only a bloody promotion for God's sake! The time for civilities and diplomacy had picked up its muddied boots and left the scene of the battle. Thomas would have to be escorted to the door and, in no uncertain terms, ask his leave until Sam at least could better control his temperament.

'Look at this, Tom.'

'Oh shit. Sam, look. I'm sorry about what happened.'

'They say that the noise made when the back of somebody's skull is wrenched off with a claw hammer is one of exquisite beauty.'

Panic took control of Thomas' trembling form. From this close distance he could clearly discern the decades of bitterness and hatred that had etched their contours onto Samuel's craggy facade.

'Sam. Now look. Let's be *reasonable* about this...'

Blackness.

The simplicity of death comes quickly.

Those wildly spoken words had proved to be the final testament of Thomas Hobson, recently appointed

Presbyterian minister of St. Oliver's on the Grey. Not much of an epitaph, I know. But suitable enough for a man whose skull was shrapnelled across the dark walls like bloodied coconut shell, whilst in the flickering candle light his old friend laughed hysterically.

Chapter Two

The Arrival Of The Nightmare.

O ctober 31st, 1998. One hundred and two years exactly have now passed and that ugly, distorted night long since forgotten.

The Victorian frontage of 'Applegate' still looks remarkably similar, although now it is bathed in a rich autumn sunlight and the youthful trees from Thomas Hobson's time have matured into well defined middle aged characters that look down upon the crescent with a profound silence.

The once proud and gothic front door of number 114 now stands blistered; peeling back in patches over various shades of indeterminate green paint.

The ostentatious brass knocker cunningly fashioned into the shape of a 'Lion's head uncomfortably gagging on a wreath of flax` has been replaced by a small wooden doorbell plaque. Testimony to the fact that the building has been converted into 'Private Accommodations'.

If you should look behind the cobwebs and the rust at the bottom right-hand corner, you might discover an ancient and otherwise unassuming protuberance. A crumpled calling card, its corner forced beneath the yellowing thumb press, which reads quite simply:

Hobson & Co. Business Headquarters.
Paranormal Investigators.
(Exorcist Surgery Thursday Afternoon.)
Flat Three.

Benjamin Foster, cramped over his writing desk,

scribbled frantically, double crossing every entry in the thick dusty ledgers with enormous gusto. It wasn't a job that he enjoyed doing but Ben was the kind who when faced with a problem knuckled down to sorting it out once and for all. Problems, as far as he was concerned, had to be solved in as short amount of time as was constructively possible in order to regain some control of his life at the first available opportunity.

Currently he was so engrossed in the task at hand that very little of him was actually visible. In fact all that any other occupant of the cluttered room might be aware of was a thick mop of curly hair embedded in the familiar pleats of the RAF trench-coat. The coat that he'd bought from 'Greyminster Market' some years before and had worn without ratification ever since.

After several protracted minutes where the scratching of a pen nib and the sounds of a partially blocked nose amplified themselves by rebounding off the creaking bookshelves, he bit furiously at the end of the tormented pen and looked up with narrowing eyes.

'Right...' When he spoke it was with a resigned timbre that was more a release of submissive breath from his nostrils than actual words. 'We've got big problems Jess. The auditors are due in tomorrow and the books don't balance.'

Jess currently occupied an armchair virtually buried under several stacks of books and paper. The statement had obviously failed to make the desired impact upon Ben's long time business partner. In fact the statement had made no impact whatsoever.

Jess Hobson—lounge lizard—intent on making it through his forties with as little effort as was humanly possible. He didn't so much as attempt to lift his stubbled head from the March edition of 'Old Kent Road' that he was investigating. Instead he simply returned an abrupt, 'So what?'

After a moment's thought however he added, with a certain amount of phlegmatic indifference, 'W'at's the odd discrepancy?'

Ben shifted uneasily and felt the cheap pen from the newsagent's starting to give beneath his teeth.

'Apparently, in our case, about twelve million quid.'

He screwed up his face in thought.

'God only knows how that's happened 'cos we haven't had a case for eight months. Our business, old friend, has about as much chance of survival as a sheep in black suspenders at the Annual Welsh Language Society Dinner Dance.'

'Ben...' Jess pulled his impressive but corpulent frame from the sagging armchair and crossed to his colleague with a slow inhalation of breath. 'Y're a sad, anaemic git. There's a very simple way of dealin' wi' ledger problems.'

Jess had an unnatural resistance to troublesome dilemmas. His shovel-like fingers grappled momentarily with the thick red ledger before pushing it off the back of the desk where it tumbled into the waste paper basket.

'We file it under 'Bankrupt' an' tell the accountants it got eaten.'

'By what, out of curiosity?' Ben drummed the shattered pen on the desktop with growing impatience. 'An eight foot cockroach with myopia? A fifteen ton blackbird with an horrendous spastic colon? A lazy, fat, bald headed bastard who sits around reading 'Old Kent Road' all day?'

Jess didn't so much as flinch. The two of them had been bombarding each other with insults since before their long term memories had begun. Comments about each other's respective parentage and doubtful sexual liaisons weren't so much used to validate a point any longer as mere punctuation.

'Tell 'em it got burnt by accident in some weird sacrificial seance last Thursday. That should scare the buggers from the Inland Revenue off.'

Benjamin sat back on the wooden chair and sought for the most direct route to the heart of Jess' obstinacy. It was pointless and he knew it. He had looked long and hard many times before and as yet, had never actually found one.

'Obviously the seriousness of our financial situation hasn't quite sunk in, has it?' he said, opting for a simple belabouring of the point. 'We're not just going under, you sad imitation of a hedgehog's pizzle. The soil's been shovelled on top, the mourners have buggered off home and the bloke from the corner shop has just written off any chance of getting back that £2.57 for the twenty fags that we owe him. The situation, in short Jess, is grim.'

Jess yawned defiantly and slouched back to his chair as Benjamin awkwardly fished the ledger out of the bin; his chin knuckled against the desktop as part of the process. He found it and attempted to wipe some old peanut butter off the cover with the sleeve of his trench-coat. As if mirroring his colleague, Jess respectively wiped his nose on his large tattooed arm.

'Ben...Y're just a pessimistic, whinging' old woman!'

'I'm not whinging.' Ben gritted his teeth. 'I'm attempting to point out a major problem with our 'Crumbling Business Empire'.'

'But y' are 'An Old Woman'!'

'To coin a metaphor Jess, we're careering down Haemorrhoid Drive with sharp and pointed heads.'

Rooting himself deeply into the loose stuffing and bent springs that over the years had moulded themselves to the exact shape of his body, Jess fumbled over the arm. His fingers made contact with the glossy magazine that he'd dropped a few moments before.

'F' God's sake, stop worryin' an' put the kettle on.' He burrowed his shiny head back into the *True Confessions* column. 'I'm sure y' massive prolapsed polyp of a brain can sort it out.'

A couple of thoughtful moments passed.

'And what do you propose I use as a tea bag? A pair of your old 'Y' fronts bound with string from last year's Christmas presents?'

Ben looked sorrowfully down at the rows of unencouraging figures.

'Let's be honest Jess, y' sad lethargic old mithin. If Mrs. Prune doesn't provide us with a case soon we might as well be bankrupt.'

Mrs. Prune lived upstairs. In actual fact, Mrs. Prune '*lived*' all over the house. Her omnipotent character had worked its worldly-wise fingers into every nook and cranny of the building she now owned.

Mrs. Prune also went under the name of 'Madame Victoria', considering herself to be a sort of 'White Witch.' She had added the 'E' to the Madam for the same esoteric reasons that she didn't regard herself as a 'Clairvoyant,'

Mrs. Prune also went under the name of 'Madame Victoria', considering herself to be a sort of 'White Witch.'

because she wasn't totally sure how to spell it. But 'Witches' and 'Clairvoyants' amounted to much the same thing anyhow and the addition of the extraneous 'E' to her 'Nom-Des-Plomb' added an air of enigmatic mystery.

It was in this particular capacity, at the exact moment that Ben Foster had mentioned her name, that Mrs. Prune was to be found. She was perched on the top of a large wooden stool resembling a heavily made-up orang-utan. And she was robed in purple velvet, intently scrutinising an old plasma ball the motor of which had long since given up the ghost.

The room was an altogether dark and dingy affair; the atmosphere enhanced by the closed curtains. One solitary candle smouldered alongside the HP Sauce bottle. Occult artefacts such as crystals, mystical pendants and skulls embossed with 'A Present From Ryegate', populated the various shelves. These were intermingled with other ornaments that one would normally purchase from cheap and tasteless novelty shops.

A lengthy purple curtain, peppered with the remnants of sequins and stars, barely managed to disguise the fitted kitchen beyond. Assorted pots and pans however, had managed to poke their inquisitive heads around the curtain's frayed hem, studying the proceedings like children that ought to have been upstairs in bed.

Mrs. Edith Norton, housewife, clutched her handbag determinedly into her lap. She cast her harsh little eyes about the colourful Tarot cards and runes that lay scattered across the cloth. At length she broke the silence, not entirely certain whether Madame Victoria had fallen asleep or not. There certainly appeared to be the rasp of snoring drifting from the old woman's position.

'Ask 'im if 'ee still wants that tub o' Brilcreem. Or can

I chuck it out?'

Seemingly startled for the briefest of moments Mrs. Prune's impressive frame swelled up dramatically, drawing in a momentous breath before responding in a deep, commanding voice that presumably resembled the dearly departed Harold Norton.

'It's of no further use t' me where I am, Edith!'

'Oh good. Only the cat 'ad some o' it by mistake last Tuesday, an' I was just wonderin'.'

One eye squinted open beneath the spangled band that was wrapped about Mrs. Prune's head. It watched Edith absentmindedly pat down the disgusting green hat that was permanently speared to the top of her skull, and then closed once more.

"Ere! W'at's 'appened t' your lisp 'Arry?"

'Lisp?'

'Yeah. Y' always 'ad a lisp w'en y' was alive.'

Mrs. Prune scarcely missed a beat, although a slightly more concentrated expression washed across her well-seasoned features.

'There are no lisps where I am now, Edith...'

'Well, y' ad a bloody lisp last week w'en you was speaking' through that Madam Bovine woman at number thirty-two!'

Edith Norton had been coming to Mrs. Prune's flat for two weeks or more now and until that moment had never noticed a damn thing wrong. However, that bloody Mrs. Bloody 'Bovine' woman, always muscled in on the act. It was becoming quite apparent to Mrs. Prune that Mrs. Dervine had set a precedent for all future spiritual entanglements with Edith's long deceased spouse.

'Yes...well...Madam `Dervine` is a frumpy fraudulent old sow.'

'Harry Norton!' It was testimony to Mrs. Prune's acting ability that Edith was still convinced her ex-husband had possession of her corpulent body. 'I never did 'ear such language!'

For a moment Mrs. Norton became profoundly introspective.

'An' why's y' voice gone s' deep? It was alwez s' bloody shrill.'

Mrs. Prune's eyes opened and a grimace shot across her wrinkled countenance.

Bugger it!

'I remember Mrs. Covington remarkin' on it, on many an occasion. 'Edith Norton,' she'd say. 'W'en's that 'usband o' yours gonna drop his b..."

'Oh dear. 'Ee's gone Mrs. Norton!'

Mrs. Prune shook her head, dislodging the ornamental star from the front of her bandanna whilst Mrs. Norton stared on in disbelief. The white witch blinked at the austere housewife sitting opposite, drew in a copious breath and wondered, momentarily, if she ought to add a yawn of confirmation. Or would that be slightly ostentatious?

'Then 'ee'd better bloody well get back 'ere! I 'aven't finished wi' 'im yet!' Edith's teeth rattled as she venomously spat forth the words and Mrs. Prune found her palm itching unwarrantedly. 'Y' not 'avin' three pound sixty off me f' forty bloody seconds o' conversation.'

A short pause, the aim of which was to diffuse the situation marginally before Mrs. Prune dug deep into her treasure chest of acceptable alternatives and tried a long shot with some apprehension.

"Ee said 'ee'll communicate through knockin' instead,' she ventured.

'Knockin'?'

'Yes, Knockin'!'

The words having been particularly emphasised hung defiantly before her client, taking on the form of an overpowering threat.

'Why won't 'ee talk t' me direct?'

' 'Cos 'ee says y're an interferin' old bag 'oo's always findin' bloody fault!' Then Mrs. Prune added as an afterthought, 'An' if y' don't shut up you'll die 'orribly.'

'Oh...'

There followed a soul searching pause.

'Well, ask 'im about the will.' Mrs. Norton nodded as if that would be quite satisfactory. 'Where's it 'idden?'

"Ow's 'ee supposed t' knock out the answer t' that, pray tell? Morse bloody code?'

'Well, ask 'im if it's 'idden in the 'ouse?'

Mrs. Prune breathed in with a quiescent air, flamboyantly throwing her fleshy arms above her head.

Entering 'Spiritual Trances' always involved; for reasons that Mrs. Prune would never divulge in polite conversation; plenty of breast heaving and a mounting display of erotic moans. The exact interpretation of this behaviour however, could be put down more to its unnerving effect on the witnesses than its actual relevance in contacting the dead. Whatever...the old woman concluded her dramatic presentation admirably in the firm belief that she had regained Edith Norton's unflinching respect.

Several loud and sensational knocks reverberated about the stupefied ornaments and the pepper pot toppled over.

'Now I saw y' do that!' exclaimed Edith with sudden vehemence.

'I think there's another message comin' through...'

'Y' bloody did that wi' your knee!'

At this point Mrs. Prune snapped—not literally—her more than ample frame put a stop to that. But inwardly she couldn't stand any more and with a swift movement she blew out the candle; plunging the room into a suffocating darkness. There followed an exciting if not *brief* scuffle that concluded with a heavy thud.

By the time the flickering match ignited the smouldering wick, the clairvoyant had deftly resumed her seat. Mrs. Edith Norton was nursing a trickle of blood dribbling from her broken nose and Mrs. Prune's fat knuckles had a growing purple bruise upon them.

She leaned across the table knowingly, her palm opened upwards.

"Arry says that if y' don't cough up t' the kind lady now, there'll be more where that came from.'

At which point the telephone started to ring, fortunately quashing any thoughts of a reprisal.

'Excuse me a moment. That's my *'spiritual otline'*—my connection t' the souls o' the deceased,' Mrs. Prune uttered, a grin breaking out across her hoary face.

'Hello? Red Bull? Is that you?' she answered, forcing the side of her head against the receiver. 'Oh...no. Thank you. I've already got double glazin'. Yes...yes...no.'

She hung up. A chill ran through her old bones. There it was again; the nagging sensation which had bothered her for some time now and was reluctant to go away. The feeling that something prodigious, dark and horrible was coming; thundering through her nerve endings as though she had cyanide in her blood.

It wasn't a psychic feeling, because Mrs. Prune was well aware she possessed no supernatural powers. It was an old woman's sixth sense, as if somehow being old brought you closer to the truth. And the truth, from where Mrs. Prune was sitting, wasn't looking good. Not good at all.

7:40 p.m. 113 Applegate. Mrs. Prune's next door neighbours. Home of Mr. and Mrs. Wambach and their son Joseph. Currently Joseph is asleep in his cot; his large eyelids and slightly damp nose highlighted in silver from the shards of moonlight that have sneaked through the curtains. Above him the mobile twists and turns in the breeze from the window.

Similar to most mobiles found the world over in children's bedrooms, it has fulfilled its function more than adequately. In the few short years of his life so far Joseph has had terrible nightmares, all based loosely on the gargolic, demented faces of the fish that adorn the ornament. Night and day the screaming haddock and the kissing plaice wait until he is left alone, then they disturb his innocent thoughts. The bright clashing colours and menacing, walleyed features are watching him now; trying against all odds to penetrate his deep slumber.

The mobile stops suddenly. Frozen within the space that it occupies, in a manner that jars with our perceptions.

On the wall above the clock suddenly ends its rhythmic

ticking. From somewhere in the dark corner, a haunted, echoing laugh rumbles up the dresser and crawls across the ceiling with a disconcerting momentum.

Joseph's dreams are being disturbed again. His face is becoming flushed and the tiny, perfect thumb has tumbled from his mouth.

Above his head the wall has started to bulge as if the very brickwork itself was made of rubber. It forms a pair of knotted hands. The wallpaper creaks, then groans and splits. The hands reach out, scrabbling dementedly at the insubstantial air.

On the highest shelf in the room a Pierot doll with a shock of purple hair, cranks round its head. The sawdust creaks and squeals beneath its weight, as with painted eyeballs it scrutinises the little boy. This time the monster has broken through.

Downstairs Mr. Wambach watched the Channel Four news with a worried frown deeply etched onto his hairless brow. He had been bothered of late by a great number of troubles.

He was bothered by his hairline that was making a persistent and unstoppable retreat across his forehead. He was bothered that his once lean and powerful calves now appeared to be adopting the overall appearance of a croquet hoop. He was bothered by the narrowing of the years themselves, and the fact that 365 days appeared to cover only half the amount of time now that they would have done in his youth. He was bothered that in recent times he had been finding his newly graduated secretary more attractive than his wife. And he was more bothered still that it was making him feel like a lecherous, aging paedophile.

But most of all what was bothering him was the growing suspicion that he was beginning to lose his marbles. There had been so many odd goings on around the old house of late. Shadows where they shouldn't have been. Bumps and bangs and howls in the dark.

And right now, an odd sensation that crept up his collar, forcing him to loosen his tie and sink farther down into the safety of the comfortable armchair. It prickled at the bristles on the back of his neck, making them stand to attention as if charged with electricity.

A fulminating, vacuous laugh suddenly drummed across the patch of air just below the ceiling. It rattled around the chandelier and vibrated through Mary's collection of glass trinkets.

With aching eyeballs, Jacob Wambach looked up at the ornamental lamp directly above him and he heard the tears of glass starting to split.

Back upstairs Joseph awoke, the corners of his tiny mouth bubbling with saliva. The ceramic denizens of the deep on their repulsive mobile swung as if caught up in some unfelt but powerful draught. Their two dimensional teeth snapped aggressively down as the creatures attempted to free themselves from their cotton restraints.

Across the cupboard tops the toys were moving threateningly. Tin soldiers marched in regimented rows with distressing clanks and groans. Grotesque Victorian replica-dolls tugged out their own stuffing, examining it with barren eyes. The ridiculous hand-stitched felt helicopter, that had appeared so friendly and safe in the toy shop window, now tried desperately to rotate its flaccid pink blades. A flabby toy covered in helpful words such as 'Wheel' and 'Red' and 'Squeak' battered senselessly against the box of a large metal dumper truck.

Confronted with all this mayhem Joseph's initial reaction was to gurgle and grunt with delight. A gurgle that was quickly replaced by an expression of confused childish fear.

The furniture itself now began to tremble and move and the little bubbling lips became a gaping red gash that defied Newton's Law on not being able to change an object's mass.

A deafening catcall ripped from his throat, charging violently throughout the infrastructure of the building. At which point the wardrobe toppled forwards with a thunderous crash.

The lounge; where the entire lamp fitting has just come loose, exploding like a bomb on the back of Jacob Wambach's armchair.

'Mary!' A sudden burst of adrenalin catapulted his fragile body from its seated position towards the door at an almost incomprehensibly fast sprint. 'Dear God! It's started again!'

Moments later Jacob reached the landing and advanced upon the bedroom door. With trembling fingers extended, he reached out for the fat, jolly knob. It had been painted with a yellow smiling face that now bore a sickening resemblance to something evil. Something better locked

Confronted with all this mayhem Joseph's initial reaction was to gurgle and grunt with delight.

up in his own nightmarish childhood's subconscious.

What happened next forced Jacob physically backwards with its gobsmacking shock.

There was the deafening roar of wind, accompanied by great sheets of blinding blue-white light that streamed through every cranny. It was followed by the dirty, demented laughter that flaunted itself on the maelstrom, cutting Jacob's goosepimpled flesh to the quick.

'Joseph!' Every thought now focused itself intently upon the vulnerable child beyond the door.

Summoning up the very last ounce of strength and courage within his wiry, delicate frame, Jacob Wambach placed his shoulder against the bulging portal and heaved with all the might he could muster.

The door creaked, then shot back into position with the buoyancy of an impenetrable jelly.

Jacob screwed up his features into a tiny knot of frustrated determination. Then, with a concentration of effort such as hadn't been witnessed since the aftermath of his mother-in-law's stodgy Christmas pudding, he attacked the wooden barrier once more. This time the door gave a scream and creaked in a similar manner to a lift-cable that was on the verge of snapping.

The door burst open, propelling Jacob's emaciated body into the undisturbed and apparently dormant bedroom of his child.

Jacob picked himself up from the floor and with abhorrence gazed about at the unexpected emptiness. As he stared, a clammy sensation trickled along his knobbled spine with tiny spectral fingers. Nothing had quite prepared him for the unanticipated calm. An ominous feeling of dread shook through his frame like a cold wind.

Jacob peered across at the cot—the cot where, up until only five minutes ago, the tiny child had been lost amongst the folds of his dreams. The empty cot which now contained only the rucked up quilt and Joseph's favourite bear. The one that he'd always depended upon to send him off to sleep, with its left ear missing and its stitching coming loose.

'Oh my God! Joseph!! What's happened?' Mary Wambach skidded to a halt just within the bedroom door, wringing her red hands together in staunch disbelief.

From behind the cupboards, from within the walls, from somewhere altogether unearthly and blasphemous, a rumble started. A rumble that built up steadily in intensity, juddering through the false oak rafters. It rattled through the household creating small whirlwinds of dust. Downstairs the goldfish bowl ground in tiny circles towards the edge of the Welsh dresser, so that Simon the goldfish swam precariously out over the pine precipice and took his first look at the floor. The rumbling grew louder until it reached an almost eardrum bursting capacity.

Then it stopped abruptly with a stomach churning belch and a small pair of pale blue slippers, each adorned with a quilted rabbit's face, were spewed out from the torn wallpaper just above the cot. They were coated in a sticky green ectoplasm that resembled phlegm.

'Right!!' Jacob fumbled for the telephone receiver, yanking it brutally off the hook, his grim features set like concrete. Despite his ordinarily impotent character, he was aware that now wasn't the time for emotional outbursts. Now was a time for getting the problem sorted once and for all, regardless of cost or inconvenience. He'd have to deal with his guilt another time.

'I said that bloody priest wasn't taking it seriously!' He cast an acrimonious frown in Mary's general direction and stumbled with the dial in his anger. 'Y' can't trust a bloke 'oo wears a dress!'

A distant chirrup rang harshly from the earpiece as Jacob straightened his back with a new found authority. 'Time for some proper bloody action!' With which words the balding accountant snorted down his nose.

Chapter Three

The Introduction Of The Box.

Beneath the bulging mattress of a certain baggy old bed there lay a box. It was hidden amongst the undergrowth of fetid socks and spiders' webs and cups with mould growing wild about their rims. A battered, rather sorry affair with one of its corners lost in some long forgotten accident. The lid was decorated with the sort of pattern that looked as though ink-bombs had been discharged upon it from a great height.

It was exactly the sort of box that one might find in a bank clerk's office, brimming with yellow contracts and official documents. It had been tied up by a mangled length of shoelace, a binding that resolved itself in a complicated knot. Nobody was meant to open this box in a hurry.

However, the box wasn't in fact crammed with lost accounts or grubby and aged manuscripts. What it held instead was a collection of secrets. A personal ensemble of private artifacts.

There follows a list of its unusual contents. Pay attention, because this is important. These are the most significant items ever in the history of the world.

Item One: A small tortoise in deep hibernation. It had the name 'Rupert' emblazoned across its shell in white vinyl.

Item Two: Two VHS video cassettes. One entitled, 'Revenge of the Chainsaw Prostitutes, 5', the other with various handwritten epithets, all of which had been scribbled into oblivion by a thick line of black ink.

Item Three: An audio cassette. This had no visible markings upon it, but a piece of chewed up paper had been forced into the recording slot in one corner.

Item Four: A torn page from a diary. It was stained with beetroot. This might not be significant.

Item Five: Several scrawled sheets of blue note-paper containing drawings and text in a number of hands.

Item Six: One glass paperweight that harboured a dead crab. On the base it bore the legend, 'A Present From Scarborough. Made in Hong Kong.'

Item Seven: A dog eared photograph of a four year old boy. One could hardly call the child 'cute' because of its cruel little eyes.

Item Eight: One simple calling card printed in black ink. The gothic lettering read, 'Hobson & Co. Paranormal Headquarters.'

Item Nine: A copy of 'Old Kent Road. The Magazine for Men.' Well thumbed to the point of almost falling apart.

Item Ten: An extremely old book, its spine torn loose like a tongue. It concerned itself with quantum mechanics and other related topics.

Item Eleven: One bus ticket purchased on the 19a. This particular item was neatly folded, undoubtedly to ensure its safe storage amongst the other pieces of rubbish.

All of the above minutiae, to the ordinary man in the street, might have appeared as junk. And in many respects, I suppose that they were. But try to remember these belongings if you could because they might yet prove to be of importance to the rest of this book.

All of them happened to matter to one man at least.

Because these were the only objects that managed to survive. The only scraps left in existence at 'The End Of The World'.

Chapter Four

How Not To Conduct A Private Investigation.

At the exact same moment that the downstairs telephone rang, Mrs. Prune happened to be expeditiously crossing her entrance hall. Theoretically speaking it was the 'Communal' telephone but Mrs. Prune considered the whole matter thus: it was unlikely that the call would turn out to be for Benjamin Foster and Jess Hobson. If it did, then they would probably have had a heart attack anyhow, and being them the only other two residents in the building, she might as well answer it herself.

Which always seemed justification in her doing just that.

Naturally Mrs. Prune had her own 'Personal Telephone' in her own 'Private Quarters'. However, as a rule, she tended to recite the downstairs number to her prospective clients. On the off-chance, she said, that she might just be 'appenin' down the entrance 'all w'en the bugger rang. Thus it would save 'er a great deal o' time and arthritic effort from 'aving to climb all the way back up those bloody stairs again.

That was Mrs. Prune's sort of logic. A logic, which on the face of it, might appear to be somewhat odd. But along with her innate sense of 'Feelin' the future' Mrs. Prune did possess an unnerving ability to be in exactly the right place at exactly the right time.

Or the 'Wrong' time. Depending on how you looked upon such matters.

But always the most 'Ironic' of places nonetheless.

Often, in the past, an unwitting Jehovah's witness had confidently reached for one of the doorbells only to have the giant front door swing open melodramatically. It was generally followed by a bucketful of grimy mop-water thrown across their heads in a very wet and unwholesome grey blanket.

When the telephone rang Mrs. Prune was 'Appenin' alongside it with her customary coincidence, and the bell had hardly time to reverberate before the receiver was up against her ear. She adopted a posture worthy of her most sophisticated telephone voice.

"Ello. Madame Victoria, Spiritual Bon-Vi-Vaunt and Raconteur. Children's parties a speciality.' Her patter was by now well rehearsed and uttered almost by instinct. 'Ah, Mr. Wambach...'

She made a mental note that she'd have to polish the skull that she kept on the sideboard.

"Ow's Mary's little problem? Y' know I've bin 'avin' a little trouble meself o' late. I could send 'er a couple o' jars o' me special 'Madame Victoria's Essence O' Nettle'. That should soon clear it up. Nothin' worse than bloody great grapes in the autumn years, I alwez say. Exceptional value too at only Ł4.56 a bottle...'

Mrs. Prune had a tendency to prattle on like an old goose.

A worried, tinny screech buzzed harshly from the earpiece with such enthusiasm that Mrs. Prune was forced to hold the receiver at a short distance from her head.

'Oh dear...' Her voice became sotto voce. 'That does

sound serious...' she added at length. 'Hold on there. I'll get the boys down.'

Gently laying down the receiver she crossed to the broom cupboard situated under the stairs.

Mrs. Prune's 'Broom Cupboard'.

It was locked from force of habit. The simple knowledge that it belonged to Mrs. Prune and was one of those 'Private' matters that nobody enquired further about, was enough.

The triangular door opened up onto a confined vault and Mrs. Prune dug deep, her doughy arms visible beneath the rolled up sleeves. Deep into the tins of brass polish and ancient yellow dusters that should have long since been put out to stud.

After a great deal of crashing and banging, during which various items were thrown roughly about the sloping walls, Mrs. Prune emerged triumphantly, holding a long wooden pole which sported a thumbscrew in one end. In all probability it had, in a previous incarnation, been a broom handle.

With a definite stride she crossed to centre of the hall and, holding the broom at arm's length, proceeded to batter the ceiling with great spirit. Several new cracks appeared in the plaster accompanied by a plethora of tiny plaster chunks which spiralled down like miniature comets in a trail of their own dust.

The room directly above Mrs. Prune's entrance hall belonged to Jess Hobson, who was currently slumbering in his shapeless armchair resembling a string-bag filled to bursting point with tripe.

It also belonged to Benjamin Foster. Having double crossed the ledgers until his tired eyes had started to feel like hot fat, Benjamin could no longer deny the onset of a vicious headache. So he had settled down for the night on the edge of the settee and was now immersed in the black and white television set.

Another bloody car advert sporting a sexually overt theme that masqueraded as the politically correct.

'Nice car. Wanna show me what it can do?'

Ben hated the superficiality of the adverts.

He was just glad that he didn't pay out on a license for this crap. However, on nights such as this, when Jess' excessive drinking more than substantially destroyed any hopes of conversation, Ben's muttered comments of dissatisfaction were about the only things preventing his mouth from healing up.

'I don't know about you mate, but if I found my missus hanging around a multistory car park dressed as a prostitute I'd think my marriage had problems,' Ben grumbled, the epileptic screen tracing patterns across his features.

At which point the square-jawed hero before him lifted up his perfect children in his perfect luxury park-like garden and gazed blandly into their middle-class faces. 'Hello boys, where's your mother?'

'Pimping, out on the South Bank no doubt,' muttered Ben.

Another advert started with an overfed trophy-making shop keeper confronting a mute child. The voice over began in plangent tones.

'He'll take good care of that. Just like Falkhursts' Opticians did with my eyes.'

'Why's he smashing the bloody thing about then?'

It had always struck Benjamin that the occupants of Advert Town were all middle-class to upper-class, Aryan in appearance and with immaculate white teeth. And they were all inanely devoted to one sad particular product around which they constructed their nondescript lives.

Women bounced out of bed first thing in the morning with perfect hairdos and unsmudged makeup. Garage workers who spent their entire existences working under filthy old wrecks always wore spotless boiler suits home from work. And babies' nappies were always full of blue water instead of tons and tons of foul smelling green shit.

Then the unthinkable happened, and the screeching wail of the 'Pelvic-Sculpture Panty-liner' advert ripped its destructive path from the ancient speaker. Ben crumpled up his face in disgust.

At which point Mrs. Prune's furious thumping below managed to work its way up through the dusty wires and ancient pipes. Free at last it echoed noisily off every wall that it came into contact with.

Benjamin reluctantly forced himself out of his seat and navigating a series of book pylons and towering boxes, found a path to the sash window.

With a certain amount of consternation it ground open, ripping several long slithers of paint along with it. He stuck his head out into the dark, crisp night beyond and his eyes made contact with Mrs. Prune's, whose respective head was jutting out of the window below and grimacing back.

'Ben?' Mrs. Prune squinted, confirming to herself that what she suspected was Benjamin Foster's shaggy head was not in fact a fern that had sprouted from the upstairs wall. 'Got a job f' y'.'

'Bloody Hell. It must be Halloween.'

The window slammed shut again whilst Mrs. Prune hobbled back to the telephone. She checked for a moment that Mr. Wambach was still breathing on the other end.

'The boys'll be round in 15 minutes,' she proclaimed.

A pause for the consideration of her business activities and how Mr. Wambach was currently fulfilling the position of a captive audience.

'By the by...'Ow're y' bowels 'olding?' No response, but Mrs. Prune was adept at dealing with personal problems. She bulldozed on. 'I've got an extra tub o' that special 'Newts' Horn & Bran' laxative.'

The silence at the far end of the line was finally broken, somewhat vivaciously.

'Oh...Yes...Well...Under the circumstances...That sort o' thing's enough to loosen anybody's stools I s'pose.'

Forty-five minutes passed before Hobson & Co. (Paranormal Investigators) found themselves gathered on the Wambachs' front doorstep. Mrs. Prune's rather conservative estimation of a quarter of an hour was something of a characteristic exaggeration.

Jess had a habit of falling asleep in the armchair with all his limbs akimbo so that he bore a noteworthy similarity to a starfish clinging to its rock. The first twenty odd minutes after being roused from a deep repose he would dedicate to 'eeking' out the various pains and twinges that his muscles had suffered as a consequence of his ungainly sleeping posture.

Now the two of them stood on the Wambachs' doorstep, Jess wrapped up in his padded ski-coat, balaclava and scarf. Their respective breaths hung like cartoon speech bubbles in front of their faces, Jess' trailing forward in a plume around Ben's head.

Jess reached up to ham-fistedly knock on the small glass window that occupied the top one third of the door. Before he got the opportunity however, Ben grabbed his arm, preventing any further movement. After an indeterminate struggle in the darkest regions of his pocket, he pulled out a sheet of crumpled paper and started to read it to himself. Every so often the slightest movements of his grey lips indicated that he was still absorbed.

'Okay...Itinerary check,' uttered Ben at length.

He was a total masochist when it came to lists and forms. Benjamin Foster and bureaucracy had become entangled in the late eighties when he'd discovered a tax leaflet on the library counter. Now the two of them were totally synonymous.

With a resigned snort, Jess suspiciously opened the green and cream bag he'd been transporting and looked down upon the assorted pieces of junked clockwork contained within it.

Ben had found a pencil and was officiously licking the lead so that it left a thick smear down the centre of his tongue.

'Multi-phase Atomic Plasma Gun with Special Cross-Over Beams?'

After a short time spent rummaging around assorted car innards and broken sections of a ZX Spectrum, Jess alighted upon the most likely looking candidate for the part. The object shone in the dim glow from the tungsten bulb above the porch.

'It's a kiddy's water pistol actually...' he muttered abjectly, squirting a drop of liquid into Ben's eye to reaffirm the point. 'Filled with 'oly water nicked from the font at St. Alban's last Saturday w'en Father Edward was drying 'is hands after christening Our Doreen's youngest.'

He sniffed the barrel and pulled a face as though he'd been stung by a forty ton bee.

'Might be a bit soiled.'

Regardless Ben added an imposing, if not damp, tick to his document and hurried on to the next item on the hastily scribbled list.

'High Energy Ectoplasm Collector and Boggart Detection Device.'

'Dustpan an' brush from Gerald's 'Ardware.'

Jess held up the instruments for examination. He was not, on the whole, impressed.

'And Madam Victoria's pet tortoise, Rupert,' he added for good measure, holding up a battered shoe-box with several holes punched in the lid.

'Yes...' Ben compressed his pale lips together as he always did before questioning the authenticity of any particular subject. 'I'm not utterly convinced of that tortoise's ability to actually detect the dead you know. Cats and dogs, yeah sure. I'll go along with that. But..' Here he pulled a discouraging face. 'It's hard to imagine a tortoise cowering in the corner of some haunted mausoleum somewhere, howling knowledgeably at a phantom encounter.'

He thought about the problem for a moment or two longer, noticed the look of growing frustration and anger on Jess' balaclava surrounded head, and hastily decided to get on with the catalogue.

'Elysium Spirit Enticer and Reinforced Trap.'

'Shoe box containin' a bit of old cheesecake.'

Much against his better judgement, doubt crept back into Benjamin's mind.

'Not exactly over equipped are we? I mean, I wouldn't like any potentially menacing Astral Warrior hordes filling their spectral 'Y' fronts from the threat of our advanced technology.'

Whereupon Jess reached the end of his tether, grappled for a hold, failed and plummeted off it. His large, hairy knuckles pounded hard on the latticed panes with an ominous accompaniment of high pitched cracks.

'Stop bloody moanin', and let's just get the job done!!' His face became lost in a rapidly expanding mushroom of white breath.

Benjamin decided it was best not to argue. Standing up on the ends of his toes, he could just make out a shape hurrying anxiously down the hallway. A blurred, amoebic form contorting itself into surreal configurations beyond the yellow glass square.

It looked vaguely female.

Ben rocked back on the heels of his boots as the front door inched cautiously open, letting the tiniest crack of light spill out across the step. It was accompanied by a half hidden, cadaverous female head that at the first sight of Jess' imposing red face hesitated timorously, reluctant to speak.

*Standing up on the ends of his toes, he could just make out a
shape hurrying anxiously down the hallway. A blurred, amoebic
form contorting itself into surreal configurations beyond the
yellow glass square.*

But fear had already taken total control of Mary's frame once tonight, and it was all she could do to allow her trust to come flooding back with a vengeance.

'QUICKLY!' The word rushed across the threshold with a sense of acute drama and finality. 'You must help!! My poor little boy's gone!'

Under pressure as it happened, as opposed to any other time, Jess was always quick to respond. His normally lethargic nature tended to stiffen into resolve. Especially if there was a reasonably attractive woman to impress. Not that he had any intention of letting her know that.

'Out o' the way old bag,' he muttered somewhat discourteously, taking his suddenly acquired machismo to insulting new depths. He hewed Mary aside roughly and forced his entry into the house. 'Let the professionals through!'

Mr. Wambach knelt beside Joseph's cot, his hands meshed together so tightly that his thin knuckles resembled a row of embarrassed oysters without their shells.

No matter how intense his recently renewed devotion was at that point, however, the prayer he was babbling at an incoherent velocity was brusquely interrupted. The lower panel on the bedroom door exploded into the room in a shower of wooden splinters off the end of Jess Hobson's Doctor Marten.

After a certain amount of struggle to dislodge itself from the hole, the boot disappeared once more. With all his mighty weight concentrated behind one shoulder, Jess smashed the remaining wooden structure totally out of its frame. That brought hinges and deadly shards of timber crashing down onto the carpet with a deafening resonance.

Mr. Wambach looked up, his terrified eyes swelling, as Jess proceeded to charge headlong into the room with an angry, determined expression on his hot and flustered visage. He skewed to a halt on the home made rug with its fluffy animals design, taking stock of the situation behind a set of glinting teeth.

'C'mon get me y' phantom bugger!' he shouted at the house in general, his sledgehammer fists clenched and trembling with the excitement that was coursing through his blood.

Mrs. Wambach nervously appeared in the opening behind him as the sawdust started to settle.

'Actually, the door was unlocked.'

Jess spotted Mr. Wambach in his subservient posture, screwed up his eyes in thought, decided that 'The Time for Thinking was Over: This was a Time for Action' and charged the balding accountant with the general delicacy of an enraged bull, wrestling Jacob's bony head into a severe, torturous arm lock.

With the sort of deftness normally associated with pick-pockets and draftsmen, he pulled the child's water pistol from where it had been surreptitiously stowed in his top ski-coat pocket. Then he rammed the damp barrel up against Jacob's concave cheek.

'Where's the kid y' disgusting, bulb 'eaded freak? Or would y' rather suffer a boat full of holy...' Jess thought for a moment about Mrs. Wambach in the doorway, and decided against using the sort of language that might offend her. '...Babies' Billy?' he added, impotently.

Ben had entered the room behind him and now stood over the intense tableaux with his arms folded across his chest.

'Excellent Jess. Our first client in eight months and you make the poor bugger look like the prize winner of the summer fete's mighty constipated beetroot contest.' Ben enjoyed long winded metaphors. God alone knew where he dredged them all up. However, there was a certain amount of truth about his statement. The strangle-hold on Mr. Wambach's head was fast converting its colour from pink to purple.

Mary approached the confusion meekly and leant down to talk to her startled looking husband.

'Jacob dear. These are the two young men from the 'Paranormal Research' Agency.'

'Gleezed 'oo 'eet 'oo.'

Ben placed a reassuring hand on Jess' shoulder and spoke with infinite patience.

'Would you like to release Mr. Wambach now Jess, before his head ejaculates?'

Embarrassed, Jess released his grip and stood erect, leaving his victim to cough up what felt like part of his oesophagus.

'Can't be too careful with demonology, Mrs. Wombat. Just letting the bast...' He coughed. '...the buggers understand that we mean business.'

The explanation was a poor excuse. Ben's eyes narrowed and his lean mouth stretched sardonically across his facade.

'Yes...I wasn't aware that the sort of business we were in meant spraying potential investors with infant urea.' Ben reflected for a moment and added, 'There's an old expression I heard somewhere that runs 'You stupid, gonad-headed git!"

'There's another old saying that goes 'Shut it, before I dislodge y' teeth with me steel toecap!"

Mary sensed an argument growing that was completely non-constructive. However, as long as she had guests to entertain then everything was sure to work out fine.

'Right, well. Would you like a cup of tea or something?'

Jacob thought he should add his own diplomatic attempts and show that he felt no animosity for what had just happened. Unfortunately diplomacy was something that Jess had little time for.

'I'm afraid we don't have any spirits in the house.'

'You tryin' to be funny y' old cretin?'

'No, I..'

'Well don't!' Jess had decided that he wasn't in the mood for pleasantries, of any sort. He had been disturbed from a drunken torpor for this rubbish and he wasn't best pleased. 'Just you and Mrs. Wanker get out and let us get on with our job,' he concluded bluntly.

The couple stared at him, transfixed.

'Okay!?'

With a couple of submissive, diminutive nods the Wambachs left, supporting each other on the way out through the landing door.

Time moves on. The hands on the clock crank forwards, brushing Brock the Badger's nose like an assiduous, troublesome moth.

November 1st. 4:30 a.m. 'Paranormal Investigation' in progress; sort of...

Actually, Jess Hobson is half asleep in the kiddy's

armchair situated in one corner of Joseph's nursery. It took a considerable amount of effort to contort his giant torso into the miniature reproduction folds. He's going to suffer for that in the morning.

The chair is surrounded by a dozen or so empty lager cans, all crushed into the shape of Jess' forehead; a practice he has performed since he first discovered alcohol at the age of twelve and has kept up ever since. Several ashtrays piled high with dog ends comparable to structurally unsound Aztec pyramids can be just discerned through the haze of smoke.

Benjamin Foster turned the page of the newspaper with stealth, but the crackle was enough for Jess to creak open one eyeball and embark upon a slurred conversation.

'Mr. and Mrs. Womble got off then?'

'Yeah. I gave them a couple of Madam Victoria's Horse Sedatives. That should do the trick.'

'I bloody 'ope so. The last person 'oo took one of them 'ad to get Little and Large to their 'ospital bed to pull 'em out of it.'

Ben checked his watch, breathing down his nose in frustration at the uneventful preceding few hours.

'Half past four in the morning and the closest we've come to any paranormal activity was that daddy long legs tickling your mouth when you fell asleep.'

Jess' nostrils contracted and he licked his dry lips as the memory swam disturbingly back.

'Bastard.'

His partner mentally surveyed the matter, turning it over in his mind and studying it from some impossible angles.

'What makes them do it? I mean, it's a bit of a spasticky life anyhow, scrabbling about in peoples' houses like Lena Zavaroni on speed, and then suddenly 'Oh look. A naked, white hot light bulb. Let's see if I can snap me spine on its searing surface!"

Tucking himself up beneath a blanket of grunts and grumbles, Jess examined his colleague.

'Ben...' The shoulder came up to act as a duvet hem. 'Shut y' flabby, purulent gob son before I fill it in wi' me fist. I'm trying to get some shut eye here.'

A thought seemed to occur to the more actively participating partner.

'Hold on a second. We're on stakeout. Y' can't just go to sleep! What if something 'Paranormal' happens?'

'Like what? Like the spirit of the splintered cranefly rises from the astral plane and comes back to flutter pathetically round me 'ead?'

Jess thought in silence for several seconds before adding, 'Actually, wake us up if that 'appens. It might land on a spectral light bulb or somethin' an' explode. It'll be the only interestin' thing that's bloody 'appened this evenin'.'

The lateness of the hour combined with the contrast of the calm and Jess' less than exemplary behaviour with the Wambachs', was all that was required to turn Benjamin's thoughts inwards. With diligence he started to make provocative enquiries after his own life and all of its shortcomings. The newspaper wasn't interesting enough to keep his attention from wandering. Bits of gossip about what priest had bonked what parishioner, what celebrity game-show host had been found in what gay club. Surely life was more important than that?

'You know I never expected it to be like this.' He spoke softly, an introverted tone to his voice. "Paranormal

Investigators'. Sounds so exciting doesn't it?'

That was rhetorical. A look of resignation settled on his tired features and started to construct a home there.

'Eight months of hanging around bored in 'The Outhouse from Hell', and then four hours of monotony watching kamikaze invertebrates do the splits at a hundred miles an hour.'

'Ben, I know that y' enjoy talking out of y'r arse, but it's goin' to be pretty difficult with me Doctor Marten wedged up it!'

Jess reached for his cumbersome shoulder in order to pull up the blanket, fumbled awkwardly, realised there wasn't actually one there, and got cross.

'So put a sock in it, pal. Before y' get to examine y'r internal organs from an external point of view!'

Back to the newspaper then. Ah, back to the old Jumbo Cryptic Crossword. Now there was something to curb the ruminations of an intellectually tired mind.

Fishing out the never forgotten pencil, Ben settled back with the absolute resolve of completing the unfinished puzzle. He carefully folded the paper in half and smoothed it out on the torn kneecaps of his ancient, crusty denims.

'He discovers the crease backwards and turns up unexpected.'

The rubber end of the pencil tapped his front teeth as he repeated the absurd statement once or twice whilst concentrating on the ceiling. It was an old habit that. And a pointless endeavour. Ben had never yet found the answer to any of his problems amongst the rafters. But he'd discovered a number of Jess' old bubble gum pellets set like concrete to the mock-stucco work on numerous previous occasions.

'What's that supposed to mean?' he went on quietly, his features screwing up into a puzzled aureole. 'He discovers the crease? What's that? Some sort of reference to buttocks?'

'WILL Y' BLOODY SHUT UP BEFORE Y' GET TO EXPERIENCE Y' FIRST TASTE OF YOUR OWN BOLLOCKS!'

That was enough of the crossword then. He folded the paper once more for the sake of neatness and placed it down upon the child's desk beside his arm. Then, in the full knowledge that overnight programmes consisted of awful adult gameshows that would offend the intelligence of primary school children he reluctantly leaned over and turned on the portable TV set.

Something dark filled the room. Something evil bore deeply into the depths of Ben's soul. A distorted face, its neck and shoulders garbed in Victorian costume, appeared on the screen and laughed an echoing, disturbing laugh. The disfigured face seemed vaguely familiar—older somehow. More bristles, fewer teeth. It gurned directly from the screen and spat out its words in a husky, broken voice.

'Now you *will* regret your stupid meddling, spawn of Satan's loins!'

'Bloody Hell. Pete Walterman's looking a bit rough.'

The head twisted and writhed, bulging uncomfortably as it drew nearer the front of the tube.

'The foul rankness of your vile stench offends me, son of Foster!'

The voice chilled the very marrow to hear it, sending messages directly into Ben's brainstem, unearthing horrors that he had long since forgotten.

'Before the morrow is done you shall be returned to the earth for the worms to feast upon.'

Ben was starting to suspect that something was definitely wrong. The suspicions grew stronger when he switched off the TV set and, having done so, discovered that this action had apparently made no difference whatsoever. He crouched down, his hands and knees digging roughly into the shagpile carpet, where his suspicions were confirmed as the whole damn set was unplugged in a dramatic flourish.

The hideous face continued to laugh down upon him.

He checked back in the direction of the tiny chair, to see if Jess had actually fallen asleep or not.

'Er, Jess? You know that scope of a cranefly we were talking about? Well, I think that something paranormal is about to take place...'

'You *are* the product of an unhealthy bowel!'

The grotesque head loomed out into the dark room, forcing itself across the threshold of the television's surrounding wooden case. It drew Ben's frightened lifetime experience from his body and sucked it through the speaker in a fragile, foggy scarf; a scarf that was crocheted from his soul.

There was nothing Ben could do to prevent it. The words 'Unhealthy' and 'Bowel' were now ringing in his bloodied ears, his whole body turgid, his consciousness precariously balanced on the very edge of splitting.

The screen exploded—Jess' solid, unpolished toecap had collided with it at a full, hefty swing. Inside, the head buckled and shook as the shards of glass shattered outwards in a myriad of directions.

There followed an eerie, spiralling scream of

'MUUUUuuuuummmmmyyyy' that cryptically evaporated into the walls. Then all was silent.

Ben uncovered his head from where he had adopted the foetal position on the rug. He peered up at the towering silhouette of Jess standing over him, fists on hips and one eye dementedly screwed up so that he now resembled Popeye.

'Well, I've 'ad me cornflakes this mornin' y' bugger! So *shit* off!'

Chapter Five

A Rhapsody in Black.

7:30 a.m, much later that same morning. The curtains remained undrawn at Mrs. Prune's 'Private Quarters.' The dawn outside was only just beginning in a frenzied symphony of golds and autumnal browns, slats of ruddy reds smudging themselves across the billowing skies resembling thumbprints. But Mrs. Prune had already had one hell of a morning. So much so, that she hadn't had time to bother with trivialities such as curtains, daylight, birdsong and such. After causing Ben and Jess so much trouble the previous night, she now sincerely believed that she owed them one.

What better way of sorting out emotional problems than a good old hearty English breakfast? Mrs. Prune was basically a stout old woman with her heart in the right place, even though some of her ideas on psychology might have strayed a little from the conventional.

Jess Hobson and Benjamin Foster sat opposite one another around the kitchen table, their respective hands wrapped around a steaming mug of coffee each. The smell of grilled sausage and the crackle of sizzling bacon wrapped itself around them in a comforting blanket of aromas.

When Mr. and Mrs. Wambach had telephoned Mrs. Prune first thing that morning she had almost lit the pilot light on the hob before the conversation was over. Every gory detail of the night's ghostly occurrences had been dwelt upon lovingly now that the phantom had been confirmed.

Mrs. Prune approached her *two boys* with a pair of brimming plates, heaped high with sausages, eggs, beans, and other assorted greasy foods. It was enough to make your arteries harden just to think about it.

Time, she decided, to broach the troublesome subject. 'I 'ear you 'ad a bit o' rumpus at the 'ouse next door, last night?'

Jess moved his mouth from the coffee mug, a moustache of froth lining his upper lip, and obligingly took the plate from her.

'Well,' he grumbled, pulling his immense physique upright and squaring it firmly against the chair back. 'Benjamin's pants expanded s' much that 'ee could 'ave stood in the Rochdale By-election, but I won't lose too much sleep over it.'

Despite the flippant attitude, there was a greater depth to his eyes this morning. A darker understanding that hinted at a totally different story. In order to reinstate his manliness, however, he added, 'Just some goblinesque TV presenter oo'd been watching too much Jeremy Paxman.'

'There was something familiar about that face...'

Ben spoke half to himself and half to the other two, still clutching his mug as if it were a teddy bear. Mrs. Prune laid down his breakfast before him and hobbled back to her oven.

'I just can't place it.' He looked up at Jess. 'Those features. That half shaven head. It left the same overall impression as a girning coconut.'

After several moments thought, he added, 'With a bad attitude problem.'

Jess was attempting to cram as many different types of food into his mouth in one go as he possibly could. A slow light of realization began to dawn as to whom the hideous old man had resembled.

Mrs. Prune returned to the table with her own greasy contribution to helping bring down the EEC food mountain and reached across for the bottle of fruit sauce. With an unerring sense of understanding, she launched herself into the discussion.

'W'en I was just a down trodden, rag-a-muffin girl,' she said, piercing a sausage so that it popped with a tiny release of air. 'Nothin' more than a gnat's chuff to a Tom cat's whisker, me grandfather used t' tell me stories.'

Ben took another mouthful of coffee and swallowed.

'He used to tell your grandmother stories as well from what I've heard.'

'Well, yes, but those was different sorts o' stories. Usually involvin' large, painted strumpets of the night 'oo 'ee was 'elping on account of 'em 'aving fallen over an' 'urt their knee or somethin'. No...'

She thought more earnestly and her voice dropped by half a decibel. 'These stories was about your great-granddaddies.'

Jess stopped eating, a half chewed sausage visible in his opened mouth. It resembled a tortoise waking up.

'My great-grandfather?'

'Ey, an' Benjamin's.' Mrs. Prune leaned conspiratorially across the table. 'They lived in this very 'ouse just over an 'undred years ago. At least, Samuel Foster did. Thomas 'Obson was always round 'ere though. 'Ee was one of the great Presbyterian ministers of the day.'

She sat back.

"Course things was very different then. All very plain an' miserly like. Right pair of skinflint old buggers they was.'

Ben carefully put his mug of coffee down, then he rested the point of his chin on his knitted-together fingers. Mrs. Prune looked from side to side, as if expecting the eavesdropping furniture to back away with embarrassment. She hoped that such an action might add a sense of drama to her words of wisdom. Knowledgeably she continued.

'Thomas 'Obson—there was a great bugger if ever there was one! Devoted 'is entire life to burnin' old biddies.'

That seemed to have the desired effect on the boys; now both gawking intently at her despite the histrionic pause.

"Ad this ambition t' purge Britain of Satan's work, 'ee did.'

She prodded her fork towards them both to emphasise the point. A circle of sausage dripped fat evocatively onto the cloth.

'Witches!! 'Ee 'ated us lot wi' a passion! Said 'ee wouldn't be 'appy 'til every last one of us was dead an' gone. Very proud man 'e was. Nothing 'e liked more than throwing an octogenarian onto a pile o' logs an' puttin' a light to it 'iself.'

She sat upright, a sort of nod that was more of a wink signifying that she knew something that most people didn't.

'The kiddies thought it was great fun.'

'Sounds like my sort o' bloke.' Jess bit into a slice of fried bread and the grease dribbled uncontrollably down his red chin. 'Gotta be a relative of mine.'

"Ad 'is own ducking stool. Built one in 'is bathroom. If the old woman floated, she was guilty. An' 'er 'ead was chopped off an' stuck on a spike! If she drowned, she was innocent an' allowed to go free.'

'Yes...' Benjamin pushed his breakfast to one side, now unable to complete it. 'There's been one or two improvements in the legal system over the past few years, hasn't there?'

'Many an old biddy was put to death just 'cos she 'ad a wart on the end of 'er nose, or a grimace 'cos of 'er piles. Then...' Mrs. Prune's voice became vibrant now, lifting up in accompaniment with her hands. 'One day, in a terrible fit o' rage, Samuel Foster clubbed the great minister t' death over dinner.'

Pause for thought.

'The sprouts must've bin over done or somethin'. Any'ow...An 'undred and one years ago yesterday, it was. In this very 'ouse. And they do say...'

She leaned a little closer again, allowing Ben and Jess into her uttermost confidence.

'That 'ee carved out 'Obson's' 'eart with a bread knife an' 'id it under the floor boards of the 'ouse next door.'

There followed several moments of introverted silence.

"Course...They could 'av bin lyin'.'

Another few moments whilst Ben allowed the drama to slowly take root. At length Jess placed his knife and fork down on the rim of his grubby plate and looked up.

'Got another fried egg, my fat woman?'

'Right!' Ben rose from his seat, screwing up the napkin that was hiding on his lap. 'Now I *am* determined to sort something out.'

And with that he marched from the room, his mouth clenched tightly with serious intent.

Time takes another crank forward. Another crank closer; 11:35 a.m, November 1st, Hobson and Co. Paranormal Research Library. The cupboard under the stairs.

Every floor in Mrs. Prune's lofty Victorian house had its own assortment of stairs, and consequently its own incommodious cupboard. For the mathematically inclined amongst us, that made three such cupboards in total. This particular rather mouldy old cupboard could be found festering just outside Jess' bedroom. It was an abandoned realm, where stray socks sometimes crawled as new life forms, entering into hibernation just behind the rug.

It was also an ideal hideaway for Ben Foster's store of mangy books. Unlike Jess, Benjamin was an habitual reader. Since before he could remember he had had a fascination with books. And with the occult.

So naturally, books concerning the occult would excite him beyond measure, forcing him into that emotional domain that belongs specifically to childhood. He'd spent many a long hour in those narrow and twisting second-hand book-shops, that coil down into the underworld of out-of-print publications. Often he would return home with a renewed, pounding heart, his fragile arms aching beneath the weight of new material.

The shelves of his library bulged and broke their backs beneath the gargantuan weight of volumes forgotten and parchments rarely seen.

There's Ben now—look. Sitting amongst his treasures

in the dim glow of a hand held torch, thumbing a leather bound volume. Jess is there also, crammed up against the sloping wall with an open publication on his knee, jotting something down inside it with a black felt tipped pen.

'Got it!'

Ben's index finger prodded the page resolutely, tapping it once or twice more as he continued to read.

'Squire Thomas Hobson. Presbyterian Minister for St. Oliver's on the Grey. Died 1896 from a blow on the head.'

He looked up excitedly.

'Buried at Druids' End Cemetery along with the frozen sausage that finished him off. His heart was never found.'

He burrowed his head back into the musty crinkling pages, tracing his finger along the rows of black letters. Without looking up he went on, 'Apparently, according to documents, his last words were, *"I vow to kill every last pagan in Britain, even from beyond the grave."*

That made him stop and think.

'Obviously not a character trait that's been handed down through the generations.'

Casting a sidelong glance at the taciturn Jess, Ben was puzzled to discover him engrossed in a vehement scribbling. Jess hadn't paid the slightest attention to a single word he'd just said. That wasn't out of character though.

'What are you doing?'

'Just drawin' a little scar on this old mithin's 'ead.'

Jess finished his masterpiece with a little flourish and drew in his tongue. The tongue that always seemed to stray from his lips whenever he was concentrating so ardently that he wasn't able to keep an eye on what it was doing. Ben leaned over his shoulder and took a jaundiced look.

'That 'Old Mithin' happens to be Sir Thomas Mallory. And he looked more distinguished without the black teeth.'

He squinted and leaned in a little closer.

'Or the willy drawn on the end of his nose.'

Ben thought quietly to himself for a short time. At length he broke the silence.

'What are we going to do about the Wambachs?'

'Charge 'em thirty quid f' the nights' work an' send 'em one of our Christmas Bonanza Leaflets?'

'I mean, what are we going to do about Joseph? The baby?'

Jess suddenly threw himself backwards with disgust, or at least as far backwards as the restricted recess would allow. He frowned as though the subject had tasted of bile.

'Grow up Ben, y' retarded horse jebby! W'at am I supposed t' do about it? Turn into a radio wave and go charging across the ethereal cosmos after 'im? That'd look good wouldn't it? Middle of Crimewatch UK and there's me as a sine-wave passin' through Nick Ross' neck.'

Another thought seemed to occur to him and he winced automatically.

'Christ! I might run into Bonnie Langford.'

Ben decided that there was no point in arguing when his partner was in this sort of mood. Very little point in ever arguing at all then, he added to himself on reflection. With a hunched back that made him resemble some sort of ape with arthritic problems, he struggled out though the doorjamb. He'd just have to attempt to sort the problems out by himself.

'I'm off down the boneyard to check this 'fossil' out,' he said, unhooking his sleeve from the one remaining hat peg. 'Try not to overtax yourself while I'm gone. Or move too violently,' he added with a sneer. 'Wouldn't want you to sprain a braincell, being it your last one and all.'

He emerged into the hallway with a stiff pain in his lower back.

'Oh yeah, Ben,' came Jess' voice, smothered by the vast quantity of paper and binders that it was struggling to traverse.

Ben thrust his head back in at the doorway and watched as Jess adolescently propelled two fingers, one up either side of his nose, in a time honoured gesture of adult puerility.

'Get stuffed y' great bolus of regurgitated spume!'

It was cold outside and Benjamin Foster was glad of the trench-coat. The autumn frosts nipped at his fingers like the tiny sharp teeth of invisible piranhas. He smacked his hands together noisily in an attempt to keep warm. His toes smarted through his laced up boots so he made a mental note that when they finally were paid he should buy himself a new pair. These had burst on one side and a tongue of asbestos-like lining accompanied by the occasional growth of sock continually poked themselves out to watch the pavement go by.

Druids' End Cemetery was on the other side of

Greyminster and to reach it Ben had to pass through the countless streets that he had known since his childhood. Row upon row of red brick terraces, all huddled together. Some were overshadowed by colossal brick chimneys and towering factory walls. Prisons erected for the sole crime of being born working-class. Monuments to the Industrial Age that had crumbled in exactly the same way as the crumbling facades of the buildings themselves and brought with it a poverty and deprivation that grew in the gutters like an unhealthy weed.

For a moment he stopped on the Drum Crevice towpath at the side of the filthy canal.

Here the cobblestones were half covered with chewed tarmac and the canal itself had a green, oily sheen. It resembled the skin of a chameleon. The forever surging debris of twigs and burger cartons that had been carried along slowly for mile upon endless mile, was forced to make a short detour around the twisted metal frame of an abandoned shopping trolley. Having met itself again upon the other side it continued sadly on its winding route into the blackened heart of the town.

Ben lit himself a desultory cigarette, the ends of his fingers turning blue with the razor edged cold. He drew down a deep lungful of refreshing tobacco smoke and studied the graffiti.

'Pis Of!'

There was that good old Lancashire wit and wisdom. The backlash of an unacceptable class. It struck him, as the thought had struck him often before, that his sort were just being treated badly by the rest of society. The *intellectuals* in charge of it all, the chosen few lucky enough to be born with a silver spoon in their facial orifices, really ought to have known better. But there was nobody amongst the uneducated council estates to champion their own cause. Perhaps social values hadn't altered much in essence since the Victorian times at all. He read on.

'My other wall is a porch.' 'Sydney is a bollock brain.' Apparently his 'knob' resembled a stunted, capital 'A'. 'Nigel Rees must be kicking himself that he missed this wall,' Ben thought, stuffing his free hand into his coat pocket and marching on.

At about 1:30 that afternoon Ben finally found the crooked gravestone of the great Thomas Hobson. It was half hidden by an entanglement of choking weeds and deadly columbine, at the Druids' End Cemetery, at the back of Great Coat Lane.

What an unkempt and dreary graveyard it was. Especially at this end, where nobody had tended to the graves for decades. Ivy spread its probing tendrils across most of the stones and the mausoleums. Needles and empty cigarette packets formed the mantle for many an angelic statue. The junkies and the courting couples, in search of a spot where no-one would interrupt their passions, had been and gone in the dead of the night.

And here was the gravestone of Jess' great grandfather. Overgrown, worn into some sort of gothic crustacean by the passage of time and leaning as if it had been dragged there in some unknown battle.

Ben crouched down beside it, removing a small matt-black box from his pocket. It was the sort of box that photographers' would use to measure the amount of light that an object reflected. It was bound in a snug leather holder and had a couple of additional antennae protruding from the top.

With an arched sweep he took a sensor reading of the immediate ground, before training it directly at the dishevelled gravestone with an expression of reluctant finality. He pulled it back up and studied the maddeningly fluctuating dial and then smacked it, hard, on the tombstone's apex. He looked again—still nothing.

'What the bloody Hell's going on in Jess' brain?' Benjamin muttered to himself, regarding the incommensurate machine with an expression of total despondency. 'Five years of male bonding on electronic courses and one 'spectra-graph' later, this is about as much bloody use as a woolen condom!'

Time groaned. Every second bulged outward like a replete sheep. Without warning a dark shadow fell across Benjamin's soul. Not an actual, physical shadow of course; this shadow had emotion. Hatred and cruelty that chilled the bones and filled the heart with an empty dread.

Thomas Hobson stared down, haggard and bent over the back of his own gravestone. His face a sunken, ashen grey. His eyes resembling hard jewels in their black retracted pockets.

'I wouldn't bugger about with the unknown if I were you, Ben Foster.' The corpse sneered contemptibly; its lip infested with cold sores. 'My great grandson has capabilities that are far beyond your limited understanding.'

Ben pulled his soul back into his body and swallowed

a lump of healthy courage. He could go along with that.

'That's true...Jess' outstanding talent to break wind to the tune of the Liberty Bell whilst fast asleep has always had a profound effect on me.'

He scrabbled awkwardly to his feet and stood unsteadily before the oppressive demon.

'You don't frighten me, Thomas Hobson. I've read loads of books on the paranormal and ghosts can't hurt the living.'

Hobson smiled. The disconcerting smile of the dead. All rotting gums and flashing brown teeth.

'Betcha life bogie? What's that sticky pudding on your sweater?'

The ghostly scrag end of a finger pointed at Benjamin's sweater as he cast down his eyes in puzzlement. The digit caught him a sharp flick beneath the chin—he hadn't expected old man Hobson's ghost to be solid.

'Made you look, made you stare,' came the evil cackle of the senile patriarch now quickly regressing to the attitude of his earliest childhood. 'Made you soil your underwear.'

Annoyed, Ben grappled for a hold of Hobson's upturned collar, found one and dragged the malicious spirit towards him so that their respective noses almost brushed.

'You've got a problem you sour and embittered old scrote,' Ben growled. 'I wouldn't have thought it possible, but it seems that you're just as obsessed with back passages and what comes out of them as your great-bloody-grandson.'

He tightened his grip whilst Hobson rolled his eyes downwards, watching the wrinkles spread out across his collar in veins.

'Now, what have you done with the child?'

'Child?' For one brief moment of vexation Hobson seemed almost at a loss for words. 'CHILD?! That disfigured abomination!? What's that sad excuse for a rectum sprout got to do with you?!'

It was difficult for Ben not to notice the puerility with which the ghostly figure spoke. 'That's my problem, y' wrinkled, old tosser.'

'No!'

The minister bolted upright with such unexpected strength that he drew Benjamin along with him, smashing his ribcage against the tombstone. 'This is your problem, impertinent boy!'

One claw-like hand grabbed Ben around the throat, crushing his windpipe and forcing him to gasp asthmatically for breath. Terror filled every last ounce of Benjamin's body as he struggled desperately to work free of the asphyxiating grip.

A green fog began to creep across his eyes from the outskirts of his vision, signifying the onset of unconsciousness. He fought bravely against the overwhelming power that constricted his every movement. Power that appeared to flow down the old man's arm, crackling and buzzing, straight into every muscle and joint of Benjamin's torso.

On the far edge of his senses Ben could perceive that something awful was happening as Hobson's supernatural talons passed by his head. They sprinkled a powder into his hair. God only knew what that was; something unpleasant, that much was certain.

Ben's senses went numb and his mind reeled backwards, collapsing in on itself, in an ever decreasing vortex of sound and colour.

Hobson laughed. A deep, guttural laugh that rattled with phlegm and strained the sinews of his ancient throat. Triumphantly he held at arm's length what had become of Benjamin Foster.

A lifeless bedraggled doll sporting a shock of purple hair, about twelve inches in length hanging debilitated between his wasted fingers. The tiny flaccid legs trailed limply in the breeze.

The storm took that opportunity to break. It struck the disused gas lamp in the corner of the graveyard with a jagged blade of lightning.

'Now cop a load of this, you arrogant little turd.'

Hobson shook the diminutive corpse maniacally, flinging it up, with great gusto, high above his head.

'You might find the experience uplifting.'

The doll somersaulted against the furious purple clouds before tumbling back down with the helplessness of a child's bean bag. Hobson swiftly brought his foot up to meet it, and with a deft punt sent the mannequin sailing across the drunken graves into the sturdy trunk of an ancient ash.

There it seemed, momentarily, to grip the rough bark before dropping to the ground, its shrunken limbs becoming entangled amongst the damp roots. Where it stopped, motionless and baggy.

'Bet that made your trussocks sting! So long, you insignificant scrap of flotsam. I'd like to say that it was *fun*, but I can't!'

With a creak the doll transformed back into the more recognisable shape of Benjamin Foster. A trickle of blood

Hobson shook the diminutive corpse maniacally, flinging it up, with great gusto, high above his head.

was meandering down across his top lip, highlighted by the forks of brilliant lightning that tore apart the heavens and danced across the oppressed town. His mop of curly hair was starting to matt in red and black patches as the blood flowed out generously from his ruptured eardrums.

'And next time, try picking on somebody your own size.'

Thomas Hobson laughed the laugh of a madman; standing with his hands on his hips, his humped back arched into the shape of a ghastly question mark. The thunder rolled above his head with a sense of acute theatre.

"Cos I'm a big nasty mother that you shouldn't have become entangled with!'

Then in an explosion that comprised a thousand tiny electrical bolts and left an impression on the eye where the figure had once stood, he vanished completely. Leaving nothing but the rank smell of rotting flesh.

10:30 p.m, Paranormal Headquarters. Time for the accounts to be concluded. Not that there's much chance of that. The ledgers were nowhere in sight.

Jess was deflated across the armchair with four days growth of stubble upon his chin, scowling at the TV set but too drunk and lethargic to be bothered reaching across for the on/off button. After several attempts at fumbling down the side of the chair he found the remote—a stick with a pen taped to one end. When the occupant of the armchair was at least sat upright, it was the exact length required to switch channels and knock down the volume control.

After several vain attempts Jess gave up with the *remote* and decided on a simpler course of action. That being to pull two cushions over his ears and shut his eyes instead.

A loud thumping echoed round the room. It was followed directly by a sharp cracking on the window made by a yard-brush handle being operated from above. The third crack was so loud that it penetrated Jess' defence system and brought him out of his homemade sensory-deprivation tank.

Muttering to himself, he stumbled over to the sash window, slammed it open hard and stuck his head out into the ice-cold night.

'Would you mind sending Benjamin along, Mr. 'Obson?' said the silhouetted but unmistakable head of Mrs. Prune from where it apparently grew like a blackened cyst out of the wall above. 'I need me pipes lookin' at.'

A somewhat revolting image sprang to the forefront of Jess' imagination making him suddenly feel nauseous.

'I know that all the other gentlemen in y'r age bracket, Mrs. Prune, might resemble walnuts,' he shouted back. 'But there's no need t' inflict Our Ben wi' such a request.'

Mrs. Prune, not entirely sure what Jess was prattling on about, and not entirely bothered either, drew the pole up, hand over hand and continued as she did so.

'There's some sort o' blockage. The washin' machine must 'ave eaten me spare drawers again.'

She successfully manoeuvred the pole back in through her window and after a short fight with the lace curtains it clattered onto the dresser. Jess turned the nagging doubt that was itching at the back of his bristled skull over and realised what it was that was bothering him.

"Ee's not back from Druids' End Boneyard yet.'

There was a short interruption whilst Mrs. Prune absorbed the statement.

'Y're not telling me that y' sent that poor boy down there all on 'is own?'

Jess made no reply. Their two heads stood out dark against the night resembling limpet mines attached to the house.

'My God, Jess 'Obson! Y're a daft, great bastard!'

Mrs. Prune, suddenly agitated, disappeared briefly from view, before re-emerging and looking down at Jess with a worry in her eyes that overpowered the anger.

'Get your 'at 'an coat! There's somethin' foul afoot 'ere, an' I'm not talkin' about me socks!'

And with that she was gone.

Sometimes the largest, most stouthearted of men transform into helpless, quivering piles of ineptitude when confronted by a stern ticking off from their diminutive mothers. A similar sort of thing applied to Jess Hobson.

Despite his massive build and commanding features, Mrs. Prune, although not an actual blood relative, had always considered herself a sort of mother figure to him. By way of a consequence this effected the sort of control over her adopted offspring that a sergeant major might exercise on the parade ground.

Within the hour, two dark figures appeared at the imposing graveyard gates; one carrying a torch, the other a battery powered lamp designed to resemble a carved pumpkin with grinning teeth.

The wrought iron gates opened sluggishly, and squealed as noisily as a couple of pot-bellied pigs during the mating season. The two figures stole inside, their individual lights searching the crisp grass.

Mrs. Prune squinted through the gloom. A ground mist was beginning to ascend about the graves, coiling in an altogether unpleasant serpent-like manner across the gravel paths.

Suddenly she raised her arm and pointed, so that the grinning orange head swung mesmerizingly from the string attached to her wrist. She exclaimed in a voice that rang of apprehension, 'Over there, by that tree!'

They hurried across to the dark, lifeless body of Benjamin Foster, crouching over it, hardly daring to breath.

'Ben?'

Jess seized hold of the trench-coat lapel, hauling the corpse upwards. Its head slumped backward against the trunk.

'Ben? Wake up y' bone idle git. Madam Victoria wants 'er drain attendin'!'

There was no response. Not so much as a twitch.

'Ben! Talk t' me y' steamin' turd!'

With a mounting desperation he violently began to shake the body, Benjamin's cranium colliding with the trunk several times. The action made it virtually impossible for Mrs. Prune to keep hold of Benjamin's wrist as she attempted to take his pulse. But dogmatically she clung on whilst the blood slowly drained from her already pallid features. At length she peered upwards.

'Its' no good, Mr. 'Obson.' Her voice sounded enervated, almost frail and fatigued. 'Nothin's gonna disturb this boy's slumber.'

She paused and then added, 'Midnight 'as come upon 'im.'

"Course it's come upon 'im,' shouted Jess, his voice rising in an uncontrollable panic. 'It's twenty t' bloody one in the morning, y' sad, fat old COW!!'

Once more he shook the docile body with a mounting aggression.

"EE'S DEAD JESS!' Mrs. Prune hollered. It was more of a scream than a precisely articulated phrase. But whatever it was, it appeared to do the trick.

Jess stopped the struggle as Mrs. Prune placed her voluminous hand on his shoulder and shook her head. The action amounted to much the same thing as saying that nothing he could do would be of any further use.

'Stone, cold dead...' she added softly.

Jess gently lowered the body back amongst the knotted roots and stared in ponderous silence at what had become of his trusted friend.

'The selfish twat!'

He leaned closer, frowning.

'W'at've y' done with that fiver y' owe me?' A tremor of helplessness entered his voice making it vibrate somewhat discordantly. 'Y' can't get out of it this way...'

From somewhere beyond the ebony contours of the copse a preternatural laugh began to thunder across the grave stones with gathering impetus.

Both Jess and Mrs. Prune raised their thick set features towards its source, a sinking sensation undulating menacingly deep within their hearts.

'There's a great evil at work round 'ere, Jess 'Obson...'

Mrs. Prune's head sank below her shoulders. She wagged her forefinger tenaciously, her voice sinking to a poetic harbinger of doom.

'It's unnatural is this. Y' can smell the flatulence o' the Devil round these stenching, twisted old stones.'

'Very dramatic.'

Mrs. Prune nodded, obviously pleased with the compliment. Funny what things can still affect you despite the trauma of the situation.

'Thank you. It's me special voice for the clients.'

She appeared to reach a swift decision and snatched hold of one of Benjamin's pliant arms.

'C'mon. Let's get this poor boy out of here before 'e catches 'is death.'

It was a figure of speech. One badly chosen.

There go Jess Hobson and Mrs. Prune now. Two hunched figures in the dead of the night carrying a body from the scene of a terrible crime. It bows in the middle after the fashion of a rolled-up carpet and sometimes scuffs along the ground leaving grooves across the frosted tips of the grass.

Both wonder what they would have said and done if they had just had that little extra time. Just one or two hours more before their companion departed this earthly province so hastily. That's how it always ends; always too late to repent when it happens. People ought to communicate more. So many people all talking at once, so many opinions, so much pent up emotion and nobody listening to anybody else.

Chapter Six

A Seance In The Dark.

There were a lot of comings and goings to 114 Applegate over the next few weeks. A great number of official looking figures in police uniforms appeared on the doorstep. They were accompanied by men in extensive brown coats carrying clip boards beneath their arms.

As the days passed the accumulation of faulty wiring and cobwebs on the wooden bell-plaque, became less and less of a hindrance. The numerous prodding fingers had driven a semblance of life back into the rusted circuitry.

It would be fair to say that the police had no suspicions about Jess and Mrs. Prune. From the outset it was obvious that the two of them had no intimate connection with the murder of Benjamin Foster.

Constable Parkins, a rather young and impressionable member of the Greyminster force, had originally been worried by Jess' overbearing bulk. Not to mention the aphoristic tattoos and the offensive, partially shaven head. But try as he might he couldn't find any motive and apart from the victim being moved which wasn't included in the official *'Homicide Handbook'*, nothing further could be affirmed.

Fortunately, as yet, people can't be arrested for bearing an offensive look. Otherwise this book might have had a completely different narrative.

Loss, as Mrs. Prune discovered, was best dealt with

by keeping others entertained and yourself as busy as possible. Therefore, a daily offering of ginger cakes and herbal teas occupied most of her waking hours. Through those dark and troubled times her kitchen table seemed forever to be surrounded by a noisy family of boys in blue. At night, however, it was a different matter.

Sunken, disheartening apparitions broke out of her in a feverish sweat—dreams about an unstoppable darkness. An approaching void that chattered on the very edge of her hearing and swallowed up the world as if it was a serpent digesting its food.

She took to catching forty winks during the afternoon; her well seasoned body curled up on the armchair. Life must go on.

The murder inquiries continued at Greyminster police station under the ever vigilant eye of Inspector Reginald Nesbit. Such an event was an uncommon occurrence in Reginald's calendar. Greyminster was not renowned for its violent streets, so the great man himself was determined to deposit every amount of available effort into finding the culprit responsible.

Undoubtedly Reginald had been brought up on a steady diet of Sherlock Holmes, but somehow never quite managed to encapsulate the craftsmanship of the detective himself. The murder remained unsolved and the Inspector himself remained unpromoted.

Eventually, on November 15th, 1998, Benjamin's body was sewn back together following extensive pathological investigations. The autopsy revealed nothing other than a severe case of dandruff, so the corpse had been released back into the world for private burial.

A depressive belt of grey drizzle pervaded the bleak Greyminster fells that morning. The occasional cough of wind would bring out the more substantial rain, previously concealed by the blanket of cloud. At such times it slanted down across the small crowd of associates gathered together at Druids' End Cemetery and stung their hands and faces like a swarm of wet bees.

Mrs. Prune appeared to have misplaced herself in a flamboyant black costume that had more lace about it than a Barbara Cartland novel. She watched in silence, as Father Wordsmith gave his finely tuned sermon.

Jess Hobson had stationed himself beside the grey haired priest, watching the rain form doleful patterns on the toecaps of his boots. The service costs had been met from his own wages; the Wambachs having delivered them personally in a brown envelope marked 'Regrets' despite the unencouraging results on Joseph. It was the least they could do, Mary had said, her voice sounding disconsolate with personal guilt.

But today his thoughts ran much deeper. Deeper perhaps than the rectangular hole into which the rainwashed coffin was slowly being lowered. Thoughts of revenge that bubbled grievously just below the surface.

The funeral service was brief; that much was a mercy. By noon the tight lipped mourners were filing out through the tall iron gates, their down-turned faces reflected in the puddles along the tarmac drive. The whole scene was overlaid by a shroud of shadowy noiselessness.

Mrs. Prune's mottled red cheeks glistened beneath the cumbersome veil that cloaked her features. It was possible that she could have been crying, but this was hard to tell for certain beneath the dense embroidered pleats.

At length, Jess broke the silence with a dramatic and unexpected outburst. 'Thirty-five slappers that bloody vicar cost me. Thirty-five quid t' tell us 'Ee was cut short in 'is prime. 'Ere's some soil an' a sprinkle o' baby slash. Now I'm off to old Ma Johnson's wake where there's some decent grub.' The Irish git!'

Don't be too harsh on Jess Hobson. Although he was mortally wounded inside, Jess was the sort of man who had been brought up never to let his more sensitive emotions surface. Anger, aggression and bigotry had all been acceptable in the household of his childhood. Anything vaguely approaching remorse, however, had been considered effeminate.

Mrs. Prune smudged her cheek with the reverse of her hand and brought the conversation back round to Ben, what with it being his special day and all.

'It's a terrible crime, Jess 'Obson. 'Ee never 'ad a bad word for no-one.'

'W'at utter crud!'

' Well...Almost...' Mrs. Prune continued, retracting her statement slightly to conform with Jess' somewhat shockingly honest approach to such matters. 'Animals thought very fondly of him,' she went on, attempting to justify her previous statement. 'Rupert alwezs looked forward to 'is lettuce leaf on 'is birthday. 'Is little eyes 'd light up and ee'd go bounding across the carpet ten to the dozen.'

Her eyes suddenly became a little misty beneath the black lace veil.

'I remember that time I shut the door on Rupert's 'ead by accident, 'ee was so excited. Couldn't get it back in the shell f'r a week. Looked like a Barbary ape's thumb it did. 'Ad to put it in a splint.'

She reflected for a few short moments on the touching, distant memory.

'Still, it came in 'andy f' leveraging the lids off me bile jars.'

During this last minor insight into Mrs. Prune's psyche, Jess had been studying certain memories of his own. More recent memories. Memories that started to disturb him now that the original fuss was subsiding into commonplace.

'Right. I'm gonna get that grey haired old twanker f' this!'

Worry spread across Mrs. Prune's features creating an accelerated face lift.

"Ee was only doin' 'is job, Mr. 'Obson.'

'I'll show 'im what ghoulies are all about.' Jess continued to himself. 'I'm gonna rip 'is off an' stuff 'em up 'is bloody ghostly arse!!'

'Y' can't blame Reverend Wordsmith f' this. Ee's very old y' know?'

Mrs. Prune was wandering off in totally the wrong direction. 'Ee'd 'ave 'ad to leave because of 'is inconstitutiancies. 'Bin round f' some o' me special 'Dry-as-a-Bone' remedy many a time. It's 'is prosperous gland', y' know?'

'Not the bloody vicar, y' bloated elephants' reproductive pouch!'

Mrs. Prune stiffened at the remark but decided to let it pass under the mitigating circumstances. Jess paused, taking a firmer hold of himself. It was his conclusion that if the job had to be done, it might as well be done thoroughly.

During his outburst the simple but violent outline of a plan had been forming in his brain.

'Get those knackered old candles with the grotesque moon faces on 'em, that y' so proud of, y' fat old warthog. Then meet me at the Wimples. I've got a surprise seance t' conduct. In 'onour of a long forgotten relative!'

In the full knowledge that Jess was tampering with things best left alone, Mrs. Prune set about gathering the required items from her cramped kitchen cupboards. However, not once in her great many years as a witch had she actually managed to establish a contact with the dead, so she proceeded without too much anxiety.

She collected her candles and skulls into an old cardboard box. Then translating Jess' parting instruction as *to meet him at the Wambachs*, she arranged the occult gathering over the telephone. It transpired that 10 o'clock that very night would be more than convenient. Which gave her just enough time to get the washing down off the line and check that Rupert was hibernating safely.

November 15th. 10:30 p.m. 113 Applegate. Site of the great seance.

Mr. and Mrs. Wambach had obligingly erected an old wallpapering table in Joseph's nursery. Now it was covered with a formal gingham table cloth that only usually saw the light of day when the Wambachs were entertaining visiting dignitaries. Exactly how appropriate the false flowers ornamenting the central section of the make-shift table were, or indeed the porcelain swan that Mary had added as an after thought, was open for discussion.

Both parents, Mrs. Prune and Jess Hobson sat around the dining table in the dim flickering swath of orange light that diffused outwards from the carved pumpkin mouth. Their hands were now spread, palms down, upon the ironed cloth.

Mary sat to the right of Mrs. Prune, a slight tremor throughout her frame making dozens of tiny goosebumps sit up to attention down her spine. Her throat was dry with expectation. The belief that action was finally being taken had wound up her psychology like a tense clockwork spring. She felt, at this point, that she ought to show her appreciation for the valiant efforts of all concerned. With an amount of uncertainty she proffered the following suggestion.

'Would anybody like a cup of tea before we begin?'

She turned to Mrs. Prune specifically, believing her to be the instigator of tonight's latest rescue attempt.

'We've got some very nice *Raspberry Leaf* Madam 'Victoria'?'

'No thanks. I don't want t' go upsettin' me tubes again.'

Jess raised an eyebrow in agreement with that.

'Not after w'at 'appened last time.' He readjusted the collar on his lime-coloured turtleneck with one probing finger and added, obligingly, 'I'm still findin' reports off the RSPCA jammed in the letterbox, makin' discreet enquires about the budgie.'

'Perhaps some Camomile then? I thought you might enjoy that,' Mary continued undeterred. She'd gone shopping especially that afternoon for such exotic beverages as Lapsang, Darjeeling and Spanish Fly—whatever her naive instincts had considered appropriate.

'No!'

'Cowslip and Parsley Herb?'

'SHUDDUP about the bloody tea, y' senile old reptile!'

Mrs. Prune looked askance at the surviving member of her household, her mounting concern for his well being evidently displayed across her troubled features.

Since turning his fortieth birthday Jess had definitely grown more irrational, more introspective, more lethargic. Certainly more intolerant, storing all his pent-up emotion deep inside and releasing it at random on unsuspecting victims. Now he was fast approaching boiling point; poised to go off like a grenade.

Unfortunately, none of the other guests around the table shared Mrs. Prune's concern. Jess' unreasonable behaviour had overstepped the bounds of polite conversation. If it hadn't have been for Benjamin's recent death clouding their more conservative judgement, then no doubt a great deal more would have been said.

A heavy, awkward tension now expanded above the heads of the gathering. Jacob Wambach fumed slightly in his seat; a normally sensitive representative of our species. When he spoke it was deliberate and about as composed as was humanly possible under the circumstances.

'My wife's got a very feeble constitution, you know?'

The distance between Jess' impenetrable head and Jacob's blanched skull narrowed disagreeably. 'She'll 'av a bloody feeble broken neck in a minute if she doesn't shut it! D' y' want to find out w'at's 'appened t' y' child, or what?'

'Yes...'

'Then keep it shtum! Or else I'll be forced t' peel y' lips back over your head an' tie y' bulbous tongue in a knot!' Jess added.

Mrs. Prune felt it prudent to intervene at this point.

'Mrs. Wambach?' she interposed in her most cultured manner, turning round to Mary who by this point bore an expression of mounting fear. 'Did y' manage t' find an item belongin' to little Joseph? At all..?'

That did the trick. Mrs. Wambach snapped back into the real world, hopeful and full of vigour once more.

'Oh...yes.'

She disappeared beneath the voluminous cloth. Seconds later she re-emerged, having produced a stained yellow potty from under her chair. Unceremoniously she plonked it down next to the vase of flowers. Mr. Wambach flinched backwards, his buckled teeth clenched.

'Bloody 'ell woman. I've got to have me breakfast off this in the morning!'

'Pathetic old slapper,' Jess hissed, chewing the words up beneath his breath. Then out loud he added aggressively, 'Now, can we get ON!?'

Mrs. Prune locked her fingers into an arch and cracked the knuckles.

'Just a moment. I've got t' prepare.'

She started by shrugging her shoulders and creaking her head round in a clockwise direction, to loosen the muscles in her neck. Shortly after, her rugged face assumed a tormented, strained expression of concentration. After several seconds a loud and disruptive fart opened everybody's eyes wide with the shock.

'Ahh. That's better.'

Mrs. Prune never stood on ceremony for long and a 'little skweeker' as she was in the habit of referring to such things, always helped to break an oppressive mood.

Mr. Wambach pushed his chair back with such violence that the legs sparked off the floorboards, and he cried in disgust, 'My God woman! That's brought tears to my eyes!'

'It 'asn't done much good t' mine mate, I can tell y'!'

And at that point Jess lost his temper. It had been a trying few weeks and he'd taken about as much as he could stand. Ascending so rapidly it sent his chair tumbling over backwards, he slammed his giant fist down on the table top, upsetting the pottery swan.

'Right!' he snarled. 'I've 'ad enough of this bloody farce!'

Through gritted teeth he stormed on.

'If there's anybody from the other side 'angin' about round here, then speak NOW!!'

The pungent taste of the air made itself known on the back of his throat.

'If y' can still breathe,' he added.

Then the remarkable happened. A voice trembled across the room. It was a haunting and hollow voice. I'm not going to say that it appeared 'out of the thin air', because by this point the atmosphere was anything but thin. However, the voice played around the assembled heads with the youthful buoyancy of a babbling stream.

'*Madam Victoria?*' it said, echoing through Mrs. Prune's skull and emerging from the other side. '*It's me…Benjamin Foster!*'

Mrs. Prune desperately cast her gaze around the company. She wasn't exactly sure what it was that she was hoping to alight upon, but her senses were now reeling with a full bloodied confusion. Somebody was actually trying to tune in to her psychic wavelength and it was obvious that nobody else at the table had heard a sound.

A trio of bewildered looking faces bore down upon her.

Whereupon, Benjamin Foster materialised in the corner of the room. His face was ashen grey; his eyes were sunken into bottomless black receptacles. His form was transparent but still quite recognisable as the Benjamin she knew so well. Mrs. Prune gawked at the figure.

'Oh, bloody 'Ell! I'm off!'

In her haste to get out the teapot was sent flying; a corkscrew of camomile twisting scaldingly across the room. Mrs. Wambach felt an elbow connect with the side of her head as Mrs. Prune's boots clattered and skidded on the slippery wooden floor.

She rounded the corner of the table with haste, Jess lunging out at her desperately but missing.

'W'at's goin' on?' she heard him shout as she collided with the wardrobe. Ben's voice echoed frighteningly from several feet just behind her.

'Mrs. Prune,' it called. 'Don't go. I've got to warn you!'

Within seconds she had clumped down the stairs and entered the porch muttering, 'Bugger me backwards. Me great giddy fat aunt!'

'Mrs. Prune. You're in terrible danger!'

She flung the front door open wide and scrabbled through it into the cold, dark night beyond.

Down a narrow cobbled street a few short minutes later Mrs. Prune gyrated to an unsteady halt, clutching at her ample bosom as if her heart was about to shatter. She hadn't expected that to happen.

Up until now, rather ironically, Mrs. Prune had never had any direct experience with the supernatural. Everything that had happened concerning the disappearance of Joseph Wambach; the bulging bedstead, the haunted TV set, everything had been handed down to her second generation. She had naturally assumed therefore, that those relating the stories were simply exaggerating for the sake of dramatisation. That was the sort of thing that she would have done and like most people the world over, she suspected everybody else as having the same character flaws that she had. But now this? Well...this was something again!

For the first time in her existence Mrs. Prune began to feel unsure about herself. She stopped, leant backwards against a brick wall and tried to catch her breath, in the hopes that doing so she might sort out the complicated information inside her head. Unfortunately, she didn't get the opportunity to complete the task.

A shape soundlessly removed itself from the dirty shadows, forming into the hunch-backed figure of Thomas Hobson. His repugnant tanned teeth opened capaciously into a damp, gummy grin.

'Well...well...well,' came the cracked voice as he approached her like a crab, leaning persuasively forwards onto his coiling rod. 'Madame Prune!'

Already Mrs. Prune had recognised the face; the sunken, viperous eyes and the chiselled coathanger cheekbones. She'd seen it before on an ancient black and white photograph that she'd found in the drawing room the day she took possession of the house.

For the second time ever, and all within the stretch of only a couple of short but action packed minutes, she understood that she was looking into the eyes of a ghost.

A solid ghost, but nonetheless, a ghastly phantom returned from the dead.

Hobson's eyes compacted into scant slots that were buried beneath the cracked and craggy cliff of his forehead. 'Or should I call you *Cynthia Bottomlash?*'

Mrs. Prune's personal history was rather dark and murky. Once times had been extremely hard on her; there had, after all, been a war on. Most people knew better than to discuss such delicate matters as Mrs. Prune's private and confidential past. Living people, generally, with noses to be broken and eyes to be blackened.

'Call me w'at y' like, deary.' Despite her better efforts, the customary amiability was now discarded from her voice. 'Y' couldn't scare the 'obnails out o' me forty year old boots!'

'I know your history, Mrs. Prune.' Hobson's accusing form closed the gap. Stubborn to the quick, Mrs. Prune refused to budge a solitary inch. 'Last of the great British Witches.'

That took her by surprise. She raised an eyebrow coquettishly, allowing for time whilst she regained the full strength of her lungs.

'Well, it's more than I bloody do, then.'

'And I know how the prime minister of this great country of yours',' Hobson flourished his arms about in an all encompassing movement. 'Was once a naughty boy.'

He forced his grotesque head ever closer, draining the blood from Mrs. Prune's.

'And how you gave him such a sound thrashing.'

A polluted, dry wheeze of a laugh cackled scratchily from his wet maw.

Mrs. Prune belted him hard in the groin with the metal-tipped point of her sturdy brolly. In agony he doubled up, clutching at the afflicted area.

'Then know this about me, Thomas 'Obson, last bastard son of a great line o' bastards. I don't give up wi'out a fight, y' hear! So y'd better 'ave a damn good needle an' cotton ready! 'Cos y'll be sewing y' ghostly gonads back on, back in the bowels of Hell where y' belong!!'

With which defiant parting words Mrs. Prune hitched up her skirts and hobbled off, her figure rapidly receding into the shadows. Thomas watched her disappear, embroiled in a world of his own personal suffering.

'Count your days wisely you voluptuous old walrus. You'll discover that there's less of them than you might suspect!' His voice ricocheted off the ginnel walls; his decrepit features awash with blue moonlight.

'You're down on my list, old sow! I'm going to kick those offensive buttocks of yours half way round the cosmic plains and back before you're done with!'

Mrs. Prune careered around the corner of the street, her 'offensive buttocks' colliding with a wall and her boots momentarily losing grip on the icy stones. Behind her, Thomas Hobson's evil, penetrating cackle rose from the darkness and pierced the heart of the night.

Chapter Seven

Jannice Applebotham's Guide To Feminist Principles.

Stop all the clocks. Crank the hour hands backwards if you would. Force 'Old Father Time' himself to look back across his scythe-mounted shoulder and watch the present contracting into the faraway distance.

Farther and farther into the past we hurtle, stripping away at the years. Watching them unwind like an orange peel beneath the blade of our regression. All the way backwards to the year of 1989. Just as the summer is about to crumble into autumn. Several years before Hobson & Co had as much as even been thought of.

A particular time when a video film was about to be recorded in the attic flat at number 12, Gasworks' Road, Greyminster.

'Hello, I'm Jannice,' said Jannice Applebotham, 'and this is Janet,' she added, pointing at her gaunt friend on the springless sofa.

'It's Janette, actually.'

'Sorry, Jar-nette then.' Jannice frowned before continuing. 'Whatever, we live in the same flat and we both go to college. I'm studying Cartesian Dualism, Modern Media Ethics and Women's Studies.'

There was a substantial pause whilst Jar-nette gathered her scatter-brained wits about her.

'And I'm taking Sociology.'

'And today we're going to discuss the attitude of the male presence in an evolving modern society.' Jannice appeared to be satisfied with that, as if the sentence was some sort of accomplishment in itself. She turned to Janet wearing a sanguine expression.

'So, Jar-nette...What do you think about the '*Modern Man*'?'

Janet drew in an abundant breath and perused her mental list of alternative options.

'I like a man with a small, tight bottom,' she said.

There followed a pause, after which Jannice leaned forwards and turned the video camera off. The final shot consisted of her scowling features becoming blurred as the focal point of the camera exceeded its minimum limits. The next time that the camera was turned back on Jannice wasn't looking quite so thunderstruck.

She sat on her bed; a sort of fractured patchwork affair, holding a paltry but lethal looking object not too dissimilar to a spin-inhaler.

'Now this is a must for every liberated woman,' she stated emphatically. 'It's a self defence mechanism, which when activated...'

Her thumb pressed a cream coloured button upon the object's crown, and a loud and horrible whine started to oscillate across the bedroom walls. Although Jannice continued to talk above it, presumably under the impression that what she heard in her own head was the same as what everybody else heard, it was impossible to understood a single word of what she was saying.

However the microphone was just about able to distinguish a loud thumping noise which started from the next door neighbours.

The next shot on the video consisted of Janet in an armchair with her knees tucked beneath her chin and her toes gripping the edge of the slouching cushion. In time honoured fashion she was using her knees as a book rest, a sizable photograph-album spread open before her vivacious gaze. Jannice had hold of the camera at this point. She dramatically closed in on the portfolio, as the following exchange took place.

'So, Jar-nette, what's this that you wanted to show me?'

'Right...' Janet looked up at the camera lens, blinked and looked back down to her most treasured item. 'This is my photograph album which is totally dedicated to Mel Gibbon.'

The camera closed in on the pages, revealing a collection of photographs. Some were cut out of newspapers; others rescued from magazines. Apart from the odd Patrick Sway that had somehow managed to avoid Janet's scrupulous censorship, every one of them involved Mel Gibbon in some manner or other.

Mel was talking. Mel was walking. Mel was looking rather haggard in the white flash of a camera bulb that had managed to get close enough to unveil the strain of too much alcohol lodged in his system. Mel was posing as a bronze-bodied warrior with a studded patch across one eye and a loin cloth padded with several socks, in his most famous, and youngest role.

Jannice couldn't help noticing however, that interspersed with all of this, various images of posteriors had been shrewdly disorganised.

'I've been collecting this since I was seventeen,' Janet affably confessed. 'When I first saw Mel in Tequila Sunset.'

'And is this really Mel Gibbon's bottom?'

'Well, no...' Janet looked a little crestfallen that her secret was out. But she recovered impressively. 'It's Keith Phegwin's actually. I cut it out of Girl Talk, but I like to pretend it's from that bit in Deadlly Weapon Ten, where Mel stands up with his bare bottom in the camera and...'

'It's a bit sad isn't it?'

That caught Janet slightly off guard.

'Sorry?'

'Don't you think that such things are perpetuating the social myth that women are dependent on the male of the species?'

An internal struggle was now clearly visible across Janet's features. After several arduous seconds she appeared to abandon the problem to its own devices. Instead, she browsed through the plastic coated pages with a new found enthusiasm.

'Actually, I've got a dead good one here.' She alighted upon a larger than average photograph of herself. Mel Gibbon's head had been cut out and stuck onto the person standing next to her. She had obviously used too much glue and he now had a thumb-smeared halo. 'This is the time that Mel and I eloped to the South of France and had a dirty weekend without his wife knowing. It's not true of course but it's one of my greatest fantasies.'

She hugged the scrapbook intimately to her little, flat chest.

'Jar-nette. This sort of behaviour is just as responsible for female repression as those men themselves. How can you let down the sisterhood in this manner?'

'Oh get stuffed y' stuck up cow! Just 'cos y' can't get a shag!' Janet's patience was only a veneer to her personality it would seem.

'I am a celibate feminist actually!'

'You're an ugly old dog who can't get a pork more like!'

The screen went blank. Several moments of grey interference supervened. Next up was a shot of a hand-scrawled title card that was pinned to the contorted trunk of a wintry tree. It read 'Jannice's Guide to Feminist Principles', and was followed by an excessive number of exclamation marks.

Jess Hobson, looking several years younger but every bit as ugly and bald as his modern counterpart, watched on from the park bench, as Jannice testily attacked the camera's remote control with the pressure of both thumbs. Jess looked wearied, unfulfilled, brimming with ennui and starting to feel humiliated already. But a promise was a promise and he'd had no alternative.

At length Jannice sorted out her technical problems and turned to face the camera, adopting what she considered to be an approachable, happy-go-lucky expression.

'In our constant struggle for recognition and equality in a chauvinistic, male dominated society,' she began. 'Women must first recognise their natural enemy.'

She turned to Jess.

'Jess here is a typical example of the anally expressive masculine.'

'W'at!?'

Jess' expression crumpled up into a mangled boxing glove of puzzlement.

'His behavioural patterns,' Jannice continued regardless. 'Are inherent within all male offspring of our society, along with socially aggressive behaviour, gender stereotyping and extreme homophobia.'

'Oy!'

'The only way in which we, as women...'

'Just a minute. Are you callin' me a queer?'

'Can combat such deeply engrained prejudices...'

'Hold on. Are you sayin' that I'm a brown hatter or somethin'?'

'Is by drawing public attention to men's fundamental faults...'

'I'm not a bloody bottom bandit!!'

'And holding them up to self scrutiny.'

'Don't call me a bender!'

At this point Jannice turned around to the increasingly vociferous Jess.

'What?'

'I'm not a shirt lifter, all right? Turn that camera off now!'

He closed in on the camera menacingly, reaching out with one giant hand that encompassed the whole of the lens.

'Y' not callin' me a queer bugger!'

Once more the video jumped forwards in time; a leap indicated by several short moments of hissing and rumbling static. Jannice reappeared once more, now standing in her room before a notice board. A board containing several complicated diagrams of what supposedly represented female organs. All had been drawn with a black marker pen.

The words 'Battery Low' had already started to flash intermittently on the screen as, ignorant of this valuable piece of information, Jannice started talking to a nonexistent audience once more.

'Now let's look at some of the ways that women can avoid a build up of pus and membrane by using the correct sanitary towel.'

Whereupon, fortunately perhaps, the recording ended somewhat abruptly. At a later point in time Jess Hobson must have reused the cassette, because the ending had been filled with cartoons recorded from satellite television.

It was important to reveal the contents of the video at this point. It might not appear so right now, but they do bear a relevance to our unfolding story. And it's as well to understand that particular part of Jess Hobson's history, in the knowledge that at some future time, one of the characters might just reappear.

The only other video that managed to survive past the point of no return, in fact the only other video that was contained within our mysterious box, bore the legend, 'Revenge of the Chainsaw Prostitutes, 5'. It was decorated with a rather gaudy cover, detailing a surgically enhanced woman in a leather thong. She was wielding a heavy looking chainsaw with globules of blood smeared across her cheeks.

There's not much point in me detailing what was contained on the cassette. I'm sure that the readers can work out that one for themselves without too much trouble.

That's enough time for the past now. Wind the clocks

forward once more. Wind them quickly and let's get on. Back through the discourse of the turbulent 90's. Back to the point before our attention was drawn away.

Chapter Eight

A Dance With The Devil.

This is Mrs. Prune's bedroom. A private boudoir where mortal man would fear to tread. Not that mortal man would want to tread in it anyhow.

Apart from the lace curtains, the ornamental ewer, a gaudy baroque gold-painted mirror with a crack down one side thrust into the corner out of harm's way, and the patchwork eiderdown mauling the huge feather mattress, it is a practical enough room.

The gigantic pine bed dominated the floor like some prehistoric animal; the eiderdown resembling a partially inflated hot air balloon. On its end, a brown earthenware hot water-bottle smouldered lethargically.

Various fluffy toys that would sell for a bomb in commendable London antique shops, shared their home with occultist souvenirs brought back from holidays around the British Isles. Cornish Tarot cards, astrological calendars from Dorset, The Bumper Book of Fortune Telling that she'd uncovered in a poky old bookshop on the Isle Of Man.

Amongst them all was Mrs. Prune, attired for bed, though somehow she was managing to wear more clothing now than she wore at any other time of the day. Several long, clumsy jumpers created an unflattering bulge beneath her nightgown and her feet had swollen to disproportionate size due to the various layers of socks she had on.

It was now 12:35 a.m.; the witching hour, and all was not well at 114 Applegate.

Here is Mrs. Prune prowling about her own bedroom, a guttering candle in its sooted tin holder clamped firmly onto the end of her thumb. Its probing branches of light ironically created patches of darkness in every nook and cranny of the misshapen room. An uneasiness had settled on Mrs. Prune's brow that was even now working its extremities towards the pith of her nervous system.

With the iron poker clutched so fixedly in her other hand that the knuckles had turned white beneath the fearsome grip, she interrogated the rug that lay under the bed. In the process she disturbed a few tired mice. Nothing of any consequence there.

Also nothing inside the 'Po' which rang stridently with the sound of china upon iron. Nothing on the top of the wardrobe either, where several fluffy bunnies got a violent whacking.

Eventually, apparently satisfied with her endeavours, Mrs. Prune climbed back into her cocoon, pulling up the bloated eiderdown so far that it fingered her ample chin. Resolutely she started to plough through an 'Old Rogers' Almanac.' But tonight, her thoughts were deeply rooted elsewhere; her concentration wholly crushed beneath her anxiety.

'No bugger's gonna frighten me out o' me beauty sleep,' she muttered stubbornly to herself.

After a moment's reflection she continued, 'Not that I need it, but principles are principles.'

'*Mrs. Prune?*' said a voice that was so close to her left ear she dropped the yellowing booklet and her old heart momentarily skipped an important beat. '*Mrs. Prune? I've* got to talk now and it's more important than...than...'

The voice trailed off as if deep in thought.

'Than a very important thing indeed,' it decided.

'Buggerin' 'Ell!'

Mrs. Prune started to flap in panic. Tugging the poker from where she had recently discreted it beneath the flamboyant pillow, she determinedly set her rumpled face against the dark.

'Calm down. It's me!'

There was no response. Mrs. Prune's jaw had locked up as solidly as a Chinese puzzle box. The voice faltered for a moment, and then continued, regardless.

'It's me...Benjamin Foster!'

'Ben Foster?' Mrs. Prune furtively scanned her immediate surroundings, finding horror in every shadow. 'The idiot 'oo looks like 'is 'eads bin stuck down a waste disposal pipe? W'at the bloody 'Ell's the idea? Prowlin' about in an 'onest woman's bedroom?'

Benjamin Foster slowly manifested himself at the foot of the great bed whilst Mrs. Prune clutched the iron poker emphatically to her bosom. His appearance was just as ghastly as she had remembered it from the seance; every minuscule detail permanently engraved across her memory by a cerebral soldering iron.

Ben looked down at his pale almost diaphanous boots, going pink with embarrassment. It was, admittedly, a rather unhealthy pink.

'Sorry, Madam Victoria. Under normal circumstances I wouldn't entertain the idea of entering your bedroom.' He held the thought for a moment and then added with some reserve, 'Not even for the largest cream cake in history. With

Mrs. Prune started to flap in panic. Tugging the poker from where she had recently discreted it beneath the flamboyant pillow, she determinedly set her rumpled face against the dark.

a cherry on the top as large as the cross-section of a Zeppelin.'

It was an immature thing to say, but it grabbed Mrs. Prune's attention.

'Talk like that gets y' a slap round the chops.' Successfully Ben had managed to overpower Mrs. Prune's dread, replacing it instead with a great sense of personal indignation. 'Now waddaya want?!'

'It's about that Presbyterian minister...' He cocked one eyebrow at a curious angle, attempting to indicate that the very mention of Hobson's name was tantamount to blasphemy. *'What with you being a witch and all.'*

Ben paused once more, sorting out his inextricable thoughts. It was his earnest intention to avoid terms such as *ducking stool* and *old biddy*. Words that he felt might offend his amiable landlady.

Mrs. Prune contorted her features into a nonchalant, unconcerned expression. 'Oh 'im? We've met. Great big puff 'ee is. Don't scare me none.'

It was a good job that Mrs. Prune wasn't made of wood. If she had have been, her nose would have no doubt smashed through the ornamental mirror on the other side of the room. Instead, she defiantly brandished the poker in front of her forehead, several specks of soot tumbling off onto the neatly stitched quilt.

'If 'ee tries it on wi' me, 'ee'll know what Jack. B. Nimble felt like w'en 'ee slipped on the candle flack wi' 'is buttocks splayed!'

She leaned forwards, her questioning tones sounding somewhat insinuatory.

'Any'ow, can't you sort 'im out?'

A twitch bewilderingly shuddered across her head. Ben

suspected that it was supposed to represent Mrs. Prune's version of a conspiratorial wink. In reality it looked as if she was trying to dislodge a cockroach from her right ear.

'W'at wi' you bein' dead an' all?'

'Dead?'

Astonishment played around the edges of Ben's indented black eyes. With apparent difficulty he struggled to sort out the jumbled events of the last few hours. At least, what appeared to him to be the 'Last Few Hours' anyhow. Time shows an altogether different perspective to the deceased. After several seconds of industrious thought, he realized that he couldn't and stared back at Mrs. Prune.

'What do you mean, dead?'

Mrs. Prune's venerable lips puckered up like a hen's bottom about to lay. She shook her head with an impressive draw of breath.

'Oh, bloody 'Ell. C'mon sit down on me commode, young Ben Foster. I'm not sure 'ow I'm going to break this to y'!'

As she watched an evanescent blue glow formed around Benjamin's outline. Then he was gone.

Mrs. Prune stared profoundly into the void where he had moments before been standing, and found herself examining a laceration in the flowery paper border. Her line of sight followed it along the wall for several feet, before it met with a lintel and reached an abrupt halt. Despite all the ghostly comings and goings that she had witnessed in such proliferation already that night, this last act particularly unnerved her.

She was just about to clamber out of bed and with ancient wisdom pass her hand through the empty space on the off chance that Benjamin hadn't really vanished at all, when a voice uncomfortably close by her ear muttered, '*Mrs. Prune?*'

The full impact of the shock knocked her backwards into the bedstead.

There was Benjamin, seated demurely, expectantly, on the renaissance Georgian commode; his hands on his knees and an expression of startled innocence pervading his anxious head. Mrs. Prune caught her breath, swallowed, checked that her heartbeat was back where it belonged and cocked him an angry glance.

'Stop buggerin' about like that!'

Her stare was returned. Benjamin appeared to have no comprehension what his landlady was talking about.

'I've got t' get six sets o' tights off t' change me drawers, y' know,' Mrs. Prune went on adamantly. 'An' it's bloody chilly in that bathroom.'

She regained enough composure to continue in a more moderate tone.

'Now.'

A thought struck her. It was quite apparent to anybody who had a brain only marginally greater than that of a goldfish, that Benjamin had no idea about his supernatural nuances. If she wasn't careful, breaking the news of his death to him might...well, it might kill him all over again. She chose her next move with extreme caution.

'W'at I'm about t' say might come as a bit of a shock t' y' system.'

With a wagging index finger she pointed at the chipped and deeply stained chamberpot embedded in the bulk of the commode's padded seat.

'S' make sure the lid on that Victorian potty's up.'

'It's not about the birds and the bees again, is it?' Ben looked aggrieved. 'The last lot of advice you gave me on that subject was about as much use as crocheted bog paper.'

'It's bugger all t' do with nuptials!'

Mrs. Prune drew in another deep breath that, had it been any stronger, would have loosened the wallpaper, and decided that it might be best if she just came straight to the point.

'You're dead Ben Foster! Stone, cold *dead!*'

This seemed to throw Ben off guard. At length he emerged from his introspection and frowned.

'What exactly do you mean by 'dead'?'

Defeated, Mrs. Prune threw her arms in the air.

'Dead! Y' know..?' She struggled to find the appropriate words that would somehow extrapolate the point. 'Dead! *Dead* as in the Labour Party's socialist policies! *Dead* as in John Merrick's sex life! *Dead* as in Douglas Bader's tap-dancing lessons!! You're a ghostly phantom with no more right to be on God's clean Earth than Attila the Hun! You're dead, Ben Foster. D. E. D. Dead!'

A remote realisation appeared to be dawning.

'Right...I wondered why that fat bird at the supermarket was ignoring me.' He thought about that. *'And only you can see me, right?'*

Mrs. Prune donned her frail, half moon spectacles and blinked through them. The lenses magnified her eyeballs so that they resembled two enormous moist eggs.

'An' from where I'm sat, Ben Foster, y' don't look in

none too good 'ealth neither.'

'Well, that's put a bit of a downer on Christmas...'

Something in the back of Ben's mind cried out for attention.

'That probably explains what it is I know...' His voice was hesitant.

'An' w'at's that?'

'There's something...horrible hanging around this house...'

Mrs. Prune visibly relaxed, the tension sagging from her shoulders so that she resembled a rubber dingy going down.

'That'll be the plumbing. It's bunged up agen. Some o' Jess' floaters are more like sentient life forms. I reckon there's an 'ole gang of 'em somew'ere actin' like performin' sealions.'

She took off her glasses, folded them squarely and laid them to rest on the bolstered pillow.

'My great grandfather...' ventured Ben, with some uncertainty. *'He must want the last of the Hobson bloodline.'*

'Y' know, Ben...' said Mrs. Prune. 'I'm glad you're back.'

She suddenly realised that had sounded somewhat sentimental. It was out of place and not in keeping with her usual down-to-earth character. Mrs. Prune wouldn't stand for that. So she added a harder edge to her voice and continued. 'I want y' t' look out f' Jess. Ee's bin acting very odd lately.'

She mulled over past events to herself and sought for the tell-tale signs amongst them.

'Very aggressive. Out o' control.'

'That's not exactly news is it?'

'Worse than usual. I think 'ee might be 'avin' a nervicular breakdown.'

At which important juncture there was an earsplitting crash from somewhere downstairs. An exorbitant clamor, that brought the conversation to a standstill. Both looked down at the carpet, stupefaction written coarsely into their respective features.

After several moments, when it had become apparent that the floor was not the cause and had nothing further to offer by the way of explanation, Mrs. Prune flung back the patchwork quilt and struggled from the bed. With outstretched toes she plonked her square feet into a pair of massive fluffy slippers; each one of which bore a plastic rabbit's face on the top.

'Bugger it!' she muttered, dragging her dressing-gown from the hook on the back of the door. 'There's no rest f' the wicked.'

Downstairs Jess Hobson was staggering about with a similar gait to that of a performing circus bear. He was roughly half a shandy off being completely paralytic. As he tumbled and wove an intricate track about the apartment, he dislodged countless towers of books that scattered across the carpet and came to rest with their pages fluttering in the draught from under the door.

During his heady progress toward the television set, Jess sang drunkenly in the sort of voice that only karaoke singers can manage.

'Oh Mary this London's a wonderful sight! It's full of old cockneys an' they're all talkin' shite!'

Somehow he reached the gimcrack set and collapsed before it in an intoxicated homage. Pointlessly he attempted to switch it on by jabbing angrily with the remote. Nothing happened. Nothing that is, apart from the Biro sliding several inches back down the tube of Sellotape. Jess clenched his fist and thumped the television several times upon the top. Then he studied the screen closely as if the set would apologize for its behaviour immediately and resume normal programmes for fear of its life.

At which point he noticed the On/Off button and made a connection in his head. Perhaps he ought to use his actual finger. After several drunken attempts the button clicked and the sudden scream of the 'Pelvic Sculpture Panty Liner' woman sent him toppling over backwards. Moments later, Jess sprawled ungracefully into the one remaining erect pile of books.

As he struggled onto all fours and crawled slowly back toward the set, his outstretched hand reaching desperately for the volume control, Jess was filled with a sudden sinking sensation. The impression that he was not alone in the dark with his suffering.

Another figure stood in the room. A gaunt and oppressive figure, its tall shadow falling over him in a translucent cloak. The figure was old, and it was bent, and it ailed from a tiny amount of wavy white hair that was attached precariously to the top of its head in the fashion of a lizard's Mohican. Samuel Foster watched the pathetic creature wretchedly beleaguered on the floor in front of him.

Then he sprang with the agility of a cat, and landed,

claws outstretched, on Jess Hobson's spine. A hirsute length of rope found its way around Jess' wide neck. Jess gagged as the hemp tightened itself, forcing his tongue from his mouth.

'Got a problem, Hobson?' The incorporeal figure expectorated the words. 'Last malicious home wrecker of the great bastard family!'

Mrs. Prune hobbled through the lamplit streets of Greyminster, her overstretched heart pounding dramatically beneath her bodice. Out of breath she turned from the sweeping tree-lined crescent and entered the private gravel driveway of a tall Victorian house.

It would have been a pleasant driveway under normal circumstances. Long austere trees stared gravely down upon the heads of those passing below. Despite its great height the house wore a somnolent character; very middle-class, extremely sensible almost to the point of hibernation. But Mrs. Prune had no time to notice such trivialities just now.

If Thomas Hobson or Samuel Foster were involved in the rumpus back at Applegate, then there wasn't a lot that she could do about it herself. So she had decided to turn to somebody who might help. Even those so closely associated with the pagan religion as Mrs. Prune sometimes needed Christianity, if only for a second opinion.

She stopped just to the side of the grand front doorstep, bent up double, clutching her creaking knees firmly with her copious hands. After several moments of intensive inhalation she finally looked up at the shiny rectangular window that occupied a good third of the whole first floor.

'I'm getting too old f' this sort o' thing,' she muttered, her cheeks flushed and her bosom still heaving up and down like a couple of bald headed pygmies. 'Father Wordsmith!'

She gave it a moment.

'FATHER BUGGERIN' WORDSMITH!!!'

This time the window opened with a sort of 'Swoosh' noise and the frowning head of the old priest poked itself out, resembling a snail emerging from its shell. He wasn't used to being so rudely disturbed at this hour of the night.

Picking up his spectacles from a table just out of sight, the father positioned them carefully on the end of his red-veined nose. Drowsily he squinted down into the gloom.

'Mrs. Prune? What's got your knickers in a flap at this ungodly hour?'

'Just get y' fat arse down 'ere Father! 'Scuse me French. I'm in need o' y' services, pretty damn sharp.'

She took another look at her aching feet as her boots pinched angrily at each individual toe. Then she raised her features once more, reflecting on the previous phrase.

'An' no smutty innuendoes neither!'

Ducking his head back in at the window, Father Wordsmith called out, 'I'll just get my bag, Mrs. Prune.'

Mrs. Prune, who was under the apprehension that men are men, even those as wears a frock, called back at the top of her mighty voice, 'Leave 'er asleep Father. Just get y' drawers on prompt.'

She watched him vanish. Then she turned to the gate, her thoughts moving rapidly on to matters altogether more important.

'I only 'opes we'll be in time.'

Jess Hobson writhed beneath the remarkably dense weight of Samuel Foster. His bloodied nose had been buried brutally into the carpet. The coarse rigging that bound his broad wrists stung, cutting deep wields in the flesh. A pair of extremely suspect and soiled socks had been pushed across his forehead and into the front line of his olfactory senses.

'Breathe them in deeply, Jess Hobson,' trembled the hideous booming voice. 'I'd like to think that your last lungful of air was made toxic by your own rank abominations. My only worry is that they might crawl off before I've done.'

Jess was fast approaching the conclusion that his new found playmate had one or two minor psychological problems.

'One hundred and one years, sixteen days and four hours.' Benjamin's great-grandfather gloated over the accomplishment. 'All that time I've spent trying to get back to this realm of *mortality*.'

The word 'mortality' had a special echo all of its own. 'All with the intent of destroying the last 'Usurper Hobson'!'

'Y're a bit of an anorak really, aren't y'?' mumbled Jess, an offensive cheesy woollen toe attempting to climb into his mouth and disintegrate his teeth.

Foster stopped struggling. This sent a shockwave through the whole of Jess' nervous system. Somehow the sudden and profound sense of calm bothered him more than the fight had done.

'Time has just run out, Jess Hobson.'

A familiar large, blood-stained frying pan appeared in Samuel Foster's right hand. Not a frying pan that would be familiar to Jess, but one that might be recognised by the more observant reader. Foster raised it determinedly above his head, concentrating upon the nodule on the back of Jess' whiskered skull.

'Goodnight,' he said softly, phlegm cracking on the back of his haggard old throat. 'Goodnight, forever, you vicious bastard!'

*A familiar large, blood-stained frying pan appeared in
Samuel Foster's right hand.*

Chapter Nine

The Ghost Of La Mancha.

1:35 a.m. November 16th, 1998. The *End Of The World* draws another step closer. Number 32, Old Bridge Lane. This is the home of Donald Keith Oakseed; a retired bank clerk of little notability.

It is also the discharge point for an unusually increased amount of paranormal activity. Which goes some way towards explaining why Donald was about to experience the full brunt of the universe's unpredictable nature.

The cellar of number thirty-two was a dark and dangerous place at night. Shadows from the arched grills that lifted themselves marginally above the lamplit street outside, fell across the stone floor resembling the bars of a cage.

Amongst the cardboard boxes; amongst the mounds of long forgotten junk; amongst the battered suitcases and the towers of old accounts; something stirred. Something barely perceptible to the untrained ear. A rattling, a scuffling, a sinister movement, shifting uneasily about, disturbing the stillness of the night without consideration. The brittle sound of a whisper breathed across the flagstones before snaking up and around the blotches of mould that peppered the damp brick walls.

A glass orb that was roughly the size of a baseball, rolled out into the columns of dusty dim light being cast from beyond the metal rods. A bright yellow orb with a purple stripe coiled around it, much as you might imagine a child's lollipop to look.

It started to spin. At first so gradually that it was hard to make out whether or not it was actually turning at all. But with every full rotation the orb gathered momentum. Faster now, and faster still. Soon so fast that its harsh edges became blurred and its molten interior resembled indistinct washing tumbling hurriedly within the heart of an out-of-control machine. Watch it spin! Try to focus on the ever more nebulous outline.

Then it stopped. Suddenly and dramatically. It had skewed to a halt with such instantaneousness that it appeared to have never been moving at all.

With a jolt the colourful object started to roll. This time it spooled across the granite floor, the glass grating crudely on the stone as if the orb was inconceivably heavy. It rotated around the boxes, over long discarded dolls and collections of useless paraphernalia that had been deposited here to satisfy the owner's hoarding requirements. Slowly and precisely it headed for the timeworn stairs, whereupon it lost itself from sight as the cobwebs enveloped it.

Let's take some time out now for a more satisfactory scrutiny of Donald Oakseed. This man's about to play a significant part in the forthcoming book, so it might be as well to examine him with a little more consideration.

Donald was a balding man aged somewhere around the middling-to-late fifties with the sort of diminutive stature that either results in world dictatorship or total apathy. Unfortunately for him perhaps, Donald filled the position of the latter. He had a uniquely moulded skull that was shaped like an upended light-bulb. Coupled with the pair of milk-bottle-bottom thick glasses that were permanently squeezed around his spreading nose, this created the overall appearance of a stereotypical mad Austrian scientist.

As he studied his sad reflection in the screen of the

television, Donald thought profoundly about how pathetic his life had become. He invented numerous incisive put-downs that he ought to have used on his ex-boss. Cruel and cutting remarks about Mr. Arthur Wagstaff, the manager of 'The Progressive Bank. Greyminster PLC.' Deep down inside, however, where his private laughter couldn't penetrate and the blackness of his soul had control, Donald knew that he'd never use them even if the perfect opportunity arose.

Donald was one of society's weaker, more apathetic, members. He'd been made redundant right at that awkward time of life; too young for a pension, too old for a new job. And all because his face didn't fit with the bank's new image.

Now he sat and watched the banality of the TV as its repetitive irrelevance mocked his pointless existence. Night in, night out. His bottom lip thrust forwards from sheer force of habit. His untidy lounge strewn with the pollution of half a dozen TV Dinners.

The 'Pelvic-Sculpture Panty Liner' advert blasted from the speaker into the flickering emptiness, drowning out all the other sounds without exception.

Drowning out one particular sound which, had Donald heard it, might have served him as a timely warning that all was not well. An agitated goblinesque grunting, inching its route from the depths of the cellar and gently pushing open the creaking door.

The ball trundled in from the inky blackness beyond the doorway, a crown of broken light momentarily winking off its matt surface. It stopped, as if somehow taking stock of the situation. At length the orb moved on, grunting all the time regardless of the fact that it didn't actually have a mouth. Moments later it collided against the armchair with a gentle soundless thud.

Defying the laws of gravity, it manoeuvred purposefully up the flowered material that covered the chair's slumping back. Seconds later the object appeared behind Donald's asymmetrical head. For a moment or so it watched the television with interest.

Donald caught a glimpse from the corner of his eye of something that, in his own instinctual manner, he knew was completely inappropriate. He snapped his head round, a puzzled expression creating stitches along his brow.

There was a blinding white flash. It was followed by a deafening, elongated and heartbreaking scream. Then the glass ball appeared to evaporate into the pungent atmosphere. Several ensuing moments of silence crowded themselves together in a dumbstruck awe.

Somewhat uncertain about what had just happened Donald checked himself over. Discovering that all of his limbs were accounted for he studied the remainder of the room with an amount of apprehension.

'What's going on?'

His lips suddenly took on a life of their own. Desperately Donald struggled to prevent the muscular spasms that were now operating his lower jaw. Very much in keeping with the story of his life so far, he failed miserably.

'I am the ghost of Miguel De Cervantes.'

Donald's voice had become deeper, more commanding and prominent. He crossed his bewildered looking eyes, attempting to focus on his independently operating mouth. The ruddy lips he had known for as long as he could remember suddenly grew pale and started to crack as if constructed from mud.

'I now have possession of your body,' he extemporised in resonant tones.

'Oh no y' bloody don't son,' he added in a mild squeak.

Whereupon an unusual scuffle broke out.

Donald struggled around the chisel-edged Chinese rug, grappling with his arms and kicking with his legs. The fight resembled the sort of modern dance routine where a woman in Doctor Martens and a badly stitched wheat sack attempts to portray 'Agony and Frustration' by pounding her fists upon the stage.

Several wine bottles were dislodged from the disorderly table top, plummeting with their contents spilling everywhere. The clock tumbled down from the wall with a humorous cogwheel and cuckoo noise. It landed, corner down on the top of Donald's angry head. Unconscious, he slumped against the television set.

Several protracted seconds bowed their reverential heads as they crawled past Donald's apparantly lifeless corpse.

Suddenly, his eyes jumped open. Eyes now wild and bloodshot, magnified greatly by the thick glass lenses. In a low-pitched booming manner Donald's alternate voice concluded with a sense of evil drama.

'Betcha life, Bogie?'

Mrs. Prune's sturdy boots clumped along Applegate, steam rising upwards from the metal toecaps. They were accompanied by Father Wordsmith's more sensible lace-ups. Both pairs ground to a halt in front of the familiar door of 114. An acute trepidation surrounded the two individuals. The understanding that both had arrived on the cusp of averting a most heinous crime.

A pause for breath; a doubled up, wheezing sort of pause. Their eyes concentrated on the tall Victorian aspect before them. A sudden, horrific crash shattered the still night from the dark window high up above.

'Oh, bugger it!' Mrs. Prune hitched up her knickerbockers. 'Now we're in trouble. If y' 'adn't 'av' stopped t' put on y' best vestal drawers, y' ronner...'

Mrs. Prune was having difficulty with the old priest's proper title, and instead used anything that happened to be close at hand.

'Then we might 'av saved the poor bugger's life.'

'Oi assure ya, Mrs. Prune,' came back the softly spoken Irish intonation. 'Oim wearin' only me pyjama bottoms beneath me cassock. There's absolutely no call for using that sort of language.'

A shrieking, vivid light ripped the clouds apart as if they were made from tissue paper, engulfing the two figures in an envelope of blinding brilliance, before disappearing with the same immense velocity with which it had arrived. A copper-bottomed frying pan of some considerable weight clattered to a halt in front of them. Following tradition it spiralled with decreasing momentum, creating circular ruts in the gravel. The pan was stained with dark red blood.

'By the great glistening gonads o' the fat holy Pope!' Father Wordsmith exclaimed with startled indecorum. 'What the shit was that?'

Mrs. Prune lifted her skirts with no apologies for the lack of dignity. From some concealed pocket, though it would be imprudent to enquire exactly where, she produced an empty Lucozade bottle and handed it to the priest.

'If y' gonna piss y'self, y' majesty,' she said with sagacity. 'Then stick this up y' wimple. We need all the 'oly water we can get.'

With which expressive words she slammed the bent old key into its lock and thundered over the doorstep in the manner of a small steamroller complete with hobnails.

Jess Hobson's flat resembled the remains of a crèche after a 400 strong party had been through it. The sort of party that left those who had to clean up such things afterwards, desperately scrabbling for the phone in order to contact the Samaritans. If the Health Authority had known then the whole apartment would have been condemned immediately.

The door burst open and Mrs. Prune charged through the blackened opening with the out of breath theologian following hard on her tail. Both were confronted by a scene of such chaos that it took them both by surprise.

In the centre of the destruction; amidst the mounds of barely recognisable furniture was Jess Hobson. His great bulk was down on all fours, lambasting the smouldering carpet. His tongue hung out resembling a damp duvet steaming quietly over a fireplace; his right hand clutching intensely at his arid painful throat.

'My God, Jess 'Obson! 'Scuse me blasph'my, y'r 'Oliness,' Mrs. Prune muttered as an aside to the clergyman. 'W'at the 'Ell 'appened 'ere? 'Ave y' been attacked?'

She was well aware that as the last word tumbled headlong from her mouth it had been the wrong thing to say. Pointless as it was however, the question had filled a nasty void in her life, where rational thought had taken the hint and succinctly scarpered.

Jess snarled, a sarcastic contempt attempting to knot his shaggy brows together.

'No! I've got a date wi' that bird from Mulberry Crescent 'oo breeds Dobermans f' Crufts. Thought I'd brush up on some foreplay techniques.'

Mrs. Prune, it had to be said, had been expecting some sort of response along those lines. At least it confirmed that Jess was behaving quite normally and hadn't succumbed to possession, or some such other diabolical thing. She avoided the comment adroitly and continued with gallant single-mindedness.

'W'at the bloody 'Ell 'appened?' She cast her eyes in a slow and analytical circle about the ruin. "Ow did y' see off that Foster character?'

'He didn't, you fraudulent old frump.'

A figure that no-one had noticed before, unwrapped itself from the dark corner. It oppressively drew up alongside Mrs. Prune.

Thomas Hobson. Still not dead! At least, not back amongst the others who had departed from this mortal coil, where the bugger belonged.

'If you had any powers of precognition at all,' Hobson leaned down upon her persuasively. 'Then you'd have known that it was I who sorted Samuel Foster out. It was I who saved the life of my fa...my grandson, Mrs. Prune. It would appear that my supernatural powers are a little more keen than those of that bastard spawn Foster. In short, Mrs. Prune, I sent Samuel's ghost packing with his tail between his legs.'

Uncoiling his fingers, Hobson gave a short demonstration of how he'd produced the devastating thunderbolt that had finished off his colleague. Then his voice became darker. His teeth winked liked a prism so keenly honed that it didn't just refract light, it neatly sliced it into points.

'And you would have predicted this as well.'

Hobson lunged, his bent and outstretched digits reaching for Mrs. Prune's scraggy throat. A crackle of blue electricity danced around the tips.

Mrs. Prune's umbrella came up smartly between his legs, ending with an unpleasant, twisted sort of snap. Thomas Hobson froze. Then lurched forward in agony, his puckered old mouth shrunken to a tightly contracted orifice.

'Looks like y' want t' watch y' crystal balls more carefully, Mr. 'Obson,' Mrs. Prune snorted. 'Father? Go on..'

She nodded at the distraught Thomas Hobson whilst winking one round little eye at Father Edward Wordsmith. However, priests are not renowned for their understanding of human deviousness and Mrs. Prune's clandestine message failed to be enough to spur him into action.

On the third attempt, however, when the nod had become more of a headbutt and the wink had become more of a frustrated snarl, an understanding of what was required clicked into place. Without further hesitation he produced a full bottle from his cassock. Expertly unscrewing the stopper, he poured the bottle's pungent contents onto the head of the hoary geriatric before him.

The result was rather more explosive than the gathering had expected. Everyone, including the sodden ghost, staggered backwards in disgust as a toxic mix of repugnant gases fizzled revoltingly from Hobson's clothing.

'Sorry,' Father Wordsmith turned crimson with embarrassment. 'Oi 'ad sprouts for me supper. Must ha' bin off.'

'Don't think you've seen the last of me, thou warty and haggard old...' Doubled up in agony, Thomas Hobson searched despairingly for the most fitting and dramatic insult. Being caught in the throes of excruciating pain was, perhaps, not the best time to worry about presentation however. 'Old...' Bugger it! 'Old cow!' he ended feebly.

A crooked grimy digit prodded Mrs. Prune on the end of her nose.

'I'll be waiting for you, you vicious old bag! Waiting in the dark shadows where you least expect to find me. Or underneath the bed, at the turn of the midnight hour, where you've forgotten to check. I'll be the bower of the tree that raps against your window pane in the dead of night. I'll be...'

'Oh, bugger off!'

And with a second unhealthy snap of gristle Mrs. Prune's solid and unreasonably swift kneecap connected with his supposedly incorporeal groin.

An echoing moan rose upwards in pitch until it had passed beyond earshot as Thomas Hobson faded from view. Moments later he seemed nothing more than a confused and distant memory. A nightmare confronted by the pale light of a winter's dawn.

Chapter Ten

The Haunting Of Wellington Hall.

For a moment we must spool back the reels of time once more. Back to October 31st, 1991. It was by tradition, a dark and stormy night. Great clouds hung like feather mattresses across the sky, slung from one horizon to the other, as five silhouetted figures struggled against the tempestuous wind. Small, insignificant figures all trudging with their heads down along the foreboding puddle-patched drive that led up to the magnificent Wellington Hall.

Benjamin Foster and Jess Hobson were amongst the five, all of whom were beginning to regret that they had agreed to spend the night in Greyminster's most famous haunted house. Each had their own personal fears and troubles, now magnified greatly by the closeness of the looming building. Mrs. Prune had put them up to it, with her usual charismatic forcefulness. To raise funds for the Albert Finney Memorial Hall Scouts—or so she said.

A flash of lightning momentarily illuminated the underbelly of the sagging heavens. As it did so Wellington Hall stood out in all its startling detail, so that no single nook or cranny could escape the blue light. Then it faded once more into a gothic silhouette, leaving nothing but a chill in the adventurers' bones.

Beneath his arm Benjamin Foster carried an old fashioned portable tape-recorder. The sort of recorder that had two mighty reels on the top and a microphone that resembled a small painted brick. Indeed the solid equipment had brought about a twinge to his back muscles and had made the walk along the claustrophobic drive appear to be almost four times as long.

The hunch-backed butler with the permanently runny nose had shown them to their quarters. It was here that the reels began to turn with the sort of uncomfortable humming noise that was usually associated with insane professors.

It was difficult to discern which voice belonged to which member of the audacious squad, but the ensuing conversation ran something along the following lines.

'Just get 'old of the damn thing.' This might have been Jess' voice. It was hard to tell.

'What are you going to do?' This voice might have been Ben's. Again it was difficult to be certain.

'Just 'old the bloody microphone. I'm gonna break wind.'

At which point another voice joined in on the conversation.

'Are you indeed, Jess Hobson of 114 Applegate, Greyminster?'

And another.

'Why are you running around the room with no clothes on—Angela Derry of Rubble Lane North, Devils' Crevice? Telephone 8759201.' The disruptive sound of flatulence being broken at extremely close range distorted the recording. So much so, that it took several moments to settle back down. At length however, the occupants of the room could be heard muttering indistinctly amongst themselves once more.

'You smelly, stinking sod!'

'Don't waft it about. I don't want your germs.'

'No, don't — Greg Monks of 49 Merlin Road West. Telephone 8944351.'

'It isn't Greg Monks' actually, is it Angela?'

'Stop suckin' me willy, Dawn Holbern of 29 Runnywart Row, Greyminster. Telephone 8770123.'

'I wouldn't suck your willy if you paid me, Jess Hobson of 114 Applegate, Greyminster. Telephone 866692. Besides which, it's so small it'd get stuck in my teeth.'

The voice that followed was altogether louder than the others that were jostling for the lead role in this pantomime. It was also much too close to the microphone for comfort, becoming almost impossible to determine due to its resonant bass. It sounded remarkably similar to Jess Hobson's on the whole though.

'This is w'at me willy sounds like.'

There followed a sort of muffled rustling noise.

'Get the bloody microphone out of your undies!'

'Urgh! Look at the big skidmarks on Greg Monks' undercrackers. Telephone 8944351.'

Here the machine was apparently turned off; a break indicated by the dull thud of the switch being twisted. After several seconds of static it was switched back on again with the same gusto, the opening gambit being a loud and raucous belch aimed directly into the microphone.

'W'at's happened to all the beer?'

'You've drunk it all, slap head!'

'Shut up and go to sleep.'

'God, 'oo's let off?'

'It was Greg Monks of 49 Merlin Road. West.'

The discussions, if such trivia could be referred to as such, continued along the same familiar lines for several more minutes. Adults, regardless of age and calling, when locked inside a tense situation, regress rapidly into the realms of bickering childhood. Especially when high spirits and alcohol are combined.

After some time, the adolescent conversations subsided. After that, the only sounds to be heard were the occasional hiss of a poor quality recording head scraping the tape, and the odd scuffle and grunt that emerged from the background. Occasionally somebody giggled through a sleeping bag. Or somebody else would make a childish little noise. The odd raspberry, closely supervened by a barely contained chortle. Eventually a worried voice broke the silence with the precision of a scalpel.

'Shut up! Everybody shut up!'

'What's that noise?'

'W'at noise?'

'That noise!'

'Listen!'

'It's comin' from Greg Monk's sleeping bag.'

For several moments the charitable ghost hunters listened profoundly.

The silence that followed was an intense and altogether embarrassed sort of silence; the noise that had so rudely interrupted the proceedings having now packed up its bags and fled. What had initially sounded like a muffled bat's wings passing by in the night was now gone. It quickly became apparent that it wasn't about to return in a hurry either.

'It's stopped now.'

'Oh my God! Who's blown the candle out?'

'What's that?!'

At this point the recording started to get crowded and confused. Anybody paying attention might have just heard the ominous sounds of a heavy chain being dragged across the old floorboards. Or the creak of various wooden beams amongst the ensuing melee. Unfortunately for those concerned these were merely minor details amongst the thunderous chaos. All the voices had now become one indecipherable clutter.

'Come on then. Stop buggerin' about!! Who's that?'

'I want to go home now, Gregory.'

'Bloody 'Ell!!!'

'The doors are opening!'

'Gregory! TAKE ME HOME NOW!'

A loud crash managed to confuse matters even more, tying up the shouts into knots. Several previously well maintained baritones had now become tenors with fright. It was almost as if the atmosphere had been swamped with a barrage of helium. All the voices in the darkness began to clamor above each other.

'Buggerin' Nora!'

'CHRIST!!'

'It's coming through the window!'

'AAARGH!!'

'HELP ME!!! MUMMMY!'

'Bog Off, Jess! BOG OFF!!'

'LET GO! LET GO!'

'Greg Monks' of Greyminster has done a dump in his trousers! Telephone 8944351.'

And at that point the recording ended—abruptly. There are not enough facts to know why this should be the case. But the concluding few moments were occupied with what sounded remarkably like Mrs. Prune's laugh from somewhere in the background.

At some point afterwards the contents of the reel must have been transferred onto normal audio-cassette. The remainder had been filled with the current top forty.

This recording *is* a most important item indeed. It belongs back in the box. Where it might be better for all concerned if we left it undisturbed.

So let's close the mottled grey and black lid once more. The cardboard lid that is our gateway to events that filled the past. And fast forward back through the intervening years. Back to where we left off before the chapter began.

Chapter Eleven

The Ghost Ventures Out.

The following morning dawn never *actually* arrived. It rarely did at this time of year. The world just gradually became less dark; the customary British weather rolling down from the fells and spreading out like a cloak across the rooftops of Greyminster. Within the familiar and comfortable sanctuary of Mrs. Prune's cosy kitchen, Jess' palms smouldered on the chipped mug that his ever beneficent landlady had shoved before him. A helter-skelter of ghostly steam now rose from the coagulated brew and dispersed above his head resembling the apparition of a tormented soul.

A collection of mechanical trinkets littered the table cloth at Jess' elbow, forming a haphazard imitation of the Tower of Babel around the pepper pot. The insides of what looked to be a 1930's radio set, jostled with lengths of wire that had turned partially brown with age. They became entangled with clumps of ancient computer organs that had been indelicately disemboweled. The mound was accompanied by a screwdriver and a slice of toast with a bite taken from it.

Mrs. Prune took her seat on the opposite side of the breakfast table, heartily digging into a slice of gammon. With a face the epitome of disconsolation Benjamin Foster stared longingly at Mrs. Prune's steak from where he sat on the opposite corner. Benjamin drooled a sort of phantasmagoric ectoplasm drool.

He figured thus; it was unlikely that ghosts would have the metabolism required to polish off something as earthly as a slab of meat. And discretion suggested that a half-digested lump of pig floating along the street might frighten the good residents of Greyminster out of their tiny wits anyhow. He could have been wrong, but Benjamin wasn't exactly willing to take that risk.

Mrs. Prune added a gravy boat full of tomato sauce to her breakfast. A distant rumble of spectral gastric juices defiantly played havoc with Benjamin's set of transparent entrails.

Jess picked up the screwdriver and started to tinker with the complicated machine. There followed a series of unconnected but amusing mechanical noises.

At length Mrs. Prune belched loudly, apologetically patted her greasy lips with a dainty fist afterwards, and wiping her fingers on a paper napkin leaned across the table to Ben.

'Somethin' big an' threatenin' is comin', Ben Foster. 'Ow come y' don't know w'at it is, bein' dead an' all?'

She was under the impression that being dead somehow let you in on all the secrets of the universe. Benjamin thought of the steak and heard his stomach growl.

'It's probably one of Jess' rumblers,' he replied facetiously. 'They're pretty big and menacing. The last one of them I saw rearing up at me from the 'U' bend had fangs! I was going to attack it with the plunger but it would probably have become a Dalek!'

'Y' know damn well w'at I mean! Can't y' find out w'at's going on? 'Ave a word with Arthur Scargill or somethin'. Ee's probably the 'ead o' the Ghosts' Union.'

'Arthur Scargill isn't dead yet, Mrs. Prune.' The fact that the leader of the Coal Miners' Union hadn't been on the telly for a few weeks was enough for Mrs. Prune to assume the worst. 'Unfortunately,' Ben added.

He looked puzzled for a moment, then spoke without making eye contact.

'What do you suppose happened to my great grandfather?'

'Back where 'ee belongs. Bowels of Hell with Beelzebub's pitchfork up 'is jacksie no doubt!' Mrs. Prune removed a stray string of gammon from her hind teeth, putting it to rest on the edge of the plate with satisfaction. 'Actually, 'ee'd probably like that! Roarin' great ponce that 'ee was!'

'One thing that bothers me though.' Ben bit his bottom lip in contemplative thought. 'If he was around in Victorian times, why was he wearing denims?'

That thought struck home. In all the confusion Mrs. Prune hadn't noticed that particular anachronism. In fact nobody had noticed that particular anachronism.

Well, it was hardly surprising really, was it? You don't go round attempting to isolate minor discrepancies when some demented ghost is trying to tear your head off.

But now that she thought about it, the faded denims, with their familiar and often advertised motif, were certainly an enigma. Not only had the ghost of Samuel Foster been wearing them, but so had Thomas Hobson. In fact he'd been wearing bloody sneakers as well.

It was definitely something that required her further investigation. However inconsequential at the time, such little flaws might be deemed of major importance in the long term. They might even hold the key to exactly *what* was going on. Possibly even why Mrs. Prune had been saturated of late with feelings of complete and utter dread.

'I don't rightly know, but...'

She stood up and crossed to the mantlepiece with purpose; small crumbs of bread tumbling from her pinny.

Three, crumpled calling cards poked their heads from behind the ornamental carriage clock. Mrs. Prune removed them with her stodgy digits and returned to the table. The rectangular objects were flung down in front of Jess. Automatically, he stopped his inventing and raised his head at the interruption.

'Take a gander at these.'

'W'at's this? We out of the quilted stuff again?'

'It's y' Christmas bonus.' Mrs. Prune resumed her seat, resolutely folding her arms across her wide chest and inconspicuously adjusting her bosom as she did so. 'That's the third call for y' 'Paranormal Services' this mornin'.'

With a knowledgable look of the sort that Jess suspected as not being terribly *knowledgable* at all she nodded smugly and sat back. 'Somethin' rotten this way comes. An' I'm not talkin' about 'Arry Norton neither!'

Jess read the words on the top card aloud.

'Madame Victoria Whiplash. All manner of unusual requests granted.'

The card was instantly snatched from his grip with such vehemence that the immediate space in front of Jess' eyes became a momentary blur. Mrs. Prune compressed her wrinkled lips awkwardly together into a self-conscious scribble.

"Ow did that get in there? Bloody kids an' their April fool pranks!'

She coughed, a little high pitched cough, then tapped the following card as if nothing had occurred.

'Look. Number thirty-three, Old Bridge Lane.

Disturbance next door.' Mrs. Prune's recovery had been remarkable and she continued without notice. 'Only just round the corner from the cemet'ry that one. Grave goin's on indeed.'

Jess had to admit that it all seemed rather coincidental. Since Hobson and Co had first been established their pathetic excuse for a business had only received four calls. Such was the lack of demand for their unusual services.

Two of the calls had been from the kids off the council estate. Kids who had found their advert in an abandoned Yellow Pages and had thought that it might be fun to wind them up by going 'Whooo' down the phone.

Apart from the Wambachs', the only other call had been from a woman who had lost her keys and was convinced that her long departed husband had stolen them from her. As it turned out, the old dear had escaped from the local retirement home. But now there'd been three calls all in one morning! It was disconcerting to say the least.

Benjamin, alert and eager as ever, was up on his feet before his partner had finished articulating the words.

'I'll pop off down there. 'Ave a quick rummage around. See what I can discover.'

"Oo d' y' think y' are?' Mrs. Prune straightened smartly. 'Randal an' bloody 'Opkirk? There's only me as can see y', y' daft sod!'

'Well, clearly, all things considered,' Benjamin cast an accusatory glance across the table cloth towards the tumour of mechanical trinkets. 'Jess would be about as much use as an elastic truss on his own. I wouldn't trust him to stand the right way round at a urinal, sad gonad-headed git that he is.'

Jess' face appeared menacingly from behind the toppling pile. It was wearing a pair of old glasses tautly strained about his cauliflower ears. As far as spectacles went, this pair had a rather odd appearance. The frame was roughly two inches thick, the front being constructed from what resembled two old camera lenses bolted into position. A hardly noticeable electronic motor was attached to one side of the disjointed arms.

Jess regarded Ben; after blinking once or twice he punched him hard on the nose. There was the sound of muffled crunching and several blue electrical bolts shot out of Benjamin's jaw. Jess removed the spectacles and turned them over in his hands, a self-satisfied expression dominating his coarse features.

'Right. Well, they appear t' be workin' okay.' He glanced across at Mrs. Prune. 'Certainly proves me theory that Ben's not a proper ghost. Seems a bit too solid f' that sort o' thing.' He rotated the buzzing glasses between his fingers, momentarily marvelling at his sudden comprehension of quantum mechanics. 'Simple 'Phase Re-alignment Mechanism.' Now I can keep tabs on Timothy Claypole 'ere. Stop him from puttin' his foot so far down 'is own gob that the bristles on his kneecap scratch 'is clacker!'

With a dramatic sweep of his shovel-like hand, Jess snatched the cards from the crumpled cloth and stood up, ready to depart.

'No rest f' the terminally greedy.'

He reached for his maroon body-warmer, cramming the new invention into one pocket.

'Work t' be done! Ben?' Jess spoke to the patch of empty air beside him that he was sure would be swearing and cussing to itself. 'W'en y've finished wiping the ectoplasm off y' chin, meet me at Old Bridge Lane. An' bring the account book.'

A greedy smile spread across Jess' broad square jaw.

'This one looks like it could keep us in Figgy Puddin' 'till the New Year.'

November 16th, 1998. Another dirty, low-slung morning where the sky was attempting to prop itself up with the help of the chimney stacks. Intermittent explosions of stinging rain burst in isolated incidents upon the shoppers exposed hands and faces.

11:34 a.m. The total annihilation of everything steps up its pace and marches swiftly towards Armageddon.

Old Croft Mill stood amongst a huddle of smaller buildings with the overbearing pretensions of a protective father. Built circa 1746 the sails hadn't turned for the whole past decade. The giant red and blistered lattices were blown off in the great storm of 1985. Now they rotted, leaning nonchalantly against the mammoth pepperpot of the mill itself and causing a nuisance to passers by.

Next door to the grubby landmark was the Barn. What had once been a red brick building with doves in its eaves had now been converted into a shop full of curiosities. It had not been one of Greyminster council's better development plans. Nothing ever managed to get sold in the Barn, its shelves of locally turned pottery and home-made peg-dolls remaining undisturbed from year to year and gathering a layer of grey dust.

Donald Keith Oakseed strolled into the rundown

square. Gone was the usual submissive worm that had been Donald's allotted personality for the past forty-something years. In its place walked an altogether more arrogant character.

He stopped beside the half-erected fir tree, prodding his dark glasses up his nose with one forefinger. Not only had his carriage altered, but Donald was now oddly attired for a man of such humble disposition. A leather jacket hung open around a brilliant white tee-shirt. His leather trousers tightly hugged his short but muscular legs, tapering into the loose fitting necks of black cowboy boots.

Most peculiar and probably most unbefitting was the brightly coloured pump-action water-cannon that he held in his right hand. A luminescent yellow and pink affair, filled so voluminously with water that several droplets plummeted from the nozzle.

When Donald spoke the voice carried a definite Scottish inflection.

'Ah, Mish Moneypenny. Ey shee the sitchuation in Bulgaria ish deteriorating again.'

Mrs. Edith Norton was leaving the 'Dried Fruit Specialists' a large tub of all-bran struggling to escape from her wiry grip. Beneath the other arm a bag full of shopping was causing her transportation problems. It would be fair to say that Edith wasn't quite sure how to respond to Donald's solicitation. She had known him for most of his life and for the majority of that he had seemed a fairly boring sod.

'Ev'ry bloody town an' ev'ry village,' Edith muttered to herself. 'There's alwez some nutter 'as to approach me!'

This is Donald's mind's eye. Things have become extremely jumbled now. Two personalities struggling for the control of one body. A square central to his vision, with a crosshair target moving soundlessly across it, genlocked itself against Croft Mill and its soiree of attendant buildings. Donald fought valiantly against the powerful influence. There wasn't much chance of his own mind successfully coming out on top. But he'd made a concerted effort anyhow and perhaps that was worthy of note.

The target focused on the summit of a baguette that was poking from Mrs. Norton's bag. It went to maximum zoom, Donald supplying his own special warning noise.

'Please put down your weapon!'

Edith backed away. The manic red eyes that glowed across the rim of the sunglasses kept a steady lock on the startled promontory of bread.

'You have twenty seconds to comply.'

This statement was obviously some sort of pointless bluff. Without waiting for even a fraction of the designated time to elapse, a stream of ice-cold water jettisoned out of the toy gun. It completely missed the rude loaf, colliding instead with the gonk-like bobble that was sewn to the woolen helmet of a delivery man. The merchandiser struggled beneath the weight of his unwieldy boxes as the water ran down his forehead in several frozen rivulets.

'Oy! W'at's your game, y' daft pillock!? Y' nearly 'ad me eye out then!'

Edith seized that opportunity to make her excuses and depart.

'Well, I must be off, Mr. Oakseed.' She studied him askance, a puzzled frown tugging down upon the central section of her brow. 'I do 'ope y' little problem clears up.'

She paused. After a couple of seconds thought she

Without waiting for even a fraction of the designated time to elapse, a stream of ice-cold water jettisoned out of the toy gun.

opened up her handbag and began to delve through the contents. Several plastic containers of Valium rattled against various old photographs of her long lost companion.

'Y' know, I've got the name of a good psychologist somewhere...'

'The name's Bonk. James Bonk.'

He's really gone this time, Edith thought. Donald raised an eyebrow, prattling on with indubitable confidence.

'Licensed to have major sex.'

Edith Norton appeared to freeze. For the slightest length of time she seemed to be partaking in a personal game of musical statues. Then her narrow eyes shrunk into pin-pricked holes.

'Not wi' bloody me, y're not mate!' The handbag snapped shut. Mrs. Norton spun dangerously on her pointed heels, creating tiny sparks that fizzled briefly upon the rainwashed cobbles.

'I'll 'ave the police onto you! If my 'Arry was still alive 'ee'd 'ave 'ad y' kidneys f' braces.'

She took to her heels. Being old and unstable at the best of times, the unrehearsed sprint resulted in a sort of half-run, half-stumbling walk. Not a terribly practical gait for someone whose sharp and undependable heels added to the general precariousness of her ancient frame. Her centre of gravity tottered dangerously on the limits of remaining upright. Shopping spilled across the stones, rolling into gutters and exploding across the ground.

Donald slid the glasses down his nose, a smug expression on his face.

'Moneypenny. I'll fight those commie buggers for you.'

Just for a brief moment the real Donald struggled to the surface. His features flickered into focus, a bewildered simper washing across his facade in a solitary wave. Then it was gone. Before the genuine Donald could utter a single word, a tidal-wave of confusion overtook him. It dragged him down, spinning into the unexplored depths of his mind, where consciousness was a barely observable state. Cervantes' re-emerged triumphantly.

'And for England. And the Queen of course.' He went on. 'Naturally, that goes without saying. I'll kick that massive backside of Robby Kiltrane's all round the British Isles with my stinger mounted boot from 'Q'. Even if it means losing my foot in his mammoth buttock cleft!'

By now, several inquisitive shoppers had appeared in the surrounding doorways. Donald was shouting defiantly after the disappearing Edith Norton. His declaration of undying love sent a nervous titter through the group of voluminous ladies.

Edith fumed as she tottered towards the main street. She was angry at being associated with the undersized creep. Down inside she wanted to hurl something abusive back at the watchers. But when she turned, Donald was already facing the mill in a reverential silence.

This is Donald's mind's eye once more. Or rather Cervantes. Whatever...its perception was startlingly different to that of the average person.

The broken-down building no longer resembled the mill that had overlooked Greyminster for as long as he could remember. It now wore a sort of fuzzy-filtered border that on films usually denotes that the hero is experiencing a dream sequence.

Croft Mill creaked, then it groaned and very slowly— expanding and contracting with the flexibility of a pregnant jellyfish—the building metamorphosed into a rather unconvincing tyrannosaurus rex.

The rubber dinosaur snarled, a huge barricade of chiselled teeth filling its scaly lips, saliva dribbling ineffectively down its incisors. Donald, after one or two moments of experimentation, threw back an uncompromising sneer that despite his best efforts defiantly bore an aspect of discomfort.

'Godzilla! Y' slitty eyed, rubber suited gargoyle! If I had my special Roboman power I'd morph to the same size and kick your alien scum butt to kingdom come!'

The enormous water-cannon was raised cautiously to the front of his glasses. Donald fired a laser bolt, aimed directly between the makeshift monster's eyeballs.

To the gathering crowd he squirted a somewhat limp column of water into the cold November air. It feebly arced into a desultory puddle.

Mrs. Edith Norton, watched the proceedings from a safe distance. Wearily she shook her head and hitched up her skirts to regain her dignity.

'Donald Oakseed. W'at a sad bugger 'ee turned out t' be,' she continued to herself. "Oo would 'ave thought it? 'Ee was alwez such a quiet man.'

This is the home of Martha Sonneman; number 33, Old Bridge Lane. It is now approximately 12:03 p.m. and the bulky figure of Jess Hobson in its quilted body-warmer, looks somewhat out of place in the dainty front room.

It was an ordinary lounge. Glistening pottery shire-

The rubber dinosaur snarled, a huge barricade of chiselled teeth filling its scaly lips, saliva dribbling ineffectively down its incisors.

horses forever towed polished carts along the corner shelves. Lattice-windowed bookcases displayed their unread contents to the educated visitors. An antique writing-bureau had been forced into the alcove beside the fireplace. Receipts stuck neatly out of the cubby holes as if whoever had placed them there had created what they believed to be a sort of organised chaos. Almost as if social decorum demanded it to act as a head rest, a large ginger cat was asleep on the armchair.

Martha Sonneman herself was a thin, pale creature with masses of auburn hair and a sprinkling of freckles that were carefully arranged about her features. She seemed content to wander around the house without wearing any shoes. Her tight fitting sweater was covered with fanciful lace roses that tried to disguise the fact that Martha had nothing much to put in it.

It wasn't that Martha was particularly thin. It was just that there had obviously never been much of Martha to start off with.

'Right, so...' Jess turned to his patiently waiting client. 'Mrs. Sausage?'

'Miss. Actually, it's Miss.'

Martha didn't have an actual voice. It was more of whisper. The sort that makes romantic icons at the cinema, but in reality forces the listener to strain their ears in order to comprehend the words.

'Yeah...Look...Personally I couldn't give a toss whether it's Miss or Mrs. It's your money. If y' wanna waste it bickerin' over details then that's your lookout.' He tucked his thumbs into his belt loops and hoisted his abundant denims.

Martha's demeanour changed dramatically.

'There's no need to be rude!'

'I charge by the 'our Mrs. Sexpot. So if y' want to discuss '*Etti Quettie*' y'd better 'ave a full purse. Otherwise, let's get down t' business.'

Flustered, but holding her pride admirably, Martha brushed the lank hair from her forehead so that her pointed nose jabbed obstinately at the air. 'Well, it's about my next-door neighbour...Donald.'

A long and uncomfortable pause followed.

Jess and Martha stared into each other's eyes, each expecting the other to re-establish the difficult conversation. After several seconds a certain amount of tension started to show itself, creating the most minuscule of tremors across their immutable aspects. At length, with a snort of breath down his nose that made the hairs in his nostrils whistle, Jess gave way.

'Mmm...' There was a sarcastic keen to his voice that denoted trouble. 'I am actually a paranormal investigator, Mrs. Saucepan—not a blasted bloody mind reader! "*It's about my next-door neighbour, Donald*", 'ardly qualifies f' any sort o' reaction. So either elaborate on w'at Donald 'as done or stop annoyin' me and wastin' my buggerin' time. I 'ave actually got more pressin' engagements. Such as removin' the winnits from me rectum!'

Martha compressed her wan lips to stave off the insult and started again.

'Well, something's happened to him.' She upturned her cow-like eyes to the ceiling and studied an indeterminate patch amongst the magnolia swirls. 'He's sort of changed...'

There followed another lengthy pause which rapidly became uncomfortable. For one so dogmatic on refinement and homeliness, Martha had a unnerving habit of putting the common visitor at unease. At length Jess took it upon himself to break the stale tension once more.

'Yes...Obviously we seem to be 'avin' a little communication difficulty 'ere!' He let his gaze wander up, his arms folded aggressively across his chest. 'It might 'elp in future if you would like to continue speaking' until, perhaps, somethin' relevant actually occurs. An' then we could avoid standin' 'ere like a pair of autistic inbred aristocrats tryin' to discuss quantum mechanics. Now, w'at was unusual about Donald's behaviour this BLOODY MORNING?'

His voice had reached a crescendo—it slammed across the room and rattled a porceline Devonshire pit-pony.

'Well, he doesn't usually have columns of green light coming out of his eyes for one thing. Or smoke coming out of his nostrils FOR ANOTHER!'

That seemed to qualify; Jess seemed more than satisfied that he had extracted a modicum of relevance.

'Right,' he muttered, stuffing his broad hands into his pockets and rocking backwards on the balls of his feet. The heels of his boots created small indentations on the plush carpet. Indentations that Martha was aware would probably never be removed. 'Now...W'at's y' relationship with Mr. Oakseed, Mrs. Sexorgan?'

'Well...'

It was obviously an uncomfortable question and one that Martha didn't feel at total liberty to answer. She contorted her face by way of dealing with the inner struggle. Jess inhaled deeply, adopting an altogether more condescending tone for the following line.

'P'raps it might 'elp if y' just spoke one syllable at a time.'

Martha turned a look of scorn, pouting her bottom lip at the proffered suggestion.

'Or p'raps we could try charades,' Jess ventured further. 'Or maybe I should just use a cricket bat round the back of y'r 'ead t' remove the mental blockage!'

'I'm trying to think! Stop pressuring me!' If she could have twisted her limbs around each other any more she would have resembled a columbine. Jess was not exactly impressed.

'It's not the bloody finals o' Mastermind is it, y' bloody stupid woman?' He was now leaning so close into Martha's head that warm gusts of alcoholic breath were flushing her cheeks into small pink patches. 'W'at's y' relationship with him?'

'I...I...I don't really like to say...'

Her voice trailed off like the last dregs of bath water going down a plug-hole.

'Awh... Why ever not? Frightened of w'at the paparazzi might make of it? I could just see it now, tomorrow's 'eadline in the Mirror, "*Sad, lonely old nobody involved with unheard of twat!*"'

Martha bit her top lip to prevent the fury from erupting, folding her arms ever more tightly across her minuscule bosom.

'No! Of course I'm not bothered about the papers!' she replied, no longer able to look Jess squarely in his encompassing face. 'But...you know what the neighbours are like?'

'NO I BLOODY DON'T! If I did I wouldn't be fartin' around tryin' to get a stupid cretin like you t' bloody tell me. Would I?'

'Mr. Hobson. Your attitude is...'

'Going t' get a lot worse if y' don't start bein' a bit more cooperative. Now!! Mrs. Sexbomb. Were y' shaggin' Mr. Oakseed or not?'

After several moments spent gnawing on her lower lip, during which time the sinews down her slender neck turned into piano wires, Martha offered a diminutive, 'Sort of...'

Jess closed his eyes, counted to fourteen slowly, and opened them again.

'Sort of?! You were *sort of* shaggin' somebody? You were just *sort of* rollin' about beneath the covers with *sort of* no clothes on. In a *sort of* innocent, *sort of* shaggin' *sort of* manner?'

'Well...yes...I suppose so...sort of...'

A grin spread across Jess' head that, had it grown any larger, might have split his cranium completely in two.

'Good,' he said, having reached a conclusion to his quandary. 'Then, y'll 'ave 'is backdoor key I suppose!'

Number 32, Old Bridge Lane; previous scene of paranormal activity. There is every reason to suspect that some other supernatural occurrences might also have their roots here.

A tremendous, rusted key—orange and brown with teeth that resembled mortuary slabs—rattled in the untended lock. At length the door swung open upon its hinges; a resonant creak shaking the spiders from their webs. Apprehensively, Jess and Martha's shadows fell across kitchen floor. The short hairs on the back of Jess' broad neck were standing to attention as the two intruders nudged their path towards the lounge.

Nothing much had changed since the previous night. Except that, perhaps, it wasn't so dark. And there was the small matter of the two round scorch marks of course. A pair of blackened circular exposures, still smouldering about halfway up the largest wall. Presumably the burns had been created by the two famous columns of green light. Several springs of chestnut-coloured smoke coiled up towards the ceiling like the shadows of pubic hairs.

Jess looked around cautiously. The sitting room appeared to be some sort of shrine to modern Anglo-American culture. Video films with gory covers occupied every available space. Jess tugged one suspicious looking item from where it was crushed beneath an overburdened bookshelf.

'He was very keen on 'Videos',' said Martha, peering over his shoulder. 'Arnold Scharzener films, Sylvester Stalon films and one or two others we shouldn't mention.'

Jess snorted. He wasn't going to ask her 'Why Not?' He had no intention of spending the next hour or so trying to coax an answer out of the woman. Instead he inserted the cassette box beneath an abandoned set of crusty dinner plates and regarded Martha from the corner of his eye. Embarrassed, she retracted her head from his shoulder, staring around at the remainder of the property.

'Mrs. Cesspit. I'd like you t' do me a favour.'

Martha's face lit up with an eager expectation.

'Of course, Mr. Hobson. Whatever I can do to...'

'I want y' t' 'Piss Off'!' Jess stuffed his hands into his pockets and ruthlessly lashed out at an unstable mound with his toecaps. 'I'm sick of y'r inane gibberin'. So if y' wouldn't mind crawlin' back beneath whatever stone y' originated from...'

'But...but...' Martha was having a really bad day. It had definitely grown worse in the past half an hour or so. 'Don't you see?' She made a sweeping gesture with her right arm. 'These videos are probably what turned him!'

'An' shut the door on the way out! I don't want the smell o' y'r feet sneakin' back in.'

Disgusted, Martha slammed shut her mouth, clenched her fists into tiny hard balls by her sides, spun on her heels and marched from the room, banging the door behind her as requested. This final act was contrived with such strength that a small cloud of sawdust broke loose from the mantle.

For several moments Jess listened attentively to the retreating foot steps that slapped across the narrow seperation between number thirty-two and the building next door. When he was sure that the irritating female had finally gone he whispered, in the sort of articulation that was more of a loud shout than anything else, 'Ben?'

No response.

'Ben Foster? D' y' read me?'

Just the ominous sounds of unsteady video turrets creaking beneath their own abandonment.

'Ben!? Come in y' dead cretin...'

Remembering something, Jess wrestled the spectacles from his pocket before purposefully thrusting them onto the bulbous crown of his nose. Immediately Benjamin Foster appeared, half way through shouting an excited sentence at such a volume that, had his throat been corporeal, would have ruptured his larynx.

Martha Sonneman herself was a thin, pale creature with masses of auburn hair and a sprinkling of freckles that were carefully arranged about her features.

'...KING IDIOT! What the Hell do you think you're doing?! Don't treat our clients like that!' A ghastly finger jabbed at the bridge-piece of the cumbersome glasses. 'One case every nine years! And you go an' treat her like a Yorkshire man treats his bloody mother!'

'The woman was obviously some sort of retard,' Jess remonstrated to little avail.

'A *paying* retard Jess!' Benjamin paused between sentences. 'There's a vital component of that little phrase that cautions diplomacy!'

'She also stank like a sumo-wrestler's gusset.' Growing jaded, Jess traced a phallus across a grime-coated video jacket, crinkling his nose into a concertina as the dust coiled up one nostril. 'I can understand why that cat was lickin' its own bottom. It was probably tryin' t' dislodge the taste of 'er skin from its tongue.'

'You're missing the point, Jess. Financially Hobson and Co is going down hill faster than Ironsides with knackered brakes.'

'Well, it doesn't exactly 'elp w'en 'alf the bloody partnership is dead, does it?'

'And whose fault was that?'

'Well it certainly wasn't mine, y' vicious little afterbirth! I told y' not t' go wanderin' off on y' own! That woman...' Jess at this point prodded in the general direction of the kitchen door with a large finger. 'That woman is an offence t' my aesthetic sensibilities.'

That's rich, thought Ben. *Coming from somebody who doesn't even know what aesthetic means.*

'She 'as the body of a decomposin' meerkat corpse an' a face that resembles an old woman's chin.'

Benjamin frowned.

'You fancy her don't you?'

'W'at?'

Jess' features appeared to drain with embarrassment. Rapidly they refilled with an altogether denser hue.

'That's it, isn't it?' Benjamin continued, latching onto the give away nuances. 'Sexual tension!'

Jess clenched his teeth so hard that a small bony lump appeared in each cheek.

'It was so thick you could run a knife through it like Camembert cheese.'

There was a moment's pause for deep reflection. The sort of hiatus that guilefully waits before a storm breaks. Whereupon Jess belted Benjamin hard in the front teeth. There was the sound of molars cracking. It was the second time since breakfast that Ben had regretted the fact that he wasn't intangible. A crackle of blue electricity loosed itself from Ben's temple, earthing along Jess' arm with such suddenness that Ben's attacker flinched backwards in shock.

'Don't be s' disgusting,' Benjamin rocked back and forth in a private world of throbbing pain, ignoring the rantings of his partner. 'I'd rather suck the pus from a schoolboy's boil.'

Jess nodded his bludgeon of a head at that, as though confirming the statement to himself.

'Through a straw,' he added to strengthen the point.

Clutching at his split lip, Benjamin slowly raised a brow that was so furrowed he could have trapped several marbles inside it.

'Now that I *can* believe. But...' His voice sank to a rumbling growl of vexation. 'Y' still want to get inside 'er drawers. Even if you'd have to use a crowbar t' do it!'

'Are y' calling me a transvestite, Ben?' This was Jess' automatic reaction to any sexual reference. 'Because unless y' want me t' stick y'r 'ead up me arse an' fart on it, thus creatin' untold damage even t' those deceased, y'd better put a sock in it pronto! Start searchin' this musky, festerin' slum f' some sort of clue as t' w'at 'appened 'ere.'

Mrs. Prune had been correct. Jess had gone beyond the edge of tetchy and was fast approaching 'schizoid'. He now resembled a juggernaut on heroin.

'Some sort of clue? And what does one of them look like?' It was a perfectly reasonable question.

'Well, let me see. It's probably gonna be purple with a yellow stripe an' a big arrow pointing to it accompanied by the words, 'This Is A Bloody Big Clue!' Or p'raps it'll just resemble another fistful of rock 'ard knuckles collidin' wi' w'at's left o' the gristle in y' stupid, PHALLIC SHAPED NOSE.'

With resignation Ben started to remove individual videos from the closest of the bookshelves. The job was undertaken with an unhealthy and sullen silence that betokened an impending sulk. He studied the well-thumbed covers with a half-hearted intent.

'Miss Sonneman reckoned that the answer might lie in the videos somewhere,' Ben proffered by way of more amicable dialogue.

'Yes...I wouldn't be too 'asty t' trust the word of a paraplegically brained symbiont if I were you.'

Having seated himself on the floor cross-legged, Jess shuffled through his own mound, constructing a circular wall for himself. Ben peered at one of the bricks.

'Extinguisher 12. Judgement Decade.' He studied a

couple more with expanding intrigue. 'Zombie Holocaust. The Revenge of the Chainsaw Prositutes, 5.'

'Let's 'ave a look at that. It might be important.'

Obviously it was, because Jess stuffed it up his sweater for further perusal at home.

'Very influential things, films.' Ben had found himself a rhythm by now, speaking whilst he downloaded the films one by one.

'When I was knee high to a grasshopper's knob there was this fat, spotty twit called Dennis Waltham. Used to live four doors up in a house that looked as if Mother Teresa belonged there. We nicknamed him 'Turd-Pipe' Waltham 'cos he had a permanent crust of snot on his top lip. His mum was always trying to polish it off with a phlegmy hanky. But every morning at nine o'clock when school started, it was back—all green and solid like the outflow pipe on Blackpool beach.'

Ben leaned back against the cupboard with an air of reflection and perused the darkest depths of his long term memory.

'One year we went to Blackpool on a field trip. We had to write an essay on *"The sights and sounds of the seaside."* Waltham put, *"Blackpool with its famous tower looked like a beach with a hard on."*

'Are y' actually goin' t' get t' the point?' Jess interupted, growing thoroughly bored by this never ending monologue. 'Or would y' rather experience the 'G' force on y' facial muscles of extreme flatulence from inside me large colon?!'

'The point was...' Ben gave Jess an unsuccessful chilling stare. 'The point was that when he was eight years old, he went to see 'Superman' with his mum and dad. Three days later he tried to fly off the top of the kitchen cupboard and impaled himself on his novelty Blackpool Tower paperweight.'

Ben shrugged his shoulders suggestively, having made his point, although Jess wasn't sure exactly what the point was.

'I knew a girl once, called Karen McDougal,' Jess replied, embarking on a recollection of his own. 'Got so involved in a book she was readin' that the 14a ran over 'er 'ead an' killed 'er.'

'That's not the same sort of thing at all.'

'Well...' Jess breathed heavily in, filling his lungs with the room's stale atmosphere and almost choking. 'As much as I'd like to get involved in an 'eated debate about the corruption of youth at this point, Ben, it 'ardly seems likely that a retired business clerk would start shootin' green lightnin' bolts out of 'is 'ead an' turn into a psychotically deranged killin' machine just because 'ee watched the 'Ewok Adventure'.'

'No...But it makes you think.'

'Which in your case might result in some 'orrific aneurysm, so just button y' gob and save y'r opinions until y'r next visit t' the toilet.'

Ben reached down behind the collection of films that he'd amassed. His anaemic fingers fumbled awkwardly for a substantial grip on the object that they'd just encountered. Moments later he extracted an orb that he hadn't noticed before. It was about the size of a child's ball; yellow and purple and made from some sort of glass. He lifted it up to the light, squinting ardently into its impenetrable bubbled depths.

'What do you think this is then?'

Chapter Twelve

The Thick Plottens.

November 16th. 2:30 p.m; *'The Caldwell Crescent Retirement Home For The Elderly and The Infirm.'* A grandiose building surmounted by an antiquated green copper roof, the only alternative from the otherwise colourless structure. The austere walls had been constructed from the finest slate that Cumbria had to offer. A slate that now had patches of pale yellow running through it, as the ravages of time had gnawed away at the surface. A hint of the gothic renaissance had found its own influence around the doorway and upper windows, as generations of owners had applied their own interpretations of good taste.

Donald Oakseed stood between the vertiginous gates, gazing up at the huge house with an air of hypnotic fixation. The manner of his attire was curious to say the least. It consisted mainly of a 'Safari Suit' such as a BBC naturalist might wear to go traipsing through the jungle. Not the most obvious apparel for a cold November's day in north Lancashire. In one hand Donald clutched at the coiled serpent of his whip; an object fabricated from a helix of dark and indiscernible hide. A circular water-flask was provisionally fastened onto a leathery sling knotted about Donald's neck, and then tucked indiscreetly beneath his moistened armpit. The brim of a large and flaccid hat covered his incandescent eyes—disturbed eyes, that pulsed between red and green like a possessed set of traffic lights.

A tormented struggle briefly distorted the muscles around Donald's brow. The genuine Donald Oakseed battled magnificently but, it must be said, in absolute vain. His personality was no contest against the squatter that currently occupied his head. With an inward primal scream the less dominant character plummeted hopelessly towards the bottom of the mental maelstrom.

After God knows how many centuries in the realms of death and malformation, the great author had returned and was about to make his mark once more upon the unsuspecting world. He aimed Donald's decrepit body at the large front doors and stepped forwards, breaking the lull before the holocaust.

.

A number of old dears were silhouetted in their chairs against the blanket of daylight that occupied one whole side of the great lounge. Humped and squat, they resembled a collection of stout cacti. Some watched the television, transfixed day and night regardless of what was showing. Terry Bogan came and went rousing the occasional false-toothed smile. Shane Michie's anarchic show had them all trembling in their undetachable chairs. Bob Ponkhouse filled their heads with memories of the war and risqué well-seasoned jokes. And Michael Darrymore, what a clean living, nice young man he was.

To be honest, the only break that the old dears achieved from the cathode ray tube, was when the sharp and spiky nurses would trundle them off for the night. Not that the poor old things had ever noticed it happening. Their consciousness hung somewhere between the real world and a permanent cerebral celebrity game show.

Clara London, on the other hand, had different ideas

on how she and her best friend, the rather docile Edna Pruitt, ought to spend the autumn years of their lives. Dominoes, gossip and a never ending procession of large cups of tea. The gossip, unfortunately, had all but dried-up long ago, when the war had become too foggy a memory to embellish any further. But the tea kept on coming, accompanied as always by the patronising 'Equal Opportunities Male Nurse,' Allan. And an eternity of domino games ran so seamlessly into each other that it had become difficult to determine where one game ended and another began.

Clara carefully positioned a 'Double-Six,' on the table in front of her, with a trembling hand that portended the onset of Parkinson's disease. She cast a cautious eye towards the armchair beside the fireplace as she did so.

The armchair was occupied by Celia D'Locksmith; a stoical, impassive woman. There she sat, perfectly motionless. Submerged so deeply in her own superiority that her nose stroked the air like the tip of missile, and her hands topped a walking cane the point of which stabbed at the carpet. She was definitely of a more refined breeding than the others around her. Regrettably, her equally proud and disassociative son had dumped her there years before and done a runner. *What a way to end your life*, Clara thought without remorse, before returning to her undefeated streak of fourteen years.

Edna Pruitt laid down a 'Double-Four' and grinned, optimistically. It was brushed angrily to one side by her impatient game's partner. Somewhat confused over the rules of the sport, despite the many decades of active participation, Edna tried again with intensified concentration.

'Christmas was much more traditional when we was young.' Her voice rang out shrilly, sounding similar to a frog with a dry throat. Her filmy wet eyes shifted their cataract obscured gaze over the bare walls and the complete lack of decoration, filled with a longing for the past. 'Not like this at all.'

'That's because it's only November, dear.'

'November...yes...' Edna was off on some voyage of her own. A voyage that by-passed reality and headed straight through the foggy precincts of Memory Lane. She leaned across the table and spoke behind the back of a hand so full of varicose veins that it resembled an orgy of blood-worms. 'We used to 'ave a great big Christmas tree. With lots of bows and ribbons and kittens on it. And we'd all stand round the 'arpsichord and sing Christmas carols.'

'It's not bloody Christmas yet!'

'Eh?' Edna had gone deaf again. That irritating selective deafness that only took her on when it chose to do so. Most convenient as far as Edna was concerned. But bloody annoying for everybody else who wanted to conduct a discussion with the slightest modicum of rationality about it.

'Christmas!' Clara leaned into her inanely smiling friend, cupping her lips in one palm so that the already substantial shout was amplified to the point of agony. *It's not bloody Christmas yet!*'

'Christmas...yes...We 'ad t' make our own entertainment back then. None of this new fangled electronic radio rubbish.'

Ignoring the constant stream of nonsense that was issuing forth from Edna's mouth, Clara suddenly thought it appropriate, after all the years spent confined to her inadequate company, to finally broach a difficult subject.

'Edna?' A hesitant moment whilst Clara hunted for the precise words. 'Edna...why 'ave y' got to repeat everythin' I say?'

'Say...yes...We all used t' get a tangerine each in our stockings.' Edna was off again, lost in a personal history that grew more evocative with every rendition. 'Oh my God!' That broke the general air of complacency across the collapsible card-table. 'Look at the state of Mr. Jefferson!'

Mrs. London's astounded eyes followed the direction of the animated digit, wavering before the apex of Mrs. Pruitt's nose. They came to rest on Mr. Jefferson; the old gentleman in question. He was snoring profoundly alongside the miniature arboretum, his head slumped over onto a tweed shoulder.

"Ee 'asn't got long f' this world,' Edna added. 'Bags I first dibs on 'is armchair w'en 'ee's gone.'

Celia D'Locksmith chanced a quick glance in the couple's direction. A mere cursory glimpse, whilst their attentions were otherwise engaged.

Sometimes Celia had wondered what it would have been like had she lowered her standards and took the other old biddies at face value. Unfortunately, Clara had noticed the impassive eyeballs swivelling back into their original position.

'I don't know what you're staring at, neither. Y' stuck up old bag!'

'Old bag...' muttered Edna, her lips syncopating almost instinctively with her friend's, before the words had so much as finished leaving Clara's thin and dangerous mouth. Clara jabbed an accusatory finger in the general direction of Mrs. D'Locksmith's chair.

'The likes of us not good enough for you 'Auty Tauty, Aristocratic Types' eh?'

'Types...'

Celia spoke. Her voice hadn't broken the vow of self-imposed silence for over four years now. It held a sort of lofty control and good command that was not normally associated with the other occupants. Unfortunately, her nose rose steadily as she uttered the words, betraying the calm and collected exterior.

'If I was 15 years younger I'd...'

'Still be a toffee nosed old cow!' Clara nodded triumphantly. Then she added as an incisive afterthought, 'With no visitors!'

'Suppositories...' muttered Edna, who had obviously not been listening hard enough.

There was a squeal of unoiled trolley wheels as Allan the day-nurse trundled in his towel-covered load. With the artistry of a barber, he removed some ancient crusted dinner from Edna's chin, smartly finishing the job off with a circular polishing motion. Edna appeared not to have noticed. The food was automatically replaced by small pond of saliva that appeared without solicitation.

'Bloody 'ooligan.' It was Clara's habit to accost anybody younger than thirty-four in this manner. Like most old people who are confined to one building for most of the time, her perception of the outside world had been slightly coloured by Crimewatch UK.

'Like all the rest of 'em!' Clara added, rather flatly. 'There was none o' this violence on the streets w'en we was bloody young.'

'No...' Allan sported a genial smile that said he'd

Shells flew in all directions, accompanied by limbs and false teeth and small parts of furniture and dominoes and jigsaw pieces.

travelled this road before. 'You were too busy killing Germans, weren't you?'

Where upon the lounge door burst off its hinges in an eruption of wooden shrapnel. Several residents ducked for cover, disturbing memories rising from their wartime graves. In the process, numerous pace-makers started to whine like abandoned puppies.

Donald Oakseed charged through the lacerated opening. He was closely pursued by a uniformed security guard, who looked as though his head had been dipped in boiling sherry. From the confined depths of his leather jacket Donald produced a sawn-off shot gun.

"Ere! What's your game?"

Allan instinctively made to grab the weapon, sentinel to the last of his old aged pensioners. He was brushed brutally aside with a strength that he hadn't anticipated.

Donald focused in on Clara's excited eyes. It was just like on Crimewatch last week, she thought, slapping her hands together and beaming with suspense.

'Clara London?'

Splinters of light pierced the sullen air, drowned out by the ear-ripping scream of gunfire. Shells flew in all directions, accompanied by limbs and false teeth and small parts of furniture and dominoes and jigsaw pieces. Windows shattered, light bulbs burst. Blood splattered up the walls in a gorefest that only the lowest of 'The Creeping Dead' sequels would stoop to recreate.

In short, it was a massacre.

From behind the remains of the sofa came a creaky, high-pitched but apparently unconcerned voice. It rattled almost musically through the excessively large springs that the settee now sported.

'We 'ad a sense of community back then...'

The voice descended into an inconspicuous mutter, as if its owner had for the first time noticed that a major disaster had befallen. One last eardrum-blasting explosion of cartridges disturbed a couple of pigeons that had been roosting in the eaves.

Then silence fell across the tangle of barely discernable items, clustered beneath the heavy quilt of gunpowder smoke. Nothing moved apart from the odd chunk of plaster giving way from the gaping holes in the ceiling.

2:35 p.m. Greyminster, being a rather reserved town by its intrinsic nature, was blissfully unaware of the impending doom that was casting a portentous shadow across the universe. But *time and tide*, as the old adage tells us, *wait for no man*, and the first sensations of hopelessness had started to creep between the rows of terraced buildings.

The 'Paranormal Investigations' continued. Now confined to the 'Small Boys' room at Mrs. Prune's boarding house.

Actually, that isn't entirely honest; whatever Jess Hobson was currently doing it could not, by any stretch of the imagination, be considered as work. Occupying the 'Throne' as he called it, Jess studiously examined a well-thumbed copy of Razzle. To say that he was *reading* the magazine would also be an unacceptable bending of the truth.

A buckled can of beer was close at hand—it was half consumed. On the opposite side of the pedestal, a box of chocolates, was being molested. Jess, trousers round his ankles and magazine on his knee, read contentedly. A great many things had been bothering him of late. But, in the time-honoured tradition of countless Hobsons' before him, several hours spent locked in the lavatory with something to occupy his mind always sorted matters out.

Mrs. Prune however was far from at peace. Outside the door with her features screwed up in frustration, she marched angrily up and down, continually clenching and unclenching her fists. The nails on her finger tips had dug deeply into her palms making tiny lacerations. Every so often she would stop and breathe deeply in, casting a glance at the lock.

Mrs. Prune had often considered having another toilet installed. Unfortunately, that was of no help under the current circumstances. Though she did make a mental note of rectifying the matter at the first opportunity.

At length her patience wore as thin as a perished elastic band. 'Jess 'Obson! W'at y' doin' in there? Givin' birth?'

'I'm not y' mother, Mrs. Prune. She's the only woman I know of 'oo ever gave birth t' a stool.'

"Ow dare *yoo*!!' The final '*Yoo*' of that statement had an altogether haughty and dignified ring about it. 'You're the only person I know as spends almost a third of 'is life on the bog.'

The same voice piped back with growing exasperation. 'Y're puttin' me off.'

A short pause for further consideration of the subject. "Ow am I s'pose t' take a dump with a warty old rhino listenin' in at the keyhole?'

There followed the rustle of what at first seemed optimistically to be something other than a magazine being thumbed. Much to Mrs. Prunes' chagrin her expectations were wrong.

'It's upsettin' me sphincter muscles.' Jess proclaimed once more. 'I can't perform wi' you standin' outside waitin' f' the splashdown.'

Mrs. Prune tightened every orifice on her body at that. It required every ounce of her will-power not to shoulder barge the door.

'Aim f' the side o' the bowl or somethin'! Just 'urry up! Before me knickers tek on the appearance o' weather balloons.'

Inside the cramped and dimly lit chamber Jess reached down into the back pocket of his crumpled denims. Moments later the enormous hand reemerged, clutching an object between its saveloy fingers. The pair of *Phase Re-alignment Glasses* were thrust onto the end of his bulbous nose.

Benjamin Foster bore down upon him urgently. He lunged the toilet roll determinedly forwards, holding it roughly about an inch in front of the lenses. Jess, startled at this unexpected visitation, jerked back his bristled scalp, an action that resulted in his cranium making contact with the cistern head. It produced an unhealthy sounding crunch.

'Jess! Finish off the paperwork quickly.' The toilet roll was flung towards him in the most undignified manner. 'I've discovered something important!'

Jess whipped off the glasses. In desperation he attempted to pull his already over-stretched sweater across his hairy pink knees, shouting at the top of his powerful voice, 'BUGGER OFF!!'

At roughly 3:30 that afternoon, Jess finally emerged from the restroom. It seemed much later, especially on his landlady's account.

Mrs. Prune now stood over a lugubrious eggplant, the dented watering-can appliquéd with orange rust, dispersing the contents of the morning's teapot over the all-consuming leaf mould. Having finally given up the ghost and paid a visit on the Wambachs', the stout landlady was now satisfied that she could continue watering her plants without going through any further mental torture.

Benjamin Foster buried his Anglo-Saxon nose between the pages of a musty volume that lay dismembered before him. He casually licked a fingertip, applied a little pressure to the page, and brought away the corner in the process.

A blackened sentiment of festering anger swamped the apartment. Heavy boots rattled through the burnt and blackened woodwork, dislodging various curtains of soot which tumbled soundlessly. As the shadow fell across the pages, Ben raised his eyes to greet his partner, one brow arched quizzically into his forehead.

'At last...I was beginning to think that the toilet had swallowed you up.'

Suddenly a thick-set, hirsute arm tangled itself about Benjamin's emaciated neck. His ghostly head became jammed in Jess' immovable vice.

'Don't EVER disturb me mid-dump again!' Jess tightened his grip like a boa constrictor. 'Or else y'll be spendin' the rest of eternity tryin' t' dislodge a kidney from the top of y'r 'ead!'

A bolt of lightening erupted from Benjamin's skull, earthing itself into the nub of his colleague's chin. At that same moment an umbrella made contact with the crest of Jess' skull. It bounced back upon impact, producing a sharp and resounding 'Thwok!' Moments later it was accompanied by the spout of a rusted watering-can making impact with his other ear.

Jess relinquished his delirious hold. An act that concluded with the sort of wheezing that someone might have made had they just swallowed a bag full of feathers.

'Leave 'im alone y' useless great brute! Don't y' think 'ee's 'ad enough buggerin' problems o' late wi'out you 'alf maulin' the poor lad t' death?!'

"Ee already is dead!

'Well, there's no need f' you t' go makin' it worse!'

Mrs. Prune struggled onto her toes, prodding his shoulder with a substantial finger that, regardless of Jess' bulk, actually made him rock backwards.

'An' y' ought t' 'ave more respect f' y'r elders! Now...Listen t' w'at Benjamin's got t' say, an' y' might learn something f' once. If y've got any braincells left in that bull's gonad of an' 'ead o' yours!'

With obvious reluctance Jess turned to Benjamin. He was straightening up the collar on his spectral pullover.

'Right. Well, let's hear it then. This '*Profound*' revelation that's goin' t' turn the world on its 'ead. Managed t' formulate an equation for Einstein's inverse-universe theorem 'ave y'? Or 'ave y' just found a nasty bump on y' noggin?'

Ben slid the crumbling manuscript across the table to his partner whilst muttering indistinctly, 'Have a close look at this.'

Jess picked up the bent and haggard tome, several chunks coming adrift in his fingers.

'Peculiarities of the Physiognomy of Quantum

Mechanics an' 'ow to set up a Nicam VCR f' the Absolute Beginner.'

He stared at the cover hoping for some great revelation, failed to see the significance, stared at Benjamin, glanced back at the book and ventured hopelessly, 'Volume one?'

He slammed the tome shut, waved it in the air with one dismissive hand and thought, *'Bugger it.'*

"Ave I missed the point? Or was Stephen Gawking s'pose t' come into the room at this juncture an' start ruminatin' on some new theory concernin' temporal physics and event horizons?'

Ben reached for the volume, noting the wrinkles that were appearing in spokes from Jess' ever tightening grip. Jess childishly snatched it back. After several seconds of competition to prove who had the fastest reflexes, Ben finally slammed the ancient manuscript back down on the table. He thumbed backwards through a couple of the crumbling leaves.

At length he pointed to the relevant line of small print at the bottom of page one, turning the book around for Jess' closer scrutiny. Jess craned his neck forward, squinting at the typeset.

'Authorship 'Thomas 'Obson and Samuel Foster.' He uprighted himself in an expression of bafflement. 'So they were a little ahead o' their time? W'at's the point y're tryin' t' make, Ben? That they've come back from the dead t' claim the 'Booker Prize of 1897'?'

'Look at the publishing date.'

Ben's voice was calm. It reeked of smugness. The sort that could penetrate down into the soul and dance amongst the gastric juices until you were sick. Jess repressed an overwhelming urge to clock him one. Instead he strenuously followed the minuscule list of required acknowledgements that book's frontispieces everywhere appeared obliged by law to print.

'Twenty forty-six.'

'I found it over there in a Sainsbury's box filled with old copies of Men Only.'

'Yeah, *'Old'* wasn't the word,' Jess reflected, having perused the top few layers of that particular container himself. 'Pre-Chaplin crap! All writin' about politics an' steam engines with the odd topless black an' white shot. No wonder I found 'em put out for the bin men at the back o' the Wambachs' house. Talk about givin' a starvin' dog a rubber *'bone'*. Any'ow, w'at were you doin' lookin' through that box?'

Strategically Ben managed to avoid the question.

'Jess...I know that on cold days like this your brain sometimes needs a jump start. But, don't you consider the publishing date just a little important? Don't you find it odd that a volume on quantum mechanics happens to have been published several years in advance of our own time?'

'So w'at? So the publishers employed the same typesetter as the Greyminster Chronicle an' got the date wrong by a hundred or so years? Find us a pen quick an' I'll inform Ripley's *Believe It Or Not!* Y' sad polyp!'

'Look Jess. I don't exactly know what this means. But it's about Thomas Hobson, so it's got to be important.'

As the conversation was unfolding, the telephone rang. Mrs. Prune feeling obsolete had answered it. She now covered the mouthpiece, confronting the boys around the burnt and unstable doorjamb, her features having expanded in alarm so that they resembled a balloon with a felt-tip face drawn upon it.

'As much as I 'ate t' break up this lovers' tiff,' she interrupted with an amount of emergency in her tone. 'But, would either of y' 'appen t' know a Donald Oakseed?'

Benjamin and Jess turned to each other. Their initial expression of confused surprise slowly reverted to one of indignation. Jess was barely able to contain the reluctance in his voice.

'Name sounds familiar. W'at's 'ee done?'

'Blown up an entire bus queue wi' an ectoplasm gun, an' caused a double decker bus on Caldwell Crescent to blow-up just by lookin' at it.' Mrs. Prune thought about that for a moment before adding, for the sake of her own mental stability, 'Apparently...Any'ow, there's a Miss Sonneman askin' for y'.'

Looking suddenly flustered, Jess clumped across the apartment, accepting the receiver with a diffident sigh.

'Mrs. Sasquatch? Don't say a word. No, DON'T! Just 'old on there an' I'll come round. Just as soon as I've finished jammin' a grotty old book up me partner's left nostril.'

Chapter Thirteen

Murder as the Evening Falls.

November 16th. 4:00 p.m. Greenwich meantime. During this narrowing month of the year the gloomy daylight hours have been curtailed by the great approach of winter's dark shroud. The shortening of the afternoons results in a reduction of the number of *'Genuinely Useful'* hours. Unbeknown to the majority of the residents of Greyminster there is much less *'Available Time'* than anybody might actually realise.

The old are aware of this situation. What's left of the old people in Greyminster anyhow, following the massacre at the rest-home earlier that day. Fewer days ahead now than behind. But for them there are other, more important matters at hand. Matters worth fighting violent battles over.

Look down. There are *lots* of old people gathered about this particular institution.

The Albert Finney Memorial Hall. A wooden Swiss-chalet based structure that rears into view along the grassy slopes of South Ringing Fell. A building that even now is caught up in the throng of the annual Jumble Sale. The resultant chaos is the once-yearly all-out-war for the possession of second hand clothes, mangled books and the sort of broken pottery that buzzes when exposed to boiling tea.

It was a typical jumble sale that was very much in progress, having that instantly recognisable fervour of religious zeal and hypocrisy about the whole affair.

Father Wordsmith fluttered excitedly behind the 'Collectors' Pot Stall'; his face alight with the excitement of being intimately involved with the pensioner's community. Around the middle-aged priest, dozens of old dears searched for that elusive bargain amongst the rubble of lampshades and old curtain fabric.

Most of them were fighting; all with varying degrees of violence. Let's concentrate on the two of them closest to hand.

Edith Norton, recently recovered from her incident with Donald Oakseed, was wrestling Mrs. P. Atkins over some tatty piece of cloth. The situation with its customary lack of elegance had escalated into one-on-one combat.

Edith, with her fingers so tightly clawed on the offending article it started to rip beneath the nails, was in full fettle by this inflamed juncture.

"Smine! Geddoff it y' old walrus!'

'You horrible old witch. I'd 'ad the vicar put this aside for me.' Mrs. Atkins, ignoring the wisdom of Solomon, was now allowing the cloth to tear.

'That's abuse o' bloody church committee privileges if y' ask me!'

Edith took a swing at Mrs. Atkin's head with her brolly. It made contact at roughly the same time as Mrs. Atkin's Zimmer frame crushed Edith's big toe through her repulsive woolen boots.

Father Wordsmith pushed through the tumultuous hordes feigning ignorance of the odd barneys that were breaking out all around. He reached the podium relatively unscathed, and climbed up to a dais at the front of the hall.

'Ladies!' His voice hollered around the vast wooden

vault. 'If I could have your attention for a moment. Ladies please! It's time for the prize tombola draw.'

Father Wordsmith leaned down to an old dear on his right hand side, speaking with an amount of worried confidentiality.

'Could y' hand me the tombola bin, Gladys?' His eyes flicked back up towards the ever-darkening anarchy. 'Before things start turning nasty!'

Compliantly, Gladys obeyed her mentor. She struggled beneath a large black plastic bin that had been filled to the point of overflowing with a mound of small pink tickets. Several vouchers broke away from the unsteady mountain, tumbling like blossom to the polished boards beneath her boots.

At which point a violent laser gun brought the noisome crowd to a shocked and hushed standstill, zigzagging its blinding path towards the rostrum. Moments later the bin exploded beneath Gladys' infirm grip, showering a storm of pink confetti over the top of everybody's heads.

As one, the crowd turned to gaze upon the heroic stance of Donald K. Oakseed. His short figure stood proudly flourishing a weapon the blade of which appeared to be constructed from a column of light. The figure moved dimly along the balcony that skirted the back of the building. He wore a costume reminiscent of a familiar space hero.

'ArTwoDeeTwo?!' cried Cervantes, his masterful voice ripping outwards from Donald's accommodating mouth; his burnished eyes staring with passion towards the refuse container. 'Don't worry ArTwoDeeTwo. I'll save you.'

With one disproportionately immense hand, he grabbed hold of a nearby rope that was hanging from the rafters.

And with a mighty Tarzan cry he swooped down into the crowd. Unfortunately in doing so Donald misjudged the length of the cord. After a gallant descending arc, full of theatrical melodrama, his body collided heavily with the ground. The old dears gathered about him in one hoary, highly compressed crescent.

The old women loomed down; united at last against the common enemy. Nobody, *but nobody*, was going to take their jumble sale away from them. Senile solidarity had taken root.

Suddenly Donald was up on his feet, old dears flying backwards in all directions. Stalls were overturned sending discharges of junk up towards the rafters. Wall-bars broke beneath the hurtled bodies of the old and geriatric.

Cowering behind the lectern with Gladys, was Father Wordsmith. 'It's perhaps a little bit more violent than usual Gladys,' he intoned in his soft Irish lilt, wondering if he could make it to the trap door lever in time, and escape. All around him the noisy confusion raged on.

Let's not hang around this hall to watch the ensuing pandemonium. Suffice it to say that the mounting pile of bodies only added to those at the retirement home. Later, Donald left the jumble sale as its only victorious member, silently disappearing down a side-street as the strobing lights of the police-cars swiftly moved to the site of the carnage.

11:30 p.m. November 16th. The residence of Miss Martha Sonneman. Martha skipped along the hallway; an almost weightless caper, in stark contrast to the violent ringing of the front doorbell. It was accompanied by the deafening hammer of Jess' fist threatening to shatter the wood from the main body of the door.

The welcome mat tickled roughly at the bare soles of her pale, freckled feet as she reached delicately for the latch as though it was some fragile glass rose. She wheezed breathlessly upon the latticed window, polished it smartly with the sleeve of her flimsy pink sweater, and peered out through the portal into the dark night beyond. With an expression of vulnerability she drew the tartan dressing-gown about her elegant frame, flicked back her hair and allowed a tender nibble to ruck up her lower lip.

Two figures occupied the front doorstep. Benjamin Foster and Jess Hobson. Martha only witnessed Jess of course, what with Ben being dead and all. But she probably wouldn't have noticed him anyhow. She was more than a little enwrapped by her own thoughts tonight, most of which centred on the enormous face that was distorting back at her through the buckled glass.

Jess for his part, was keenly attired. Not a crease, wrinkle or curry stain in sight. To be honest, he felt uncomfortable and out of place; the funeral suit pinching painfully at various parts of his bulky anatomy, and looking peculiarly unfilled at various others. With a purposeful, almost strangulating movement he adjusted the magnificent kipper tie.

Benjamin inhaled a lungful of the night air through his dark nostrils and pulled an uncomfortable face. 'What's that smell?'

'Probably the turd comin' out o' y' gob.'

The aroma was rather excessive. Its pungency left a burning sensation on the back of the throat.

'It's Old Kung Fu, that bloody aftershave! Auntie

Maureen bought you a bottle about four years ago.'
Benjamin dug deeper for his more recent recollections.
'It's been gathering dust behind the cistern ever since.
The only time you opened it was when you ran out of
alcohol last Easter.'

The front door swung open beneath Martha's dainty
grip. She adjusted her dressing-gown carefully, in the hopes
that it might make her appear slightly more endowed. As
she did so, Jess unashamedly belted Ben bluntly on the
nose with one mighty fist. The electricity crackled in
bafflement around the cube of digits before earthing itself
elsewhere.

Jess caught the aspect of bemusement that was scribbled
across Martha's face. In embarrassment he pretended to
be scratching his Velcro head instead. Benjamin Foster
staggered backwards, clutching with silent ferocity at his
doubled up proboscis. Beneath his breath he swore
violently.

Tucking his tie into the top of his sweater Jess smiled.

'Ah, Mrs. Sassenach. I got 'ere as soon as I could.'

'Why, Mr. Hobson...' Martha wondered why she
suddenly sounded like a Victorian maid but couldn't do a
thing about it, and shook the thought from her head. 'I
was beginning to think that you couldn't come.'

There was a moment of embarrassed silence.

"Oo the bloody 'Ell told y' that?"

'Nobody.' Martha's voice trailed off. 'It's just that I
called this afternoon and...'

'Oh...Yes...' Jess straightened up, his heavy brow lifting
like a storm cloud. 'Of course...I had to feed Mrs. Prune's
tortoise.'

Martha paused, a little mental arithmetic questioning the integrity of that statement. 'For seven and a half hours?'

'Yes...well, its jaw got stuck.'

'How?'

'W'en I was kicking it under the chin f askin' too many STUPID QUESTIONS!'

'I ought to get the RSPCA onto you.'

'I wouldn't do that Mrs. Cesarean. They'd probably cart y' off an' 'ave y' destroyed for 'avin' an incurable varicose VEIN FOR AN 'EAD.'

By this point their voices had risen so dramatically that several lights had come on along the crescent. Following suit, various dark faces were now squashed against the windows of the terrace in an attempt to get a clearer view of number thirty-three.

'Jess?' Benjamin hissed at his colleague through his ice-cold teeth. Unfortunately Martha was in full swing. The road to romance was going to be slightly more rocky than anticipated, it would seem.

'I'd rather have a haemorrhoid for a head, Mr. Hobson, than a...a...BOLLOCK!'

'Jess!' Ben tried again to attract his partner's attention. This time his frustrating persistence resulted in success.

Jess Hobson, teeth gritted in vexation and fist tightly clenched, swung round upon Benjamin who ducked instinctively. For a moment Jess became dizzy as the whole of his perspective changed.

The offending glasses were grabbed from the summit of Jess' nose and following a brief inspection were hidden in the depths of Benjamin's trench-coat pocket. Whereupon Benjamin vanished completely from Jess' sights with an almost silent 'plop'.

For a moment or two longer Jess stared angrily into the remaining empty space. After which the enormous skinhead suddenly doubled up in agony, clutching at his groin as if something or someone had placed a well-aimed kick at his genitalia.

Martha's fuming anger dropped as the object of her distractions crumpled before her. An expression of worried concern drew down her features in an avalanche of surprise.

'Are you all right, Mr. Hobson?'

A muffled whimper seemed to indicate that perhaps he wasn't.

'Apart from the rather obvious fact that me scrotum appears t' 'ave burst, y' mean?'

Jess attempted to straighten up without tearing any ligaments, hobbled across the doorstep clutching at the gusset of his trousers and turned a furious shade of purple. Martha stooped over, taking him gently by the elbow.

'I think you'd better come inside for a moment. We'll have a look for some ointment.'

Begrudgingly Jess allowed her to drag him in through the door.

'P'raps a needle an' thread might be better.' Jess staggered, adopting a curious gait. It resembled a mongoose that was suffering from a bad bout of rickets. 'An' y're not touching my privates with y'r 'orrible 'arpy claws!'

'Don't be such a baby, Mr. Hobson. It's nothing I haven't seen before.'

Jess looked up horrified, straight at the back of Martha's retreating head.

'Why? W'en did you sneak a gander at me gonads?'

The door closed behind them.

114 Applegate. Apartment Four. The Hobson & Co Library, to be exact. At about roughly the same time that Jess Hobson was receiving a lesson in manners from his acrimonious business partner, Mrs. Prune was making a most important discovery of her own.

If the reader would accompany me, let us enter the fetid underworld of the cramped and sloping cupboard. There's Mrs. Prune, hunch-backed amongst the collection of old books that was once Benjamin Foster's pride and joy.

Two large volumes lay open; spread across her extensive square knees. Mrs. Prune's eyes grew ever larger beneath her tiny spectacles. Her puckered mouth had fallen open into a pleated gawk. To all intents and purposes it resembled a hungry barnacle waiting for its supper.

'Bugger me fat Aunt Nellie with a cucumber.'

Another page was turned with little consideration for the book's great age. Rigidly she scanned the lines. 'So that's what's goin' on,' Mrs. Prune added to herself, with an amount of growing consternation.

She looked up thoughtfully, grabbed her hat and coat from the hook above her head and struggled to lift her ancient heavy frame. Moments later Mrs. Prune was plonking the hat upon her topknot with a degree of grim determination, and having wrapped the long coat haphazardly around her wide shoulders she breathed in deeply. It was the sort of inhalation that made her swell to about three times her normal size. Then Mrs. Prune made a secret resolution to herself.

'Time for action!'

And with that, she left the building.

Chapter Fourteen

The Phantom Returns.

There was a rattle of a teaspoon from Martha Sonneman's kitchen. It chinked around an expensive mug and was eventually laid to rest on a bone-china saucer.

The front room of number thirty-three, Old Bridge Lane, appeared to struggle beneath an oppressive bank of barely contained animosity. Jess Hobson nursed his battered pride. It was proving difficult to regain any dignity whatsoever; especially considering that he was perched rather awkwardly on a cushion obviously designed for the ease of the discomfort normally brought about by haemorrhoids.

Martha emerged from the dimly lit doorway, transporting a silver tray. Two mugs of simmering coffee rattled about on their ill-fitting saucers. They were surrounded by a selection of chocolate Hob Nobs and custard creams. Regardless of modern political-correctness, Martha still found a healthy enjoyment from tending to men's needs.

'Feeling better now?' The refreshments were placed on the smoked-glass coffee table, the glutinous coffee washing over the broad rims and forming stalactites down the sides of the mugs.

'I was! 'Til that great Rottweiler fleabag decided t' use the gusset of me denims as a scratchin' post!'

Jess narrowed his eyes at the shapeless hot water-bottle

that was currently clinging onto the sofa. Two sapphire eyes glinted menacingly back from the expanse of orange fur.

'Oh Ginger's just a great big softy really.'

Ginger obviously didn't think so. Jess growled at the overweight animal before remembering something important from much earlier in the day.

'Well, as much as I enjoy our little *'Tete a Tits'*, Mrs. Suspect,' he began with his usual aplomb and diplomacy. 'W'at the buggerin' 'Ell did y' actually want, any'ow?'

'Ah...' Martha lifted the coffee to her wan lips and blew the cloud of steam sensitively from the surface. For a moment the top half of her face disappeared. 'It's my neighbour, Mr. Oakseed. Something odd's turned up in his cellar.'

There followed a protracted and altogether familiar silence. A pause that carried itself on for that fraction too long.

Suddenly Jess was scrambling up onto his feet, wearing the sort of formidable frown that said, *'This interview is now over!'* Or words of one syllable to that effect.

'Right! I'm goin' home t' dunk me testicles in some 'orse lineament. W'en y' finally discover 'ow t' communicate properly, Mrs. Sausage, then please don't hesitate t' phone a priest or someone. In fact, y' could try a plumber. To unblock y' cerebral cortex first.'

'It's torn Mr. Hobson!'

The sudden remark made him stop, one solitary word stupidly hanging off the edge of his teeth. Jess gathered his tired wits together before carrying on.

'Yes...It probably is! That's why I'm goin' 'ome.'

Martha grabbed him. Having witnessed the smouldering expression that burned across Jess' shoulder she repositioned her pallid hands carefully together on her knee. Sitting primly she went on to explain what she'd discovered about number thirty-two.

'The fabric of reality in Mr. Oakseed's cellar. It's got a great big rip in it!'

Now it was Jess who was taciturn. An obviously difficult thought process worked its way out through the muscles of his brow and mouth.

'It's the wrong time o' month isn't it? Women's matters. Greenwich Menstrual Time, or w'atever. Go an' 'ave a word with y'r local GP, Mrs. Sorespot. I've no doubt 'ee'll be able to 'ave you committed.'

'No, Mr. Hobson.' Martha attempted to force Jess' suspicions aside with her genuine concern. 'It was like a gash. A sort of long pulsating hole...With multicoloured balls coming out of it.'

'Are y' sure y're not getting confused with me little accident?'

She sprang to her feet in such an impassioned motion that Ginger visibly expanded.

'Something bad's torn through from the other side!' Martha was working herself up into a frenzy now. The veins on her temples had begun to stand out after the fashion of miniature giblets. 'Whatever it is, it's taken possession of Donald. Something bigger and uglier than even you! And something's got to be done. It must be stopped before it destroys us all!'

Martha concluded this outburst having vehemently shouted the final words into Jess' countenance from a range of mere inches. He arched an eyebrow in a dismissive manner.

"Ow come the smell of y' revolting feet didn't see this *'Anomaly'* off then?' Jess wasn't in the mood for being described as *'Ugly'*. Especially by somebody whose hairstyle had gone out of fashion in the summer of 1975.

'Listen, y' great muscle skull! If *you* don't stop whatever it is that's controlling Donald then *nobody* will.' Archly she added, 'Call yourself a *'Paranormal Investigator'?'*

As suspected, that struck an inharmonious chord deep within Jess' psyche. A slander against his *'Detective Talents!'* was the equivalent of calling him *'A worthless great pratt!'* He stiffened his tendons and pulled himself up to his full impressive height.

'Right then! Where's Donald, the four-eyed little toss rag?'

A look of relief swept across Martha's sly facade.

'Well, usually at this time he's staggering home from the Ruptured Duck.' She cast her mind back to the many chauvinistic hours indulged in Donald's company. 'Singing sea shanties with the words slightly altered to make them rude.'

Jess' gaze fell to the shiny new boots he had acquired from Benjamin's wardrobe. Boots that were all laced up wrong and had been tweaking the joints of his toes since leaving Applegate.

'Time t' try out me new *exorcise boots* I think!'

Midnight; the witching hour. Cold and icy and bathed in a lush November blue moonlight. Mrs. Prune hadn't much time for such matters of aestheticism. Atmospheric graveyards had the same amount of appeal to her sensibilites as a basket full of washing that needed to be done. To Mrs. Prune, the *witchin' thing* as she so expertly called it, was all about purple robes and sewn-on sequins and giving susceptible old biddies something new to believe in. Some sort of tangible optimism that their tired old religion seemed unable to provide. There was the odd crucifix positioned around the apartments at Applegate. For that touch of familiarity that the old could relate to. But other than these nods toward convention, Mrs. Prune's was the sort of *witchcraft* that you bought from a cheap stall on Greyminster Market. All pink and yellow skull candles, and Tarot decks designed by the local school children.

Her rugged fell-walking boots crunched along the winding gravel drive. Small drifts of marsh fog separated around her ankles like gossimer. It would be fair to say that there was no pointed hat pinned down cockeyed upon Mrs. Prune's head. No suggestion of a birch twig broom. None of that crap. Just her trusty old boots and a thick woolen coat, buttoned up tightly enough to keep out the intrusive night. And an umbrella. *Important bit o' the 'Occultin' Craft'*, was that.

Thomas Hobson's burial plot was currently occupied. The breathless young couple in the middle of the first throes of courtship procedures had little consideration for what lay beneath the scrub.

Emma Wilkins was fast approaching sixteen years of age—fifteen years, five months and thirteen days to be exact, and she was still counting.

The misapprehension that all of her fifth form colleagues were no longer virgins, found Emma herself labouring under a great deal of pressure to join the initiated before she attained the legal age. Reaching 16 would, after all, destroy the incentive.

Grant Warrenhurst was also a fumbling adolescent. He was hoping to gain his first sexual experience tonight.

A pair of heavy boots crunched inconsiderately across the distant sepulchres. Startled by the echo, Emma sat up straight; wide eyed and horrified. Hastily, she rebuttoned her blouse.

'Did you hear something Grant?' Her whispered breath turned into an icy white gas which hung before her pale lips, slowly breaking into spirals and lurking away.

Grant sat upright; frustration etched across his acne-infested features.

'I couldn't hear anything above the groans of your pleasure.'

'What bloody groans?' Emma stared at the spotty youth thoughtfully for a moment, realising for the first time how much more mature she seemed than him. 'You're not gonna tell your mates at school about this, are y'?' A slight hint of worry accented itself on the back of her voice. Grant blushed in embarrassment, avoiding the topic.

'Was it any good?'

Was it any good? thought Emma, pulling a puzzled expression mixed with disgust. *One bloody grope through a fastened-up bra, and he wants me to compliment him on his sexual technique.* The Earth had hardly moved had it, for God's sake? All those books that she'd found on the top of her parents' wardrobe, full of drawings of men who looked like Quakers with big, bushy beards embroiled in sexual pleasures with female social workers. All that stuff about *'Erogenous Zones'* and *'Clitoral Stimulation.'* She hadn't exactly experienced much of that lot tonight.

'We haven't bloody done *anything* yet.'

'No! An' y' bloody not goin' to, neither!'

Mrs. Prune stepped out of the bushes. The point of her brolly brought Grant a dexterous crack about the nape of his neck. It wasn't exactly a life threatening blow. But under the circumstances, it was enough to dampen the adolescent's ardour.

'Get off that grave! No bleedin' respect f' the dead.'

Emma scrabbled to her feet; a bemused and mentally shattered Grant following suit.

'Last o' the great romantics, eh?' Mrs. Prune regarded the flattened grass sprouting up from the sacrilegious oblong, one eye screwed up with an amount sarcastic measurement. 'Y' ought t' be 'ome in bed be now, any'ows. Y' parents'll be worried sick!'

With just enough momentum to pound the brutal message of guilt through their impetuous skulls, she belted them both a couple more times with her trusted umbrella. Moments later the adolescents made their escape across the dismal landscape of the dead.

'Just cos y' too old for a good shag y'self! Y' frumpy, old Weeble!' Grant's voice echoed off the wretched monoliths, in the time-honoured tradition of inexperienced youth. 'Who's grave is it any'ow? Yours?'

'I know your mother, Grant Warrenhurst.' Mrs. Prune's own voice rang out as sharp as a bell, without her even bothering to look up from the studious prodding of the ground with her brolly. 'Don't think I'm so old as I can't bloody see straight!'

There followed a brief moment of indulgent and self-absorbed thought.

'An' yours, Emma Wilkins. All dressed up like a forties slapper. She'll be gettin' more than pile ointment off me w'en I next catches up wi' er.' The muffled cracks of frosted brambles breaking beneath the worried and disappearing feet of the youths, reached her ears with gratification.

To herself, Mrs. Prune added quietly, 'Treatin' the dead like they was livin'! No buggerin' respect no more!'

Then she turned to the gravestone and kicked it violently with the toughened toecap of her indefatigable right boot.

'Oy! 'Obson, y' wrinkled, retarded old stiff! Get y' bony corpse out o' that pile of soil! I wants a word with y'!'

A worried owl hooted stupidly in the nearby copse. Mrs. Prune patiently waited. At length:

'I know y' there!' The consonants split through the night with contempt, taunting the dead from their final resting places. 'Watchin' what was goin' on! Or comin' off! Or whatever! Y' sick Tom Jones.'

'The expression, Mrs. Prune you turgid walnut, is *John Doe.*' And every corpse has a right to keep guard over his own property.'

Thomas Hobson appeared, leaning over the gravestone with his familiar crooked back; his eyes smouldering dimly in a mesmerising stare.

'Not wi' 'is flies undone!' Mrs. Prune squinted through one eye. 'I knows w'at y're up t', Thomas 'Obson! Witch Destroyer an' Defender of the Faith, me big, fat arse! If y' come from the past then Cyril Smith is the lead ballerina wi' the Bolshoi!'

Thomas leaned another inch or two forwards, sucking in his cheeks so that his whole facade resembled a piece of brown paper drawn across a vacuum cleaner nozzle.

His voice strolled across the intervening gap with the same predatory skill as a tiger. 'What makes you think I couldn't crush you? Like that bastard Foster?'

'Y' can't 'urt me. Not whilst I'm wearin' me protective.'

For some unknown reason, that last statement sounded quite rude to Mrs. Prune. But she couldn't for the life of her understand why. Self-complacently, her bent old fingers fumbled for the immense pentangle that was hung around her neck as though it was the Mayoress' badge of office. With a firm grunt the medallion was shoved beneath Hobson's twitching nose. Thomas Hobson moved back slightly, a sneer of disgust hidden beneath his expression of contemptible disbelief.

'You bought that in Patels' Novelty Souvenir Emporium in Stoke-on-Trent. On a Mothers' Union Outing! Cheap, worthless plastic made in Taiwan!' Hobson concluded with a gummy grin that glanced and coruscated in the moonlight.

'Bloody works though, don't it?'

That much was true, as Hobson's expression revealed, despite every effort he had made to disguise it.

Aggressively he leaned forwards again, his bones scratching against the potmarked rim of the gravestone. Putting a curled snarl into his crabbed old voice he said, 'One day, you sour old mutton, you'll not be wearing it. It'll be on the bedside cabinet, forgotten. Or down the gutter with a broken chain...And when that happens I *will* destroy you. Splattered across the nearest wall like a leg that's burst from dropsy.'

'Now, BUGGER OFF you obese toad and leave the dead alone!'

Then he vanished.

Mrs. Prune looked about herself, checking to ensure that he hadn't suddenly reappeared behind her. In the copse the owl fluttered off with the sound of snapping twigs, startled by the ensuing shouts.

'I'll put a stop t' y'r evil games, Thomas 'Obson.' Mrs. Prune's voice carried the weight of the dead and the wounded, as she shook her clenched fist at the oppressive night. 'God 'elp me if I don't!'

12:35 p.m. The ultimate demise of the universe is already well underway. Not that anybody from around these parts would actually be aware of this particular fact. Nonetheless, the creeping edge of destruction is drawing in from all directions.

There had been a rumpus around the old town that night. The general public, due to one or more vociferous local newsmongers, were already calling tonight's incident, *'The Great Ruptured Duck Massacre.'* In spirit, it had followed a similar path to what had been named, *'The Great Retirement Home Massacre.'* And in substance it was remarkably similar to what was aptly called, *'The Great Massacre of the Albert Finney Memorial Hall.'*

With a head full of violent images, Miguel De Cervantes now steered the body of Donald Oakseed back onto the often traversed grounds of Old Bridge Lane. The figure lurched forwards, its reptilian eyes weeping like ghastly sores as it headed for home.

In the cellar of number thirty-two a narrow ivory light pulsated. Momentarily it highlighted a collection of mouldy furniture whose history, along with the rest of the cellar contents, was now forgotten. It crackled and spun on a slither wide axis; picking out the sharp corners of the untouched coal and the atmospheric spider's webs.

Jess and Martha were seated nervously to one side, sunk into a debilitated sofa that resembled a Yorkshire pudding. Look at them both—two middle-aged adolescents.

Almost snuggled down together. Almost, but not quite. Both concentrating upon the convoluted phenomenon before them, neither knowing what might emerge at any moment to confront their darkest fears.

'What do you think it is then?' Martha spoke, a scarcely audible voice that lapped over her mug's lipstick-coated rim.

'Well...it's obvious.' Jess sorted the words out in his head; attempting to formulate an explanation that might appease the layman. 'It's a sort o' line of white light that sort o' goes up an' down.' He narrowed his nostrils thoughtfully. 'An' pulses...'

Taking hold of Jess' thickset arm Martha edged a little closer across the cushion. Jess made no apparent attempt to stop her from doing so. Although, it should be noted, that he did thrust one finger down his sweater collar because it had suddenly appeared to tighten.

'Tell me, Mr. Hobson...Are you scared?'

'God no...' Jess shrugged and felt his cheekbones sear. 'Women are always comin' on t' me. Must be me natural charm.'

'You will protect me, won't you Jess?'

She studied his profile with her large brown eyes; the pupils wide and flawlessly shining against the closeness of the dark. Romantically Martha snuggled herself down. Her cheek brushed against his sweater sleeve. Nothing could ever destroy this moment together...

'What the BLOODY HELL IS THAT!?' Martha's scream shattered the serenity.

The unannounced materialisation of Benjamin Foster produced a burst of adrenaline in Martha that nearly removed the top of her head. Jess took control, attempting to pat Martha's scalp in what was presumably a comforting manner.

'That's just me partner, *Benjamin Foster*. He had a little accident with a madman...'

'It nearly made me have a little accident myself.' Martha released her grip slightly from Jess' chest, realised what she was doing and slowly tightened it again.

'So...How come Miss Sonneman can see me when *I* wear the spectacles?' Benjamin enquired, his magnified eyeballs ogling the cellar and squinting ridiculously into the dark corners.

'Y' probably wouldn't understand, bein' a bald brained afterbirth.' Jess wasn't sure that he understood the principle of 'Phase Re-alignment' himself exactly. It had just been an idea that had seemed to suggest itself to him at exactly the right time.

'Your ghostly form is just out o' phase with our reality,' he explained, not so much dragging the concept out of his head, but having the words appear there as if invited in by somebody else. 'So the glasses twist their surroundin' environs back into a neutral phase lock.'

'A bit like Scooby Doo?'

'W'at?'

'A bit like Scooby Doo? The dog? You know? Scooby, Dooby Dooby Dooooo?'

'Not really...' His business partner sought around for a more in depth explanation. 'On Scooby Doo...it always turned out t' be the janitor with a projection unit.'

Benjamin chewed his bottom lip thoughtfully, turning over half-remembered past experiences in his head.

'I must admit, it always bothered me that.' He blinked straight at Martha, giving her an excuse to snuggle just that bit closer to her magnificent protector. 'How the Hell did the janitor always manage to create a three-dimensional holographic image using a Super 8mm projector?'

Ben paused. The gnawing doubt about Jess' skill with all matters mechanical was still bothering him.

'So how come when you wear them...' He lined up the words into single file and allowed them to exit by his ashen mouth. 'How come...you don't go out of phase...as far as everyone else is concerned?'

'Buggered if I know,' Jess said at length.

This is the upstairs lounge at number thirty-two, Old Bridge Lane. It is threateningly dark and deathly still. A strange growing yell begins to fill the empty atmosphere. A resonant high-pitched rumbling that seems to arc across the hollow void and shake the building with angry, invisible hands.

A good half of the living room wall comes crashing down in a confusion of projectile bricks and choking dust. The crash is deafening. The closest furniture crumples up beneath the maelstrom of tumbling masonry.

Gradually the eruption cleared and started to settle. Donald Keith Oakseed strolled out of the billowing smoke that coiled from the debris as though it was a serpent surrounding its prey. He wore a multicoloured poncho and a black cowboy hat that was pulled down across his alligator eyes. From a holster—a leather object that was slung casually around his thin waist—he drew a Colt 45. With five rapid rounds he disposed of various ornaments that had previously been adorning what was left of the mantelpiece.

Moments later Donald embarked upon a total demolition of the lounge, removing any obstacles in his path. Scattered ornaments and videos became dismembered beneath the heels of his pointed boots; the glass of the coffee table shattering outwards with great effect when applied with the same pressure. Any item of furniture that had obviously gotten on his nerves was held aloft above his head with incredible strength. After which it was hurled against the walls, breaking up into dozens of tiny sharpened fragments.

Downstairs, Martha held ever more tenaciously onto Jess, now out of genuine fear for what was happening elsewhere in the alarming household. Jess himself stared almost vacantly up at the ceiling directly above, apparently nonplussed. He was attempting to work out Donald's position from where the chunks of plaster were giving way in inverted volcanoes. A massive crash followed by an explosion, clattered deep into the night. That one *must* have woken the neighbours up all along the street. As for what had caused it the most possible explanation was a gas cooker colliding with a fridge freezer at high velocity.

The noises stopped somewhat abruptly. For some time the only sounds that could be heard were those of an unsettling scuffle being enacted overhead. At length Jess breathed deeply in.

'Donald's 'ome then?'

At which point the cellar door burst open in an eruption of light, so broad and deafening that it framed Donald Oakseed's silhouette. A silhouette that now was clutching maniacally onto an enormous dripping knife. Teardrops of something black and sickening plummeted soundlessly onto the cold cellar steps.

Donald's eyes crackled and buzzed with an ominous jade green glow.

His voice echoed down into the cellar, making their blood turn as cold as ice.

'Norman? Have you got a girl down there?'

Chapter Fifteen

The Thunder Breaks.

Jess struggled laboriously onto his feet. In the process Martha was ungallantly hurled downwards. Moments later she found herself sprawled across the defective sofa like a rag doll.

With an ostentatious sweep of his muscular arm Jess extracted a weighty crowbar from where it had been tacitly Sellotaped beneath his sweater sleeve. His jaw had set firmly into position, his eyes taking on the appearance of a pair of thin sluice-gates.

Gunfire and flashes pumped through the dark cellar in combustible fists, setting it alight as if bonfire night had been bottled indoors. Chunks of stonework detonated into showers of chippings, drumming deadly raindrops down across their incarcerated heads.

In confusion Jess Hobson scanned his immediate environment, only to discover that Donald Oakseed had somehow worked an untraceable path directly behind him. A hand grabbed hold of his sweater, with a strength that was far in excess of what its stature suggested. Cervantes crammed Donald's demented features up close to Jess' own.

His voice bore an uncanny resemblance to a rasping file being dragged across the edge of a metal bench.

'Now I guess that in all the confusion I kinda lost count of the number of bullets that I fired myself.'

Sixteen, thought Jess, not that he'd been counting.

'So, do you feel *lucky* PUNK?'

A lethal looking carving knife was brought slowly level with his sweating features.

'Do you know what sound an eyeball makes when it's punctured?'

'A sort o' poppin' noise?' Jess shrugged, staring deep into Donald's dark, emotionless eyes. "Oo *are* you?'

'You're a smart kid...' Donald's features filled the whole of Jess' vision, distorting into potmarked landscapes due to the intimate lack of distance. 'Figure it out for yourself.'

The grip was released. Seconds later two large, old fashioned pennies were produced apparently from out of the thin air. With the sort of concentration usually required of a bomb-disposal expert, Donald started to push the coins on the surface of Jess' eyeballs. Jess vaguely remembered a similar thing being done to his Uncle Albert in the coffin.

'W'at exactly is y' problem mate?' He flinched, unsuccessfully trying to prevent the currency from being forced any deeper into the painful sockets. 'I know that chartered accountin' isn't exactly a fulfillin' job, but this is goin' a bit far!'

'I am the ghost of Miguel De Cervantes...' Donald vomited the words as if they had been a liberal helping of rancid spinach. 'For centuries I have struggled in the vain and twisted hope of returning to the world of mortal man...Now let's see how mortal *you* are!'

Jess screwed up his features into what resembled a package of bacon off-cuts and prepared himself for the final sensation of death. The sort of noise that a wooden gavel hitting an oak bench might have made had it been slowed down and played through an extremely bass speaker, ripped through his ears, echoing around the hollow bone that encased his terrified brain. Then silence.

Jess opened one eye with extreme caution. Donald had collapsed on the dusty cellar floor, clutching the back of his skull. A weird blue cloud emerged in anguish from the back of his potato shaped head.

There was Benjamin; stooped over the body brandishing the cricket bat from his schooldays in his ethereal hands. A blue contour of electrical current outlined the metaphysical weapon.

'Out for another century then!' An expression of complaiscancy spread across his ghostly features.

The cloud retreated into the glass orb that had rolled from Martha's feet. The globe then whistled and spun, blurring into what appeared to be several images before eventually coming to a halt near the spacial rift.

Which seemed an advantageous point for Jess to bring down his boot heel upon it. With splintering effect, a nebula of tiny glass shards expanded outwards, hovered briefly and then descended to the stone floor in a curtain of fine powder.

'Sorted!!' Self congratulations scrawled themselves all over Jess' gigantic face. 'Right, Mrs. Sespit, that's forty quid f' the call out fee an' twenty quid f'r expenses.' A thoughtful expression washed across his crude but satisfied countenance. 'But a pint in The Cockerel's Sphincter tomorrow night should suffice.'

Then he saw her. Martha was down on her hands and knees amongst the coal dust administering aid to the rather groggy, but fast recovering Mr. Oakseed. The sort of aid that only those of long time intimacy could administer.

Donald Oakseed now had a great deal of lipstick prints plastered across his bulb shaped skull. It looked vaguely as if he was being attacked by a swarm of red admiral butterflies.

'It's over now, Donald.' Martha, totally enveloped in her maternal instincts, had forgotten that Jess had ever existed. 'Let's go upstairs and I'll dig out your Baywatch collection...'

Jess felt his heart sink; when he spoke it was more to himself than to Martha.

'On the other 'and, business 'as been rather poor of late. P'raps the money would be more convenient.'

More convenient or not, Martha was no longer listening.

Instead, she was leading the disconcerted Donald towards the cellar steps, donating her shoulder as a walking frame. Benjamin turned to his old friend, unsure what to say. Eventually he thought of something.

'C'mon Jess. We'd better let them sort this out for themselves.'

He placed his hand on Jess' shoulder as warmly as it was possible for a ghost to achieve. Absorbed in deep rumination Jess followed the couple up the stairs and out of the dingy cellar.

1:35 a.m. November 17th, 1998. The old ferry boat house. A ramshackle wooden structure built as an appendage to the river Grey. A small jetty bordered by an ornamental railing, leads down to the rusted ferry boat.

Across the mysterious waters of the river's mouth, lies the patchwork countryside known locally as 'Devil's Crevice.' An eiderdown of feudal horticulture, washed in the silver-grey moonlight of this sad November night.

Benjamin Foster leaned over the aforementioned railings; his arms folded so that they formed a comfortable rest for his insubstantial chin. Jess Hobson on the other hand, sat dejectedly upon the damp slate flagstones. Each had their own respective troubles and fears. Each had their own respective bottles of alcohol—both were impressively potted.

On the off chance that the reader might be wondering at this point, Benjamin had just discovered that ghosts *could* become drunk. He was now attempting to ascertain, purely as an experiment you understand, by how *much*. Several phantom bottles would frequently appear from time to time, pouring into a supernatural tankard.

'W'en I was a young boy...I use' t' come 'ere a lot.'

His voice was slurred, sounding rather as though his head was submerged in a bucket of treacle. Jess raised an eyebrow at the drunken innuendo that entered his intoxicated mind.

'Most afternoons anyhow...' Ben added the words, sensing the inevitable derisive comment from his partner and curtailing it promptly. 'I'd watch all the stupid, poxy little ferry boats strugglin' across the yawning mouth of the river.'

He was starting to sound quite philosophical by now. The sort of melancholic philosophy that most people of a more sober disposition would describe as, '*Talking Bull.*'

'Stupid, cruddy little boat...strugglin' over the silt,

Benjamin had just discovered that ghosts could become drunk. He was now attempting to ascertain, purely as an experiment you understand, by how much.

before anchorin' alongside the slimy tongue o' Devil's Crevice jetty. Every day...Regardless o' the storms; regardless o' the number o' passengers, it'd struggle across.'

Benjamin cast one transparent arm about himself with a vague demonstration of the ferry boat's trouble. The 'Phase Realignment Spectacles' slid bizarrely down his nose at a skewed angle.

'An' I always thought...*'What's the point?'* For some unexplained reason, alcohol always coaxed his Lancashire accent out that little more. *"W'at's the bloody point, eh? If there's nobody on the bloody thing, what's the point o' battlin' across, fightin' the elements? Salt water lashin' y'r face an' hands! Coarse ropes rippin' the 'ard skin off y' palms?"*

He paused, reflectively studying the murky depths of the almost depleted bottle.

'Then one day...years later...I was standing in the pourin' rain watchin' the stupid buggers doin' the usual 'ard slog. W''en I thought...*'Just a minute...W'at the bloody 'Ell's the point o' me standin' 'ere?'*

'Bollocks!' Jess knew what he meant, although the word that had actually emerged sounded more like 'Rororks' in his inebriated state. 'Bloody women, eh Benjamin? Bloody Women! Y' can't live with 'em. But it's against the law t' murder 'em!'

With a trembling arm that could no longer support his dead weight, Benjamin uprighted himself, moving unsteadily towards the slouched form of his colleague.

'C'mon, y' fat bastard. Let's be 'avin' y'.'

'Geddoff, y' sad shirt lifter!' Jess waved the bottle rather dangerously in a misshapen ellipse above his balding head. 'An' I'm not a FAT BASTARD!'

'Actually, you *are* a fat bastard, Jess. The other day I

thought that four o' the houses down Mulberry Crescent 'ad shifted in some sort of landslide.' Benjamin shook his head wearily at the foggy recollection. 'But it was just that the light was 'avin' t' bend around you.'

'I'M NOT A FAT BASTARD!'

Look at them now. Lost and forgotten by the residents of Greyminster for the deeds that they have done. Unsung heroes, drowning in their own self-glory and misplaced resentment. Not to mention about seven bottles of extremely strong spirits.

Watch as we pull slowly back from the tableaux in order to study the events from a much greater, less obtrusive, height. A police van surrounded by its own eerie blue light, draws casually in upon the downhearted scene. Benjamin, with an almost paranormal sixth-sense, removes the glasses from his nose and, promptly disappears.

Jess' shouts echo up into the calmness of the evening, caught and muffled by the dragnet of the imprisoning clouds. 'I'm not a Fat Bastard! Y' mop 'eaded scope!'

Mrs. Prune sat behind Benjamin Foster's old desk, partially hidden by an enormous dusty volume of considerable antiquity. Up until that moment she had been completely engrossed in its ancient words of menace. So much so, only her hoary fingers had been visible holding the edges. On its cover were a large embossed pentangle, gold against red leather, and the words '*Malius Malafacturum!*'

'Oh...My Goodness!'

Tilting the book down with wide, horror-struck eyes

Mrs. Prune pressed her nose against the darkened window, squinting out into cloudy night.

Donald Oakseed's cellar. Number 32, Old Bridge Lane. Adjacent to the spatial rift, several multicoloured orbs begin to judder mechanically.

An echoing laugh hauntingly branches around the room; twisting and writhing. The thin line of light suddenly starts to tremble violently and with a loud rip the column dramatically doubles in height. Shredding and creaking in blinding white flashes, it continues its rapid growth into the roof.

Mrs. Prune stared from the dimly lit window. In the general direction of Old Bridge Lane a finger of light briefly prodded at the clouds, lighting their underbelly with an oppressive lining of silver. The illumination ripped a path of destruction up above the rooftops, shredding right across the sky. It was accompanied by an unhealthy and blasphemous noise.

'Oh...Bloody 'Ell!'

Mrs. Prune stumbled backwards, her excited breath steaming up the pane in a fog through which the blinding light struggled. Something about her haggard expression suggested that the unavoidable end had finally begun.

'That's torn it now!'

Chapter Sixteen

Another Dip Into The Box.

W hen all was said and done—when all the
universe and its contents had been lost to
posterity and there was nobody left around to
argue the toss—the following article somehow managed
to find its passage into the last remaining box to survive
beyond the Armageddon. The extract was from a page
that had been removed from Martha Sonneman's personal
Diary.

There follows a transcript in full, such as it is. Martha's
meagre handwriting style wouldn't allow for too much
accuracy in translation. And the additions in black ink
could only be guessed at, on the whole.

> *Dear Diary,*
> *Sometimes I look at my reflection in the mirror,*
> *And wonder who it is, that's staring back at me.*

The inscription, 'An old bat' had been inserted in the
same black ink.

> *Sometimes I am sad, and sometimes I'm down,*
> *And sometimes like a bird, I want to be free.*
> *Sometimes I watch the autumn rain,*
> *Running down my window pane,*
> *And sometimes I feel,*
> *That I am not real.*
> *Who am I?*

The poem was completed by an illustration of a flower
crying, in the same coloured ink as the composition itself.
Beneath this in black and accompanied by thirteen

exclamation marks were the words, '*A stupid old bag*'.

What makes one scrap of nonsense more suitable than another to survive to the very end of time itself, and beyond? This is a question that on the face of it seems impossible to answer under the present circumstances.

The existence of the world is rapidly draining away. Like a fine and powdered sand through the larger than average neck of some gigantic eggtimer. No time left now for such inquests into the nature of the universe. Let us, therefore, press on with great haste.

Chapter Seventeen

When The Bowels Of Hell Burst.

December 5th, 1998. 8:30 p.m. There was nobody at home when it happened. Jess Hobson was down at the Stag's Head. He was engaged in a game of darts that he was losing spectacularly, being somewhat the worse for wear after far too much drink.

Mrs. Prune had volunteered to do the cub-scouts' jamboree. She had taken along several trays of what she called 'Spastic Toffee' and was now unlocking various jaws and removing broken teeth.

In the centre of Greyminster, a terraced house was cordoned off. Number 32 Old Bridge Lane to be precise. The police had thought that restricting public access to this now celebrated curiosity would be a wise move. At least, until they had managed to find out exactly what the voluminous column of pulsing light was. The column itself had torn through the roof and its summit now disappeared into the heavens. Several ministers had said over the telephone from London that they would come down and investigate as soon as they got the chance. That had been nearly three weeks ago now, and no men in bowler hats had been sighted around Greyminster yet.

Let's have a closer look ourselves. The column of light was roughly four and a half feet thick in diameter. It appeared to be rotating slightly in an anticlockwise direction, various crackles of electrical discharge spiralling around its girth.

The unusual phenomenon had attracted large crowds

of inquisitive people at first. But after several long days, when it had failed to produce anything deadlier than the occasional tanning of susceptible bald heads it became nothing more than another feature of the town.

Constable Parkins at that moment couldn't have cared less. He stubbed out his dog-end, grinding the speckled brown filter into the pavement with the toe of his highly polished boot.

8:31; only another seven hours of boring watch duty to go. His thoughts turned to an open log fire. Warm slippers being toasted, watching the smoke curl up the chimney. That was when it happened.

A Lancaster bomber emerged from the column and screamed through the night with an orange and black scarf of flames in its wake. It lit up the sky as though it was some giant Chinese demon; a great fist of molten metal pumping mountains of smoke from its ruptured fuselage. The engines howled, the effluvium painting shadows across the floodlit rooftops with an ominous feeling of dread.

It crashed—headfirst—with an explosion approximating that of a small atomic bomb, straight through the front of 114 Applegate. The building toppled in on itself in a mushroom of bricks, sending bayonets of flame ninety feet into the air like a fiery crown.

For a moment Constable Parkins remained perfectly motionless. His hands were still knitted together in front of his pursed lips, frozen in the midst of breathing out. Then the shock-wave ripped across him, tearing at his hair and tugging hard upon his trench-coat.

Fire engines screamed. Blinding strobes illuminated the tall facades of the terraced crescent. Distant voices ran amok amongst the confusion.

A swelling crowd of dog walkers accompanied by women in dressing-gowns, slippers and mudpacks, suddenly gathered about the blazing inferno. Butterflies of smouldering timber were pursued in chaotic patterns by blackened moths of charred brickwork. Jacob Wambach stood and watched; his arms folded across his chest, his breathing slow and regular.

The tail of the enormous plane was projecting upwards from the burning ruin at an angle of approximately 45 degrees. Every so often it would creak and the crowd would shuffle backwards. The flames crackled and spat, licking higher up the disembowelled building; the tiled roof collapsing inwards with a volley of rubble.

The smoke stung Jacob's eyes. It caught on the back of his throat, making its presence known tartly upon his uncomfortable tastebuds. Through the tears and the grime he caught a glimpse of a figure. A tall, dark and masculine form. The top half was enlarged by an RAF bomber jacket, the fur lapel of which was smouldering sluggishly. The stranger walked with great purpose from the terrible wreckage; teeth glinting like piano keys beneath a handle bar moustache. The crowd cheered as he approached carrying a small and solid bundle.

A bundle of pyjamas with tiny pink toes. A small sleeping child, with its thumb in its mouth and its eyes tightly shut, oblivious to all of the disorder surrounding him.

'Joseph...?'

Jacob ran forwards now as if lost in a dream.

'Morning Captain.' The pilot spoke with an English accent that was so pronounced it sounded as if he'd swallowed a whole bag of best plums. 'Sorry about the bloody mess. Bought a mortar on the sausage side. Barely made it back to Good Old Blighty in one piece.'

Jacob carefully relieved him of the wondrous bundle. The aviator continued through a beaming, toothy smile, the edges of his whiskers releasing occasional corkscrews of smoke.

'Still, taught the bloody Hun a lesson in manners, eh?'

For a moment his expression sank.

'Old Wog bought a sticky wicket though. Grenade through the gun turret. Decent chap, Wog. The lads'll miss him.'

Mary had appeared. The two thankful parents were now more concerned with Joseph than anything that the aviator had to say. But a sensation of concern began to grow in Jacob's stomach. A feeling, that all was far from over. He cast a glance across his shoulder at the column of energy that, now he came to look again, resembled a searchlight from the second world war.

A smudge of black smoke that the bomber had scribbled from its heart, scored across the clouds resembling a thick line of graphite.

'Where did you come from?' Jacob's voice was so depleted that the question could only have been asked of himself. 'I don't understand. What the Hell is actually in that thing, anyhow?'

'Sorry about the bloody mess. Bought a mortar on the sausage side. Barely made it back to Good Old Blighty in one piece.'

Brian Hughes

8:35 p.m. The sweat down Geoff Askew's temples ran as thickly as slug trails, his whole corpulent head resembling a urinal being flushed of its contents.

Tonight was his *big night*. Months of standing in front of the full-length mirror in his mother's bedroom, perfecting his timing over and over, had lead with a beating heart to this very special occasion. And now here he was, engulfed by the shadows of the imposing stage.

The location, 'The Partridge Road Workers' Union Club.' A yellow-tiled structure that wore the portentous Gasometer across its back as though it was some sort of towering socialist emblem.

The agenda, *'Billy Badger's Gag In.'* A raucous night out for the lads. Blue jokes and strong ale with a 70's sing-along to follow.

Geoff bore the general mien of a pot bellied pig. If it wasn't for his jokes he would have amounted to absolutely nothing in life. This was the career move that he'd been struggling for. The gig that would lift him off the shop floor and hurl him with great ceremony into the limelight.

Beads of moisture ran down his neck, collecting about the grubby shirt collar.

'Ladies and gentlemen...' The tinny voice of the compere thrummed around Geoff's numbing skull. 'Billy Bodger!'

A roar of expectancy went up from the crowd of cloth caps and glasses. *'Badger! It's Badger y' pillock!'*

Billy scrambled up on stage, taking a firm grip on the microphone stand with his podgy white fingers. His startled eyes peered out across an ocean of thin faces. *Right—this is for the North!*

'A Pakistani, a Scotsman and a Jew walked into a pub.'

And that was the end of his act.

A great many newcomers to the comedy circuit have died on stage the first night. But none quite as unexpectedly and horrifically as Geoff Askew. And none, as far as my knowledge goes, by a telephone box materializing with a thud upon the top of their heads.

The door of the red latticed kiosk opened slowly. A short man carrying an unusual umbrella, his features lost beneath an oversized Panama hat, stepped out. He looked down at the trickle of blood that was forcing itself into several small rivers across the stage.

'Bloody rubbish!'

A projectile in the form of an over ripe tomato hit him squarely on the jaw. Then another; this time a blackened sprout that bounced off his shoulder and spun into the safety curtain.

'Bloody talentless crap!' The hostile crowd swelled antagonistically. 'Where's the stripper?!' Working class critics were not the best renowned of audiences to play for. 'Geddoff the stage, y' poncy little slut. An' get Bertha on!' Every insult was accompanied by a harboured item of decaying vegetation.

Moments later the embarrassed interloper vanished. The telephone-box door slammed shut with a definite thump. He was followed by a chorus of laughter and the chant of, *'piss off, piss off'* that had been cunningly reassembled into the style of a hymn.

The machine partially dissolved from the venomous line of the assemblage's sight, the gradual tick over of its engines increasing in resonance until the tankards rattled across the oval tables.

Moments later, the box rose; spearing its pinnacle

through the rotating mirrored-globe just above it. One of the arched windows of the Union Club pulverised in a profusion of minuscule glass fragments, as the telephone-box hurtled indifferently through it, escaping at high velocity into the dark night beyond.

8:45 p.m. Walking Edge, a bleak and barren rock on the Greyminster Fells.

Old Lancashire legend tells of a mysterious entrance hewn from the living rock itself, by the druids in a time that had long since passed. It was surrounded by mystical runes, appearing only once every 1,000 years and only then to the pure of heart and in times of great trouble. Nobody in living memory had actually come across 'Merlin's Entrance' as it was known locally. A suggestive title, that was seldom mentioned without a cocked eyebrow or two. But a few industrious myth-makers had carved their own mysterious symbols along 'The Edge.' Symbols such as 'Mandy is a slag' and 'Greyminster United for the Cup'.

However, on this night, the great stone gates were visible for all and sundry to gaze upon. A colossal limestone entrance mounted with ancient craggy pillars, topped with a plinth that was carved into the very 'Edge' itself. The momentous doors had been opened just the tiniest of cracks so that a light spilled from underground, accompanied by twists of sulphurous smoke.

What a shame then that there was nobody around to bear witness to such an event.

Deep down in the cavernous subterranean vaults of the dead. Here lie the sleepers in wait for the world's end.

Row upon row of snoring, prostrate bodies. Bodies

that are clothed from head to foot in rusted chainmail; surmounted by long rune-carved swords with indecipherable inscriptions. Arthur's Knights—the brotherhood of the fabled Round Table, lost in their slumber beneath the Greyminster Fells.

'Obstreperous Vortigern. Well met by death.'

A cracked and aged voice with a diction seemingly older than the hills themselves, pierced the stillness.

'Arise now for England, on the Great Dragon's Breath.'

The figures stirred, almost imperceptibly, apart from a slight clattering of armour leggings against shields that were fashioned from the highest quality steel. Amongst the protracted yawns, the wizened old man to whom the voice had belonged stepped out of the folded shadows and into the phosphorescent glow. He was old—incredibly old, with a beard as pure white as the fresh fallen snow that reached down to the floor and coiled off around his feet. On the apex of his enlarged balding pate sat a grubby cotton night-cap. In one geriatric hand the ancient immortal clutched a mighty carved staff that was almost twice the height of the wizard himself.

'Arthur?'

The giant gnarled stick prodded the grumbling body of a shrunken old man with a five foot beard, who was settling himself back down for the night on an altar.

'Arthur? Are you awake?'

'Bugger off.' When Arthur spoke his gums gnashed together, the fermented juices from several centuries of sleep cracking in the pits of his crevassed mouth.

Another prod in the ribs and despite his heavy mail, Arthur winced. Muttered obscenities loudly pierced the tranquility as his eyelids creaked open once more.

'*Come Arthur. There is work to be done.*'

'What time is it?'

Arthur yawned, then he extended his arms, as was customary for those awaking. Barely able to keep the lids from leadenly closing, Arthur surveyed his disordered fellowship now all in various stages of getting up for a hearty breakfast.

'*Time enough!*' snapped Merlin authoritatively, turning his bent spine upon the fraternity with an air of mysterious drama. It was accompanied by a creak that brought the contours of Merlin's face to a point.

'About eight-thirty then...' Lancelot had rejoined the world of mortal man. Only just though. The centuries had not treated his tired frame well. It was now haggard and toothless, sporting only the odd patch of yellowing hair. Not much like the romantic artists of 19th Century had portrayed him, it must be said.

'*Time...*' Merlin continued, glancing ambiguously into the roof of the vaults.

With a motion of such swiftness that Lancelot noticeably jumped, Merlin threw his soiled night-cap into a pit close to hand. The flaccid length of material toppled over and over, until eventually it disappeared into the dark murky depths. Then he conjured up a well-used and crumpled pointed hat. Firmly gripping the rim with his crooked thumb Merlin slammed it onto his wizened cranium extremely hard. '*...Time for The Last Great Battlefield.*'

The minuscule soothsayer turned back to his old associates, most of whom were still having trouble setting their false teeth into position.

'*Time...*' he said with a sneer that ripped his beard apart. '*For the End of the World!*'

9 o'clock sharp. The enormous clock on St. Oliver's struck the hour.

Number 32, Old Bridge Lane, Greyminster; the cellar. Or more precisely the base of the column of erratic blinding light that now roared with the volume of a forest fire. Its mighty girth pulsated rapidly, tendrils of flailing static scratching at the dark corners.

Constable Parkins was on guard duty outside. And whilst guarding the building from nosy vandals and stray cats was obviously of a high importance to the Greyminster boys in blue, there was currently nobody to bear witness to what was taking place in the cellar.

What exactly was taking place?

Well, the column had taken on a more frantic appearance for one thing. For the last hour and a half it had vomited out orbs at ever increasing intervals. Some were striped; others spotted. But all were constructed from the same bubbled glass and all of the unidentifiable articles carried a density that was completely inappropriate to its size. The orbs ground on the rough stone floor, rolling under boxes, apparently searching for unoccupied places to retreat. From each of these orbs crawled a deadlier threat than before.

Some were goblins with sharp and pointed ears, who took up playing poker in one dusty corner. Their upturned ruddy noses jabbed the air, as sharp as pointed knife blades. One or two sat around on the suitcases, rolling the orbs in their sticky little hands.

Small, oppressive demons scurried in and out of the mounds of unattended junk, frightening worried spiders with their glistening ochre fangs. Small balls of red fur, with wide mouths that stretched almost completely round their heads. They snarled and they snapped and their toes went scrabble, scrabble.

Patches of grey against the blackness drifted intransigently through the gathering melee. Strange translucent creatures from the other side of time, phasing dangerously between universes as they attempted to occupy new and sacrilegious shapes.

Twisted and gruesome characters from history built bridges from the books that had been left in the dark for storage. They now drove squawking Dodos bound with rope to model steam trains, beneath their perilous constructions. Dickens, The Wright Brothers, Cook and Thomas Hardy. Hunched figures creating gothic shadows with their long pointed fingers and twisted old bones.

With humped back and crooked smile upon his rotting lips, Thomas Hobson circumscribed the crowded cellar with curiosity. Leaning forward heavily both his hands upon the knob of his stick, he rubbed his skeletal fingers against each other, laughing as he did so. In this light the ghastly phantom could have easily been mistake for Lucifer himself.

The clock at St. Oliver's on the Grey tolled the ninth beleaguered bell. A doleful sound that rumbled across the old town and hid itself in the darkest corners. Whilst the figure of a distorted Pierot doll played its fiddle with a maniacal delight on the ancient crumbling spire of the silhouetted church.

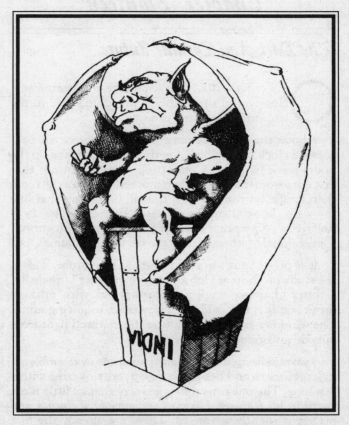

Small, oppressive demons scurried in and out of the mounds of unattended junk, frightening worried spiders with their glistening ochre fangs.

Chapter Eighteen

The Dark And Distant Future.

October 30th, 2037. The actual time is indeterminate. However, it's probably approaching 5:30 in the late afternoon, early evening.

Above the richly ornamented mantelpiece an oak-encased clock clicks slowly, methodically chewing up the hours piece by piece. Comforting, familiar sounds that first echo from the cobweb hammocked rafters of the room then muffle on contact with the tall bookcases that line the walls. Look at the books here. 'Einstein's Theory of Relativity', 'Quantum Mechanics and Event Horizons', 'Dimensional Mathematics for the Beginner. Volume One.'

It is now about forty-odd years in the future. This is the study of Thomas Hobson at Greyminster University, a dusty chamber equipped throughout with antique furniture. It is the study of a powerful, inquiring mind. The windows are tall and diffuse the matured light from outside into great dusty sheets.

Two middle-aged men, bearing an uncanny resemblance to Jess Hobson and Benjamin Foster, are tinkering with a machine. The one resembling Jess is perhaps a little more gaunt in his features. His eyes are somewhat harder and his age is slightly advanced. There are already the first signs of a curvature meddling with the discs of his spine, and a tremble in his fingers hints at neurological trouble ahead. The figure resembling Benjamin Foster is perhaps a little taller than his namesake. A little wider round the stomach. A little more cynical around the eyes.

Thomas Hobson toiled diligently, confined beneath the restrictive wooden machine. His narrow fingers pulled at the web of loose wiring; experimentally turning various hand-carved dials that resembled Victorian spinning tops.

This is a future built from a thinly veiled renaissance. This is the hour of inventions constructed of oak and pine, all lavishly embellished with carved wooden gargoyles and miniature mice and multicoloured glass orbs, that hold the note papers down.

'I've got to get it finished!' came a crabby voice from beneath the console. Thomas' back creaked audibly as a testimony to the long hours of labour he'd put into his work. 'Hand me the screwdriver.'

'The one that looks like a French tickler? Or the one like a carrot with a knob on its head?'

'Either. I'm not bloody bothered!'

Thomas' bony fingers grappled desperately for the phallic-shaped tool before dragging it out of sight beneath the walnut overhang.

'It's the bloody university fund holding committee!' Bastards want to withdraw the expenses 'cos some git from the *arts*' hall wants to make some poncy film about hermaphrodites and how badly society treats them!'

'It's an odd little contraption.'

Samuel stuck a finger into a suspicious looking hole and felt the full brunt of an electrical shock that made his glasses pop off his forehead and left his hair standing up on end so that he resembled a startled toilet brush.

'How does it work?' he went on, nursing his black tipped digit.

'That's a little difficult to explain.' There was a thud

and a bump and the air turned momentarily blue. 'Especially to a mentally retarded stool like yourself.' *Fizzzzz. Pop.* 'Bastard! Have a look at the manual if you're so bloody interested.'

Samuel hunted around the cluttered surface and unearthed a glossy brochure that had been jammed unceremoniously between two silver column-levers. He picked the prospectus up before short-sightedly squinting at the front cover, struggling hard not to move his lips in time to the words.

'Sheep Shagger's Monthly?'

A hand, almost violently, grabbed it from him. Moments later another thick tome was urged sternly into the empty space.

Adjusting his granddad-shirt collar, Samuel regarded the manual for some time. Judging from the contorted expression the concepts were obviously of an extremely complex disposition. At length he gave up.

'So this thing'll go, will it? Or is it just some expensive sex aid that bleats?'

Fortunately Thomas hadn't heard the latter comment. 'Like the bloody clappers mate. Whunsh! Straight out of time!'

'It's not some sort of antique coffee percolator or something, then?'

'Not exactly.' Thomas wormed out from beneath his invention; grime etched into African tattoos across his prominent cheekbones. 'Look, why don't you go and help matron molest the students or something? Give your arse crack a rest.'

'I just don't understand the notes...' Sam stared down at the book once more in an attempt to remove his concentration from the black smudge that had taken up residence along the length of Thomas' nose.

'What notes in particular?'

'All of them.'

He pointed to a long line of symbols. 'What's this massive equation?'

'Quantum theory expounded, my dear Foster. You see, I've exploded the mathematics to encompass the fifth dimension.'

'Right...' At this point a cloud of incomprehension fleetingly crossed Samuel's aspect. 'So it's a record player then?'

It took Thomas a few seconds to work out the connection in his mind. When he had finally managed to do so, he shook his gaunt head in despair and pulled himself up by a brass handle.

'The '*Mathematical*' fifth dimension, Foster—the fourth being time. Very tricky thing to do that, five dimensional mathematics. Have to have a brain the size of an elephant's genitalia injected with steroids.'

Thomas fiddled in an abstracted manner with a few levers, speaking all the while with his slightly curved back turned upon his old partner.

'In order to get a working formula you initially have to take Einstein's original equation of $E = MC^2$. Then divide the whole thing by nought.'

He turned, wiping the oil from his emaciated hands onto a monogrammed rag.

'Nought and infinity, y' see? It's all the same thing. A bit like your brain actually. There's sod all of it there, but it's infinitely dense. A little complicated to understand but it's pretty straight forward once you've got the hang of it.'

'But...' Samuel shook his head, trying to comprehend but somehow failing completely to grasp the nub of the issue by its precarious hilt. 'How can you have another dimension then? Sort of like a black hole that sucks everything into a tiny space, you mean? Like Maidenhead?'

Thomas thought for a moment then adopted a fresh track.

'Imagine a circle, right?'

He was sure that even Samuel was capable of that. Nonetheless he grabbed a 2B pencil from his waistcoat pocket and started to sketch one down upon a sheet of blank paper.

'Now...If you lived in two dimensions that would be a straight line.' With a cursory glance he noticed the confusion written into Samuel's eyes. 'There would be no other way to draw it, right?'

Samuel nodded. It was the sort of nod that suggested in principle he agreed, but right down he hadn't actually understood a solitary word of what had just been said.

'If you lived in three dimensions it would be impossible to imagine what a sphere would look like. The closest you could get to it would be the circle, yeah?'

'Yeah...' Samuel consented reluctantly.

'Imagine trying to work out the volume of a sphere using Pi when you don't even know what *volume* is. But if you added a fourth dimension, such as time, then the whole mathematical substance becomes *exploded*.'

Samuel looked up, not because he understood, but because the silent pause that ensued was starting to bother him.

'Right. I've just about got that.' Actually, he hadn't. But what the Hell? 'So what's that got to do with all this?'

He waved an encompassing hand in the general direction of the machine that Thomas had been so industriously working upon.

'What does it actually do?'

Thomas blinked. He now stood in genuine awe that someone could be so utterly stupid. One last bloody try then.

'No matter how many dimensions you live in, right, there's always got to be another 'Fixed Dimension' for the others to actually exist. Now, if you wanted to travel backwards and forwards in time, you'd need to create a stable environment in which there was a fifth dimension.'

That really *had* puzzled Samuel, no end.

'What would that dimension consist of exactly?'

Thomas leaned forward with intimidation, seizing his colleague by the wrist that protracted itself beneath Samuel's copious shirt cuff.

'That's what I'm about to find out!'

And with the flick of a switch, followed closely by a blinding white flash, the two were engulfed and had vanished from time.

That was all a long, long time ago; now...in the future...

December 6th, 1998. About 11:45 on a grim and overbearing winter's morning. 114 Applegate,

Greyminster. Or at least what was left of the terraced building that hadn't yet tumbled down.

Mrs. Prune paused, blinked at Benjamin and expectantly waited for some sort of response. Her crabapple of a chin rested on her fat crinkled hands which in turn rested resolutely on the top of the yard brush handle.

'So they both ended up trapped in 1896? That explains a lot.'

What could be seen of Benjamin's face around the *phase realignment* spectacles, still bore the expression of a troubled and thoughtful mind. 'But what about all the other stuff? All the ghosties and ghoulies and things that go bump in the night? And the Lancaster bomber? And the number of phonecalls?'

There had been another fifteen telephone calls that morning.

'Dunno.' Mrs. Prune shrugged her shoulders, dislodged her head from the broom and started to brush up the snow around Benjamin's ghostly scuffed boots. 'All I know is w'at I read. An' w'at I read was those notes. Found 'em 'idden between the pages of another of 'Obson's bloody books. About murderin' witches an' choppin' off their 'eads!'

There was a clatter of bricks sliding across one another from close at hand. The knoll of wreckage situated several feet behind the two of them, pushed itself up into the shape of a small pyramid. Three or four individual bricks rolled off to reveal a rough looking Jess. He narrowed his aching eyeballs in response to the sudden overwhelming brightness of the daylight. Eyeballs that were yellow and road-mapped with intricate veins.

'W'at's 'appened to the 'ouse?' The words stumbled out of his head. 'Last thing I remember was staggerin' 'ome from the pub about 'alf eleven.'

'You mean you didn't notice?' Ben jumped down from the rubble, casting a despondent glance that Mrs. Prune in mute agreement reflected back.

'Well, I 'ave t' be honest. I thought the bed was a bit more uncomfortable than normal. But I just put that down t' me liver developin' a crust.'

Jess winced, grabbing desperately at the small of his back, as the nerve endings started to turn themselves on one by one.

Let's just interrupt the proceedings of this book for a closer perusal of what had become of the once noble Victorian building. Nothing much remains now that could be associated with how things once stood. Just a smouldering heap comprised of twisted metal stumps that protrude at fantastic angles from the fragmented walls. A construction that had been chewed up and spat out because it tasted unpleasant. Melted wiring holds the shreds together in the same fashion that jungle vines would keep erect a lost Peruvian temple.

Roughly one third of Mrs. Prune's boarding house was occupied by the fragile skeleton of a smoking Lancaster bomber. A prehistoric relic that creaked and complained as it hung from a precariously tottering wall. The whole ruin had been dowsed by a light fall of snow that, by 9 o'clock that self same morning, had become a soiled blanket.

Jannice Applebotham clenched her fist and poised it, hesitantly, above the bell plaque. At that moment the front door burst open and Mrs. Prune cheerily hoisted a broom head of brick dust and slush over the doorstep. It travelled at an angle of forty-five degrees. Straight over the duffle coat that Jannice was wearing. Several modest chunks of plaster landed squarely in her short red hair. Mrs. Prune blinked apologetically.

'Sorry love. I didn't see y' there.'

With unsteady hands she attempted to remove the muck from Jannice's shoulders. An energetic and rather boisterous confusion quickly followed that somehow managed to entangle Mrs. Prune's prodigious digits with Jannice's own pallid fingers. The operation was halted with an embarrassed abruptness.

'Is Jess in?' Jannice peered upwards through her enormous owl-like eyes.

For a moment Mrs. Prune fumbled, rather stunned at the enquiry. It wasn't often that Jess received female callers. At least, not ones that looked sociable or wanted to see him without having been paid first. Jannice noticed the consternation as it stomped across the old woman's features.

'We used to be on the same electronics course together, at college.' She successfully managed to reassure the astonished Mrs. Prune. 'We made a film together once.'

Mrs. Prune cocked one eyebrow, the hulking form of Jess himself looming over her gooseberry head.

'Oh God! Not you?! W'at d' y want now?' Jess' voice had the dismissive tones of one merely asking the question out of politeness rather than somebody actually interested in the answer. 'Finally come f' the cure from bein' a thespian?'

He silently noted the bright yellow insignia on Jannice's duffel-coat that read; *All Men Are Potential Rapists.*

Not in your case, he thought.

'No I haven't. And it's *'lesbian!'* for your information'

Mrs. Prune looked over the visitor in an attempt to ascertain whether she actually liked her or not. Jannice was a solid girl, late-twenties/early-thirties, with the sort of legs that you could use to stand umbrellas upright in. In an effort to disguise them, she had worn loose-fitting pantaloons striped in blue and cream.

Now they no longer resembled tree trunks so much as a couple of odd looking deckchairs. The colours clashed with the red and white granddad shirt and the heavy grey duffel-coat. She was so bedecked with cheap, colourful plastic jewelry that she rattled like a marionette every time she moved forwards.

Although not unattractive had she lost about three stones, most of her better features were hidden by a stratum of foundation. Her eyes were surrounded by thickly applied shadow so that she resembled a panda, and her lips maintained the consistency of two rosy-red cushions. Mrs. Prune reached the conclusion that she liked what she saw.

'So, w'at d' y' want?' Jess snapped out the words..

Jannice replied with a commanding voice that walked rough shod over his impropriety.

'I'm now in the fourth year of my women's studies at the uni'. As part of the course I'm preparing a thesis on *'Ethnic Attitudes towards Women in Modern Society."*

Jess wore a frown of incomprehension that had lowered his brow by several gnarled and knotted inches.

'You're about as ethnic as it gets in Greyminster, I'm afraid,' Jannice reluctantly admitted.

'So, y' want a job?'

'Not as such. I just want to take notes and watch your methods.'

'It'll cost y'!'

'Don't be such a daft great pillock!' Mrs. Prune bustled indignantly past him, retreating through the door with the stubbornness of an enraged warthog. "Course 'ee'll employ y' me dear. An' 'ee'll pay y' as well.'

She hadn't quite understood the exchange of words, but she understood Jess and his bigoted attitude. Taking Jannice vigorously by the sleeve she led the uncomplaining feminist through the interior of the grubby bombsight. Jannice gazed about herself and then blinked in disbelief at the utter devastation.

'Is this the house that was hit by the plane last night?'

'W'at shall we employ y' as? A psychic?' Jess knocked the soot from the Lancaster bomber's nose with an amount of mocking condescension. Suddenly Mrs. Prune was upon him, the leathery face turning purple with frustration.

'You listen 'ere, Jess 'Obson. This young woman wants to 'elp. An' from what I've seen s' far, y' need all the bloody 'elp y' can get!'

Prodding his nose with a muscular digit, Mrs. Prune turned back to Jannice who stood meekly in the door. Her eyes had now become narrow gun slits across the pill box of her forehead.

'Don't let this 'un give y' any trouble, dear. 'Ee's a bully an' a bastard. But 'ee also knows w'at's good f'r 'im.'

She snapped back around to Jess, who flinched automatically.

'The 'ole of 'Ell's breakin' loose out there! So go an'

answer some o' these calls we've bin 'avin'. We've got t' find out w'at's goin' on. There's still something we don't know, an' it's obviously very important. There's somethin' 'orrible an' nasty 'appenin' round Greyminster. An' it's definitely all bloody wrong!'

'Like w'at?'

"Ow the 'Ell do I know? But none o' this adds up. So get off y' fat, lazy arse an' go an' do a decent day's labour f' bloody once.'

With his head hung down slightly, and a disgruntled grumbling barely audible from his lips, Jess snatched the cards from the telephone table. He shouldered self-righteously past Jannice, barging her into a skewed position, flung himself out of the front door and headed resolutely towards the slush-covered street beyond.

Benjamin, who had been watching all of this decided to follow his partner to their first destination. Mrs. Prune grabbed his arm.

'I've booked us into a room at the Waldorf 'Otel,' she said, checking that Jannice and Jess were out of earshot by now. 'No point in stayin' 'ere tonight. Gets a bit chilly sleepin' rough in December. Even f'r a ghost.'

'The Waldorf?' Benjamin's eyes widened in surprise beneath the unwieldy lenses. 'That's dead expensive.'

'Well, I 'as the odd favour owin'.' Mrs. Prune tapped the side of her nose with a boomerang shaped forefinger. The action signified that now was the time to put a discreet clamp on his enquiries.

There were still certain dignitaries entertaining in Greyminster who, despite their advanced dotage, required their histories to remain a secret. From time to time Mrs. Prune called the odd favour *'Back in'*.

'Rooms 8 to 14,' she went on. 'Just 'til the insurance pays up an' the 'ouse is rebuilt. Y'd better warn Jess.'

Ah, now that was going to be the problem. Having 114 Applegate rebuilt. There wasn't any insurance. Mrs. Prune had never bothered with it. So now it looked as if the boarding house would join the ever growing list to be totally demolished. In reality, she had known that already. But she hadn't wanted to cause any undue alarm.

Deep in her heart Mrs. Prune, with a terrible precognition, was now totally certain that she'd never set eyes on the old house again. Whatever it looked like, knackered or otherwise. Her old bones were warning her not to expect another Christmas...Or another morning...Or another sunset...Not a sausage...

Because the *'End Of The World'* was rounding the corner and thundering up the drive with its horns aimed straight ahead.

Chapter Nineteen

A Collection Of Sinister Characters.

12:45 p.m, Blackberry Row, Greyminster. Jess prodded the yellowing doorbell with such determination that his solid joist of a digit bent almost double in the process. The Westminster Chimes sounded mechanically down the hallway.

Jannice dolefully studied her ungainly feet. It occurred to her that now was an ideal opportunity to broach a most troublesome subject. A topic that had been screaming down the walls of her anxious mind since arriving at Applegate.

'Jess...' Jess' name emerged from her throat in the form of an uncomfortable cough. She took a deep breath, swallowed and tried again. 'Jess....I've got something to tell you.'

Steeling herself, Jannice slowly raised her eyes. Unfortunately, the aggravating leviathan turned out to be ignorantly squinting through the ornamental window that was situated at the top of the front door.

'It's about the real reason that I called.' Undaunted Jannice continued. 'Quite a difficult subject to talk about actually.'

Jess spoke from one corner of his downturned mouth without bothering to turn his bristled head.

'Don't worry. I'll finish this job an' then, if y' lucky an' I'm not totally knackered, things might get a bit raunchy later on.'

'What?' An expression of disdain drifted across Jannice's features. 'You've got a bloody hope, haven't y'? Mel Gibbon coming round or something?'

'I don't remember y' complainin' on the back of 19a that night.' Despite only catching his profile, Jannice knew that there was now a smug grin torn revoltingly across his features.

Dear God! The useless great oaf still remembered that? Jannice had completely lost track of what it was that she'd found so important to tell him. Instead she was now scrabbling in desperation for excuses concerning her past misconduct.

'That was four years ago, and I was drunk Jess. *And bloody desperate!*' Something struck a chord in her head. She relaxed all the tendons in her gullet and staring thoughtfully down at her frozen toes she composed the next line with a little less haste. 'Actually, that's what I wanted to talk about...'

'I'm sure y' 'aven't forgotten me fourteen incher.' *For crying out loud! Jess really was a childish sod at times. Nothing had changed. Just like a man!* 'Eh? Babies' arm 'oldin' an apple ring any bells?'

'This *'New Man'* thing just passed you by, didn't it Jess?'

There was no oral response to that. Just a blank, formal stare. She carried on. 'I bet you don't even know what a clitoris is?'

Ahha. Jess brightened up. He wasn't as stupid as Jannice suspected.

'It's a swimmin' costume.' The surprising phrase was proclaimed with utter conviction.

'What?'

'What?' An expression of disdain drifted across Jannice's features.
'You've got a bloody hope, haven't y'? Mel Gibbon coming round or
something?'

'It's a bikini.' Uncertainty, however, was now creeping clumsily back into his features. 'Y' know? *Peaches* by The Stranglers. '*My God. Is she trying to get out of that clitoris?*'

'You really haven't got a clue, have y'?'

'W'at y' talkin' about woman?'

'Have you actually got *any* idea what turns a woman on, Jess?'

'Yeah. A great big knob an' a big pile of dosh.'

'You sad deluded bollock brain.'

At which point the door opened and the argument dropped dead. A head emerged from the gap, shaped not unlike a turnip tied up in a bun, with a polished red chin jutting forward from a baggy sailcloth neck.

'Mrs. Forest?' Jess glanced down to the rectangular card in his broad hands and then double checked the conker of a face.

'Mrs. Forsyth,' corrected the head.

'Yeah...whatever...just show us the problem. I'm a very busy man.'

Jess pushed the door open fully, the safety chain snapping from the rotten structure apathetically, and muscled his gigantic frame inside. He wasn't one to stand on ceremony, that much about Jess had to be said, but he was always determined to make clients feel as worthless as possible from the earliest opportunity.

'*Very* busy,' added Jannice to the puzzled old lady, following suit and crossing the threshold. 'Spelt: 'B, I, Double Z, Y.'"

Mrs. Forsyth's front room turned out to be an altogether twee affair. A secret museum of ancient chintz artefacts and antimacassars carefully positioned over the backs of the arm chairs. Bone-china teacups perched on lace clothed tables with doilies.

Somehow Beethoven managed to appear 'Not Out Of Place' amongst such finery. His distorted magnificent figure sat hunchbacked upon the creaking piano-stool, playing gasps of twiddly sonatas whilst scribbling disjointed markings across a large wedge of paper. Every so often a sheet of notation would be flung dramatically above his head, in an outburst of either merriment or extreme self-disgust.

Jannice watched him for a moment or so, enwrapped with personal awe.

'Is that Beethoven?'

'Well, 'ee's certainly got the fore'ead for it.' Jess noted the almost perpendicular stove of the composer's frontal cranium. Mrs. Forsyth bustled in, patting her bun with an expression of acknowledgement.

'There's another four of them in the kitchen.'

'W'at?'

'Another four of them,' she repeated, nodding. Curling her thumb into the palm of her hand whilst extending the other digits, she began to mark them off one by one. 'Charles Dickens, Oscar Wilde, Mary Shelly and Martin Korgette.'

'Martin Korgette? The children's entertainer?'

'Yes...' A puzzled expression took up residence on the old woman's brow. 'I thought that was a little odd myself. I don't actually remember him passing on.'

Jess lumbered across the carpet with the ferocity of a mountain troll, accidentally uprooting a cat from the sofa in the process. A flea-bitten, partially bald animal that had, until that point, been minding its own business quite successfully.

'Mr. Beethoven. Oy! Lug-wig!'

'He's deaf,' said Jannice.

'Oh yes.' Mrs. Forsyth seemed to know all about that. 'That's why he's a ghost.'

'No...no, he's deaf, Mrs. Forsyth. Not dead!'

'What?'

'He's deaf.'

'Yes, I know. That's why he's a ghost.'

Jess was evidently growing annoyed as the patchy conversation took place.

'Look. GO AND PUT THE KETTLE ON Y' SENILE OLD BAG.'

He leaned into the words as if he was shouting against the wind.

'What?'

'THE KETTLE!' Two beady eyes stared back at him from an uncomprehending facade. 'GO ON! OUT!!' He'd had enough.

Mrs. Forsyth was forcibly hoisted through the living-room door like a sack of old coal. Not that it was a particularly violent hoisting, but the act concluded in her pint-sized body clumsily disappearing into the kitchen. Jannice watched as Jess re-emerged, dusting the labour from his broad palms.

'What was all that about?' Pushing her screwed up fists angrily into her ample hips, Jannice glowered in what she considered to be a menacing manner. 'You can't treat old women like that?'

'Why not?' Jess brushed the remaining dust from his sweater-clad chest, satisfied that now he could get on with his job.

'Because they're old, that's why not! What harm was she doing you?'

'W'at 'arm?'

He screwed up his face so that it resembled an infant evacuating its bowels. 'Bloody 'Ell! I'm sick o' listenin' to it! This town is swarmin' with aggravatin' old swines like that.'

'You agist git!'

Actually, Jess was well aware that Jannice was probably correct. His normal attitude towards the aged wasn't quite so vehement. But the words kept on coming into his head, suggesting themselves randomly as indisputable facts and then finding an exit by storm-trooping his mouth. For a moment he wasn't sure whose opinion it actually was.

'If you just took a little time out to hear their side of the story you might learn one or two things that'd make you a better person.' Jannice had adopted her stalwart pose. 'You're gonna be old one day y' know.'

'Christ, I 'ope not. I don't wanna end up talkin' utter crap an' dribblin' in me porridge.'

'Old people do not talk crap!' Jannice was now working herself up into a mutinous frenzy. 'That's just a stereotypical bigoted point of view.'

'Don't talk crap?'

Jess' voice was rapidly reaching a strained crescendo once more, his huge body swinging forwards with an amount of mockery distorting the limbs.

"There was none of this violence on the street when I was young."

The words were uttered in mimicry of an aged remonstrance, and the impersonation was surprisingly accurate.

'Well, that's true,' he went on. 'All the blokes were off bayonettin' 'Arry Hun or shootin' 'Arry Jap through the lungs. *'The streets were a safe place to walk back then.'* Not with a bloody Mesherschmidt dropping bombs on y'r 'ead it bastard wasn't!! No bloody violence? What d' y' call droppin' two nuclear warheads an' meltin' God knows 'ow many million people then? The old idiots seem t' think that the bloody war was some sort o' musical 'all show.'

'Those old people,' shouted Jannice. 'Those old people fought that war and lost countless millions of lives so that you could spend your life free from fascist oppression. And this is how you treat them!!'

'Fascist oppression?' He thrust his expansive face up against Jannice's. Resolutely she set her jaw against the intrusion of personal airspace as if it was constructed from iron. 'W'at gives with the attitude *We fought the war to keep the facists out'* then! I've got news f' the old sods; they all bloody voted conservative in 79!'

'That's slanderous.' By this point Jannice had become so infuriated that a tiny bubble of spit hit Jess in the eye. 'You've just got no tolerance for anyone other than yourself, that's all! You disgust me Jess Hobson. You ought to be grateful for what these people did without reward.'

'Well I never bloody asked THEM, DID I!!!?' His puissant intonations rattled powerfully through the dainty pot tea-service, ringing in shrill echoes from their bone-china rims.

Whereupon, Beethoven threw down his quill, covered his ears and with his large head going a decidedly dangerous shade of purple he cried, 'SHUDDDUP!!!!!'

1:07 p.m. December 6th, 1998. The narrow streets of the old town of Greyminster were rapidly filling with a great swollen fog. A clammy, impenetrable mantle that emanated from the cracks in the stone walls and the gaps between the flagstones.

People headed home and pressed their noses against the damp window panes, unable to see any farther than just a few feet. Diffused light from lamp-posts along the roads spread through the all pervading greyness in weak translucent banners.

Initially strong bars of sunlight had managed to force a path through the cloud bank, but such reluctant illumination soon became nothing more than a ghostly water-colour and was eventually consumed by the hungry creature that the fog had evolved into.

It rose from the river like the wraiths of dead elephants, fumbling its fingers into every nook and cranny of the houses along the dock front. Slowly expanding, coiling and smothering, drawing a veil across the buildings.

Then they came...out of the grids, and from their secret locations around the backs of the houses. From under the flagstones and out of the gutters.Sometimes on their own, sometimes in groups of large numbers. Dancing, and screaming, and inquisitively prying. Scratching at the fog with their cruel intrusive talons.

Mrs. Prune happened upon them as she was hobbling down what she suspected to be the Old Arcadia Road. The fog had become so glutinous by now that it pressed against her features and weighted down her clothes. She found herself fumbling slowly along, almost blindly. Her sturdy boots clattered through the empty stillness as she probed her way forwards with the umbrella point.

Why was the Waldorf so far across town? It was the sort of petty thought that Mrs. Prune would occupy herself with in most confrontational situations, and this situation definitely had the sense of confrontation about it. *Bloody inconvenient! An' bloody inconsiderate too!*

Something clutched at her stockings. Something sharp and nasty. It bit with prickly teeth. And it lacerated the fabric with harsh thorny claws.

'W'at the 'Ell?'

Mrs. Prune looked down, only to find herself confronted by the most repulsive little creature that she had ever encountered. Despite the draining light, its teeth glinted demonically.

The creature was small; about a foot long from the bristled point of its elongated skull to the scrabbling tips of its fearsome toenails. It was vaguely human in form, but with a disproportionately large nose hooked over on the end like the bill of a heron. And it was thin—so desperately thin that it appeared to be on brink of breaking in half at any moment. For a brief, indecisive second or two Mrs. Prune felt sorry for the poor half-starved little thing, but when it bit her again, any previous misgivings were hastily replaced by an indignant anger.

With a ruddy great whack Mrs. Prune dislodged the offensive savage in the same manner that one might dislodge an old scab. It spun off into a heap, before lying unconscious on the flagstones. Moments later it was caught up and devoured by the enveloping blanket of vapour.

In the distance Mrs. Prune heard a scream echo off the unfamiliar walls; footsteps running wildly, snarling and snapping and the sounds of teeth entering flesh. She waited for a moment, her heart floundering dramatically beneath her tight ribs, listening to the scattered volleys of sound that rushed up to accost her.

Greyminster appeared to be under some sort of siege, spearheaded by an army of grotesque goblins. Unable to find the source of the confusing noises that resounded about her she struck out again. This time it was with purpose, thrashing stubbornly through the fog bank in an attempt to reach safety. After several wrong turnings, the terrible truth began to dawn that she was now totally and utterly lost.

Bugger it!

Then something unexpected happened. All right, something *else* unexpected then.

As she forced a tunnel through the dampness, the point of her umbrella fizzled impulsively. Seconds later it detonated in a shower of black moths. Mrs. Prune brought the brolly up to eye level, turning it over in her hands. Whatever the black fragments were, her brolly had never done that before.

Experimentally she poked it forwards. Just to test if there was something in front of her that had been responsible for the blast. As it happened, there was.

The shifting wall of mist bit back with a vengeance. The brolly vanished almost completely in a shower that consisted of 80% black confetti and 20% shrapnel right up to the small, metal clasp. Mrs. Prune sprang backwards in surprise, then stood perfectly motionless, waiting to see what was going to happen next.

What happened was this—up above her the fog slowly started to retract, gradually folding itself over so that it resembled a giant duvet being bundled into a bag. It billowed and spiralled in ever thickening clots.

Overhead the sky portentously gathered itself up into the udders of a thunder storm. Then, with the noise of two steam-trains colliding in the heart of an ancient brick tunnel, it thundered across the heavens.

That was when Mrs. Prune realised that she was on the outskirts of Greyminster; on Jack's Ladder, the ledge that overlooked the back end of the old metropolis. Horrible events were enacting themselves down below. A blood-soaked battle raged relentlessly across the whole panorama that stretched before her sights like the Bayeux Tapestry.

Goblins! Millions of the little buggers! Wrestling the residents! Dragging people across the cobblestones by one or both legs. Pulling old ladies' hair out and nailing up cats. Evil little bastards and so many of them!

And heading down the main street appeared to be a group of old men on Zimmer frames, in armour that shone in the pale remains of the threadbare sunlight.

Mrs. Prune turned and stared out across the craggy moors of the Greyminster Fells. Somehow she felt that the answer to all of this might lie out there somewhere, amongst the black rocks and the sad lonely sheep.

What she saw made her suddenly feel nauseous to the point of staggering backwards, shaking her senses to the very marrow. Instead of the rocky outcrops and the bleak lonely crags, there was nothing—just an expanding void of blackness. An endless wall of empty space that appeared to retreat upon itself indefinitely. The *'End of the World'* had arrived.

Jess regarded the four twisted figures that were gathered around the kitchen table. Their subnormal behaviour had now led onto torturing Mrs. Forsyth. He'd never had much regard for those who dedicated their lives to literature. All fops with limp wrists and floppy hats and velvet jackets. And as for Martin Korgette. Anybody who had made millions out of sticking his hand up a bear's bottom and then squirting a water pistol into some special guest's eyeball, was either a genius or just the luckiest sod that ever walked the face of the Earth.

Even Jess was aware however, that Martin Corgette wasn't actually dead. And not once did he recall Smutty Bear jamming pencils maliciously up an old woman's nostrils.

Jannice started to cross to the coarsely laughing group, ready to strike another blow for women's liberation. Jess' broad arm blocked her path.

'Don't interfere. Not even *you* could take on that sort of evil. However…' At this point his face broke out into a demented grin so that his features resembled a liver that had violently burst. 'I've got a cunning plan.'

There followed an expectant but apparently motiveless lull, no sign of even a stupid plan rearing its cunning head. Jannice waited, her impatience visibly straining. At length Jess turned.

'That Dickens bloke's not much of a 'umanitarian, is 'ee?'

'He was when he was alive. Dickens was a great altruist.'

'No 'ee bloody wasn't.' It didn't matter that Jess had no idea what an *'altruist'* was. He could work out the general implication. "Ave y' ever read any of 'is books?'

Dickens was currently applying a pair of pliers to Mrs. Forsyth's front teeth. But principles were principles and this wasn't the Dickens that Jannice recalled from her college education.

'I have actually, yes. It was required as part of the sociology studies. He was a brilliant philanthropist. A champion of the poor.'

'Rubbish! 'Ee was a multimillionaire, 'oo exploited the working class for 'is novels.'

'What?'

'It's true!' Jess regarded the expression of astonishment unfolding across Jannice's facade. 'All of the villains in his books are workin' class, whereas all of the heroes are members of the 'ierarchy fallen on 'ard times.'

For the briefest moment Jannice scrutinised what she knew about the Victorian author. 'What about Oliver Twist?'

'My point exactly! The Artful Dodger an' 'is mates are all criminals from the underclass. But Oliver turns out to be descended from the landed bloody gentry. W'at a surprise. Champion of the proletariat, my arse crack!'

'How would you know, anyhow?' Jannice appeared to have somehow grown larger. 'You've never actually read a book that doesn't contain speech bubbles.'

Dickens was currently applying a pair of pliers to Mrs. Forsyth's front teeth.

Oscar Wilde, looking every bit the dandy apart from the pulsing red eyes beneath the flop of his fringe, belted Mrs. Forsyth on the temple with his brass-topped walking cane.

'There is only one thing in the world worse than being ignored.' When he spoke it was pretentiously melancholic. 'And that is being an old battle-axe who's about to be disembowelled.'

Jannice gritted her teeth. With her corpulent fists clenched into suet cannon balls, she struggled defiantly against Jess' prominent left arm.

'I don't remember Oscar Wilde being evil and malicious!'

'Can't say as I'd know meself. I've never read any of 'is books. 'Ee looks like a puff though.'

'You what!?'

It wasn't so much Jess' attitude towards the literary greats that distressed her, as the word *puff* being used so bluntly in the same context.

"Ee looks like a limp-wristed charmer of the pink snake,' Jess added irreverently, on the off chance that she hadn't in fact understood.

'That's a grossly unfair thing to say. You always were a homophobe, weren't you?'

That almost threw him, but past experience allowed him to rally back triumphantly.

'I've got nothin' against 'em. Some of me best 'Ex-friends' 'appen t' be shirt lifters.'

'I suppose you're gonna come out with some bullshit as to why they all ought to be exterminated now, are you?'

This caused an inner struggle that Jess fought intrepidly

against. Political correctness was never his forte, but he hated the term bigot because he wasn't sure what it meant.

'On average about four hours of telly a week are devoted t' *'Gay Issues'* right? But only 'alf an hour is donated regularly t' disabled issues. Now one in ev'ry ten people in Britain is disabled, whereas only one in an 'undred is bent.'

'And how long have you been a supporter for disabled issues?'

'Since it suited me!' He craned his neck downwards, drawing his imposing face closer than Jannice would have liked. 'Come t' that matter, w'en was the last time y' saw all o' the queers complainin' about the lack o' disabled facilities? Can't remember? Well, I'll tell y'! Never, that's w'en. But w'en it comes t' their problems they expect everyone t' rally round them! The selfish BLOODY BASTARDS!'

Jess stopped, clutching his head. A speckled red mist had formed in some rarefied maelstrom, gyrating dementedly before his clouding eyes. Something was wrong. Something heavy was overbalancing his equilibrium. That hadn't been his voice. Those hadn't been his points of view.

Undeniably, Jess was a bigot. But all his life he'd made a point not to hold polemical convictions. It was almost as if he was becoming a caricature of himself, as ghastly and tormented as the creatures that were currently tearing the strips from his venerable client.

He shook the words from his head, tried not to think about them, and blinking, looked about himself.

'Where's Benjamin?'

'Who?'

'Benjamin Foster. Me business partner.'

Jannice cast Jess a glance that was bloated with concern for his sanity.

'I thought he was dead.' With uncertainty her voice plunged to a lower, barely audible level. 'I read in the Greyminster Chronicle that he had died. In *mysterious circumstances.*'

'One can 'ope.'

As if waiting for his cue, Benjamin's incorporeal form surfaced from the underworld. It shimmered for a moment or two, fierce electrical vines flickering wildly up and down the torso as if charged with wild blue static. In one cadaverous hand Benjamin clutched dogmatically at a supernatural cricket bat that had manifested itself slowly in an eerie radiance. He blinked through the milk-bottle-bottoms of his spectacles.

'At last...' Jess broke out into a grin that almost halved his clay head. 'The cunning plan's arrived.'

Benjamin swung the unearthly implement experimentally, following its line with a degree of schoolboy expertise. A trace of preternatural images pursued the bat upon its calculated arc.

'Right....There's work to be done.'

Benjamin Foster wasn't a violent man—come to that, he wasn't a violent ghost either, but he didn't enjoy seeing old ladies being roughly handled by anomalous hooligans. With the length of willow gripped intently in both hands he marched upon the grotesque soiree and dealt the first of several devastating blows.

Dickens screamed as the back of his head crumpled up like an egg-box. A pall of blue smoke gushed from the screaming mouth, retreating fearfully up the flank of the sink unit resembling a flimsy slug. Somewhere behind the bread-bin the gaseous abnormality vanished from sight, its fizzing crackle stopping abruptly.

Benjamin approached the sink with an eyebrow arched in caution. Reaching behind the metal container, his grey tongue prizing his even greyer lips apart with serious concentration, his fingers fumbled tentatively around for some time. At length a green and yellow orb was extracted. Ben promptly smashed the offensive object on the floor beneath the sole of his boot.

Right...Next!

Oscar Wilde's frantic screaming came to a brusque halt, as the apparition of a flaming cricket ball made contact with the dome of his ostentatious skull. The manic eyes crossed, the body slumped and the ebullient contents spilled out, finding refuge in a purple and pink orb that was surreptitiously hidden beneath the Kenwood Chef. Benjamin prodded it dexterously from its hiding place with his bat, then he smashed it sending pearls of razor sharp glass spinning off in all directions.

Benjamin turned back to the remaining affray, determination embodied throughout his metaphysical frame.

Mary Shelly didn't put up much of a struggle; following an immoderate thunderbolt that seared from Benjamin's pale fingertips her phantasm unobtrusively skulked off. Benjamin blew the smoke from his digits, satisfied with his growing abilities. Being dead wasn't so bad after all. He watched as the spectre entered the colourful orb that was secretly housed inside the cooker. The door was slammed tightly shut behind her, Benjamin turning the oven on to gas mark twelve. He waited for the bang—it came and the oven shook.

Finally, for this room at any rate, Benjamin turned to confront Martin Korgette, the children's entertainer. This time an electrical golf club was raised above his head in mocking reverence of the grim reaper's scythe. A tiny twinkle in his magnified eyes said that he was going to enjoy this.

Beethoven played another inharmonious chord, not entirely certain whether to include it on his augmented mound of notations. It was debatable that he had heard Korgette's final sickening thud. A blow closely followed by the conclusive scream, which in turn was closely pursued by the decisive smash. All the sounds that emanated from the adjoining chamber would probably never have penetrated his almost nonexistent hearing abilities.

A few seconds later, several figures appeared in the doorway, Mrs. Forsyth, it must be said, looking rather the worse for wear. Jannice considerately held the old woman upright with a benevolent arm. Nonetheless, the old dear bore a grateful expression. Benjamin pounded the liberating ghostly cricket bat determinedly in his palm.

'Four down, one to go.'

Beethoven never knew what hit him; though he might have surmised that it was large and made of wood.

His immense bulbous forehead smashed straight through the music stand that was attached to the piano top. A grimace of yellowing teeth, surmounted by a greasy flop of curled hair, erupted from the other side in an explosion of paper fragments. For a moment the great composer looked bewildered; the expression rapidly gave way beneath a devastating shriek. Another mighty thwack brought the screaming to an end.

The familiar cloud left the corpse from one worthless ear in a ribbon of swirling fumes. Unable to compose itself any further the creature hurtled around the cluttered room, as though seizing the opportunity for one last erratic waltz. Its waspish tail disappeared into the toe of Mrs. Forsyth's slipper.

Benjamin stooped over, picking up the moccasin with his free hand. It let out a prolonged sonorous rasp as the last couple of inches of Beethoven's rear appendage struggled to gain access into the orb.

'W'at was that noise?' Jess took the object, Benjamin shrugging noncommittally in response to the question.

'Beethoven's last movement?'

'W'at is this thing, any'ow?' Jess turned the orb over in his hands, studying its pot marked surface for clues—an inscription, a nameplate, a *Made in Taiwan* sticker. Unfortunately, nothing presented itself. Just the odd flaw deep within its heart where the occasional air bubble had been imprisoned.

'Some sort of transportation device, I think.' Benjamin slid the glasses down his nose and, having managed not to vanish, peered over the bridge inquisitively. 'They all seem to have one.'

A nagging annoyance tickled vaguely at the back of Jess' skull. He scratched it thoughtfully.

'W'at about that Lancaster bomber, then? Where's the ball that belongs t' that?'

As soon as the words left his lips Jess regretted having said them. *Never tempt fate*, as Mrs. Prune was always so damned fond of drumming into him.

Beyond the latticed window panes Jess could just about determine some sort of battle that was being conducted with a great deal of confusion. What appeared to be thousands of grubby, undersized creatures with flat skulls and pointed noses were jumping up and down on the townsfolk. People were being ridden with great ceremony along the length of the cobbled street, goblins tugging on their locks of hair and using them for reins.

Then the rumble started. Slow and drawn out at first, similar in pitch to an approaching diesel engine. Only more violent and foreboding. It seemed to take an eternity, growing sluggishly; moving in the fashion of giant slabs from the heart of the column.

Blackberry Row was only just around the corner from Old Bridge Lane. The front room at Mrs. Forsyth's commanded an excellent panorama of the rip in reality. It towered boundlessly above the rooftops opposite before disappearing in an arc of perspective up above the December clouds. Stilll the grumbling grew; a resonance so bassy that it disturbed the lining of the stomach. Then it emerged resembling a huge, glass turd. The size of the great dome on the Ashton Memorial and by the looks of things burdened with about four times the mass.

Just for a second it tottered on some sort of unnoticeable precipice, as if the mighty glass bomb was undecided as to what to do next—then it plummeted; down amongst the screaming crowd who had no time to retreat beneath its gigantic expanding shadow. It landed with a thump that rocked the houses down the streets, toppled over the chimney pots and sent a tremor clear across every part of the town. Cracks ran out all around it mimicking the roots of a powerful tree, and the sounds of the screams echoed down the broken boulevards, battering around the corners and becoming entangled with the foundering lamp posts.

Chapter Twenty

Mrs. Prune's Last Waltz.

The Waldorf Hotel had a name far in exaggeration of its genuine worth. A name along those lines suggested something imposing. Something elegant with huge balconies and great sweeping stairwells. But the truth was that the Waldorf was only a pompous, squat building.

The ground floor was a pub, the only way into the *hotel* being up the wide flight of stairs in the centre. The entire building was jointly owned by Councillors Meldrew, Wicker and Thorpe. So it was anybody's guess as to which one had let the rooms to Mrs. Prune. It might have been all three, come to that.

Jannice and Jess were still arguing as they walked back across town. The *Waldorf* wasn't hard to miss, being situated directly at the back of St. Oliver's. It was cornered by the four tallest trees in Greyminster and with a little imagination could be made to resemble a four poster bed.

'If I'm such an almighty great bastard...' muttered Jess, stomping his foot down with great strength upon the flagstones. 'Then why're y' still hangin' around with me?'

A stubborn hairy goblin had wrapped itself around the sole of his Doctor Marten, clinging dogmatically to his boot-laces and refusing to let go. Intermittently it giggled and bit hard at his ankle. He scraped the remains off his boot and onto the curb.

'I didn't invite y' round. So, why don't y' just sod off!?'

'It's not quite so simple as that.'

Jannice tried to keep pace, staring abstractedly behind her at the sad patch of goblin that had been left twitching in the grid. Seconds later she followed Jess through the Waldorf door.

'Nothin' ever bloody is simple wi' you!'

Jess now shouted above the heady din. The public bar filled their senses from every direction. He strode purposefully across the sticky carpet, steering a path between the upturned barrels that supposedly represented the tables. Jannice relentlessly followed up the constricted staircase, into the ceiling of blue cigarette smoke.

'Y're like a bloody Siamese afterbirth.' The words emerged from Jess' mouth, skillfully riding a snarl bareback. 'Sod off an' leave me alone!'

'Jess...We really have to talk.'

'W'at about? Feminist bloody issues? Why pre-menstrual tension is an excuse to let murderers free to kill someone else next time the moon is full?'

'No Jess...'

Jess unlocked the door to room six with the appropriate key. He stormed inside, his features screwed into a purple cabbage of frustration with the irritating student behind him.

'It's about our little boy,' Jannice shouted from the hallway, as the door began to close somewhat harshly.

A moment's pause. A reflective time dedicated to some difficult thought processes that threatened to choke Jess' brain at its stem. Very gradually, as if its full weight was being moved upon a solitary strand of gossamer, the door once more creaked open as Jannice watched. Jess' puzzled head appeared around the jamb. Wearing an expression half constructed of astonishment, the other half sagging into irksome disbelief, it leaned obtusely into the long narrow hallway.

'W'at?'

Jannice struggled with the words. To her shame she discovered that there was no way she could look Jess in the eyes after all. Turning crimson with embarrassment she spoke confidentially to her stubby toes instead, her voice nothing greater than a worried, whispery sound.

'Our little boy...'

Despite the complicated movement of Jess' twitching lips, no sound was audible other than the slow shuffling of nervous feet. His eyes flicked backwards and forwards, the lids going up and down like the curtains at an amateur production night. Jannice filled the empty silence with a murmured explanation.

'Our brief encounter on the 19a? I...we...had a child, as a result.'

Mrs. Prune, who had been standing inside the door with her corpulent hand wrapped around the knob, listening as the conversation unfolded itself, now muscled the gawking giant to one side. She took Jannice by the arm; an action so unexpected that it made the self-conscious scholar raise her head, startled.

'Come on in, dear.' Jannice stared blankly into Mrs. Prune's well-seasoned face. 'Would y' like a nice cup o' tea?'

One elbow connected roughly with Jess' ribs as Jannice was led into the sanctuary of the quarters beyond.

'W'at?'

'An' shut the bloody door. We don't want 'er catchin' any draughts, do we?'

This was all very difficult for Jannice. She had an urge to point out to her congenial host that she wasn't actually pregnant. More than that, the little boy was approaching three years old now and growing. But she couldn't find the heart and, instead, was lead compliantly to the sofa where submissively she sat down amongst a garnish of cushions. An idea struck. Jannice obligingly delved into the pocket of her striped granddad shirt.

'This is a photograph of him.' Mrs. Prune donned her spectacles, after the fashion of school mistresses the world over, preparing her ancient eyeballs for a thorough examination of the image. 'Little Thomas.'

'Oh yes...'Ee's lovely.'

'W'at?'

'Look at 'is piggy little toes...'

The ancient matriarch grimaced, apathetically cocking her head on one side with the sort of wisdom that years of past experience bring to such occasions. Actually, 'ee was an ugly little bugger, like most bloody babies were. But Mrs. Prune knew that she ought to appeal to Jannice's maternal instincts in order to...hold on.

'I wasn't going to tell you, Jess.' Jannice raised her eyes from the rug apologetically as Mrs. Prune snatched the photograph from her hand and held it up to her nose. 'I was going to raise him myself. You know; as an independent woman.'

'W'at?'

'But, recently he's started...doing things. Man's things. And...' Jannice found it hard to part with the following collection of thoughts. However, the whole situation had gone too far to turn back by this point. 'I thought he ought to meet his father.'

She swallowed and looked acutely into Jess' astounded eyes, searching somewhat vainly for any signs of comprehension.

Mrs. Prune was occupying the battered suitcase that she'd used to transport all of her remaining untoasted memorabilia to the Waldorf. There was a great deal of rummaging and shuffling and thumping, projectiles flying out across the room like haywire fireworks.

'Man's things?' Jess frowned, the whole weight of what was happening still sinking in. 'Man's things? At three?'

'Yes...you know...'

Jannice raised an eyebrow, nodding ambiguously at the carpet.

'W'at? Gettin' drunk, eatin' curries an' goin' f'r a slash in a telephone box?'

'No...Y' know...?'

Jannice repeated the same motions with her head as before; this time adding, 'He got his first... *erection*...'

'Ah...' Fatherhood. Jess appeared to have succumbed to his newly appointed position as patriarch. 'Takin' after 'is old dad then.' Anything that would improve the local myths about his sexual prowess was guaranteed to hold power over his towering ego. 'Bring the little sod over an' I'll soon sort 'im out.'

'Got it!'

Mrs. Prune emerged triumphantly from behind the beaten suitcase, clutching an ancient black and white photograph in one hand and waving it triumphantly above her round head. It was creased rather badly and had a top corner missing. Nonetheless, she hobbled across to the walnut dining-table that dominated the floor, placing the two of them down side by side on a mat.

'Bugger me fat arse with a coconut! I knew there was somethin' important we was missin'!'

Mrs. Prune reared her features, suddenly concerned.

'Where's Benjamin?'

That brought an abrupt halt to the conversation. The unexpected fear in Mrs. Prune's voice with its almost caustic inflection made Jess stop in his tracks and concentrate profoundly upon the question.

"Ee's gone off...'

'Gone off?' Mrs. Prune made it sound as if Jess was suggesting that Benjamin had turned rancid and mouldy.

'Yeah...Gone off to...' Jess puffed out his cheeks in thought. 'Old Bridge Lane.'

'Old Bridge Lane?'

Jess stared at Mrs. Prune. After a moment he added, 'Yes...Old...Bridge...Lane.'

He emphasised each word, because his redoubtable landlady appeared to be having some difficulty understanding them. 'Y' know? The place where Dodgy Donald and Maudlin' Martha enjoy slaughterin' people!'

'Oh my God! Y're a stupid great...' Mrs. Prune lost control, anger swelling in the manner of some inflammatory disease that had taken over the muscles of her mouth. *Great bald headed Bastard!*

Jess stood upright; his eyebrows raised at this commentary on his appearance and ancestry.

'He said he was confident enough to sort out Mr.

Oakseed's cellar now,' interrupted Jannice in an attempt to diffuse tempers.

'W'at's the problem?' Jess shook his broad head in confusion. Mrs. Prune was growing ever more alarmed with each passing moment. 'Ee's not likely t' get hurt is 'ee? Ee's already bloody dead!'

'W'at about Samuel Foster?' Mrs. Prune glowered, the great cement-mixer of Jess' chin overshadowing her tiny frame. 'Was 'ee bloody indestructible?'

It was more of a statement than a question. Mrs. Prune continued. 'And w'at d' y' think this is?'

She lifted the stump of her brolly, shaking it ferociously about beneath his kneecap of a nose.

'No idea...A sheep's tampon?'

'It's me brolly!'

'Very good. At least it won't 'ave much chance of pokin' me bloody eyeball out next time it rains!'

'It's the end of the world!' Mrs. Prune was reaching new depths of emotion, whilst her voice had achieved new summits of bone-grating pitch. 'That's w'at it is! I stuck the bloody thing out by accident on the way down 'ere. An' the end disappeared up its own jacksie. 'Cos there was nothin' there!'

Jess cast a sideways stare at the forward sitting Jannice. A somewhat baffled aspect was making its presence known plainly across her features. Mrs. Prune thought it prudent to elaborate.

'Greyminster! Lancashire! The World! Everythin'! It's all gone. Eaten up by somethin' nasty! Somethin' big an' black an' orrible! Its' got t' be stopped!'

'Stopped?'

'Yes! STOPPED! The 'ole world's gettin' smaller an' smaller. Soon it'll be s' small y' won't be able t' stand upright on it! Understand?!'

'No...'

Well, Jess didn't understand. And the fact that Jannice appeared to be impersonating a hungry goldfish seemed to indicate that she was still rather confused about the issue as well.

'Nobody's buggerin' doin' nowt!! Y' just all stood around arguin'. Like there's all the time in the world. Well, there ain't! It's 'appenin'! An' if y' don't stop it now, y'll be dead!!'

'Madame Victoria. It's bin a particularly tryin' time lately...'

'Get y' bloody big gormless 'ands off me, Jess 'Obson. I'm off out!' Mrs. Prune hoisted her tenant's heavy digits from where they had patronizingly clamped her frail shoulder. 'Got t' see a ghost about a photograph!'

In a huff of resolution, she grabbed her coat and lanced a woolly hat to her head, before snatching the old photograph off the table and turning to Jannice.

'Make sure this bastard don't nick off without marryin' y', dear, bloody men. They're all about as much use as a chocolate kettle.'

A substantial finger came so close to the end of Jess' astonished nose that he could feel it brushing against the tiny invisible hairs extending from each nostril.

'Give that a kiddy a father. An' stop avoidin' responsibility! It's not got much of a bloody future as it is.' She thought about that for a moment then lowered her finger again, sadly this time. 'If it's got any future at all...'

After which, Mrs. Prune spun dramatically on her thick rubber soles, marched determinedly from the apartment and slammed the door shut behind her. It was supposed to represent one final defiant parting gesture, satiated with the knowledge that those would be her closing words. The ultimate aphorism that any other living soul would ever hear from her wise old lips.

An awkwardness occupied the hotel chamber. There was no room left any more for words. Too much to comprehend all at once. Best to let it all simmer in silence for now.

The door onto the landing opened slowly once more. Ineptitude spilled across the threshold in an invisible wave. Mrs. Prune hobbled in, avoiding everybody's gaze. She'd made a right fudge of that dramatic exit, and no mistake.

Without deviation, she crossed to the cabinet that was bolted onto the far wall and taking a handle apiece in each podgy mitt, swung the doors apart with great effect. The humiliated sage raised her eyes from the carpet where they had been intensely tracing the pattern.

Inside the cupboard sat an old woman—a very old woman. The distressed creature was more of a skeleton, on the whole. A collection of grey bones with a loose-fitting skin draped around it. In several places the membrane had torn, revealing muscles that resembled cables; the only things stopping her joints from dropping from their sockets. As the first barrage of light thundered through the doors, the hideous female started to scream. An ear piercing wail that cut through the bones and vibrated the light-fittings brutally. Mrs. Prune crooked one thumb, using it to indicate the oddity across her shoulder.

'And while y're about it, sort this one out, will y'?'

Greyminster and its surrounding environs were shrinking. Being nibbled away slice by slice; chunk by chunk. Meanwhile the Victorian town itself was growing steadily more crowded. The gentry who lived on the outskirts very infrequently set foot onto the likes of Greyminster's cobbled old streets. Today, however, there was a general consensus among them that a change of heart might be more appropriate.

Giles Barley, the owner of *Nine Acres Farm*, had watched the ever encroaching darkness chomp off the copse at the far corner of his field of prize winning rams. The end of the world had little time for preferential treatment, it would appear.

Nine Acres Farm had been in the family's capable hands for several centuries and so had the same set of genes. After many generations, where 'Nepotism' was a commonly used business term and 'Incest' was part and parcel of local tradition, Giles had been sportingly produced. It wouldn't be an over-exaggeration to say that Giles had the sort of mentality more normally associated with boxer dogs; in other words, Farmer Barley was a dullard.

Unlike most people, the aggressive imbecile hadn't jumped off the stile at the approach of the world's end. Instead, he had watched the empty void moving forlornly down upon him. A solid black shadow, swallowing everything in its path.

The sheep had more sense, of course. Unfortunately

they also had less option to do anything about the situation. Until the very last moment they had huddled together in one corner, their little legs trembling like cornstalks; their plaintive bleats rising sullenly.

Then the darkness came and enveloped them with little fuss. After one or two minutes more it had crept up on Farmer Barley. With the curiosity of a pre-school toddler, he thrust his arm somewhat lackadaisically into the hollow curtain. Moments later he pulled back a foreshortened stump. After studying what remained of his appendage for some short time, Giles Barley discovered that his knees had taken the same course. And then...

Well...then there was nothing. Just an emptiness, receding relentlessly into an immeasurable distance as it chewed up the landscape.

Farmer Barley had gone to join the rest of his blue blood.

His wife on the other hand—or niece, or whatever you wanted to call the huge slab of red and white cutlet that had shared Giles' bed—watched her husband's demise through the latticed window of the farmhouse kitchen. Carefully Anne laid down the bloodstained knife next to the severed sheep's head that she had been working dutifully upon, unhooked her coat from the hatstand that was standing by the kitchen door, picked up the multicoloured bead shopping-bag that she'd inherited from her grandmother, and buggered off sharpish. Behind her the deadly wall marched ruthlessly onwards.

Town wasn't quite what Mrs. Barley had expected. Not that she had expected an awful lot, having little time in her hectic schedule to stand about deliberating on such matters.

A bustling throng crushed against her down the narrow darkened streets. The walls of the buildings were starting to creak beneath the strain of human bodies. She fought through the frantic townsfolk with courageous vehemence, heading for as close to the town centre as she could reach. The wake filled in behind her with a sea of frightened people.

The massive bubbled orb that had plunged from the monumental phenomenon was firmly embedded in the cobblestones of Old Bridge Lane. Inconveniently the obstacle now blocked Anne's further progress, sparkling and glinting in the spinning shards of light. The hilt of a broad sword hit the farmer's wife squarely on the top of her head. She slumped to the cobblestones, oblivious to what was left of the world.

'Merlin? For God's sake! Speak to me Merlin!'

Arthur tugged at the loose tendrils of his prominent white moustache, dragging them reluctantly from his mouth and spluttering the words in a moist, gummy tone. Lancelot's tiny wrinkled fingers gripped his shoulder with the strength of a claw.

'Nobody could've survived that Arthur. If 'ee was only short before, 'ee'll be even shorter now.'

Together the two knights both studied one particular point, about two feet from the bottom of the orb and three feet down below the surface of the cobbles. At positions, evenly spaced around the circumference of the giant globe, various ancient knights had dug their walking sticks into the minutest of cracks. With a great deal of heaving and shouting they attempted, rather pointlessly perhaps, to summon up enough strength to lift the

Then, with a thunderous rush of wind that sliced the air in half as though it was a loaf, Arthur brought the mighty sword crashing down onto the dark glass.

enormous death trap from its moorings. One or two backs could be heard going crack, followed shortly by one or two stifled, toothless moans.

Bedevere, a diminutive figure with a face that was more of a dried leather sporran than actual features, feverishly leaned onto an out-jutting pike. The shrivelled old man was using his whole body weight for leverage, almost swallowing his cratered chin in the process. His Zimmer frame, decorated with an 'I LUV THE NORTH OF ENGLAND' sticker, buckled beneath him. It skittered rather noisily across the road, colliding at length with the curb. Losing balance on the vibrating pike, Bedevere tumbled. The ground rose up to meet his fragile frame with such force that his false teeth shot out of his head, gnashing as they were spat into the air. Moments later the unleashed dentures bounced resoundingly off the back of Sir Percival's balding pate with a 'snick.'

A strategically placed lance shattered beneath the immense amount of coercion being applied to it. Splinters of white painted wood expanded upwards into a toadstool of tatters, reaching a height that was level with the third story windows.

'Oh, shit!' muttered Galahad, clutching his blackening thumbnail. A voice bellowed authoritatively behind him, curtailing his culpability.

'Stand aside. STAND ASIDE!'

Despite his obvious dotage, Arthur's voice was still commanding.

Clutching at backs and holding down hernias, the old men started to hobble apart, a faltering optimism re-igniting their hopes that Arthur had some noble and reassuring idea that the rest of the knights hadn't thought of. As it happened, he did.

With both hands gripped firmly around the ornamental hilt, Arthur held aloft Excalibur and swung it triumphantly above his head. For a moment his ancient arms almost gave way. The light sang from the tense blade, creating miniature rainbows that twinkled with the brightness of a prism.

Then, with a thunderous rush of wind that sliced the air in half as though it was a loaf, Arthur brought the mighty sword crashing down onto the dark glass—it struck. Connecting angrily, with the sound of an anvil falling through a corrugated-iron roof...and snapped in half. The top part somersaulted across the road, embedding itself in Martha Sonneman's front door.

Arthur gawked in bewilderment at the stubby remains of the once potent sword.

'You have *broken* that which *could not* be broken...' Lancelot spoke with a grave sounding voice.

'The bloody thing snapped in 'alf in me 'ands!' The wizened monarch held up the stump and his baggy eyes moistened.

'Can I borrow y' weapon a minute?'

Mrs. Prune had not exactly forged a path through the crowd, so much as the crowd had somehow knowingly made a bubble for Mrs. Prune to move freely within. Now she plucked Excalibur from Arthur's trembling hands and set about attacking the wall of tape that Inspector Nesbit had been so anxious to surround number thirty-two with.

'Madam...I beg your pardon?' There was a ring of petulance about the old man's cracked intonations.

'Ta, very much.'

With a hack and a slash the adventurous witch created a hole that was just the right size for a stout old woman to squeeze through. The sort of gorge that could be traversed with the minimum of difficulty despite her copious backside. Apparently satisfied by this accomplishment, Mrs. Prune handed the sword back and studied its rather forsaken form.

'Not a very big dagger, is it?'

Arthur's cheeks grew red with embarrassed innuendo.

'Still, it got the job done, eh? And, y' know w'at they say..? About size not bein' important?'

Apparently a similar saying must have been around in the dark-ages judging by Arthur's pained expression as he retrieved Excalibur and attempted to hide the dishonorable euphemism back inside its scabbard.

He lifted a finger to embark upon some innocuous comment, but was confronted by the remains of an ample bottom. The behind wriggled its pear-shaped path through the hewn plastic barrier that had previously protected the dangerous front door.

3:05 p.m, December 6th, 1998, 113 Applegate, Greyminster. Joseph sat and played. A nonsensical childish game that involved his favourite one-eyed teddy bear being beaten about the head with a colourful rattle. The child was incarcerated now by the wooden cot that had been forced beneath the front windows of the lounge. Upstairs his parents slept, the sleep of the dead. Every ounce of their energy having been spent on the emotional turmoil of the past few weeks and the resultant outburst of feelings from the previous night.

Now they dreamed. Scattered dreams; the sort that

exhaustion tends to generate. Secure in the knowledge that the nursery — the source of all the evil — had been well and truly boarded up. Three broad oak planks had been hammered across from one side of the doorjamb to the other, using twelve inch nails. Nails that had been embedded with determined ferocity, right up to their hammer-marked heads.

For double the security measures an old chest of drawers had been dragged in front of that, leaving grooves across the landing carpet. This had been filled with the heaviest objects that the Wambachs' could find. The iron coal scuttle, brimming with rubble from next door. The iron poker, the iron lid off the range, the iron itself—that was heavy.

Ironically the door actually opened inwards. It was the sort of oversight that only those who had done everything possible to secure the future might have managed. Consequently the nursery door blew open. The wooden structure slammed angrily on an item of furniture within the bedroom. Such a slam that, had the parents not been so exhausted from all their endeavours, would most certainly have awoken them.

With a vibrant swiftness a gaseous form shot out into the hallway beyond, resembling some sort of transparent dart. Seconds later, it hurtled down the stairs screeching to a halt as it approached the front door. There it paused, performed a reconnaissance of its current situation, then shot off hastily towards the portal leading off the downstairs' hallway.

Entering soundlessly it skimmed a manic trajectory across the carpet before reaching the rectangular wooden cage that now rattled against the window ledge. The wooden cage containing the bouncing baby boy.

Joseph gripped tightly at the painted bars, standing up on tiptoes, his bulbous head jammed firmly against the barricade. From here the innocent child could study all the events that were taking place through the thicket of trees beyond the window panes. He gurgled in delight at the encroaching black cloud that was hiking resolutely up the drive.

The wraith took this impeccable opportunity to strike, and strike quickly. It diffused, with a struggle, through the back of Joseph's perfectly round skull. Then it wriggled and squirmed, thrashing its tail about in the fashion of a landed sea bass, until the whole of its ethereal body had managed to battle inside.

Joseph turned, his eyes now a smouldering red. No more gurgles, just a sadistic sounding hiss. The whip-like tongue of a venomous adder shot from his mouth. With an unpleasant series of miniature snaps it crushed a half - dead fly that had been hoping to survive until the start of next spring.

Mrs. Prune's trusted old boots 'clacked' resoundingly down the cellar steps, with the sort of hollow noise that shire-horses being lead across a courtyard at night might have created. She was getting too old for this nonsense. God knows; she'd done her bit for 'King and Country' in her time. And most of the members of the Houses of Parliament as well. And where had it gotten her? Absolutely, buggerin' nowhere, that's where. All that hard work—and all those hard members—and now, as far as she could determine, there was hardly any bloody country left. Virtually no world, no universe.

Mrs. Prune wanted answers and, by God, she was going to get them, if it was the last thing she ever did. That postulation made her stop in her solidly stomped tracks. A momentary worry, just a little one about the size of a spark, fleeted gracefully through her troubled mind. Mrs. Prune shook the thought from her head before clopping adamantly down the few remaining steps.

The stone ground reared up and reached her dependable boots. Gingerly prodding the dust-strewn floor with her scuffed but solid toecap, the venerable dame attempted to ascertain that it wasn't some illusion or other. Following several sparking punts, convinced that the floor was substantial enough to venture further, she lowered herself begrudgingly onto its surface. Then haughtily she paced the column of light several times, inspecting the murderous aberration with dignified curiosity. Bloody arrogant thing it was; thundering away with the noise of a generator.

'I knows y'r 'idin' 'ere somew'ere!' Mrs. Prune called at length. She stopped in her tracks, cautiously encompassing her surroundings.

'Ah, Mrs. Prune.' It was a deep, craggy voice that rose to greet her. That particular variety of voice that had an edge to it of razor sharp sarcasm. 'How very nice to see you.'

The stooped and convoluted figure of Thomas Hobson materialised obnoxiously on the top of a crate in one corner. A figure looking rather below par, it must be said. The skin around the features now hung from the bones in leathery strips. Hobson flashed a toothless smile, broken only by a single blackened stump around which his vocabulary whistled disjointedly. When he spoke, the membranous build up of phlegm rattled harshly against the rungs of gristle down his throat.

'I was wondering how long it'd be before you arrived.'

Nonchalantly he passed an orb from one bony hand to the other. Occasionally he would pause to rub one hooked, emaciated finger in concentric circles around the sphere's northern pole.

'I wants t' talk wi' y'. 'Bout this!' she declared.

Mrs. Prune held up the crumpled photograph, thrusting it unpleasantly onto the apex of Hobson's rancid nose. The apparition flinched backwards, not out of fear but to gain a better focus on the article before him. He raised a frayed eyebrow ironically.

'Ah yes...I recognize that. Rather good, isn't it?' His voice almost crackled like a log fire. 'I always was a handsome child.'

'All you ever was, was a bloody great bastard!'

With a flourish, the photograph disappeared into Mrs. Prune's unfathomable coat pocket again.

'That's probably very true, Mrs. Prune. Especially when you come to consider the nature of my family history.'

'So y' never were Jess' bloody great grandfather then?'

'What?' Hobson bolted himself upright, apparently startled at Mrs. Prune's question. Then his flinty eyes twinkled with the steely glint of a pair of ball-bearings. 'Oh, Mrs. Prune. And there was I, thinking that you'd finally got all of the answers together in one spot.'

Mrs. Prune shuffled disconcertedly, hoping for that one strand of knowledge that might help to put a stop to whatever it was that was destroying her world.

'Of course I was his great-grandfather, you stupid, hideous old FRUMP!!'

Thomas clutched the orb tightly in his lean, wasted hands, grinding his splintered nails across its irregular exterior.

"Ow?"

'What?'

'I said "*Ow*"? It's a question.'

'I'm well aware of that, Mrs. Prune, you grotesque little sideshow freak. I didn't think you'd taken up learning to talk Apache Indian.' Hobson scratched the orb once more. This time it sent an uncontrollable shiver running the full length of Mrs. Prune's sympathetic spine. 'The 'How' is rather obvious. So obvious that I'd assumed that even a foetal-faced old hamster like yourself could have worked it out.'

'Right...' Mrs. Prune tensed herself up into an intellectual bovine. ''Y' invented a machine, that took y' backwards in time. But...y' can't be both of 'em.'

She mulled that one over, checking out its shape from various psychological directions. 'Not both of 'em. Not both 'is great-granddad an' 'is son!?'

Mrs. Prune frowned. As she did so a sort of realisation joined her corrugated brow, slotting uncomfortably into place. 'That would make y' an abomnally,' she ventured.

'An '*Anomaly*',' Thomas corrected her mispronunciation. 'And yes, it does rather doesn't it?'

'But, somethin' went wrong with the machine?' Mrs. Prune was working overtime again, the pistons thumping in her head. 'Somethin' bloody stupid! An', w'atever it was, it's caused the end of the world?'

'Keep going Mrs. Prune, you sad ruptured, flabby old teat.' Hobson suddenly loomed forwards, his emblazoned features standing out with an unexpected strength. 'Can you guess what it was? Can you guess why this is happening?' He leaned closer, the repellent aroma from his gums hitting Mrs. Prune's nose in much the same manner that a boxing glove would.

There was a crunch beneath Mrs. Prune's boot as she took a step backwards automatically. Looking down to investigate, she discovered that she had broken a pair of familiar spectacles—rather *thick* spectacles. The sort that had a miniature engine attached to one side. She glanced sharply up at Hobson, who now wore a licentious, diabolical smirk that ran haphazardly along the right-hand side of his gaunt face.

'W'at 'ave y' done wi' Our Ben?'

Thomas Hobson erupted triumphantly in a loud peal of laughter that ripped his rank mouth apart like a set of bagpipes tearing. It echoed around the intimidating vault with remarkable strength. The old villain rocked backwards and forwards; his deformed back creaking and cracking, tossing the ball in the air and coughing from the decomposed pit of his stomach. He caught the orb, brought it up to his nose and spoke with a cruel sneer inflected through his voice.

'Have a guess...You tiresome old bag!'

And he looked through the transparent sphere at the honourable old madam, his unyielding eye magnified by the refraction of the glass. Then he blinked, somewhat ambiguously. Deep in the orb's heart, Mrs. Prune could just about discern the faintest wisp of coloured smoke moving around in an anxious spiral.

'Let 'im out!'

'Or what?'

'Or by God I'll..' She raised the stump of her brolly above her head, realised how ineffective that would be, glanced around the cellar for another promising weapon, couldn't actually find one, so added instead, 'I'll rip y' worthless old bollocks off an' push 'em down y' neck.'

Hobson laughed again. This time the echoes petered off into an almost morose sigh. The despicable figure tossed the spheroid across his angular shoulder dismissively.

Mrs. Prune made an exceptionally agile dive, considering her advanced age. Unfortunately, however, the ball spun across her finger tips. It changed direction with the impact and thundered irreversibly into the column of light, accompanied by a sickening traumatised howl. Mrs. Prune hit the floor with the same momentum as a sack of King Edward's.

'Tsk...tsk.' Hobson's voice pierced the ensuing stillness. 'Now look what you've done.'

The depraved miscreant sprang down from the upturned crate; his sneakers squeaking menacingly upon the stone as he landed.

'Time to die...'

Mrs. Prune raised her head; one side of her folded face coated with grey dust. Despite the circumstances, her tone was still defiant.

'Y' know y' can't 'urt me, Thomas 'Obson! Not whilst I'm wearin' me prot...'

One adipose hand fumbled awkwardly for the elusive length of string that was normally tied about her sturdy old neck—it wasn't there.

Look now. Far away, across the cramped and bowing rooftops. Somewhere back amongst the smoking mounds of rubble that were formerly 114 Applegate. Fused into the top of a charcoaled bedside cabinet. Nothing more than a twisted molten victim of the terrible accident. Recognise it? You should...this is Mrs. Prune's lucky pendant. Abandoned and forgotten during the overwhelming events of the last couple of days, it'd take a razor-edged spatula to remove the amulet from where it had bonded itself into the varnish.

'Betcha life...Bogie?' Thomas Hobson raised one erudite eyebrow.

The knuckled fingers arthritically straightened themselves, cracking painfully as they did so. The scrawny arm extended to full length and an ear-splitting, eyeball-burning fireball, struck out from the ends of Hobson's broken digits. It snaked across the cellar, hitting Mrs. Prune at the section where her rib cage met with the base of her sternum, with such undiluted force that her tired old body was lifted completely off the floor. The ancient witch was flung grotesquely against the wall.

For several heart-rending seconds her whole frame shook epileptically, dancing convulsively with probing blue sparks. Her torso was outlined by a luminescent white glow. Then it started to expand in the manner of a bicycle tyre that was dangerously attached to the end of a car pump.

Mrs. Prune tried to scream, but unfortunately her old lungs never got the chance to open. Then she burst. Impressively, it must be said, giving the general impression of an over-ripe tomato being trodden on by a spiteful schoolboy.

In a splutter of intestines, the old woman suddenly occupied a space and shape that was no longer recognisable. Just a morphous damp smear across the fabric of peeling brickwork. The only clue left to suggest that it had once borne human form, was a pair of bloodshot eyeballs, situated ridiculously close to the top. Eyeballs that bore a wild look of intensified fear.

The remnants slid down across the pointing, tracing angular patterns between the bricks. Large blackened red globules jostling soddenly to the stone floor. Thoroughly satisfied, the figure of Thomas Hobson turned its hideous spine upon the scene of brutal horror and with ponderous decrepitude lurched arduously away.

Chapter Twenty One

Banshees In The Cupboard. Zombies in the Church Yard.

Jess paced up and down in front of the cupboard that contained the withered old woman. Rhythmically he slapped the chair leg that he held in one hand against the palm of the other. Behind him stood Jannice, who now gazed on somewhat anxiously.

At length Jess stopped, forcing his features into a semblance of a deflated medicine ball at the Banshee's awful wail. He turned around to Jannice, wearing the sort of facial cast that said, 'W'at the Hell am I supposed t' do now?'

'Actually, I recall something from a book I read once.' Jannice looked up optimistically, having previously been engrossed in deep thought.

'I 'ardly think that burnin' y' bra's goin' t' be a great 'elp in this situation.' Jess pondered the predicament and added, 'Besides which, it looks like *she* should 'ave worn one 'erself a bit more often.'

He examined the timbered ribcage and the other overexposed parts of the banshee's anatomy. After some deliberation he added, 'She could tuck that bloody thing into 'er sock.'

Jannice paid no attention to the remark. Right now, the liberation of anorexic women would have to wait. Instead she signalled her accomplice closer, whispering something important in his right ear. It was obviously something disagreeable, because Jess bolted upright with a sharp movement.

'Y' can't be serious? Y' want to me to do what?'

Jannice beckoned him down again, repeating the same muttered comments. Only this time a conspiratorial hand cupped itself over his ear denying access to inquisitive bystanders. Jess' expression set as solid as a jelly that had been moulded out of concrete.

'W'at? Wi' that wrinkly old saggy-titted cow?'

'Apparently,' Jannice continued aloud. 'That way she'll think you're her long lost son and grant you three wishes. Or something.'

'That's not enough.' Jess shook his head, biting his bottom lip pensively. Jannice's suggested course of action was definitely one for the back boiler. One that was going to bloody stay there as well.

'Besides, I'd never 'ave done a thing like that t' *my* bloody mother,' he went on, the mental image that had formed becoming ever more acidic. 'Especially if *she'd* 'ave borne a strikin' resemblance to a raisin pickled in vinegar!'

Almost as if it had taken offence at that description, the banshee started to howl. Moments later the emaciated female leapt from the cupboard with surprising dexterity. With a dull thud it landed in a crouched position, checking maniacally around. Time for action.

Jess heroically pushed Jannice from the reach of its keen claws. Defensively the chair leg was brandished before him, in the absence of anything more substantial such as a baseball bat.

'C'mon then, y' shrivelled old bitch!'

The ends of Jannice's fingernails pierced the flesh on

Jess' shoulder blades as she stiffened apprehensively behind him. He tried not to wince at the sudden sensation of pain.

Unfortunately, Jannice convulsed with surprise when the banshee rushed unexpectedly across the carpet, woefully shrieking—Jess also screeched. Through watering slits he watched the malicious spirit scurry perplexingly into the fireplace. It vanished up the chimney with an apathetic whimper. The last they both saw were a pair of scrawny legs scrabbling up the brickwork disturbing columns of dust.

Jannice felt the tension sag from Jess' shoulders and unhooked her fingernails. She was embarrassed about her stereotypical reaction to the encounter, hung-over on guilt at having let down every woman in the world.

'Did it look frightened to you?' This was an attempt to put her own self-loathing behind her.

'It would 'ave done if its 'ead 'ad connected wi' this!'

Jess hadn't noticed her humiliation. Instead, he swung the chair leg in front of his nose several times, concentrating on the flow of the swing whilst it followed the curve of his grin.

'It looked terrified to me,' said Jannice.

Something bothered her about the banshee's exit. The vile creature hadn't exactly struck her as being the sort that would be so easily dominated by the threat of a gormless middle-aged bloke.

She searched around the living-room with the vague hope of *not* actually discovering whatever it was that had really disturbed it. She discovered the truth with a sensation that was similar to having her innards removed.

Not only had the corner of the room gone, but most

Almost as if it had taken offence at that description, the banshee started to howl. Moments later the emaciated female leapt from the cupboard with surprising dexterity. With a dull thud it landed in a crouched position, checking maniacally around. Time for action.

of the wall, half of the dresser, half of the sink and the whole of the door.

Jannice screamed, regardless of what that might say about her show of *'feminine solidarity.'* In panic Jess swung around and pointlessly lashed out at the emptiness with his weapon.

On the backswing it became apparent that the top of his club had gone missing. He stared at the hopeless stump as it spluttered in his hands.

'What the Hell is THAT!!?' Jannice blasted, mesmerised by the great wall of darkness before her.

'The window!'

'A window onto what?'

'NOT THAT! THE BLOODY WINDOW BE'IND Y'!' Jess didn't have time for this crap. He grabbed the slow-witted feminist by the collar and heavy handedly dragged her backwards, kicking violently. Without a pause, he shouldered aggressively through the glass pane in a loud smash, pulling Jannice's struggling carcass behind him.

The human body is capable of a great many wonders. Under pressure it produces an automatic release of adrenaline. Millions of microscopic globules, all bustling and charging through the veins, causing a traffic jam in the occipital lobe. The entire experiences of a lifetime can often be relived, under intense situations, in a matter of seconds.

Observation slows down as well, to let those experiencing some terrible danger at first-hand observe the futility of attempting to alter their fate. Unfortunately, due to some evolutionary oversight, the muscles of the body don't actually react any faster. Exactly why this is, nobody has a satisfactory explanation, but it certainly allows the individual a lot more time to worry about the fact that they don't.

As he hurtled downwards, Jess had ample duration to reflect upon several pressing issues. It crossed his mind that he ought to have opened the window first. It also crossed his mind that Jannice had parted company with him somewhere en route, all that was left in his grip being a torn section of cloth, presumably what remained of her granddad-shirt collar.

Then Jess realised with an ominous dread that the window had been on the first floor. Now he, and several thousand shards of sharp pointed glass, were hurtling at maximum velocity towards the cobbled pavement below. Not much of a cushion from thirty-odd feet...twenty...ten.

There was a loud accompaniment of bones snapping. Jess dementedly forced his eyelids into two clefts of anguished determination and waited for the delayed stabs of pain to arrive.

Several seconds passed during which there was nothing more uncomfortable than the jab of an elbow in his ribs. It was accompanied by the devastating squawk of the squashed banshee as it rattled down his lughole and slammed against his ear drum.

Jess opened his eyes. Only to discover where Jannice had gotten to on her personal wanderings.

'You bloody stupid...'

The cork soles of her sandals grappled for a foothold on the slippery bricks. Pressed against one cheek the oxidized drainpipe gave an ominous creak as it attempted to withstand her onerous weight.

'Bloody bald headed bastard!'

Jannice was no longer proud of being *'a large woman'*. Odd that; how highly threatening circumstances can *momentarily* affect one's lifelong beliefs. Instead, for the time being, she would have preferred to be a bulimic wastrel. The drainpipe pulled away from the wall at the clamps. Small, irregular triangles of metal started pinging from where the duct joined up with itself, lower down.

'Let go y' bloated SLUG!!'

'How dare you?! You chauvinistic...'

Creak!

'Petty minded...'

Crack!

'Penis brained...'

Groan!

'Aggravating...'

Splinter!

'AAAAAAAARGH!'

The whole world rushed upwards in a blur. With an unhealthy jolt the drainpipe stopped, at an angle of 45 degrees. It shuddered precariously, Jannice dangling below it resembling a teabag on a string. She kicked out her solid legs so that her feet just managed to scrape the surface of the bricks. Just a little more and she might be able to reach out and grab hold of the...

CrrrRRRRRACK!!

Jannice fell with the weight of a mattress, sandals

above her head, legs ungainly splayed, the back draught whistling noisily through the gaps between her toes. Ten chipped toenails glinted sharply in the softening sunlight as she toppled, her scream spiralling along the helix of its own Doppler effect.

She landed. Like a child, on top of Jess. Caught in his big, strong arms. A sixteen and a half stone child admittedly; the full, unexpected weight of which brought him down onto his knees. He met the ground with a painful crack, sending Jannice sprawling into the Waldorf's wall. After several moments Jannice cautiously opened her eyes.

There was Jess, clutching his stomach in an attempt to recapture his plundered breath. Otherwise he appeared to be remarkably unharmed.

Up above, with the faintest fizzle, the enveloping blackness gnawed slowly at the horizon about 14 feet in front of them. It was closing fast down the side of the Waldorf Hotel. A white line edged the roof where the emptiness of the space devoured the red tiles with invisible teeth.

'Get y' fat arse into gear!'

For once Jannice didn't stop to argue the finer points. Almost by common consent they both hurdled the stone wall of St. Oliver's, before stumbling, half blind, across the collection of graves.

St. Oliver's on the Grey was no ordinary churchyard. Only those who had made considerable effort towards the Presbyterian cause could rot away beneath this sanctimonious soil.

Have a good perusal of the philanthropic and the benevolent dead, if you would. Here's the grave of Albert Bailey, inventor of some insignificant item. He had died a very rich and successful tycoon.

Lady Antonia Spreight. The last woman to be executed in Greyminster for the bizarre murder of her husband. The crime had involved a bedstead, a breadknife, a fish bone and a slab of granite for some enigmatic reason. Despite her rather heretical end it was decided that she'd paid enough capital to the church coffers to be given a decent burial here.

Sir Reginald Montgomery whose penchant for willing sheep was not reason enough to forfeit his right to the hallowed plot of ground. His vast amounts of money had secured his inhumation amongst the other notorieties.

All the filthy and despotic slept beneath the soil in St. Oliver's black museum of the macabre. The sleep of the damned, that no amount of money could stave off in the end.

Or rather *had* slept...

The pounding of Jess and Jannice's feet penetrated down through the inhibited earth, drumming ominously through the low roots and bickering insatiably around the dead. Have you ever watched a lugwormer call up worms for his bucket? What he does is take a garden fork and push it into the ground. Then he drums on the handle and the worms, sensing the vibrations, think that it's raining up above. Not wanting to drown, the invertebrates then crawl towards the surface. A similar occurrence was happening now, only on a much grander scale.

St. Oliver's grounds had begun to tear into great mouths of turf, spewing up bodies as though they were lumps of old phlegm. They broke through the grass as if it was nothing more encumbering than a pie crust—all putrid and rotten. Various costumes traced the local

St. Oliver's grounds had begun to tear into great mouths of turf, spewing up bodies as though they were lumps of old phlegm. They broke through the grass as if it was nothing more encumbering than a pie crust—all putrid and rotten.

ancestry over the centuries. The older and more distinct the style, the less actual flesh the clothes' occupants appeared to possess.

The mouldy skull of Agnes Moorhen, a long forgotten civic dignitary, reared up. An earthworm writhed within its soiled eye sockets; disturbed from its tunneling by the form uprooting itself and howling despondently. Jannice bellowed as the foul ancient head blocked her view, a mere four inches from the end of her nose.

She felt her arm being grabbed. Jess with his usual gentility, almost pulled the thickset spectator from her rock steady feet.

'It's only a zombie...Look...'

Armed with harshly gained expertise, Jess' anvil of a fist walloped straight through Agnes' head and emerged from the back of the skull, creating a shower of tiny splinters. Instantly Jess regretted having committed himself to such an outrageous maneuver. It took him all of several uncomfortable seconds to dislodge the head from his wrist.

Pulling a face not unlike a bulldog with chronic indigestion, he grabbed hold of Jannice by the hand once more, before dragging her off through the throng of the dead.

Zombies, for reasons that Jess wasn't sure about, tended to walk in the same fashion as scarecrows. All stiff arms and inflexible legs, as if their muscles had been manufactured from unyielding poles. He figured, as he watched them stomp around the upturned headstones, that it must have been rigor mortis that was responsible for their unbendable condition. However, since rigor mortis only lasted for a few hours after death, on reflection that wasn't very likely at all. Jess put it down to artistic interpretation and left the matter at that.

Drawing up alongside the grey stone corner of the gothic church tower, he slowed to a curious saunter. An ancient dwarfed door cryptically led down several steps and eventually found an exit beneath the pulpit inside. He reached a standstill, hands on knees, exhaustedly gasping for breath. Jannice mirrored his stance, wheezing expressively.

The darkness had reached the church grounds. It silently munched at the privet hedge that lined the bent stone walls, swallowing the railings that were topped off with iron spikes. Zombies pathetically tottered and span on the edge of the world, like tin soldiers on a shelf. Cart-wheeling and staggering, before plummeting into total oblivion.

Jannice was the first to stand upright. Unable to speak, she tugged desperately at Jess' shoulder; an indication that it was now time to move on before the opportunity had passed.

"Old on a moment.'

An insignificant grave had been placed against the building. You could tell that it didn't belong to anybody special because the down spout from the roof was situated about twenty-odd feet above it. Every time the slightest drizzle occurred, all the water gathered along the gutters and poured down onto the top of the headstone. A constant, relentless gurgle of precipitation, slowly eroding the memorial away.

Without any apparent motive, Jess thumped the inscription as if attempting to wake the grave's occupant. A few short moments later the ground began to crumble. A mangy head — half of it still covered with flesh, the other half riddled with maggots — emerged from the degenerated soil pushing the pointed blue chippings to one side. It was wearing a sort of stupid lopsided grin where the lips had rotted away and were no longer adequate covering for the wedge of blackened teeth.

One steel toecapped clog collided with the grinning features somewhat rudely. The neglected head burst against the tomb stone behind it. Thoroughly satisfied, Jess turned to Jannice, who was suffering from shock. She backed away slightly, astonished by his unprecedented conduct.

'Me old geography teacher.' Jess brushed his hands, whilst smiling broadly. Compensation at last for all those terrible hours spent in his company as a child. 'Last time that old bastard gives me the ruler f' drawing breasts on 'is map o' Europe!'

Moments later the two fugitives emerged at full pelt from the cramped and narrow ginnel that skirted the church. Straight into a vast living wall of terrified townsfolk. Jess pulled up short, Jannice careering into his back so that the resultant chain reaction resembled a domino rally.

The crowd appeared impenetrable. However, the faint crackle behind them was enough inspiration for Jannice to lurch forwards, forcing Jess and herself through the smallest of openings. Moments later they had become completely engulfed, being carried along on the crowd's drifting undercurrent.

An expectant fear swamped the senses from all around them. It flickered and discharged itself violently in the quickening air. Something new and ever more ominous was approaching.

Previously animated people now stood frozen in terror as an extensive lattice-work shadow fell across their heads.

There was a creak and a thud and all the sky turned seriously black.

Up above the rooftops, sagging and groaning, rose an unnatural creature. Tall enough to stride the houses; flimsy enough to let the wind whistle spookily through its frame.

A figure constructed entirely from stalks of wicker; knotted together at the joints by reeds that the colossal degenerate seemed to be having some difficulty in articulating. The towering demon leaned itself heavily upon the tree tops in order, one would suppose, to steady its gigantic and pendulant chassis.

A huge wicker foot impacted destructively upon the struggling victims below it, creating a myriad of muffled groans that presently turned into a singularly unpleasant crunch.

The body of this enormous automaton appeared to be some sort of huge wicker scaffold that was constructed from a collection of smaller, self-contained cages. Occupying these receptacles were various items of farm produce. Some carried apples that bounced about the infra-structure resembling colourful Ping-Pong balls. Others enclosed cabbages of the prize-winning variety. Whilst others still imprisoned cucumbers that would have made Mrs. Prune blush.

A larger than average bantam with wild bulging eyes gawked out through the bars across the chest. It clucked and squawked amidst a snowstorm of feathers, apparently having control of the elevated figure through a system of pulleys and frayed bits of rope. Using its wings and various levers, it had managed to steer the Colossus onto the street where it tottered in the general direction of Jannice Applebotham and Jess Hobson. The bantam's eyes glowed the colours of Hell's cavern walls as they focused themselves on the two worried victims.

Jess breathed heavily down his nose and let go of Jannice's hand.

'Now, that's just takin' the piss!'

The streets attempted to empty themselves. Unfortunately it was an attempt that, under the circumstances, was hardly likely to meet with any great success. Several old people became trampled underfoot as the fearful crowd began to detonate in all directions. Screaming children in prams were left abandoned to their fate. Barking dogs performed acrobatics around the conflicting legs of the would-be escapoligists.

The other huge foot now swung itself forwards and crushed another small army of tiny humans beneath its ballast.

Decision time—forwards or backwards? Not much of a choice for either direction on the whole. Jess searched across his shoulder, surveying the path that they had already taken. The ever progressive darkness had already consumed the vestry of St. Oliver's and was even now ploughing a steady but relentless furrow through the front porch.

'It's a choice between the Devil and the dark black sea,' Jess muttered. *Ah well. Better the Devil you know than the omnipotent dark black presence that you don't.*

He grabbed Jannice by the first available piece of clothing that came to hand. With a certain amount of irony this just happened to be her bra strap. Before he had time to contemplate the outcome of such an ill-mannered faux pas, the hefty woman was pulled off at a sprint. Jess' own substantial body darted between the towering wicker pylons that constituted the demonic creature's legs.

The elastic reached its limit and Jannice, with her mouth opened wide so that it resembled a Venus Fly Trap, was twanged in his direction, slipping ungainly. The two of them collided, before Jess dragged her startled carcass through the dark gothic archway that led onto Abattoir Row.

This was where Lady Spreight had annihilated her long suffering husband. An indelible scribble on the brick wall beside the drainpipe bore testimony to that fact. A scribble that read *'Mr. Spreight was murdered here and Joanna Beardsley was shagged by me.'* The well-constructed sentence was accompanied by a wriggly arrow and a drawing that supposedly depicted the act in question.

At that moment in time the couple were re-enacting their personal histories once more. *No!* Not Joanna Beardsley and her boyfriend, whoever he was. Lord and Lady Spreight, demonstrating the danger in keeping the gene pool too narrow. Just quite what she was doing with that fish bone was an education in itself and local scandal had apparently overlooked the pound of fresh lard.

'What the Hell is going on?' Jannice exhaled the words so that they came out somewhat strained. The couple had ground to a halt and now watched the homicide reconstitute itself over and over again, in every graphic colourful detail.

'I've no idea. But I think it's about time we found out.' Jess' words were punctuated by clouds of spasmodically exhaled breath. 'That bloody thing was after me. Did y' see the look on that chicken's face?'

'Jess...we're all going to die, aren't we?'

'Why me?' Jess was now rambling, completely ignorant of his partner's queries. 'W'at 'ave I done wrong? Apart from pullin' the legs off spiders w'en I was too small t' know better.' He considered that carefully, dredging up a guilty admission from the depths of his long term memory. 'An' I did keep a wasp in a matchbox once. It got cooked.'

A look of horror crossed the contours of his plastercine face. 'This can't be all 'appenin' 'cos I cremated a wasp, surely t' God?'

'Jess!? You're talking bollocks! Calm down and let's try t' figure this thing out.'

Unfortunately there wasn't time. The respite was short lived and on reflection might have been put to better usage. A tumultuous grinding whistle signified that their troubles had started once more.

One mammoth wicker hand crashed through the cracked plaster ceiling in a shower of wreckage. Jannice and Jess backed away, flattening themselves against the wall. With their hearts beating loudly, the couple held tightly to each other.

The digits probed and prodded, going 'Fizz' as they connected with the tableaux of the ghostly assassination that continued regardless. As a coil of electricity wrapped itself around them, the fingers snatched themselves back in surprise. Then the whole hand appeared to sense something. It hovered indecisively for a moment, swinging ponderously. Then it creaked and it turned as if suspended by some invisible chain.

Then it struck. Jannice felt a sharp stab as she was grabbed by the left leg and hoisted upwards. With one desperate movement Jess snatched the other appendage.

A tug-of-war broke out using Jannice for the rope. She screamed as the knowledge of what it was like for a sixteen and a half stone woman to do the splits against her will became a regrettable experience.

It was no good. Jess reached the conclusion that the hand wouldn't stop and if he held onto her much longer, then he'd get one part of Jannice whilst the maniacal bantam got the other. So he let go and with a sudden violent movement Jannice smashed through the hole that had been hewn into the roof.

Jess checked about himself. Suddenly he felt more alone than he had ever felt before in his whole life.

He emerged from the alleyway a grimmer, fitter man. His heart pounded in his head; determination etched sternly into every cranny of his expression. His hulking torso hurtled out with the velocity of a bullet, almost colliding with the wicker legs that were straddling the heaving street beyond.

Above him Jannice struggled and kicked. That was typical. She'd forgotten all about the techniques that she had learned in the many 'Women's Self Defense Classes.' As the creaking hand tightened its grip, she reverted to the good old school of fighting that everyone, male or female, always reverted to in genuine confrontational situations. Punching and kicking and screaming very loudly. One sandal came loose in the struggle. It toppled down, spinning rabidly onto the pavement.

Behind her the darkness was filling the whole of Jess' vision as though the wicker man was just a cardboard cut-out stuck onto the front of oblivion.

'Jess...' Jannice screamed above the turmoil of the

threshing arms. 'Try and stop it. Whatever '*It*' is...'

So Jess, panic-stricken and with his usual cultured approach, hunched up his shoulders, put the top of his head forwards and charged the great structure in the fashion of a nuclear missile.

He collided. And part of his ear cut itself on a splinter from the cane.

For a moment the wicker man teetered on the edge of the void. It trembled uncertainly, rocking backwards and forwards, then it tumbled.

The ocean of nullity into which the whole world appeared to be falling ran the full length of its arm. The arm that terminated in the badly mimicked cluster of fingers. The fingers that were clutching with stubborn reticence at Jannice and it toppled unavoidably into the pool of endless emptiness.

Jannice hit the pavement and Jess felt a jolt as his heart momentarily stopped beating. At least what was left of Jannice hit the pavement. Still surrounded by strands of vegetation Jannice stared up in an expression of augmented horror.

She was only half there now, what remained was disintegrating slowly.

'Now look what you've done.'

Sometimes when the end comes, certain people just knuckle down and get on with it. Jannice was obviously one of those people. She pushed Jess' arm aside as he struggled to pull her back in the full knowledge that it would be awful to spend the rest of her life existing only from the bottom rib upwards. She didn't even 'want' to contemplate how she'd use the toilet. She felt a calmness breaking through the overwhelming abhorrence.

'For Gods' sake Jess, put a stop to this, all of this...the world shouldn't end this way now. Not so dreadfully!'

'How?' Jess wanted to say more. But even now the words caught up in a tangled knot about a third of the way along his arid, taut throat. Stupid, selfish macho pride. Dominating his character, right up until the end.

'I don't know.' Jannice swallowed and sensed a hollowness creeping up her spinal cord. 'But you'd better hurry up and find out.'

With a fizzle the darkness reached her chin and Jannice wore it like a collar.

'I love you Jess...'

He closed his eyes, unable to watch the finale come, There followed an indistinct pop. It sounded similar to the sort of noise that a toy gun would make when it was firing its cork. When he circumspectly opened one eye once more, Jannice had gone.

Chapter Twenty Two

In The Windsock Of Eternity.

N o date...no time...no place...just Death. The great barrier that we all must cross sooner or later.

What's it like on the other side then? What does eternity consist of? Does mankind genuinely have an eternal soul and a case to answer for?

Or was the whole concept just an inevitable con trick? A humbug, invented by the men who wear frocks whilst preaching messages against amoral sexualities? A horrible deception that was designed to make us all conform to more acceptable social standards?

Jannice Applebotham was just about to find out.

'Hello...?' A frightened ineffectual voice echoed softly across the swirling confrontational void. An emptiness consisting of pastel lilacs and watery creams, as if somebody had dropped magnificent globules of ink onto a sodden page of Bockingford. 'Is there anybody there?'

A shimmer, an undulation of ethereal sound that crossed the drawn ghostly spaces in the same way that ripples cross a pond when a stickleback breaks the surface.

"Ave you arrived 'ere now then, dear?" A slither of purple, something similar to a stroke that had been painted by a Japanese brush, appeared faintly in front of Jannice. It spoke in a rich Lancashire accent. Jannice stared, though with what neither party could determine. She too had a body of sorts. It was thin and transparent, with no limbs. But it was a body of some description, and it must be said, that was a start.

'Mrs. Prune? Is that you?' There was a tremble of fear in Jannice's fragile voice. 'Are you dead?'

'I bloody 'ope so, dear. I don't want t' spend the rest of me autumn years as a morfuzz red blob wearin' me intestines f'r an overcoat.'

'Where are we?'

'Limbo, dear.' There was a moment's thoughtful pause. 'Where the dance comes from.'

Jannice's vision appeared to allow her to see through mile upon mile of colourful cumuli.

'Where's everybody gone to?' Another thought, somewhat more substantial, came swimming to the front of her mind with apprehension. 'Shouldn't somebody be around to meet us?'

'I 'spect 'Ee's just nipped out f'r a fag.'

'He?' Jannice was obviously beginning to feel a soupcon more comfortable. It was always encouraging to know that no matter how disturbing the situation had become, there was always her firmly held beliefs to help get her through the bad times. 'I always thought that God would probably be a woman.'

'Wouldn't 'ave thought so.' Mrs. Prune appeared to stiffen, or at least her form increased its density. 'Not with the bloody great mess 'ee's got the world in. That's the work of a man, that is. Bloody useless great 'unks of meat with gonads f' brains, the lot of 'em.'

That had the desired effect. If a slither of pink light could have grinned then Jannice's would have done so right now. Instead she gave off a short glow of warmth that Mrs. Prune felt deep down in her soul. Jannice softened.

'Some people reckon it's all a test, you know?' There was no forthcoming answer so she carried on with her hypothesis regardless. 'To ensure that we're good enough to enter the Kingdom of Heaven.'

'Christ, I 'ope not! Pardon my French,' Mrs. Prune added reverentially. 'All the bloody exams I ever took meant that somethin' worse was comin' up. God 'elp us if it's worse than what we've just bin through!'

'So what's this place then?' Jannice wasn't altogether convinced that Mrs. Prune's blasphemous attitude was the best to adopt. Not under the circumstances. 'Is it Purgatory?' No response. 'Are we stuck here? Imprisoned?'

'Y' sound like y've 'ad enough o' this already, dear. W'at's the rush?' Mrs. Prune attempted to subdue any fears that Jannice might have had. 'Might as well enjoy it...while it lasts.'

Jannice was confused slightly by this comment. The distraction appeared as a faint reddish-blue towards the front of the area that Mrs. Prune had allotted for Jannice's face. The old woman decided to elaborate on the subject to put her cohort's mind at ease.

'Let's put it this way. Once y' get in there, wherever '*There*' might be, y' there for eternity.' She lowered her voice, such as it was, by half a decibel or so. 'That's f'r ever if y' didn't already know.'

'I did,' said Jannice.

'Well...' Mrs. Prune's gaseous form uprighted itself, becoming a straightened pinion of vapours. 'That's long enough f' anyone t' go worshippin' 'is *Almighty Greatness*' bloody, smelly feet. An' playin' bloody 'arps on clouds, singin' songs about 'ow bloody marv'lous 'Ee is.' After a short pause, 'I'll take me chances and 'ang around 'ere f'r a bit.'

Unfortunately Mrs. Prune didn't get the opportunity. Which was a shame, because she was starting to enjoy her temporary spell in Oblivion.

Just as the thoughts shuffled psychically from her diaphanous purple form, a small door appeared noiselessly off to one side of them. It was surrounded by yellow light bulbs after the fashion of a dressing room mirror, and plinthed with a painted sign that read *'WAITING ROOM. Please Take A Ticket'*.

The door opened with an unearthly creak and a four foot five man hobbled out in some obvious discomfort. He was very old; the warped staff being tightly gripped in the bends of his disfigured hand a requisition it would seem, to holding his ancient frame upright.

Partially folded in the manner of an elderly ape, the aged minister thudded forward with a disjointed rhythm. A length of whisker breaking free from the outlandish beard, curled itself accidentally around the irregular crutch. An unfortunate occurrence that resulted in the old man stumbling awkwardly. Jannice and Mrs. Prune simultaneously emitted a worried gasp.

However, the image managed to steady himself. With the expression of somebody who's just unwittingly broken wind and now wants to pretend that it wasn't him, he continued towards them. His playful gait creaked rather violently, bringing an expression of resolute pain to his eyes.

'I'm sorry to have kept you waiting, ladies.'

Extracting a clipboard from somewhere deep beneath his dazzling robe, the archaic gentleman began a contemplative check of the numerous columns that were drawn along its length.

'Bureaucracy and all that sort of nonsense.' His voice

sounded familiar. Not unlike the woodpecker bookend that had lived in Bagpuss' shop. 'What with it being the *'END OF THE WORLD'* today. And those bloody awful quills they keep sending us. Never have worked properly. I've ordered ten boxes but the damn things still leak. Look at my fingers.'

He held up one wizened hand, the tips of the fingers stained with blotches of blue ink.

'And it doesn't wash off,' he added resentfully.

'I like the beard.' Mrs. Prune was feeling altogether too cocksure for her own good. 'Though I must admit, I was expecting somebody slightly taller.'

The diminutive rabbi cocked an unimpressed eyebrow in the old woman's direction.

'Right. Let me introduce myself.' Taking in a deep breath, he spoke with a powerful all-pervading voice. A different voice entirely than the one that he had used just moments before.

'I AM THE ALL SEEING, ALL KNOWING, ALL FORGIVING. . .THE GUARDIAN OF TIME AT THE PORTAL OF CHOICES!'

The words continued to echo for a few moments after the old gentleman had stopped, and with some relief he broke out into a cheerful grin that revealed a row of little rotten pegs.

'Very impressive,' said Mrs. Prune. 'Can y' do Tommy Cooper?'

Consulting his notes once more, the withered Rabbi uneasily shifted several pages into a disorganized heap. He had noticed a certain resentment towards him in Mrs. Prune's sardonic tone. He thought it best to ignore it, on the off chance that it would pass as soon as it had dawned

'I AM THE ALL SEEING, ALL KNOWING, ALL FORGIVING ... THE GUARDIAN OF TIME AT THE PORTAL OF CHOICES!'

on the old dear that she was in fact dead.

'So...It's Mrs. Agatha Boyle and Miss Priscilla Dewhurst then, is it?'

'Do I bloody look like an Agatha Boyle t' you?'

'To be honest, you don't look like anything much,' the old man retorted, attempting to quell the rush of blood to his nose.

'There's no need f' rudeness.'

Jannice's pale form leaned over the host's knobbled shoulder, checking through the long list of names as he drew out a pair of half-moon spectacles. After several minutes of intense dissection, Mrs. Prune broke the silence. Something had been bothering her. Not just of late, but throughout her entire lifetime. There was something that she had always intended to do and now appeared to be the most appropriate time in which to do it.

'I've got one or two complaints t' make...'

A frayed and yellowing scroll appeared in front of her purple ribbon, unfurling for approximately four hundred feet across the tempestuous sky. The little old man raised his head from the bureaucracy, slightly shaken but devoting his undivided attention to her stately form nonetheless.

'Now then...first. Number One.' Mrs. Prune attempted to raise a finger that she didn't have. 'Cancer an' other rather nasty diseases.'

Somehow Mrs. Prune lowered the scroll once more, giving the impression of peering over the top of her spectacles like a house-keeper.

'Now there's not much call f' that sort o' thing really, is there? I mean! W'at d' y' think y' playin' at? Y' can't blame that on Mankind. God knows, they've done all that they can do t' try an' stop it. C'mon. Give 'em a break.'

The little man blinked, nonplussed, staring in silence as the scroll was lifted back up.

'Number Two. Adolf 'Itler.' It went down again. 'W'at an 'orrible sod 'e was. What the 'Ell was goin' through y'r 'ead w'en y' came up wi' that one?'

'Yes...' The stunted Hebrew paused, cocking his head on one side so that he resembled a terminally ill parrot. 'I think you might actually be operating under a misapprehension.'

'Number Three.' Mrs. Prune marched on valiantly. She had a long list to get through and there wasn't time for arguments. 'Virginia Bottom bein' minister f'r 'ospitals. Now that's just goin' too far.'

If she could have wagged a bodacious finger then Mrs. Prune would have done so.

'Yes. Right. Mrs..?' The word trailed off, inflecting itself into a questioning accent.

'It's Prune. P. R. U. N. E. As in the laxative!'

This brought a genuine look of surprise to the old man's features, a horrid toothy smile rippling out beneath his whiskers.

'Ah...Albert Prune's wife? We had him through here a number of years back. Splendid fellow.'

That threw her for a moment. It threw Jannice as well. Somewhere in the back of Jannice's mind she must have known that Mrs. Prune had at one point been married. However, she was such an independent woman that it was hard to imagine what sort of husband he'd been. Probably just a harmless old man on reflection. Nevertheless, the broaching of the subject had brought Mrs. Prune's complaints to a halt long enough for the rabbinical school graduate to throw in his tuppence worth.

'I'm not altogether sure who you actually think I am, Mrs. Prune.'

There was another pause, this time appropriated by confusion.

'Aren't *you* God?'

'God? Good God no.' There was a tremble of shock in his creaky old voice that was fast turning into humorous wonder.

'Well 'oo the bloody 'Ell are y' then? Wastin' me bleedin' time moanin' at y'.'

'Didn't I tell you? Oh, I'm so sorry...I could have sworn that I had done.' His voice had acquired a conceited almost ironic tone. 'Oh well, here we go...'

The aged representative of the after-life took a breath and mouthed in a voice the volume of planets colliding just to ram the point home, 'I AM THE ALL SEEING, ALL KNOWING, ALL FORGIVING...THE GUARDIAN OF TIME AT THE PORTAL OF CHOICES!'

Mrs. Prune took her metaphysical fingers from her ears, cocking a transcendental eyebrow at the sarcastic little Jew.

'An' w'at does one o' them do w'en 'ee's bleedin' at 'ome?'

'Well...Now...Let me show you...'

Curling his hairy toes up at the ends and spreading out his arms ostentatiously, the little gentleman thumped an invisible surface with his staff.

The heavens began to rumble as if they were constructed on pistons. Clouds loosened and parted. A table sized relief map slowly appeared between them, lifting itself up into a secure position. It ground to thunderous halt before the three onlookers, with a mighty and echoing click. The diminutive immortal looked around at the two esoteric figures, beaming.

'What's this?' gasped Jannice.

The little man dropped his voice to a low, passionate whisper.

'This is a map of *all* the universes!'

The three of them leaned over the highly detailed object. Millions of tiny galaxies no bigger than thumbnails, all spinning in the vast eternities of space. It was odd, but if you looked hard you could travel anywhere across the broad three-dimensional map, picking out the individual planets, the individual countries, even the people. All those humans, milling around; getting on with their lives without a care in the worlds.

One universe in particular was having some problems. It was smaller and more apathetic than the others. Like a brown sprout that gets shuffled surreptitiously to the side of a Christmas dinner plate. *I wonder 'oo's that is*, Mrs. Prune thought to herself.

'So...Where's God?' she asked, not one to let go of an idea once it had planted itself in her head. She'd planned on having a go at the bugger all her life and it seemed a pity that she wasn't going to get the chance.

'I've no idea,' replied the guardian. 'I'm not a religious man myself. Have you tried the state of nirvana?'

'Where's that? America?'

'It's my job,' he went on heedlessly. 'To sort people out. You know; help them decide where to go.'

'What do you mean '*Where to go*'?' Jannice was growing ever more intrigued.

'There are two forms of life.' The guardian erected two of his fingers and pointed knowledgeably at the first of them. 'One's physical.' He pointed at the other. 'One's spiritual. The consciousness. The Spirit? The Soul?'

Jannice was staring at the tanned walnut of his head beneath its suffocating beard; her expression somewhat blank. She'd understood what he'd said, it was just rather hard to tell the difference without any distinguishing features to gauge for reactions.

"I think therefore I am', and all that rot.' He girned a smile surrounded by hair.

'And the two things are separate?' Jannice asked the question with an amount of uncertainty weighing down her voice.

'Sort of...The 'Spiritual Being' needs the 'The Physical Body' to survive. It sort of anchors itself automatically. Drifting through universes to find a body to call its home.'

'What about the other way round? I mean...' Jannice struggled momentarily before regaining her mental footing. 'The physical body? Does that not work without a soul inside?'

'Goodness, of course it does, young lady. At least, it does...but not properly. There are thousands of people wandering about out there without any souls. Automatons if you like, waiting for a life-force to plug them in. Or into them.'

'How do you know the difference?'

'Oh, it's obvious. Just watch them. They're the ones that play rap music on their car stereos on hot summer afternoons, when the last thing you want to add to the stifling heat is something fast that clogs up the brain. Those that work from nine 'til five for all of their lives and never question why they do it or if there's any more to life than that. People who think that Michael Borrymore is entertaining. You've got to admit, that's a sad excuse for a life.'

'So, God's not 'ere then?' said Mrs. Prune.

The guardian wearily relented, shaking his head so that his beard swung. 'Not unless he's hiding from us.' The ancient Hebrew pulled down the corner of a frown across his right eye, in a sarcastic manner. 'Playing 'Peek-a-boo."

'Double bugger!!'

Jannice, whose concentration was now transfixed on solving the Meaning of Life, caught the old man's attention again. Her mental agility struggled further to establish a conclusion concerning all things philosophical.

'So, how come the spiritual '*Us*" She used the term carefully, pondering the implications of such an ambiguous phrase. 'How come '*We*' actually exist in the first place?'

'Ah...Now that *is* the Mystery Of Life.' The guardian's tone had suddenly acquired a sense of drama. He wagged a crooked, ink-stained finger knowingly, beckoning Jannice into his private confidence.

'Bugger, damn an' bugger.' said a petulant voice from somewhere behind. 'W'at a bloody waste o' time!'

Speaking that little louder in an attempt to drown out the profanities, the venerable rabbi continued.

'Imagine what it would be like if you didn't exist.' He

stooped down to what he considered must have been a rough approximation of Jannice's ear hole. Then grinned.

'I'm afraid I can't...' muttered Jannice, disappointed by her honest answer.

'Exactly. That's because we exist simply because we cannot do otherwise.'

Jannice thought about that. It was impossible for her not to exist. All she'd ever known was being alive. Therefore it logically followed that if she didn't exist she wouldn't even have been asking the question. Ipso facto, she existed, therefore she had to exist and that was that.

'Got any sandwiches?' said Mrs. Prune, not one to be left out on a conversation.

'My job,' said the host, who was now growing selectively deaf in one ear, 'is to help you choose what body you want from here on end. Give you a push in the general direction and hope for the best.'

"Ow d' y' get a job like that then?' Mrs. Prune muscled in. There was a certain amount of scepticism in her voice, as if she was making a statement rather than asking.

'It's voluntary work actually.' The old man leaned into his staff with resolution, reluctant to talk with Mrs. Prune on that particular subject. Not that you could blame him. Mrs. Prune had to admit that the thought of it being 'Unpaid' and 'Unskilled' did tend to put the mockers on the fancy voice with the echoes a bit.

'Voluntary? Why d' y' do it, then?'

'Well...' She'd caught his attention now. There's nothing better for catching people's attention when they don't want to talk to you, than getting other people to start talking about themselves. 'The hours are all right. And you get your own uniform...'

Pulling out the toga with his clawed hand, an expression of disdain visibly traced itself across his jaded features. 'Such as it is.'

It wasn't exactly the height of fashion. Traditional perhaps. But not exactly practical for wearing in a place that was chock-full of high-rise breezes.

'And you get to meet people!' the distinguished scribe added, with perhaps some reserve.

'Get a lot of 'em round 'ere, then?'

'One or two. Some rum buggers amongst them. We had one a few years back. What was his name now?'

The guardian brought a contemplative finger to his lips, studying his memories intently.

'Adolf Hitler,' he said at length, recalling something that seemed important now. 'You mentioned him before.'

He drew in a deep breath, what was visible of his mouth beneath the carpet of white hair puckered up like a tiny volcano.

'Not the sort to have as a neighbour that one. Tried to bite Danny on the head.'

'Who's Danny?' asked Jannice.

'Danny. Oh, he's the tea boy. Helps out with odd jobs around the place.'

Mrs. Prune and Jannice both nodded at each other. That sort of Danny.

'What 'appened to 'im?' Mrs. Prune ventured further. ''Itler I mean.'

'Don't know exactly. He did a runner with the tea coffers shortly after he'd arrived. I had meant to lock him up somewhere safe. Out of harm's way. Still you can't win them all. I can't be sure about this...' His voice trailed off into speculation. 'But I think he ended up as a member of the Conservative party. On Earth, you know?'

The rumpled Jew shook the reverie from his decrepit balding head and fixed a reverential focal point upon the map that breathed before them. The time for conversation was over.

'Now then ladies? What do you fancy?'

'I want t' go 'ome.' Mrs. Prune's wraith spoke out with grim determination.

'Ah...' The dwarfish figure of the old man set; his voice faltering slightly. 'That's a little bit impractical.' And he pointed at the grey smudge that was now even smaller and more insignificant than before. 'There's not much left going for that particular universe.'

That much was true. It was such a small universe by now that it resembled nothing more than a grubby fleck.

The rabbi felt that Mrs. Prune was giving him a dirty look, though he couldn't be sure. It wasn't as though it was his fault. After all, he had no say in the '*Great Design*' of things. Nonetheless, he found himself melting beneath her invisible but highly reprimanding gaze, and proffered an almost apathetic and diminutive, 'Sorry..'

'Then I'll just wait 'ere an' see w'at 'appens. Thank you!'

At which statement, the guardian suddenly grew flustered. The prospect of having Mrs. Prune hanging around his comfortable workshop for the rest of eternity was not very favourable. She looked like the sort that'd have away with all the tea bags. And never brew up for herself. And make sure that the stock cupboard was always kept clean and tidy. And no smoking. Definitely no smoking. No. She'd have to go, somehow.

'It's down to about half a square mile,' he pointed out, an oscillation appearing uncontrollably along the length of his voice. 'And closing fast. Not much that anyone can do to save it, I'm afraid.'

And he presented her with a crooked brown smile that represented an end to the matter hopefully once and for all. It had about as much effect on Mrs. Prune as discovering that the test cricket had been cancelled due to rain. In other words, bugger all.

'I'll still wait,' Mrs. Prune established. 'I 'ave ev'ry confidence in Our Jess.'

Somehow the purple smear managed to victoriously fold its arms and assume a haughty appearance. Clever if you could do it. But then Mrs. Prune had a knack for the 'Clever' and the 'Smart.' Confused by such a display of down-right stubbornness the guardian turned his attention back to the more compliant Jannice. Slightly dubious but ever optimistic, he cast an open palm across the map.

Mrs. Prune shuddered briefly as she felt a ghostly timid hand grab onto hers. She squeezed it gently in as reassuring a manner as was inhumanly possible.

'No...Thank you all the same,' said Jannice politely. 'But, I think I'll stay with Mrs. Prune.'

Chapter Twenty Three

Darkness Falls.

3:55 p.m. December 6th, 1998 The still smouldering ruins of 114 Applegate. The snow has now cleared, but the soot and the grime remain.

Jess Hobson rummaged ardently beneath the charcoaled remains of his trusty old bed. A bed that now resembled a construction of burnt and blackened match stalks, all bent and twisted upwards at peculiar angles.

Following the somewhat dramatic end of the wicker man, not to mention Jannice, Jess had gathered his shattered thoughts together in one place. Having stuffed them higgardly piggardly back into his aching head, he had set off rather determinedly in the first direction that had actually suggested itself—which was fortuitously the opposite direction to the great wall of darkness.

Somehow Jess had managed to work his tracks across the town. Anybody blocking his path had received an unfriendly elbow in the mouth or a gentle shove to one side. Greyminster was rapidly becoming the shape of a kidney dish and with equal rapidity it was diminishing in stature.

The darkness moved on, gathering momentum with every lamp-post it devoured. It had nibbled at the gates of the Sword Street Municipal Park and licked the statues of Greyminster's famous as if they were lollipops made out of stone. But most peculiarly, it had followed the exact same sweeping curve that Jess had taken on his struggle to sprint right across the town. That was suspicious.

Charging around the bustling chasm was a badly sketched ghost train, as if somebody had drawn the engine in with a very soft pencil and then couldn't be bothered to finish the job off properly.

There was a grunt and a snort and a collection of assorted ancient sports socks were hurled from their secret lair beneath Jess' bed. Moments later, several offensive articles stuck with an unappetizing squelch, to the piles of bricks where the walls of the building had once proudly stood. Jess had definitely had better days.

Several long forgotten boxer shorts were unearthed and thrown unceremoniously onto public display. Sad rigid squares of material with legs that had survived the inferno by evolving into some sort of flame retardant monsters.

It was at the great Bogg Street Terminus, a huge, Victorian cylinder of latticed windows and pigeon droppings, that the most bixarre sight had caught his attention. Probably the most stupidly bizarre image that his eyes had borne witness to throughout the entire day.

Charging around the bustling chasm was a badly sketched ghost train, as if somebody had drawn the engine in with a very soft pencil and then couldn't be bothered to finish the job off properly. Child-sized in proportions, the ridiculous machine was controlled by an extremely ugly phantom. With a shock of purple hair and eyeballs that resembled fried eggs, the damned abomination clung to the funnel with its toes. The whole cacophony hurtled round in erratic circles, crashing into people as though they were nothing more than straw bales at a demolition derby.

It was at that moment that Jess decided that he'd just about had enough of all this nonsense. After wrenching off the cast iron shutters that stopped the public from invading the platforms, he had settled down upon the painted lines that ran along the platform's edge. He allowed his legs to dangle precipitously over the tracks, his head in his hands whilst he indulged himself in a good delve into personal thoughts.

It wasn't the ghosts or the goblins that were bothering him now—far from it. Most of the goblins that were skulking around the platform were eyeing him suspiciously and keeping a discreet distance.

No...he could handle himself against that particular variety of terror. All that he needed were his sturdy boots and a strong, steadfast stomach. But the ever encroaching darkness; now that was the altogether more undeniable problem. There was nothing that Jess could recall from Benjamin's Nursery book on ghosties and ghoulies, that actually dealt with the whole universe disappearing in a sickening fizzle.

The darkness was in some way connected to all the other problems; he'd figured that much out. After that it grew a trifle vague. It had something to do with the column of light—the rip in reality as Benjamin had called it. And Thomas Hobson and possibly Samuel Foster and definitely the end of the world.

Suddenly Jess felt the urge to do something positive— he didn't know what, but the tiniest seed of a thought began to germinate.

He wanted his box. The famous box of personal belongings that could be currently found beneath the remnants of his bed.

There wasn't much that could be said for what Jess had secretly interred within it. Just a few odds and ends that he'd collected together, representative of his personal history. Nonetheless, Jess wanted to find his box now. If he was going to die then he wanted something that would remind people of who he was. Even if he was only a sad, lonely middle-aged cynic with no ambition in life and even if there wouldn't be a world left to remind.

The thought grew into determination, then obsession.

Then suddenly, that was all that seemed to matter any more. Somehow it seemed important. That was what had driven Jess home. Full of purpose and intention.

So there he was, buried beneath the blackened berth in a frantic search for the personal possessions that he'd collected together over the decades into his cardboard receptacle.

At length Jess emerged, an ankle sock draped across the top of his stubbled head and a grey, mottled box in one hand. A satisfied grin ran along a stolid line across his sweating features. Suddenly, a scrabbling noise across the pyramid of bricks startled Jess into vigilance.

'*Here we go again.*' He turned, an expression of stoic acceptance engraved across his lumbersome face. He stared straight into the eyes of Joseph Wambach. Not the Joseph Wambach that he remembered from the photographs he'd been given on that fateful night back in November, but a sharper, more demonic child, with pointed fangs that were glistening with bubbled saliva and verdant slime.

Behind the child, number 113 was slowly vanishing. The darkness had arrived, devouring the ground with what appeared to be an unstoppable force.

The infant spoke. A dry, scratchy rasp of a sound that resembled the snapping fronds on a long since dead bush.

'The *Master* would like to see you now...'

Ignoring the mysterious invitation, Jess narrowed his eyes. With his package of possessions tucked securely beneath his right arm, he approached the diminutive imp in as threatening and aggressive a manner as was possible.

'Y're the cause of all this, aren't y'?'

'What?'

A genuine expression of surprise crossed the child's aspect. For the briefest of moments Joseph almost looked human again. An innocent toddler on the edge of having his bottom paddled severely.

'It all started the night y' first disappeared!'

Jess closed the gap. His left hand clenched into a tight fist, the knuckles turning white and standing up to attention.

'The Master would like to see you...' the demonic juvenile reiterated.

'W'at Master?' he asked.

'*THE* Master.'

Yes, the little bastard was obviously asking for a smack in the gob. However, Jess reluctantly held down his patience. If he could only get some sort of answer to his enquiries before he booted the annoying scab into the darkness.

"Oo is the Master?' Jess carefully pronounced each individual word, alternating them with short pauses so that the sentence had an edge to it.

'*THE* Master.'

Jess further tightened his fist, so that his knuckles now cracked like old knots. He breathed out through his nostrils. This produced the sort of noise that a tyre would make should you remove a six inch nail embedded in its tread.

'The *creator* and *destroyer* of the *universe...*'

That wasn't good enough. Jess gritted his teeth, ready to strike. Demons evidently aren't as dumb as most people would have themselves believe. At least this one had the good sense to recognise danger when it was so patently imminent.

'Mr. Hobson...' The submission was hissed in a voice as dry as flames.

The muscles around Jess' knuckles relaxed slightly as he thought about the revelation.

'*Thomas 'Obson*? Creator o' the bloody universe? So is it that bastard then 'oo's be'ind all this?'

Jess might have been about as quick witted as a bull that thought its holiday destination was a place called '*Be Castrated*,' but with a little mental effort he always got there in the end.

'Where is the '*Great Master*' then?' Jess almost spat the words from his mouth as if they tasted of vomit.

'At the source of all *reality*.'

The incubus studied Jess' features for a moment, before realising that it was receiving the sort of blank stare in return that said a great deal more than a thousand words might.

'Number 32, Old Bridge Lane,' Joseph ended rather meekly.

'Thanks!' Jess' boot collided abruptly with the creature's sheepish grin. A grin that instantaneously vanished into a collapsed hole of broken flesh. With a scream of disappointment the diminutive devil spun off the bricks, its nappy coming embarrassingly undone in the process. It was gorged by the massive wall of darkness beyond and there was a fizzle as the demonic infant crumbled to dust and disappeared.

'I'll find me own way, ta very much,' Jess added. Before

the darkness managed to grab hold and swallow him up as well, he turned and headed off towards the centre of the town.

What was left of Greyminster screamed and it writhed and it thronged with frightened pedestrians.

Attention from the knights of the round table had now turned from the huge glass paperweight and concentrated itself instead upon an extraordinary light-bulb covered figure that was squirming about in the gutter.

'Hold his head,' bellowed Arthur, 'and I'll see if I can cut him free.'

He attacked the crackling figure with a great amount of enthusiasm.

'How the Hell did he get entangled in that lot, anyhow?' asked Sir Bedevere of Sir Percival.

'Well,' Percival began, casting a glance at the metallic hook that was protruding from the corner of number thirty-nine. It was a lethal looking ornament, situated about half way up the side of the first floor. 'He was attempting to climb on the top of that damn glass thing. Said he'd got an idea from some acrobat he'd seen once at Camelot. Rolling about on some damn ball or other.'

'Sounds nasty...' Bedevere nodded, an amount of knowledgeable sympathy in the incline of his head. Glancing back at Sir Gawain, enmeshed by the stranglehold of Christmas lights, he continued. 'And he got caught up in this lot when he leapt from the window ledge, right?'

'Bloody awkward thing that.' Percival leaned upon his misshapen walking stick, prodding his upper molars back onto the gum with a slippery tongue. 'No idea what sort of creature it is. But once it's got a lock on you, it doesn't bloody let up.'

At which point Jess' silhouette appeared at the farthest end of the shrinking avenue. An outline, sprinting to all intents and purposes, with the dispatch of an Olympic runner. So strenuous was this work-out that his knees were almost touching his chin, as they rose with every giant leap, forcing his huge frame forwards. Behind Jess the massive barrier of the darkness was evidently in close pursuit. He skidded to a halt when the Green Knight blocked his path. A few speckles of blood mixed with dust sprayed up from his boots, dappling the Green Knight's armour.

'Thou shalt *not* enter!'

'W'at?' That one solitary word was the last that his aching lungs could contain. Without a single breath left in his body Jess doubled up, gasping and wheezing, his hands gripping tightly round his knee-caps.

'All who wish to enter must first battle with the *Green Knight.*'

Jess took in another difficult breath, feeling his chest tighten as though somebody had squeezed it into a tiny elastic band.

Vicar's Underpants!

'Look mate—the worlds' about to end an'..'

'*None* shall pass!'

Behind him Jess could faintly hear Martha Sonneman's voice. It fluttered rather harshly from the open window at number thirty-two. It was followed by a sound that bore a resemblance to the sort of laser gun often used in tacky science fiction programmes. Then a screech and a smell of burning, then finally an undignified, yet diffident silence.

Jess inhaled through his nose, tilting up his features. The gargantuan warrior was standing guard with stubborn pointlessness. He wasn't exactly sure why the knight felt it so important to do this, but it was probably connected with the fact that Mrs. Prune had gone inside already and no-one had actually come back out again.

The Green Knight was totally armoured in green shiny metal. Not even Jess' hobnailed boots would have made any more than a slight dent in that lot. Unlike the colossal onyx sword that the knight nonchalantly rested upon. One simple swing from that would completely heave Jess in half. He'd need a bloody tin opener before he stood any chance at all.

Then he saw the one tiny flaw in the guardian's stubborn plan. Just one small patch of fabric that, no matter how tightly filled, was undoubtedly penetrable.

Fortunately Jess wasn't terribly chivalrous, and whereas knights had a tendency towards fair play and the British way of going about things, he didn't. The phrase 'It's Just Not Cricket' in Jess' vocabulary simply translated into 'Well, It's Probably Football Then.'

Seconds later the Green Knight doubled-up in surprise, his eyes watering. With the speed of a jaguar, Jess muscled him aside, darting beneath the tape, his boots scrabbling defiantly across the cobbles. Then he was gone.

Behind him the darkness confidently ate into the tremendous ball. Arthur and his knights staunchly attended to the last, each one being picked off individually and swallowed whole.

'*Cry Havoc!*' Arthur shouted bravely against the unstoppable tide. '*And let slip...ah...no...*'

He took a step backwards, rocked on the bubbled dome and had another attempt.

'*My Horse, my horse. England is a horse.*' Gazing down at his dimly shining boots, Arthur frowned.

'No, no. That wasn't it.' He gazed back up into the face of death and added, '*Bollocks.*'

Then there was nothing. Nothing apart from number thirty-two, Old Bridge Lane, with its column of light growing out of the roof. Nothing apart from the sounds of Jess' boots scrabbling through the front door, before retreating into the building's nucleus.

Chapter Twenty Four

A Confrontation At The World's End.

4:21 p.m, December 6th, 1998-not that it matters. In about seven minutes time there'll be no-one left to bother about such things. No universe remaining for such matters to be appropriate in and with nobody about to measure them, there'll be no more hours, no more years—no more time.

Just the cold isolation of death and a fathomless emptiness where the universe once stood. With nobody there to remember it, it won't even be a memory.

Just a handful of minutes to go, all piled up against one another as if backing away from the very edge of time itself. Where the Hell is Jess?

Take one last look at the cellar of number thirty-two. This is where the adventure ends. It's already taken a bite from one corner of the ceiling, creating an eruption of terrified spiders that are now seeking sanctuary amongst the boxes of junk down below. It continues to feast steadily; chewing up the beams across the roof and crackling down the plaster work that hangs off the bricks in great broken folds.

From India, an upturned crate that once carried dried tea-leaves across many a storm tossed ocean now serves as a seat to a twisted, hump-backed figure—a figure dressed in Victorian garb with anachronistic denims and a pair of time-worn sneakers rotting upon his feet. He leans heavily upon his contorted stick, eyes pulsing red through the band of shadow that rings his forehead. A shadow that is cast from the brim of his hat. His teeth appear to be constructed from the finest amber and his skin appears to be sewn together from scraps of mouldering canvas.

At last there comes the thundering of heavy boots upon a gritty floor. The crash of the cellar door flying open as if whoever was approaching had ignored its presence entirely. Jess' body advances, bounding down the cellar steps, taking several precipitous stairs at a time. His face is flushed. His head shines red as if it's been sunburnt, his Velcro hair resembling miniature grey saplings growing up from a sandstone rock. He hits the floor beyond the final step and hears the crackle of the emptiness against the column's mighty roar.

Then Jess turns to the ancient hobgoblin, who cackles the laugh of an imbecile whilst stomping his stick upon the ground. He points a meaty finger accusingly at the grotesque, shrivelled head.

'What the f...? Right...W'at's goin' on? 'Ow do I stop this, y' shitty old weasel?' Jess demanded

'You don't!'

Old man Hobson clutched his knees, rocking backwards and forwards; a clucking noise in his throat and a mischievous glint in his evil diminished eyes.

'Oh yes y' do!' Jess grabbed him tenaciously around the trachea with one muscular hand, feeling his bitten-down nails pinching strenuously into the rough flesh beneath. 'Y're not tellin' me that y'd start the end of the world an' allow y'self t' get killed along with it! Not after God knows 'ow many centuries o' trying t' get back!'

Despite his windpipe being partially crushed, Thomas Hobson still managed a laugh. A laugh full of hollow irony that bit deep into Jess' nerve endings. The edge of the darkness took another noiseless step, progressing languidly upon the couple from every direction.

'Jess...My boy.'

Jess felt a bony hand attach itself to his shoulder. A weird little squeak escaped from Old Man Hobson's oesophagus as Jess tightened his grip substantially. From that point on the aging reptile sounded as if he was puking his words up with some difficulty.

'Jess?'

A pause to reconsider the next approach.

'Or should I say...Father...?' Thomas tried to cock his head on one side but found it pushed back upright with a sudden and almost deadly wrench. 'I'm not responsible for all of this.' His tone sounded almost sincere.

But Jess had grown older. Now he knew that every good lie was built on a foundation of truth. He closed his fingers another fraction as the darkness followed his every movement.

'Just remember that one little squeeze might be enough t' snap y' spinal cord!'

He narrowed his eyes as Thomas felt another slight increase of pressure. It was accompanied by what might have been a trickle of blood struggling upwards from his larynx.

'If you're not responsible...' Jess chose the words carefully, making sure that there was no room for misunderstanding. 'Then, 'oo the 'Ell is?'

Thomas attempted to clear his throat, but his Adam's apple scraped on the tightening grip. He tried to swallow, but there was nowhere for the saliva to go. So instead he watched the walls as the darkness pruned them into weird and spectacular shapes.

'Why? *You* are, my dear boy...' he said with a grin.

Jess had already suffered several nasty shocks to his system that day. In fact, it was a wonder that his system hadn't entirely collapsed beneath the full onslaught. But nothing had prepared him for that snippet of information. It had opened up a whole new Pandora's box of devastating notions.

It was of course possible that Hobson was lying. That thought had occurred to Jess, but he decided to discard it. If Hobson wasn't being honest then it was probably the most bloody pointless tale that he could actually think of. And even then it would be pointless of Jess, with such a small amount of time left, to bother not believing it. The simple truth was he had no choice.

There was a gurgle and Jess stared down. He released his hand, realising that if Thomas Hobson was to have his windpipe crushed, entertaining as the concept might have been, then Jess wouldn't get the chance to understand what had caused all of this. Not before the world reached its closure anyhow. Clutching the box of possessions tightly beneath his arm, Jess took a step backwards, nodding at his wrinkled son.

'I want to *understand!*'

'There's not enough *time!*' Thomas Hobson rubbed the scrag of creased skin around his scrawny neck. He coughed what appeared to be a slither of tissue into the air before him. 'It'd take too long to explain it to a dullard like yourself.'

'Try me...' Jess collected his nerves, watching another corner of the ceiling start to buckle.

'There's no point, Jess. There's not enough time for explanations.'

'MAKE TIME!!' shouted Jess, overpowered by frustration and fatigue. 'That's what you do isn't it? *Make Time!?*'

He brought his purple face up against the old man's. Hobson attempted to flinch backwards, feeling his throat tearing beneath Jess' considerable purchase.

'You don't make time.' Thomas shook his head thoughtfully, bringing up a little more phlegm. 'You just break into it...What you make is the space, to let the time roam free.'

"Ow?'

'How? What do you mean 'how?' You add another dimension. Like turning an architect's two- dimensional drawings into a real building. Add another dimension and let it all hang out.'

He obviously found that remark highly amusing. A sort of private witticism that appealed to his sordid sense of humour, and *his* sordid sense of humour alone. He squeezed out a fragment of a laugh from his gagging mouth.

Jess looked around at the blackening walls. Almost all gone and still no bloody closer to an answer. Thoughts buzzed around his head, taunting him like a batch of aphids. He threw one in Hobson's direction to see what would happen.

'So, you an' Samuel Foster made a time machine?'

'No...No!' Old man Hobson sounded cross at that suggestion. He licked his dry lips, studying his own thoughts with great intensity. 'I made the bloody thing. I put it together. They were my scientific principles, my equations. They were even my bloody carved mice for Christ's sake!'

Carved Mice, thought Jess, his mind going off at a tangent. *What the Hell was this bloke on? No wonder the world was under threat.*

'That bloody fool, Samuel bloody Foster, the pillock! He just came along for the ride.' Thomas lifted an anorexic finger, stabbing the space before his nose, as if Foster himself had been occupying it. 'He resented what I'd done. He resented everything I did. Bloody idiot.'

Jess thought about that scrupulously, and as he did so tiny pieces seemed to join together inside his head. After barely a moment's pause, he presented the following assumption, more to himself than the choking cadaver in his clench.

'An' most of all 'ee resented gettin' stuck in the past!? 'Ee didn't go along for the ride. *You* made 'im go! An' 'ee resented that.'

That made sense; Jess knew it made sense and the expression across Thomas Hobson's haggard features did nothing but confirm it.

'Y' took 'im away from 'is 'ome, an' 'is family, an' the bloody thing broke down, an' y' couldn't get back!'

Thomas Hobson scowled, anger written across his countenance. 'Yes...so that filthy bastard went and killed me! But I came back to finish him off! I returned to put an end to the bugger's bloodline...no matter what the cost!'

"Ee killed y' because...because...' Jess' mind was now charging. The darkness descended further with every passing second. He could sense it drawing across him like death. That set off his adrenal glands, forcing his mind into fourth gear. It was starting to make sense and he was running out of time. Racing neck and neck with the end of the universe itself. "Ee killed y' because...w'en 'ee'd finally sorted out 'is new life, new family, new children, y' screwed it all up agen, by gettin' that promotion. The last great bastard. Up until the end.'

Jess concluded this magnificent exposé with a thump applied to Hobson's resonant skull.

'He killed me 'cos he was a great bastard, with no bloody standards. But he never understood what I'd done; he never understood the full implications of my work.'

Hobson paused, drawing in as much of a breath as Jess would allow.

'I couldn't die, y' see. Not here, not where we'd ended up. So I was willing to destroy everything to sort him out and I mean bloody *everything!*' The old man was screaming, now enwrapped in his own revenge once more.

'The end of the *World*.' Jess spoke in a hushed and cogitative tone. 'It was you comin' back that brought about the end of time—the end of *everything*.' He paused to study the hideous old gargoyle who was by now sitting apathetically on the edge of the upturned tea-chest. 'W'at did y' do wrong?'

'Nothing...' Hobson laughed again, only instead of echoing off the walls this time it fell down dead in the fashion of a partridge being shot. There were no longer any walls for the sound to bounce off; the darkness sluggishly consuming the cellar floor.

'Y' did somethin' wrong...' Jess was talking half to himself. 'Somethin' stupid. Somethin' y' missed. Somethin' so terrible that it brought an end to absolutely everythin'.'

'It was your fault, Jess!' Hobson dropped his voice to a croak. He jabbed a finger at Jess' nose.

'Why was it MY FAULT?!' Jess shouted, feeling the sinews of his neck strain. 'Tell me!!' His mind started to wander. He wanted answers before everything was swallowed into oblivion and there was no time left to ask any more. 'W'at about the glass balls? W'at about the goblins? An' the plane crash? What about...' He gritted his teeth, staring maniacally in front of himself. 'Everythin' y' OLD FART?! W'at about EVERYTHIN'?!'

'Figure it out for yourself, Jess.' The twisted lunatic seemed resigned, almost pleased that it was ending. 'You wouldn't let me take possession of your head before. Now you find the answer.'

'Take possession?' Jess randomly searched his recollection of events from the past few days. All those times when he'd said and done things against his better nature. Things he'd regretted. Opinions he'd never had. 'That was YOU?! You were inside me 'ead? Y' scabby old bastard!'

There was that laugh again. It stopped without warning as Jess tore the debilitated skeleton from the tea- chest by inserting a finger up his nostril. Yanking it hard, he threw the frail body onto the floor. There was a crunch as his boot came down heavily upon Hobson's neck.

'Go ahead, destroy me!' The embittered veteran stared upwards without concern, the red glow in his eyes growing dimmer all the time. 'Go ahead. It won't alter a damned thing. It's over Jess and there's nowt you can do to stop it! The world *has* to end this way.'

'I can't kill you; no, I *won't* kill you. We might be related but genetics don't account f'r everythin'.' Jess gently moved his boot up and down, figuring out his next move with some caution. 'But I can make it so uncomfortable that y' will beg me f' death t' come quickly.' That had sounded dramatic. Now to add a little emphasis to the words with some physical action. The heel of his boot ground into a ring of gristle and old Hobson choked, a furrowed grey tongue flapping unrestrainedly from his puckered lips.

'Now! W'at went wrong?' Jess asked the question with infinite patience, twisting his heel that bit more as Thomas tried to move it from his neck with his wretched hands. "Urry up. 'Cos Y' might find it 'ard t' speak with a mouth full o' blood.'

It wasn't the words, or even the image, that made the old man stop struggling. It was the heavy honest threat that pervaded Jess' voice. He suspended his conflict, made a decision and started to confess.

'That paperweight in your box...' A crooked, skinny finger pointed at the tied up parcel. 'That's where the end came from.'

'W'at?' The light switches on the skirting board disappeared from view with faintest of crackles.

'You're an anomaly, Jess. Just like me. We're both bloody paradoxes. For one to exist we both need the other.'

'So? D' y' want a bloody medal?'

'You still haven't figured it out, have you?' Hobson fought against the obstructing foot. He failed to lift it a single inch. 'This isn't *reality* at all, you arse. The whole bloody thing is just fiction!'

Sometimes some topics are difficult to comprehend all at once. It takes time to digest them, sort them out in your head. So it'll come as no surprise to learn that Jess found it difficult to approach that last statement from no matter which angle he regarded it.

'W'at the 'Ell are y' talkin' about?' He wasn't sure whether another turn of his boot would snap the old bastard's neck or not. So he left it and hoped for the best. Behind him a suitcase went fizzle and vanished.

'This world, this universe—it isn't real. It never was!'

Hobson choked, attempting to wriggle his gullet out of the vice, but the boot came down that little harder, bringing a pass to the futile struggle. Jess might have been many things, but most of all he was incredibly strong— especially from the ankle down.

Reluctantly Hobson carried on with the thread of his jumbled explanation. 'We're all anomalies. You created me, I created your grandfather. There's no ancestry further back than me and no descendants further on. I created *all* of this.'

His little hands made a sweeping gesture of what was left of the darkening room. If there had been more, he would have tried to encompass that as well. 'I unleashed time from its boundaries by creating this fantasy. Everything you've ever known was the gate that caged time in, until I opened it. This, Jess, is the *fifth* dimension.'

'This isn't real?'

'No. None of it ever was.'

'It's all an invented extra dimension?'

'Christ...It's a good job I was the quantum mechanic and not you.'

Another crunch brought an abrupt halt to Hobson's condescension.

'When you unrestrain time,' he continued, feeling the back of his neck grinding down against the stone floor. 'It expands. Like turning a circle into a sphere.'

'I don't understand,' admitted Jess with reluctant honesty.

'But it's simple...'

'No it isn't!'

'What's the problem? I've explained the bloody thing for God's sakes!'

'No y' 'aven't.' Jess wanted to kill him. He wanted to crush his jugular into a flattened tube, thus destroying the creature that had annihilated all of his friends.

'If..' He struggled to form the words. 'W'at...' Get them in the correct order, Jess Hobson. Breathe deeply in and start again. "Ow can y' come from the future, if the future doesn't actually exist?'

Thomas Hobson returned Jess' questioning stare as if the answer to his query was so glaringly obvious that nobody in their right mind should have to ask it in the first instance.

'Simple temporal mechanics,' he ventured. 'Why should the past affect the future if its already happened?'

'Because it should!' There was the minutest pause before Jess added, somewhat noncommittally, 'Shouldn't it?'

'If you move a pepper pot from a table does it upset the cutlery?' Jess frowned and shook his head. 'If you drew a straight line and then rubbed out one end, would it alter the other?'

If he'd have had the time then Jess would have taken this logic to greater lengths. But the disappearance of a hat-stand acted as a reminder that time was not something he had much of.

'So, w'at about the goblins an' the ghosties an' the...' Jess confronted the unhappy memory as if a bitter taste had just placed itself upon his tongue. 'That bastard chicken inside the wicker man?'

'All fiction,' squealed Thomas. 'All inventions from the realm of reality. All thoughts from the sad and erroneous imaginations of men and women...'

'Right...So, 'ow come they weren't all around 'ere before? I mean, why did it all start at once an' then suddenly decide that it could never actually stop?'

'Because Samuel *bloody* Foster brought that bloody paperweight through with him. He bloody brought reality into a world where reality doesn't exist. It was like anti-matter meeting matter. Bloody stupid thing to do!'

'But there were loads of them! Not one—bloody 'undreds o' the buggers.'

'Bollockin' Hell! It's like trying teach elocution to a Clanger!' There was a thud as Thomas' frail old head received a boot beneath the chin and a trickle of fresh blood sprang from his nostrils. 'Circle to sphere!' he screamed with a hasty voice. 'Expansion. The creation of millions of choices. Understand?'

'No, I bloody *don't* understand.' Jess thought profoundly about everything he'd been told. So many things still weren't adding up. 'What about the chicken?' he said again, not one to let a subject drop.

'It was an explosion; anti-reality. Passive truth meets excited fiction and '*Caboom!*"

Several bubbles of spit left Hobson's rank mouth with the vibrant demonstration. Momentarily Jess thought that he'd understood. So, that was why Charles Dickens and Beethoven and Cervantes had all been grotesques? Because they had just been fictionalised representations of themselves.

This was unreal—all of it. Mrs. Prune and Benjamin, Jannice, even Jess himself.

There was a faint sizzling noise as the darkness partially removed the brim from Hobson's hat. The wrinkled spirit flinched away in desperation. But the strong boot held him back.

'But Samuel Foster. An' you? You come from reality. 'Ow come y' didn't create all this chaos w'en y' first arrived back in eighteen ninety-odd?'

'But I don't come from reality, Jess. I come from you and you're *not real*. It's all very recursive. It just goes round and round in circles like a snake trying to eat its own head by starting on the tail. Every time it does a loop it gets more and more twisted and more and more bent. Its impossible Jess; it's a fiction, an anomaly...That's how it all started...that's how it all ends!'

Although he wasn't sure that he fully comprehended, Jess was beginning to form the impression that any last minute attempt to save the world was out of the question. But one or two queries still required some clarification. He looked down at the prostrate old fool and changed the track that his thoughts were hurtling along.

'It started with the child,' he said. 'Why did y' take the Wambach child?'

'Let me go and I'll tell you.' Thomas Hobson wheezed optimistically, his voice not much more than a chirrup of insanity.

'If y' don't tell me, I'll snap y' neck like a twig,' Jess reiterated calmly.

Thomas Hobson relented in disappointment, managing to add a tiny amount of shrug to his shoulders. 'I just wanted to attract your attention.'

'W'at?' Of all the things that had been said, this particular admission puzzled Jess most of all. 'Attract me attention. W'at for?'

'Because I knew that Samuel Foster would come,' came the final divulgence. 'If I could come back, then so could he.'

'So that's it, is it?' said Jess yieldingly. 'The whole soddin' universe destroyed f' the sake of bloody revenge.'

'Hmm?' Hobson shrugged again. 'If you like.'

Then the senile abnormality started singing in an asphyxiated infantile voice. A voice filled with mockery at the hopeless plight of all creation and vulgar disregard for the mass genocide of everything that Jess had ever known.

'Round and round the mulberry bush. All around the steeple.'

He wheezed and embarked on the next line with vigour.

'That's the way the universe goes. 'Pop' goes the weasel.'

'So w'at did Mrs. Prune know that warranted y' death threats?'

'Nothing.'

'Nothin'?'

'Not a bloody sausage, dear boy. I just couldn't stand

the old bag. All that goodness in one body. I always 'ated witches. They weren't scientific enough.' He tapped his forehead with a straying finger. 'No mathematical possibilities. No prospect of progress.'

'And that's why, is it?' Jess was almost dumbfounded by the sorry truth of it all. 'You're a bigot and a bastard. And if this is your idea of progress I'll take stagnation any time!'

Another chunk of floor gave way and Thomas felt the sleeve of his coat give. 'Whatever,' he said. 'It's all academic now, anyhow. Isn't it?'

His eyes glowed as brightly as a pair of red brake-lights in the night.

'So that's it, is it then? There's no bloody answer 'cos there's no bloody question? Y' can't stop the world from ending 'cos it never existed in the first place?'

Thomas cackled once more. 'That's right my boy.'

'Right.' Jess looked sadly at his collection of valuables all tied-up with a bit of old shoe lace and reached a decision.

'Then *fuck off* y' old twat!'

With one mighty lunge Jess brought his foot down in an arc. It had the power of an ice berg, connecting with pin-point precision on the outcrop of the ancient retard's ruddy chin. There was a sickening crunch as the body doubled backwards towards the brink of the dark. And with a scream that seemed to last forever, like a piano chord hanging in the mind long after all known vibrations could continue, the hunch-backed old demon toppled over.

It swallowed him whole. Nothing more than a morsel of food. Not enough for a belch to compliment the meal.

A sad pathetic rag-doll falling deep into a well of resentment. No-one would miss him...no-one would know.

Now Jess was all alone. On a piece of stone floor about one foot in width. Nowhere to run to... nowhere to hide. The darkness closed in.

He sat down on the edge of death with his knees tucked resolutely beneath his chin; his back against the roaring column of light, holding the box to his chest and sensing a fizzle round his boots.

He waited for the final end to arrive and whilst he waited he thought about it all, with a certain amount of confused regret.

All going round in circles. A whole universe that had never existed, but had existed briefly, somewhere.

It was just like life when you thought about it carefully. A tiny slither of light in an eternity of darkness must be so infinitely small by comparison that it could never have existed at all, but for one brief, twinkling moment in time.

Jess hadn't woken up that morning thinking *'This is where the fun stops'*. Nobody had told him that it was time to curl up and end his life. There would be no more tomorrows. No more time to make amends,

He regretted never having carved a future for himself. He regretted all the chances he had failed to take because he couldn't be bothered at the time. He regretted all those things that he'd said to so many people that he'd liked deep down inside. No more time for regrets.

'Somewhere,' he thought. *'At the core of all this madness, there's a reality. A reality that's closing its door on an experiment that went sadly wrong. So let me get this straight. Forty years into the future, Thomas Hobson built a time*

machine and to travel backwards in time he had to create another dimension. That dimension turned out to be us, but we didn't know, because to us it had always been reality. Samuel Foster took a glass orb with him into this fictional universe and the result was an explosion of highly unstable, imaginary creatures.'

But if that was the case, where the Hell did Samuel Foster get the real object from? Because both he and Thomas Hobson came from the fictional universe also. Somewhere there must be a real universe, with real things and real people. So why did he say that it was all my fault?

Jess thought about that and he thought, and he thought, and the answer struck him at the same time that the darkness chewed one corner from his box.

'Because *I'm real*,' he said. 'I'm the *only real thing*, in a whole invented universe. I *had* to be here to start the whole damn thing off.'

Then he turned. A brief spark of light, no matter how bright or how long, in an infinity of darkness would be so inconsequential as to never have existed at all.

But if infinity were to go around in a never ending loop, then a brief glimpse of brightness somewhere along its length would matter and make a difference. All the difference in the world.

A look of worry crossed his features. A puzzled mien of something half realised as the darkness stroked the end of his nose.

He got to his feet, breathed in deeply and walked into the electrical column of light, with the box tucked securely under his arm.

Chapter Twenty Five

One Last Perusal Of The Contents Of The Box.

There follows a transcript lifted almost verbatim from several sheets of note-paper that had been added to the box at some time in the future. It was written in Jess' scrawled, almost child-like handwriting, with an accompaniment of doodles and coffee mug rings. The whole contention covered several small blue pages that had been lined using a pencil and ruler.

June 6th. 1999.

There was some doubt concerning this date as it was blotchy and smeared. A large thumb print occupied the majority of its centre.

Over the past six months I...

This word was crossed out and the word 'We' inserted above it in red ink in a neater handwriting .

...have been trying to figure out what actually brought about the End Of The World. It is complecks...

This word had been altered to read 'Complex' by the same red pen.

...and I have found that it is to...

An 'O' was added here .

...much for my brain to handle. So I—We—have decided to write it all down and see if it might be

easier to understand like this...

I will attempt to set things out in a Chronological order. Please bare with me...us.

There was a drawing here that supposedly represented a penis and testicles, although the species was unknown. What relevance it had must remain a mystery.

Four years ago I—We—had a son—Thomas—In another forty years time, that boy—Thomas—will be a leading figure in the world of Cwontuum— Quantum —mechanics. In order to create time travel he must first create a fiff —Altered to Fifth — dimension. This dimension, he discovers, is a dimension of thought. It is not a real dimension in our sense of the word. It is a fiction. Once created, it will release time so that he can travel through it.

Most of this Paragraph was covered with black thumb prints. A smile had been added in red ink at the bottom. And a scrawled note in the margin, that had been later scribbled out, read, 'Jannice Applebotham Is A Interfering SL.'

Unfortunately he—Thomas—travels backwards in time and becomes trapped along with a colleague of his. Samuel... Samual...Samuel...

All of this was crossed out and a simple SAM squeezed in the space directly above it.

Unable to do anything about it, he marries and has a son. This boy grows up, has a child of his own, who then has a son also and that son turns out to be me.

I grow—GREW—up and have—Had—a son. The same son who goes backwards in time and gets trapped. And so it goes on. Round and round in circles. I believe this is called recursion.

There was a drawing in red ink of a snake eating its own tail. Added to it in black, presumably under some misunderstanding; were several drops of liquid that appeared to be squirting from its head.

> *Unfortunately, that makes me a bit of a paradox. My own son is also my own Great Grandfather. Therefore, I am an anomaly. An anomaly in reality is one thing. But an anomaly in a fiction is another.*

This was followed by several large red question marks, the final dot of which had been so vigorously added in black that the rest of the note paper contained puncture holes. These holes matched exactly with the hole in the boxes' lid.

> *According to mathematics if you add one negative to another negative you end up with a positive.(Coffee ring) The same happens with an anomaly within a paradox. It becomes a reality. Therefore I was the only real thing in an unreal world.*

> *Question?*

In tiny red lettering above the word 'Question' with an arrow pointing to it, 'You don't need a question mark here'

> *Why were there dozens of glass balls everywhere?*

In red letters, 'So that gypsies can see what's coming?

> *Answer—they were paperweights brought by Samuel Foster. Actually he only brought one with him, which he handed down through the generations to Ben, who then gave it to me as a birthday present and the reason there was more than one was because—this is a bit hard to understand—when another dimension is added it increases everything in volume.*

Red Ink, 'What?'

> Therefore one becomes many. Like a circle in two
> dimensions becoming a sphere in three.

The side of the page was covered with drawings of small ungainly creatures climbing up the words and hanging from a cobweb drawn in black in the corner. Curly black hair had been added to one along with the single word 'Ben' with an arrow pointing at it.

> Question—Why was number 32 Old Bridge Lane so important?

> Answer—It was Thomas Hobson's home—before he died—and the place where Samuel Foster eventually hid his heart.

> Question 4 —What happened to one, two and three? — How could altering the past not affect the future? Wouldn't the Universe being destroyed, mean that Thomas Hobson could never have invented his time machine in the first place?

This was accompanied by a red stain, presumably tomato sauce.

> Answer —Once the future has happened, it becomes the past, regardless of which direction you travel in time. The future was already the past to Thomas Hobson and everything

> Question—Why didn't Thomas and Samuel's involvement in a fictional Universe actually create an anti-reality explosion itself?

> Answer—I haven't got a clue. It's a conundurudrum ...conundrum...isn't it? And a condomrumnom ...conundrum in a fiction becomes a reality. And a reality combined with their reality, becomes a fiction. It's all sort of recursive.

All of this section was underlined twice and had another couple of spiders' webs drawn across the bottom of the words.

> To be honest, I still don't understand. But that's the problem isn't it? What will become of little Thomas when he grows up? Ballet classes? Factory work? Anything but mathematics and science!

> I suppose we'd better just wait around and see.

Drawing of a sideways face with an enormous hooked nose. Probably also not relevant.

> The more that I think about this, the more twisted and difficult the explanations become.

> But that's it isn't it? It's all paradoxical. Every time a question is answered another one pops up. Help, I think my brain is about to explode...

Drawing of a red brain exploding with the word—'BBOOOM!' in the middle of it in a cartoon style of cloud. It had been scribbled over in black.

> Addenudum—Why was Thomas Hobson's book at the bottom of the Wambachs' rubbish? And Thomas Hobson's photograph found at Mrs. Prunes?

> Answer—Because originally number 114 and number 113 Applegate were all one house.

Red Ink 'Thanks To Mrs. Prune digging out the House deeds for that one'

Drawing that resembled a balloon with a boil stuck on it, accompanied by the words 'Mrs. Prune' and an arrow.

> Addendum Addendum.(B) All of this gives rise to many more questions. How could Ben be out of phase in a reality that didn't use time? Why didn't

> Ben recognize the orb in Donald Oakseed's house?
> Come to that matter why didn't I? After all, I've
> actually got one in my box. Was there something we
> didn't know about??? Why did Thomas become a
> Presbiterian ...

This word was crossed out, rewritten and underlined

> ...Minister? Why did my personal thoughts become
> reality? Was it because I was real and so were my
> thoughts, therefore...

By this stage the writing had become extremely small
and cramped. Presumably it was written on a Sunday
and Jess was unable to get hold of any more note paper.
The letter concluded with the word 'BOLLOX' scrawled
across the other words in big blotchy letters with four
exclamation marks after it. There was obviously no more
room left for further speculations.

Still, it makes you think, doesn't it?

Chapter Twenty Six

The Dark And Distant Now.

B rightness. An omnipotent wall of light, so bright that it's actually blue. Crackling and twisting; spinning and falling.

Then come the first splashes of colour, initially nothing more than mere hints. An explosion of corn yellow, an ink bomb of apple green. Semblances of pastel watercolours, pale lilac and ocean blue, flowing down the inside of a rotating cylinder and forced into sensational patterns by the centrifugal force. Down we tumble.

Down, down, down. Everything grows darker as we fall. Then silence. Nothing but the blackness of pitch.

Jess can feel it pressing heavily against his face, suffocating in its intensity. So close that he can almost taste it. It tastes of dark.

He breathes slowly, feeling his chest rise and fall. Feeling his heart beating steadily. Feeling the air cram his nostrils.

Where is he now?

From a corner of the darkness comes a familiar coughing splutter. Not a human splutter of the sort made by a smoker waking-up on a clammy morning, but a diesel sort of splutter. From the bus stop about four houses further along the Victorian terrace of Applegate. Outside

'Mrs. Evesham's Dancing School for Young Girls' to be precise.

Jess lifts one heavy eyelid, as though it's made of lead. He looks out with a watering eyeball onto a brave new world.

At first everything was blurred, as if Jess was viewing it all through the pane of glass in the bathroom window. But slowly and carefully the panorama began to take on substance. Recognisable shapes came into focus. The bookcase, with its tall ladder of shelves, all crammed with multicoloured and many angled volumes. The standard lamp, gathering dust around its top-heavy, flower-covered shade. Dust motes spinning in clusters in the weak slice of daylight that squeezed between the curtains. All recognisable objects that informed him that finally Jess was home.

There was the sofa; a creaky arrangement of springs and chewed up foam. It was occupied by the prostrate body of a soundly asleep Benjamin. Benjamin stirred, muttered something unintelligible in his sleep and licked his dry lips before burrowing himself back down into the settee's comfortable back.

Then the memories started to return one by one. Jumbled and confused. Some obvious and brightly coloured, others just strands, deeply interwoven. All juxtaposed and at the same time entwined.

One said that Benjamin had been his partner and had died. The other told a different tale. That Benjamin Foster was in fact Benjamin Hobson, the younger brother that he had cared for since his mother had died.

Jess himself was sitting upright in his trusted armchair, gripping the arms as if they were about to take off and fly towards the ceiling. His legs were stretched out before him. His boots were on the cluttered table.

So this was reality? Subtly different; but somehow, very much the same?

It was altogether more sober. Jess remembered having a nightmare once in which every time he had a pint of beer the effect, instead of making him more intoxicated, actually brought more sobriety to the world. This was remarkably similar and he wasn't sure that he approved.

114 Applegate, upstairs in the attic. An aged woman with her grey hair in a bun, rather ample round the waist and deeply embedded in the slumber of dotage, occupied the bloated armchair. An old dear, dreaming a dream of a childhood long ago. The clock on the mantelpiece announced the hour in a tinny attempt to reproduce the Westminster Chimes.

Mrs. Prune blinked, accidentally dislodged the knitting from her knees and yawned. Her top set of false teeth almost let go of the shrivelled gum.

She was just an old woman who was having trouble these days climbing those long stairs up into the roof. She really ought to come to some arrangement with the folk on the ground floor. The Wambachs' or the Wotsanames'—the middle-aged couple with the cute little boy. She must have words with them anyhow, about swapping the rooms over. All those stairs were no good for her old aching back. She didn't seem to have enough energy left these days.

Mrs. Prune also has two sets of memories.

One set, bright and clear that concerned ordering an

extra pint of milk and a packet of rice from Mr. Gordon. She'd planned on making the boys downstairs one of her famous rice puddings the following night. Jess and Benjamin always liked that. Well, y've got to do y' bit, 'aven't y'?

But another distant memory skulked at the back of her mind. A memory half-hidden by the consequences of the day, concerning a strange and wondrous place outside of time. A place where she could recall holding the frightened hand of a lonely girl. A girl called Jannice, a place of choices, a place where life and death combined.

Perhaps it had all been just a dream. Something ticking away at her ancient subconscious. After all, how on Earth could she have been a fictional character? Pah! It didn't make sense to contemplate the damn thing.

One memory, however, appeared to be quite strong. It involved Benjamin being tossed into a column of light. Accidentally the glass orb that Ben had become had bounced off Mrs. Prune's finger tips. Benjamin himself had been sent spinning to his death. But she knew he wasn't dead; that the accident had saved him. Pushing him from the fictional world, through a rip between realities. Then the memory subtly changed and the way that she remembered it now, was that it hadn't been an accident at all, but a deliberate action.

Some characters are larger than life, larger than fiction. Mrs. Prune was one such character.

She leaned over and picked up her grey knitting needles, watching the ball of wool unravel across the carpet. Then she sat up straight and clutched the hollow in her back, puckering her lips into a chewed up fruit pastel as she felt a small muscle give way.

Here is the kitchen. Familiar, warm and inviting. But a strange greasy feel to the air and a dry little noise have set it slightly on edge.

Jess opened the kitchen cupboard doors, staring purposefully into the gloom beyond. He watched the splinter of crackling light, about twelve inches long and resembling a ivy wrapped around a doweling rod of brilliance. The last remnants of a gateway that had led to another dimension. Another dimension that had by now presumably all gone.

He made a mental note, *'Better get a lock fixed on that tomorrow. Wouldn't want anybody opening it by mistake. Better make it a big lock and throw away the key.'*

Then he closed the doors, filled the kettle and thought about everything that was crowding his head.

He thought about Mrs. Prune. What a sod he'd been to her, eh? He'd have to treat her with a bit more respect from now on. She was getting on in years and he was rather fond of her really, deep down.

And Benjamin, his little brother—he'd spent too long ignoring him. Starting tomorrow he'd try and become more involved with his adventurous business plans. Live life a little more. Become an altogether better person.

Then there was Jannice; perhaps he ought to call her. He'd judged her rather harshly in the past. Somewhere deep inside all that feminist mess, he considered, was a frightened little girl just wanting to be loved. Yes, tomorrow he'd go round there with a dozen roses and try to make amends for what he'd done.

Benjamin grunted in his sleep, turning over onto his side with his arms folded across his chest. Jess walked slowly through the kitchen door and back to his favourite armchair. His mind was tired and his eyes were still heavy, so he settled himself down with a book on his knee. One of Benjamin's books. About quantum mechanics and VCR units.

He would try to read a little more from here on end. Indulge himself in the odd novel, half a chapter a day. He turned the book over in his hands, squinting at the minuscule print. All right, just a couple of pages perhaps. For the sake of his eyes—his sight wasn't what it once was.

There was much that he didn't understand about what had happened, but some questions are too great to be answered all in one go. Besides, there are always questions in life. There wouldn't be much of a future if we already knew all of the answers before they actually happened. Well, would there?

He opened the book at page one and started to read. Tomorrow he'd be an improved man. A kinder, simpler, more tolerant man.

*Ah...*But there's the rub. Since the beginning of time no matter what lessons have been learned by mortal creatures, it always comes back to the concept of tomorrow; never today. Six months down the road, tomorrow has long since been forgotten and everything is as it was.

Underneath the bulging mattress on the bed, there was a box. The sort of box that people who work in offices all day long use to keep files inside.

This one was tied up with a mouldy old shoelace. It

didn't belong in this world. It was a fictional object filled with unreal things.

But there wasn't an explosion. Just the odd fizzle here and there. Reality, when all else is said and done, is much stronger than fiction. It's more important. It can withstand a few knocks and a few bruises.

But the contents of the box were important enough for Jess to have brought them all this way.

A box out of time. Out of place. Out of mind. The last remnants of the universe. The only things left to remind them of the end of their world.

A box full of junk.

This, you may be relieved to know, is the end of this particular tale —let it be a warning to us all...